ON EVERY SIDE

This Large Print Book carries the
Seal of Approval of N.A.V.H.

ON EVERY SIDE

KAREN KINGSBURY

CHRISTIAN LARGE PRINT
A part of Gale, Cengage Learning

GALE
CENGAGE Learning·

Detroit • New York • San Francisco • New Haven, Conn • Waterville, Maine • London

GALE
CENGAGE Learning

Copyright © 2001 by Karen Kingsbury.
Scripture quotations are taken from *The Holy Bible*, New International Version © 1973, 1984 by International Bible Society, used by permission of Zondervan Publishing House.
Christian Large Print, a part of Gale, Cengage Learning.

Christian Large Print Originals.
The text of this Large Print edition is unabridged.
Other aspects of the book may vary from the original edition.
Set in 16 pt. Plantin.
Printed on permanent paper.

LIBRARY OF CONGRESS CATALOGING-IN-PUBLICATION DATA

Kingsbury, Karen.
  On every side / by Karen Kingsbury.
    p. cm.
    ISBN-13: 978-1-59415-177-4 (softcover : alk. paper)
    ISBN-10: 1-59415-177-6 (softcover : alk. paper)
    1. Large type books. 2. Domestic fiction. I. Title.
  PS3561.I4873O52 2007
  813'.54—dc22   2006033499

Published in 2007 by arrangement with Multnomah Publishers, Inc.

Printed in the United States of America
  3 4 5 6 7   15 14 13 12 11
ED003

DEDICATED TO . . .

DONALD, my closest friend, my other half, the best husband always and forever. I love you more today than a hundred yesterdays, laugh more at the silliness between us, and live more with one eye on the rearview mirror, only too aware of how fast the days go. With you all of life is a series of memories and blessed magical moments, a roller coaster of thrills in which you are constantly at my side, steady and strong. Remember when you told me you loved the Lord more than me? Let's just say I'm glad it's still true. It's what makes it all so good.

KELSEY, my sweet and precious little Norm, who can boot a soccer ball like no one else and still be the prettiest girl around. I thank God that He lives within you, helping you know right from wrong, helping you understand the plans He alone has for you. Your tender heart has more discernment than most adults. As you told me the other day, you don't need a "play" boyfriend to feel good about yourself. You need the Lord. And I'm so thankful you have Him in a way that shows in everything you do . . . your eyes, your smile, and the joy you bring me and your dad every day of our lives.

TYLER, my strapping eight-year-old treasure, who has no idea how talented and bright and kindhearted he truly is. If only you could see the picture God is painting of you, the one your dad and I see more clearly every day. Please know that I'm glad you're not rushing the process, grateful that for a little while longer I might hear your humming, happy voice making up the music of our lives. Congratulations on winning statewide honors on your "Reflections" story, Ty. One day I'll be reading *your* dedications!

AUSTIN, who is still Michael Jordan. The marvel of you, my precious child, is not that at three years old you can slip into your No. 23 jersey and dribble a ball between your legs, watching wide-eyed when your dad coaches the big guys and taking in every bit of it. It isn't the way you can reverse dunk on your kid-size hoop, or shoot nothing-but-nets all afternoon. Rather, it's the way your eyes fill with tears when you hear a song about Jesus. We knew from the beginning that your heart was special . . . we're beginning to see how very special it really is.

E. J. and SEAN — As I write this I am twelve days from taking a plane to Haiti where I will pick you up and bring you home to live with us forever. My prayer for you, my chosen sons, is that God will impress upon your hearts how very special you both are, how great the plans He has for you. As surely as night follows day, He has amazing reasons why He brought you here to be a part of our family. We have prayed and planned for this moment for a very long time and are humbly awed at the privilege of being your parents. We — all of us — love you more than you could know or understand.

And to GOD ALMIGHTY, who has, for now, blessed me with these.

ACKNOWLEDGMENTS

As always, when I put together a novel there are people to thank, people without whom the entire process simply would not have been possible. On that note I thank the Lord first and foremost for allowing me the dream of writing stories straight from my heart while still being a stay-at-home mom. Also thanks to my husband and kids for not complaining when dinner is little more than a cold tuna sandwich and a sliced apple. You guys are the best family in the world.

Thanks to Kristy and Jeff Blake for continuing to take my little Austin on days when there's no other way the writing will get done. My heart is always at ease knowing my little boy is in your care. And to Sorena Wagner, the best nanny and all-around helper anyone could have. Truly, Sorena, I couldn't have gone to the next place in my writing career — the place God was calling me to go — without your help.

There are a number of people I am indebted to professionally, and top of the list is my agent, Greg Johnson. Greg, your God-given ideas and ways of making books come together are truly awe-inspiring. I thank the Lord for the day Terri Blackstock introduced us . . . and I look forward along with you to many, many more books and shared blessings together.

Thanks also to my amazing editor, Karen Ball. So often someone comments on a certain scene in my books or on a character's personality, and I smile proudly and tell them the truth: That came from Karen Ball! You're blessed at what you do, and I am doubly so for working with you.

The staff at Multnomah Publishers always deserves a great big thank-you for being the amazing people you are. Every one of you, from Don Jacobson to the staff of sales and marketing and editorial, is driven by God's purpose. Clearly the Lord is blessing your efforts on His behalf, and I pray He continues to do so a hundredfold in the years to come. Thank you for believing in me four years ago when I first set out to write inspirational fiction.

It may not be customary to thank the cover designer, but in our world a book truly is judged by its cover. That being the case, I attribute much of my recent success to the God-given talents of Kirk DouPonce from Uttley/DouPonce DesignWorks. You have a way of bringing all the emotion of my stories — the heartache and joy, the highs and lows — into a single illustration. And you do it better than anyone around. I am humbly grateful for your work on my books.

There are always certain friends who take my books and make them topics of conversation at their work places or among their social circles. In my life those faithful friends and public relations experts include my sisters Tricia, Sue, and Lynne; my parents, Anne and Ted Kingsbury; my niece, Shannon Kane; Phyllis Cummins; Betty Russell; Lisa Alexander; Joan Westfall; Debbie Kimsie; Tish Baum; the Chapman family; Christine Wessel; Pastor Mark Atteberry and his wife, Marilyn; Sylvia and Walt Wallgren; Ann Hudson; Vicki Graves; Barbara Okel; the Provo family; Sherry Heidenreich; Peggy Babbitts; Amber Santiago; the Daves family; Connie Schlonga; and dozens of friends from my Crossroads Church family, along with many others. Thank you for being my first line of encouragement and constant prayer support. Especially the handful of you who literally pray for my writing ministry and me every day. How can I ever thank you for your love and prayers other than to say please, please keep praying. It's only by His power that any of this ever comes together in a way that might change lives for His glory.

A special thanks goes to the hundreds of readers who have written me at my e-mail address, which is listed in the back of my books. I feel as though I'm friends with so many of you and I continue to look forward to your occasional updates and letters of encouragement regarding my books. You know who you are. You're the best group of readers an author could ever hope to have!

Finally, to the Skyview basketball team, who this year went from being a new school with one league win to a second-place league finish under the best coach (and husband) in the state. Thanks for giving me a reason to cheer — even on deadline. Go, Storm!

ONE

Joshua Nunn shuffled between a closet full of file cabinets and the boxes lining his office floor. He hadn't expected it to be this hard — packing up his dead partner's things and facing whatever was left of his own future. There was a heaviness in the air, a somber silence as though even the walls grieved the loss of the charismatic man whose presence had once consumed the place.

Joshua sighed. He had never felt so alone in all his life.

Bob Moses, senior attorney and Joshua's lifelong friend, opened the Religious Freedom Institute in Bethany, Pennsylvania, for one reason only: To take back ground lost to the enemy. "Join me," Bob had said when he presented the idea to Joshua three years earlier. "The promised land awaits!"

And so it had. They'd won two local Pennsylvania cases in the past six months

— one in which a group opposed to religious freedom sued a school district to prevent students from praying before football games. The case threatened to capture national attention — much like the one in Texas a few years back. But this time, when the opposition faced Bob and Joshua, they backed off.

"God has His hand on this office," Bob would say. "I can feel it, Joshua. He's taking us somewhere big."

There were dreams of hiring more attorneys, buying a bigger office building, and finding a place on America's legal center stage where they could join similar organizations in the national fight for religious freedom.

But every one of those dreams seemed to die the day Bob Moses slumped over his office desk, dead of a heart attack at age fifty-seven.

Now there were bills to pay, office expenses to maintain, and not a single viable case on the horizon. With Bob gone, clients apparently assumed the firm was closed, and now, after just three weeks of Joshua working on his own, the phone calls were few and far between.

He grabbed another stack of files, carried them across the office, and dropped them in a box. When he was finished clearing out his partner's things, he would deliver them to Bob's widow. The woman was taking it well, but many nights since Bob's death Joshua had come home to find his partner's wife sitting with his own dear Helen at the dining room table, tears in their eyes.

Poor Betty.

I know he's in a better place, Lord, but why? He still had so much to do . . .

Be strong, Joshua.

Be strong? It was the answer he seemed to be getting from the Lord more and more these days and it seemed an odd bit of advice. He *was* being strong, wasn't he? He hadn't broken down or refused to get out of bed. No, he'd been at the office every day since the funeral, and still not a call or case had come his way. He'd researched potential lawsuits, made phone calls, written letters — but still nothing.

The facts were simple. If he didn't start bringing in cases soon, he would have to close up shop and face the reality that at fifty-six years he was as desperately in need of a job as he'd been his first month out of college. A shallow laugh made its way to the surface, and Joshua shook his head.

Be strong?

He and Bob had worked as trial lawyers

with Jones, Garner, and Schmidt for thirty years before joining forces in this religious freedom venture. In addition to their lofty goals for the Institute, there were other benefits. No more commutes to the big city, extra time for evening card games and barbecues when any of their kids were home, more time in the town they loved. Joshua felt the sting of tears in his eyes and he blinked hard as he remembered how his partner seemed to have a bounce in his step at the idea of spending more time with his wife.

And with Faith.

There was a lump in Joshua's throat and he coughed so it would ease up. Much as he missed his friend and partner, young Faith missed the man more. Especially now, when it was supposed to be —

He couldn't bear to think of Faith, of how difficult her father's death had been on her. Instead he drifted back to the beginning, back to the early 1970s where it had all begun. The year he was hired by the big city firm, he and Helen and their two girls moved to Bethany — the most beautiful place in all the world. Bob, Betty, and their daughters followed suit two years later, and the families had been practically related ever since. Joshua and Bob would tease each other about being surrounded by women.

"Not a son among us, can you believe it?" Bob would throw his hands in the air.

The memories faded. Joshua carried a stack of books across the room and finished filling the box. As he did he glanced at the portraits on the wall. Bob Moses and Joshua Nunn, attorneys at law. *We were the luckiest guys in all of Bethany, Bob.*

These days everything was different. Bob was gone. Joshua's kids were both married and lived a few hours' drive away, and Bob's oldest daughter lived in Chicago. All that remained was Bob's youngest — Faith — still single at twenty-nine and trying to find her way in a world that offered little assistance, especially when the chips were down. Faith lived in Bethany and commuted fifteen minutes to Philadelphia's WKZN affiliate station where she anchored the nightly news. Joshua pictured her as she had been a few weeks back at her father's funeral: Long, blond hair and far-off, pale blue eyes. Beautiful girl; a celebrity really.

And very close to her father.

Bob hadn't talked about it much, but Joshua knew Faith was part of the reason he wanted to work in Bethany. "I worry about her," Bob would say now and then. "She's had a rough go of it."

The plan to open a law office in Bethany seemed like a winner from every angle. They could leave the high-powered, high-pressured firm and would work from a leased office anchored in the center of the city's quaint downtown district, just minutes from their homes in Maple Heights. They would spend hours building cases and strategizing trial appearances and swapping stories of the good old days — back when they ran cross-country for rival Philadelphia high schools and squared off more than once on opposing debate teams.

Bob was so sure of himself, so full of energy and desire, convinced beyond discussion that God's hand was in this venture. And from the get-go God blessed their intentions in a way that made it look as though Bob had been right.

Joshua knelt down and yanked packing tape across the flaps of the full box.

"Retirement is for old people." Joshua could still hear Bob's voice as it rang loudly through the office. "We could run this law office another twenty years." A smile would fill his face. "Remember, Joshua . . . where God guides, God provides."

The memory faded on a wave of doubt. Joshua stopped for a moment, gazing outside at the late summer green in the leaves that lined Main Street. *Why would You guide us here . . . take us from our steady jobs . . . just to leave me all alone? How will I provide stability for Helen now? For Faith?*

Joshua, hear me, son. You are not alone . . .

The voice was as strong and certain as ever, a constant reminder that Joshua's relationship with a mighty God was intact, the single guiding force in his life. He opened another box and struggled to his feet. Once Bob's things were gone, maybe he could advertise for a partner. Someone who didn't need to make money up-front. Joshua huffed at the thought. How likely was that? The situation was hopeless.

There was something else, too.

With Bob gone, Joshua wondered whether he was actually up to the task of fighting religious freedom cases. Bob was the outgoing one, the lawyer with flair and style and conviction. Joshua? He was merely a simple man who loved God above everything and everyone else; a man whose arguments in court were succinct and heartfelt rather than memorable. Bob had said more profound things at lunch over a cheeseburger and fries than Joshua had ever said in court. Joshua had figured he'd enjoy fighting nearly any cause at Bob Moses' side.

But without him?

His doubts were rampant as barn mice.

Joshua pulled himself into a nearby chair and hung his head. What was he supposed to do now? The firm wouldn't hire him back . . . His retirement fund was intact, so it wasn't a financial concern. But with Bob gone Joshua felt as though he'd lost his sense of direction, his focus as a man. He looked up and studied the office, taking in the way Helen and Betty had arranged the plants just so, how the windows on three sides allowed the light to fill the room. Joshua closed his eyes. *This was Bob's dream, God . . . tell me if I'm supposed to let it go. Please . . .*

As I was with Bob Moses so I will be with you. I will never leave you nor forsake you.

Joshua let the silent thought settle on his heart. It was true of course; God would be with him. But what about the law office? What of the dream to fight tyrannical forces bent on destroying religious freedom?

Joshua was suddenly more tired than he'd been in weeks. He rested his head on his desk and closed his eyes. *As I was with Bob Moses . . . As I was with Bob Moses . . . As I was with Bob Moses . . .* Joshua remembered the two cases he and Bob had battled together, how God had indeed been with them, bringing both victory and visibility, a presence in the Philadelphia area that had caused certain political groups to take notice. *But that was then, God . . . I'm all alone now. I can't do it on my own.*

Be strong and courageous . . . you will lead the people of this town to inherit the land . . .

Joshua closed his eyes tighter. *Are You talking to me, God? Lead the people of the town to inherit* what *land?* He shook his head slightly to clear the strange words. He probably needed more sleep. He might even be coming down with something. That could explain this heavy, tired feeling . . .

Inherit the land? He couldn't scrounge up a single case, let alone inherit the land.

Before he could pull himself up from his desk he heard a voice. Not the kind of inner knowing that comes when God whispers . . . but an audible voice.

"Be strong and very courageous, Joshua. Be careful to follow all the ways My servant Bob Moses showed you; do not turn from them to the right or to the left, that you may be successful wherever you go."

Joshua sat straight up, eyes wide. A clamminess came over his hands and neck, and he glanced about the room. The boxes were no longer scattered over the floor, but stacked neatly by the door. And one of the photos on the wall looked different. In place of Bob's picture hung one of a younger man — a man with angry eyes and a handsome, chiseled face. *What in the . . . ?*

"If . . . if that's You talking, God . . . I want to be strong for You." Joshua's eyes darted about the room, but the windows offered none of the familiar views — only golden light almost too brilliant to take in. His heart began to race. "I . . . I can't do it alone . . ."

"Have I not commanded you?"

Joshua sat stone still in his chair as the voice rang out again. It was booming, yet it warmed the room the way Joshua's heater warmed his car on winter days.

"Be strong and courageous. Do not be terrified; do not be discouraged, for the Lord your God will be with you wherever you go. Remember the command that Bob Moses, servant of the Lord, gave you. The Lord your God is giving you rest and has granted you this land. You will cross My Jordan, and take possession of the land the Lord your God is giving you for your own."

Joshua banged his head twice against the

palm of his hand. Was he having a stroke? No, maybe it was an inner ear infection, something that made sounds form into sentences when he was the only one in the room. There was a flash of light — and then he saw it.

In the corner of the room, there in front of Bob's old bookcase, stood a man wearing the finest armor, a man whose eyes blazed with shining light. A golden man unlike anyone Joshua had ever seen before. His breath caught in his throat and his jaw dropped as the man drew his sword. Joshua's teeth and even the tips of his fingers trembled, but something deep in his gut told him he was not in danger. He could trust this man.

He stood, his knees knocking, and made his way closer to the soldier. "Are you . . . are you friend or foe?" Joshua forced his voice to cooperate and then waited stiffly, as though his feet were planted in cement.

"Neither. I have come as commander of the army of the Lord."

Joshua felt his eyes fly open even wider than before. *Commander of the army of the Lord?* That meant the man was an . . . an *angel?* It was impossible . . . but what other explanation was there? Joshua fell facedown to the ground, managing in a muffled voice,

"What message does my Lord have for me?"

The strangely peaceful soldier studied Joshua for a moment. "Take off your shoes, Joshua, for you stand on holy ground."

Immediately Joshua fumbled with his laces, loosened their grip on his feet, and slid his shoes off, arranging them neatly so they faced Bob's bookcase. Who was this man and where had he come from? If he was an angel did he know about Bob? Had he spoken with him? Was this God's way of getting Joshua's attention? And what of the strange light outside and the odd picture on the wall?

But before he could ask any of the hundreds of questions pelting the roof of his heart, the phone rang. Joshua groped about, but nothing was where it should have been.

Again and again the phone rang, until Joshua sat bolt upright and opened his eyes, his mouth dry, heart pounding. He was breathing fast and he glanced around the room, stunned at the sight that met him.

The man was gone. In his place were all the boxes and piles of papers and books that had been there minutes earlier. His eyes darted to the photographs on the wall and he exhaled his relief. Bob's picture was back, and there was no sign of the angry young man whose picture had been there a moment ago.

Joshua remembered the voice and what had been said. What land? How could he be crossing the Lord's Jordan when the Holy Land was thousands of miles away?

None of it made sense.

The phone rang once more and the sound of it startled Joshua, jerking him further back to reality. There was wetness at the corner of his mouth, and he wiped it with the back of his hand as everything became utterly clear. He hadn't heard a voice or been visited by a commander in the Lord's army. Of course not.

He had fallen asleep and it had all been a dream.

He reached for the receiver and snapped it to his ear. "Religious Freedom Institute, Joshua Nunn."

"Good. You're in." It was Frank Furlong the town's mayor. Joshua eased back into his chair and willed his heart to slow down. He and Frank had been friends for twenty years.

"Yeah . . . sorry, I was busy. What's up, Frank?"

There was a pause. "I got wind of something today. Could be big, could be nothing, but I'd like to talk about it. How about over lunch tomorrow?"

Images of the golden soldier and the sound of a booming voice like none he'd ever heard before still clamored for Joshua's attention. "Tomorrow's Saturday. Can't it wait?" He and Helen had plans to drive to the lake and take in an afternoon of fishing. Joshua figured they'd talk about his work plans — especially now that it seemed clear the law office wasn't going to survive.

Again the mayor hesitated. "This is very big, Joshua. If it happens, it'll come down on Monday, and we'll need your help. In fact, you'll be the primary counsel." There was a beat. "Tomorrow at noon, okay? Alvins on Walnut."

The fog was still clearing from Joshua's head, but he heard the urgency in Frank's voice. He and Helen could fish Sunday after church. "I'll be there."

He hung up the phone, staring at it, pondering. What could possibly be so urgent? Whatever it was, it involved the city of Bethany, and Frank wanted him as primary counsel. A surge of hope wound its way through Joshua's being. Was this the answer he'd been praying for? Was God going to let him keep the office after all? He considered the idea when a draft from the air conditioning sifted between his toes.

Frowning, he glanced down. He had only

socks on his feet. *What's this about?* In the dream there'd been something about taking off his shoes because the place was holy, but that had only been a dream, right? So where were his shoes? He looked around the room and finally spotted them several feet away.

Sitting neatly, side by side, facing Bob's old bookcase.

Two

Jordan Riley paced confidently in front of the judge like a caged and hungry animal, feeding off the fact that every eye in the room was on him. These were his closing arguments, and in the New York courtroom where the drama was taking place he had already claimed victory more times than he could remember.

He was certain this case would end in similar fashion.

"Finally, Your Honor, Mr. Campbell completely disregarded school policy by praying with a child during school hours." Jordan reached for a document from the plaintiff's table and found the highlighted section. "Page four, section thirteen, states clearly that if a teacher ignores the existing separation between church and state he or she shall be terminated immediately."

Jordan set the paper down and stared hard at the simple man across the courtroom.

Flanked by frustrated attorneys from the local branch of the teacher's union, the man looked calm, almost serene. As though he didn't understand the ramifications of what was about to take place. Or perhaps he believed, thanks to some misguided faith in God Almighty, that the battle might end miraculously in his favor.

A bitter feeling as familiar as his own name oozed from the crevices of Jordan's heart and seeped into the core of his being. *We'll see where your God gets you this time.*

He faced the judge again and motioned toward the defendant. "The religious right threaten to take over this country every day, Your Honor. Their agenda is clear: to evangelize all those around them to their way of thinking." Jordan took several steps toward the peaceful teacher and gestured in his direction. "Your Honor, the danger here is clear. If we allow people such as Mr. Campbell to control the minds of our youth, we lose the free society our forefathers fought to give us. In its place we will have a culture of robots controlled by some mystical belief in a God that doesn't exist. Human robots without compassion for people different from themselves. Robots who teach hatred toward people with alternative lifestyles or differing religions. All of this under the guise of public education?" Jordan waited a beat. "It's a travesty of the most frightening kind, Your Honor."

Mr. Campbell's attorneys shifted, glancing furtively at their notes and avoiding eye contact with their client. Jordan resisted a smile. Even Campbell's counsel could tell which way the case was going. It was all over but the celebrating.

"For that reason, it is my recommendation that Mr. Campbell be fired by the school district for violating this country's separation of church and state. In doing so, this court will send a message to other teachers, other school districts that prayer of any sort simply will not be tolerated on public school grounds." He nodded. "Thank you, Your Honor."

He took his seat and watched one of Campbell's attorney's weakly take the floor. The man adjusted his glasses and cleared his throat. "Our stance in this matter, Your Honor, is of course the matter of freedom." He checked his notes. "Freedom of speech and religious freedom."

Jordan was up immediately. "Objection, Your Honor." He smiled in a practiced way that fell just short of condescending. "Mr. Campbell's right to religious freedom has never been the issue. No one told him he couldn't pray. He just can't pray with a student in a public school setting."

The judge — an icy woman in her late forties whose patience for the religious right was limited at best — nodded her chin pointedly. "Sustained." She tossed a disdainful look at Campbell's counsel. "You will stick to the issue at hand."

The man looked lost. "Yes, Your Honor." His eyes fell again to the file in his hand, and Jordan shifted his gaze back to the teacher, still seated peacefully at the table. *Where's your God now, Campbell? You're going down in flames.* Jordan relished the thought. One less do-gooder trying to change the landscape of American culture on a belief that was no more substantiated than Santa Claus.

Without warning, a picture flashed through Jordan's mind of himself at age thirteen, kneeling in prayer, tears streaming down his face and —

For a single moment, Jordan's heart ached for the child he'd been. He blinked and the image disappeared.

Campbell's attorney finally gathered himself together enough to speak. "Uh . . . very well, Your Honor, our stance will focus entirely on Mr. Campbell's freedom of speech."

The man looked at his partner, and Jordan almost felt sorry for him. None of the attorneys he knew working for a national teacher's union would want the job of defending an instructor in a religious freedom case. Obviously the legal team was ill-prepared, and the way they glanced at their watches every few minutes confirmed the fact that they were merely marking time until they could get back to the office.

"Your Honor, you'll remember that the student Mr. Campbell was praying with had lost her best friend in a car accident the day before."

Jordan refrained from wincing, but he couldn't stop his heart from remembering a sorrow that could never be resolved. Praying in the wake of a friend's death did more harm than good. After all, how would the girl in question face life now, knowing that God — assuming there was a God — had chosen not to help her friend?

Campbell's attorney was droning on, and Jordan glanced again at the teacher. Much as he disliked what the man had done, what he stood for, Jordan had to admit there was something likable about the guy. Besides that, something about Campbell's eyes looked familiar. Where had he seen eyes like that before?

Another image filled Jordan's mind, and he flinched as he remembered. Long, long ago . . . the eyes had belonged to a man he'd trusted . . . a man he'd loved like a father . . . a man who'd lied to him.

Jordan brought himself back to the present and made a mental note to stay in tune with the proceedings. This was no time to be drifting back to the hardest days of his life. Back when people's prayers had been for him . . . back when his mother —

"And so, Your Honor, we'd like you to consider the spirit of the law in this case." Campbell's attorney actually sounded as though he meant it. "The defendant was not leading his class in prayer, nor was he teaching on prayer in the classroom. Rather he was doing what comes naturally for someone of his religion. He was praying with a student who looked as if she needed prayer." The counsel shuffled his notes into a different order and cast a last glance at the judge. "Thank you, Your Honor."

Without missing a beat the judge slid back her chair and leaned into the microphone. "There will be a ten-minute break while I evaluate the information. After that time I will return with my decision." She rapped her gavel on the desk and left through a door behind her chair.

Jordan caught himself watching Campbell's attorneys, how they whispered to their client and shook their heads, their eyes narrow and dark. Jordan looked back at the file on the table in front of him. Why was he so drawn to Campbell, anyway? The man deserved to lose his job; indeed, whatever punishment the court might decide would not be enough to undo the damage done to that student. She would have trusted Campbell. He was an adult — a *teacher,* no less — and clearly the girl was suffering through one of the hardest times of her life. Now she had only two choices: Buy into the faith lie or be scarred for life knowing God had failed to help her friend — and in the process probably doubting whether He even existed. Jordan knew where that went. He never wanted to go there again.

"Great job, Riley." The hand on his shoulder belonged to Peter T. Hawkins, president of Humanity Organized and United in Responsibility, better known as HOUR. The legal group ranked up there with any other civil liberties organization fighting against the religious right. Jordan had been working with HOUR for nearly six years and was considered young and brilliant, talented in a way that made his superiors salivate over the cases they might win at his hand.

"Thanks, sir." Jordan grinned. "Looks pretty good."

"Another slam dunk." Hawkins crossed his arms and smiled hard at Jordan. The senior lawyer had been a brilliant litigator in his day and now made only occasional appearances for closing arguments in the cases of his attorneys. It was considered an honor when he showed up, and he showed up often at Jordan's cases.

Hawkins shook his head. "Lady Luck was smiling on us the day we hired you, my friend. By the time you're done with this country's Jesus freaks, they'll be meeting in barns at night and prayer will be little more than a state of mind. I'm telling you, Riley, you've got the gift. We have big things planned for you, real big."

The long ago memory of the man's face — of eyes filled with compassion, a voice lowered in prayer — came to mind again, and Jordan willed it away. This was no time to be sucked into the past, not with his career taking off before his eyes. "Right, thanks."

The judge entered the courtroom and resumed her place at the bench, rapping her gavel until the crowd quieted. Hawkins's smile faded into an appropriately somber expression as he took a seat next to Jordan.

"Here we go," he whispered.

"Order. I have a decision in the case of Humanity Organized and United in Responsibility versus The New York School District." The judge sifted through several pieces of paper and looked at Campbell. "This case is not about emotions, Mr. Campbell. It is not about car accidents or grieving high school students. It is about following the rules as they are spelled out." She sighed and Jordan could taste the victory at hand. "You are a state employee, paid by the state to impart education to the children of this state. The rules — as Mr. Riley pointed out — are very clear in this case: A teacher may not pray with a student because to do so would be a violation of the separation of church and state." She sat back in her chair and angled her head. "The consequences are also clearly spelled out. And since you chose to ignore them, I have no choice but to do as Mr. Riley has recommended and order the New York School District to terminate your contract immediately."

The thrill of notching another win filled Jordan's senses, but rather than revel in the victory he glanced over his shoulder at Campbell. The man lowered his head for the briefest moment — and Jordan had the disconcerting feeling that the disappointment was a mere speed bump on whatever private journey Campbell was a part of. Then Campbell looked up and smiled at the judge, his eyes still full of that strangely disquieting peace.

Doesn't he get it? No one'll hire him now. Jordan wanted to shake the man, make him renounce the faith that had gotten him into this mess in the first place. Instead Campbell looked surer of himself than ever.

It was often the way his opponents looked in defeat, and that baffled Jordan beyond understanding.

The proceedings were over and Hawkins was pumping his hand, patting him on the arm and telling him he was a god among men. Even as he did so, a handful of local reporters circled around Jordan hungry for quotes and sound bites. He paid no attention to any of it. His eyes were glued on Campbell, watching as the man stood and shook the hands of his two attorneys. That done, he moved toward the spectator section of the courtroom and embraced a pretty woman whose eyes were filled with unshed tears. Campbell placed his hand alongside the woman's face and stroked her cheek with his thumb, his face lowered close to hers. Whatever he was saying to her, she smiled and nodded in response, circling her arms around his neck and holding him tight.

Seems like a nice couple . . .

They stayed together longer than any standard hug, and Jordan felt a knot form deep in his gut. They were praying. Anger worked its way into his bloodstream, quickening his heart and turning his stomach. Here, in the aftermath of what had to be the greatest blow of their lives, they were praying. Talking to the same God who had let them down and asking . . . for what? Another job to replace the one Campbell had just lost? Money to fall from the sky? What possible good could it do to pray now, when praying had already cost him everything?

"Mr. Riley . . . Mr. Riley . . ." Jordan faced the reporters with an easy smile he knew would make the next day's *New York Times.* Hawkins had told him from the beginning that image was everything and Jordan prided himself on doing his part to keep the firm in a good light. "Mr. Riley, what message do you think this sends to teachers across the state?"

Jordan opened his mouth to answer and for an instant caught a peripheral view of Campbell and the woman walking out of the courtroom, their arms around each other. *I refuse to feel bad.* He faced the cameras squarely. "This case sends a message to every instructor in America: We will not allow teachers to use a public classroom to impose religion on innocent children."

The questions went on for thirty minutes, long after Hawkins winked at him and left through the double doors. When it was over, Jordan loaded a stack of papers into his briefcase and made his way to the parking lot and his shiny, white Lexus. It was quarter after four and he had a date that night with Ashley Janes. Beautiful, plastic-coated Ashley, the well-known model he'd met at a corporate dinner the year before. She was a welcome distraction, but too caught up in the jet-set crowd and her own popularity for anything long-term.

"You're fun, Jordan," Ashley had told him after they'd gone out a few times. "Just as good-looking on my arm as I am on yours."

At the time her words had felt like a slap in the face and he'd regretted his attraction to her. But since then he'd come to understand what she meant. Their looks were just one of the aspects they enjoyed about each other, and since neither of them was looking for a commitment, their relationship was ideal.

Jordan tossed his briefcase in the backseat

and headed toward his apartment in the heart of the city, where a forest of dirty buildings made up the landscape and the hum and screech of traffic was constant. Jordan wouldn't have it any other way. The distractions of city life kept him from thinking about the ghosts of his past — ghosts he'd spent a lifetime outrunning.

He smiled to himself. After Monday he'd have one less memory to run from.

He'd already shared his thoughts with Hawkins, and again more recently at a general meeting with the firm's three partners and twenty-one attorneys. To a man the group was excited about Jordan's plan, and why not? Suing a conservative little town such as Bethany, Pennsylvania, over something that should have been taken care of decades ago was right up their alley. Since it was Jordan's idea, he was given the go-ahead to spend a few days in Bethany, where he would file the suit, then round up the city officials and see if they were interested in complying without going to trial.

If not, the suit would inevitably make headlines across the country. Victorious headlines. And a victory in Bethany would go a long way toward helping him forget the past and the things that had gone wrong in that town so many years ago.

Jordan took the elevator to the twelfth floor and made his way into his apartment. The building was nice, security guards and a workout room that Jordan used every morning at five. He grabbed a glass of ice water, took it into the living room, and kicked back in a white, leather recliner. The view from his front window was standard city fare: No sky, only the angular walls and windows of a handful of buildings.

Jordan loosened his tie. No, there was nothing homey about his apartment. Professional decorators had appointed it with leather, chrome, and glass, but there were no personal details, no photographs or sentimental knickknacks. Just a place to unwind at the end of the day and sometimes — when he couldn't help himself — a place to wonder what if . . .

What if his mother hadn't died that awful summer in 1985? What if she'd lived long enough to see him and his sister through school, to be a part of their lives, to make them a family? What if God had seen fit to let her live instead of . . .

He shook his head. What if the state hadn't placed him and Heidi in separate foster homes? What if — wherever his little sister was, whoever she'd grown up to be — she still remembered him? And what if he hadn't lost track of his childhood friend, a beautiful girl with blond hair and blue eyes as innocent as a baby's?

Most of all what if there really was a God who had loved him?

Jordan took a sip of ice water, and the questions ceased. If there was a God then He was unreliable and inept. Or perhaps sinister and judgmental — striking people down at random. Because that summer in Bethany, Pennsylvania, Jordan had prayed his heart out, begging God to spare his mother and believing all the while He would. But Evelyn Riley died anyway. At first Jordan figured there was nothing God could have done to help his mother's sickness. Later he realized the truth: Either God didn't exist or He didn't care about a young boy's prayers. And so Jordan had turned to the courtroom, determined to push what remained of society's religious deceptions into hiding or expose them for the lies they were.

That was why he needed to go back to Bethany — to even the score. With God.

He stood up and set the glass in the kitchen. There were places in his heart that he was sure weren't ready to visit his hometown again, to walk the streets where the old Jordan — the naive, trusting Jordan —

had died alongside his mother. Where the person he was today had been birthed in bitterness. The place where he'd lost the three women who had ever really mattered to him.

His mother, his sister . . . and a girl he had never quite been able to forget.

A girl named Faith.

THREE

Faith Evans checked her look in the mirror and made certain every strand of her long, blond hair was tucked neatly into the knot at the back of her head. Dick Baker, the station manager at the WKZN affiliate where she worked, had frowned on her hair from the beginning, giving her two options: cut it or wear it up. "Makes you look too young," he'd grumbled. "Don't make me work to justify having you on the air, Evans."

Faith had seen other anchors with hair similar to hers — halfway to their waists — but the issue wasn't worth arguing about. Besides, she was under enough scrutiny already.

She made her way back to the soundstage, but before taking her place she saw one of the associate producers. "It's Wednesday . . . are we running the special?"

The man stopped what he was doing and stared at her, unblinking. "Special?"

"*Wednesday's Child.* Remember?" Faith held her breath. This segment was especially important. He had to include it in the lineup.

She'd started the *Wednesday's Child* program six months earlier and used her own time to put together the two-minute segments. Each one highlighted a special-needs child who was up for adoption through the state's social services department. So far more than half the children featured had been adopted, and more than once her boss had said the program was a success. But without her constant reminders, the station executives tended to forget the segment altogether.

"So what're we talking?" A tired look crossed the man's face. "One minute, two?"

Faith kept her frustration in check. "Two."

He checked his chart. "Okay, immediately after sports."

"Thanks." Faith felt the familiar surge of hope. There were reasons for her attachment to the state's homeless children. Reasons that went far beyond good citizenship or Christian character. Faith headed back across the soundstage and eased herself onto the stool opposite the one where Ron Leonard already sat studying his notes. *Okay, Lord, these next thirty minutes*

are for You . . . help me make You proud.
"You ready?" She smiled the question at her coanchor.

Ron was fifteen years older and his position anchoring for the Philadelphia station had clearly been a demotion for him. Generally his mood reflected that truth and tonight was no exception. Rather than answer, he bunched his eyebrows together and looked hard at his watch. "When the producer says 10:45, he means 10:45. Not 10:47."

Faith swallowed. "Thank you, Ron. I'll try to keep that in mind." Her voice held not a trace of sarcasm. She respected Ron and knew he was right. Every minute counted. "I had to check on the *Wednesday's Child* segment."

Ron's shoulders dropped several inches. "It's not on the schedule."

"I guess we should write it in. Two minutes, right after sports."

A heavy sigh escaped through Ron's clenched teeth. "We're a news station, not a church."

Faith ignored his comment and studied her notes. In many ways she was marked by her beliefs and the fact that she was Bob Moses' daughter. It was why she'd agreed to use her middle name at work. Faith

Evans. Bob Moses was well known locally and by using Faith's middle name, her boss hoped viewers wouldn't identify her as religious or one-sided.

It was something he had worried about since the day he hired her.

Before that first newscast Dick pulled her aside and gave her a warning she remembered to this day: "The viewers may not know who you are, but I do. Bob Moses is a visible person with extreme religious views." He'd tapped his pencil on his desk. "I like your work, Evans, but the executives expect me to keep my anchors in line. This station is not a pulpit for you to preach your doctrine, do you hear me?"

Faith had been shocked by his warning. After four years at Penn State and five years working her way up the ladder as a sports reporter, Faith had still believed there was fairness in reporting. But in the two years since taking the position as nighttime news anchor, there were many times when she'd seen otherwise. Too often stories that favored a conservative, Christian worldview were cut or changed or balanced with opposing interviews that lasted longer and sounded more professional. It was as though the executives had mandated a certain politically correct response for most news topics, and the station manager's role was to see that response carried out.

Occasionally a child's outstanding achievement or the way a family survived a personal tragedy might be worthy of a news story, but not without heavy editing. Stories along those lines tended to feature Christians who attributed their success or survival to God, but rarely did their statements of belief make the final televised piece.

There wasn't much Faith could do about it. It was an industry rule that anchors and reporters be unbiased in their work. It was written that way in her contract. If she used her visible position in any way other than to report the news without opinion, it was grounds for dismissal. She knew the rules and she had no intention of breaking them. Not with all that had happened over the last few years.

"Three minutes . . ." The off-stage warning caused Faith to sit straighter in her seat as she memorized the story order. Ron had the first segment: Gunman takes a hostage. She had the next one: budget cuts at the city hospital. Two more follow-up segments, including cutaways to taped interviews, and they'd have their first commercial break. One more eight-minute news segment with additional footage, another commercial break, weather, and then sports.

"Three, two, one . . . and . . . go!" The voice stopped abruptly as intense, upbeat music filled the soundstage. Faith and Ron adjusted themselves on their seats and sorted briefly through their individual stacks of paper as they faced the camera, serious expressions in place.

"A gunman takes three hostages in a shootout today that left one local man dead and another critically injured . . ." Ron's voice was crisp and upbeat with the polish that comes from years of working the cameras.

"And good news for the city hospital. Budget woes may be over but at whose expense . . . ?" On cue Faith glanced at Ron.

"Good evening everyone, I'm Ron Leonard."

Back at the camera. "And I'm Faith Evans. Welcome to tonight's edition of WKZN News."

Faith angled her head toward Ron and he kicked in with precision timing. "A burst of gunfire ripped through a family home in the two-thousand block of Westchester Avenue this morning as an escaped convict broke in and took three people hostage. We have more on that from Alicia Rodriguez who was there at the scene." A thirty-second segment filled the screen with live reports and statements from family members. Faith and Ron checked the story order again and prepared once more to go live.

The newscast continued without a hitch, and Faith prayed between stories for the little girl in tonight's *Wednesday's Child* segment. Rosa Lee, a six-year-old biracial Asian sweetheart abandoned by her parents at birth and shuffled through five foster homes since then. She was legally free for adoption but she had a problem: She had been born with just two fingers and a thumb on her left hand.

Faith had spent an afternoon with Rosa and her social worker over the weekend, amazed at how well the child worked to compensate for her handicap. Even so, the missing fingers were another strike against her. Chances were Rosa might never be adopted, unless God used the news segment to touch someone's heart.

Ben Bloom, the weatherman, was wrapping up.

Lord, prepare the right person's heart even now . . . Faith loved talking to God even in the middle of a newscast. It was something her dad had taught her when she was only a child. *Father, please . . . find a home for little Rosa, please.*

A brief commercial break ended and the sports segment began. Chase Wilson was a former college athlete with model-like looks, a beautiful wife, and three children. He was in his early thirties, and rumor was the network had plans to move him into the national spotlight sometime soon. Women viewers often wrote to the station saying Chase was the reason they tuned in at all. He smiled and began talking into the camera.

"We've got baseball scores from around the league and stories from NFL camps, but before we get to that we have breaking news on a player out of Dallas. Tight end Mike Dillan's name is back in court tonight after two women — longtime friends — filed paternity suits claiming he was the father of both their children."

Faith felt the blood drain from her face. Mike Dillan? Not tonight . . . she couldn't think about him now. But images of the rugged athlete filled her mind as Chase continued.

"The women claim he impregnated both of them at a party three years ago . . ."

Three years ago? That was when she and Mike . . .

Faith forced herself to remain in position and prayed that she didn't look as shaken as she felt.

The monitor showed taped footage of Coach Graves at a press conference admonishing Mike Dillan and any other player who continued to act irresponsibly.

Faith struggled to focus while Chase finished and looked first at her and then at Ron, a casual smile draped across his face. "Exciting time of year in sports . . ."

Ron straightened a stack of papers and tapped them on his desk as he grinned at Chase. "Days of October right around the corner."

Faith lowered her chin and raised her eyebrows in a manner intended to be teasing and lighthearted. She doubted she was fooling anyone, including the viewers. Everyone in Philadelphia probably knew about her and Mike. "Doesn't look like my Mets'll be anywhere near a field by then."

Chase chuckled and flashed a handsome smile in her direction. "That's the nice thing about August. Everybody has a chance. Even your Mets, Faith."

A round of easy laughter died out, and Faith took the cue as the camera zoomed in on her. *Focus, Faith, focus.* "Each week for the past six months we've been bringing you a segment called *Wednesday's Child,* highlighting special-needs children who are up for adoption in Philadelphia's social services system. Tonight we take a look at six-year-old Rosa Lee."

Saxophones led the way as the haunting strains of a child's lullaby filled the station and faded into the laughter of children playing at Jericho Park. Rosa was living with a foster family in Bethany, and the park was her favorite place to play. Faith noticed that the cameraman had avoided the hundred-year-old Jesus statue, anchored just to the right of the play area.

Throughout the piece, a phone number remained on the screen for viewers interested in adopting Rosa. Faith watched the monitor as the camera panned in past the other children and settled on the dark-haired little beauty. Mike Dillan forgotten, Faith again savored the child's giggles as she'd done over the weekend when they'd been together for the interview. From the moment she met Rosa, Faith had felt captured by her, desperate to find her a family. Faith heard her own voice begin to sound over the footage.

"Rosa Lee's life has never been easy. Not since the morning her mother abandoned her on the steps of a Philadelphia hospital days after her birth." The camera zoomed out from Faith strolling the park grounds, her face serious, eyes on the camera, to Rosa running alongside three other children, chasing butterflies across the park's grassy hillside. An edit showed the same children eating a picnic lunch and a close-in shot gave the television audience a first glimpse of Rosa's deformed hand. "Rosa was born with just two fingers and a thumb on her left hand, making her one of thousands of special-needs children up for adoption across the United States."

The monitor showed Rosa brushing the crumbs from her play clothes and running back to the swings and slides. "Rosa will always have special needs, but don't tell her that. When it comes to using her hands, she's more determined than most kids twice her age."

The footage showed Rosa using a pencil, catching a ball, and playing tennis at the city courts. The segment finally cut to Rosa, her head tilted, long silky eyelashes batting shyly at Faith as they sat together on a park bench. ". . . A mommy who'll stay with me forever. That's what I want."

What?

From where Faith sat staring at her monitor she felt the piercing sting of betrayal. Someone had gotten to the segment and edited out the first part of Rosa's statement.

She remembered how the girl's words had pierced her heart when she'd smiled and said, "I'm praying for a mommy who'll stay with me forever. That's what I want."

God, I can't fight this battle any more . . .

Be strong and courageous, daughter. I will go before you in the battle you are about to fight.

What battle? The muscles in her stomach tightened at the thought. Had she correctly heard the still small voice she knew so well? *I can't fight the system, Lord . . . You must be thinking of someone else.*

Be strong, daughter. The battle belongs to Me.

Faith felt the reassuring presence of the Lord and her anger eased. *It's so unfair, Father . . .*

How could the station allow references to everything but a person's faith in God? And how could that be considered unbiased reporting when it was nothing *but* biased. Bias and censorship, pure and simple, and though Faith was not a fighter, it made her tempted to take a more vocal stand for her beliefs.

The footage of Rosa faded to a still shot of the child swinging high in the air against a deep blue sky, her eyes sparkling with love and hope and light. The camera angled back in on Faith live in the studio.

"Rosa is an Asian biracial child who is currently available for adoption to anyone with a valid home study. If you're interested in adopting this precious little one call the number at the bottom of your screen and someone will help you through the process." She glanced at her prompt and looked pleasantly at her partner. "Ron?"

"We'll take a break for a moment, but when we come back, a look at Julia Roberts's box-office hit, *Where Yesterday Lives*."

Faith nodded. "Bring a *box* of tissues for this one . . ."

The break played out, and in five minutes the newscast was over.

"That's a wrap," a director yelled from behind the camera. "See ya tomorrow. Same bat time, same bat channel."

A technician flipped a series of switches to cut the studio bright lights and stop the whir of the cameras just as Ron's smile faded. *Right on cue.* Faith watched, somewhat amazed. It was almost as though her partner's facial expressions were on the same electrical current as the camera equipment.

Faith studied him as he turned to leave. "See ya, Ron."

He held a hand up in her direction, not

even looking back. *At least he's a good actor.* She turned and was headed for her purse and car keys when Dick Baker caught her attention. "Come here, Faith. I need a word with you."

She felt the familiar knot in her stomach. What had she done now? Had he read her mind and known she was praying just to survive the half hour? Could he see on her face the way Mike Dillan's name had made her feel? She approached him and felt the corner of her lips raise a fraction of an inch. "Yes?"

Mr. Baker was in his sixties, a gruff, hard-core veteran of television news determined to gain the favor of the network executives. For the most part Faith thought he was her ally, a professional who appreciated the quality of her work. But there were times when whatever pressure he must have been getting from the higher ups took its toll and turned him into a tyrant.

Faith had a feeling this was about to be one of those times.

She had only seen his soft side once — after her father's heart attack the month before. The station covered the story, portraying her father in a flattering light, stating that he died chasing after his life's passion: maintaining rights for the people of

Pennsylvania and the United States. Mr. Baker himself had helped edit the story, making sure it included the fact that Bob Moses was survived by a wife, Betty, and two daughters — one of which was their very own Faith Evans.

The man standing before her now looked far less compassionate. "Haven't we warned you about references to prayer?" His words sounded as if they were leaking from a pressure cooker.

Faith was tempted to look ignorant, but instead she folded her arms and maintained eye contact with her boss. "Yes. But that wasn't *my* reference, it was —"

"Let me finish!" Mr. Baker's face was a mass of angry knots. "If I hadn't checked that *Wednesday's Child* segment first it would have aired that way, with that girl sharing her private prayers for all the world to hear."

Faith felt her face grow hot. "It's what she wanted to —"

Mr. Baker raised his hand. "Don't speak. I'm not done." His head was nearly bald, and in his frustration it had grown damp with sweat. "We've been over this before, Evans. It's bad enough that our Bethany *viewers* know your religious stance. But surely you understand the network execs know about it, too. 'Watch her, Baker,' they tell me." He shook his head and a choked, sarcastic huff escaped him. "And to tell you the truth I try, Evans, honest I do. You know why I had to fix that segment?"

"No, sir, it didn't need fixing if you'd —"

Her boss gave a quick shake of his head and glared at her. "I'm not finished! If I hadn't made that cut that would have been five God stories in two weeks. Five, for cryin' out loud, Evans. Your stories include mentions of God and prayer ten times more than the stories from other reporters. If that doesn't change, you and I both know the executives will talk." He leveled his gaze at her. "You remember that contract you signed?" He paused, but not long enough for her to answer. "You start giving biased reports, and if I don't fire you the network executives will fire me. It's that simple."

His voice was louder than before, and Faith noticed various cameramen and technical staff members scurrying off the soundstage. "Do I make myself clear?"

Faith had to fight back tears.

Go forth, daughter. Be gentle and take up the fight . . .

Not now, Lord, I can't . . . Her knees began to tremble.

Her boss's face grew still darker. "I said,

do I make myself clear?"

Be strong and courageous. I will go before you . . .

Send someone else, Father. I'm not strong enough.

Daughter, nothing is impossible with Me . . .

But it was no use. Her knees were already weak; if she stood up to Dick Baker now she was likely to faint flat across the man's feet. "Yes, sir."

At Faith's compliant answer, her boss's scowl eased. "You're a darn good reporter. Don't get me wrong. We've . . ." He paused as though he didn't want to share this information with her. "Well, we've had calls about you and Chase. There's talk about moving you up." He pointed at her, his finger inches from the bridge of her nose. "The network's watching, Faith. Don't do anything to ruin it for yourself."

Her heart felt as though it had been shredded by competing emotions. The network? Was it possible? Were they really interested in her for a potential national spot? Hope surged through her, then dimmed as her boss's words rang in her mind again: _Don't do anything to mess it up . . . to mess it up . . . to mess it up._

In other words, don't be a fanatic. Don't

wear your beliefs on your sleeve. Don't be sold out to God.

Faith sighed. "I won't, sir."

Her boss smiled. "Thatta girl. When you look good, we all look good. Remember that." He started to turn, but paused. "Don't let me see that prayer thing again, Faith. I mean it."

She caught herself nodding, and the sensation made her picture Peter two thousand years ago sitting around the fire outside the room where his friend, Jesus, was being interrogated. *I swear, I don't know the man . . .* She could almost hear the ancient words of the apostle's betrayal, feel the way his heart must have sank as he met the eyes of Jesus at that very moment.

Faith walked slowly to her car. Was she any different from Peter? Drawn and pulled and tempted to give up pieces of her soul — bit by bit — in a proud climb toward a position of power. The feeling clung to her like a damp blanket in summer time, and she couldn't will it away no matter how hard she tried. *What's this feeling, Lord? As if trouble's brewing and I'm not hearing Your will for me. And my enemies are rallying against me on every side.*

Be strong and courageous . . . the days ahead will bring testing.

Testing? Great. Haven't I been tested enough, Father?

She climbed into her Jeep and headed back to Bethany, wishing her father were still alive. Mom always turned in just after nine o'clock when she wasn't out at a fund-raiser or charity event. Once a week she'd tape the news and the next morning she and Faith would watch it over coffee. Her mother always said the same thing. *You look lovely, dear . . . your father and I have always been so proud of you.* Faith loved that time with her mother, but Dad . . . he was something else. He'd stay up until the news was over waiting for Faith's call. She would never forget those conversations as long as she lived.

She'd call him from her cell phone the minute she climbed in her Jeep. "Dad, it's me. What'd you think?"

"Sweetheart, you were more beautiful than ever. One of these days the network suits are gonna give you a call, and then everyone'll know what a wonderful reporter you are!"

The memories dissipated and Faith drove home in silence. What would her father think of Rosa's words being edited? Or of the way Dick Baker had practically threatened to fire her if she used stories that mentioned prayer or God? The worst part of it all was that Baker was right — Faith *had* signed the contract knowing the rules up-front.

The heaviness grew worse. She knew what her father would think. He'd tell her the same thing the famous Jim Elliott said before he was killed on the mission field: "He is no fool who gives what he cannot keep to gain what he cannot lose."

It was her father's favorite quote outside of Scripture.

Fifteen minutes later she pulled into her driveway, climbed out, and headed straight for her bedroom. How strange it had been to hear Mike Dillan's name after so many years. Strange to think that she had survived not only the breakup with him, but also the accident that followed. No one had ever broken her heart the way Mike had. At least not since she was thirteen, the year she lost Jordan. Her heart drifted still further downstream. Jordan Riley. The boy she'd grown up with, the one she thought she'd marry some day.

As she walked back through the milestones of the past, she realized that at every turn her father had been there. Always it was Dad who held her close and convinced her that through prayer and trust in the Lord her losses would turn into something beautiful. It was only months after she'd taken the Philadelphia job that he quit working for the big city law firm and opened an office with his best friend.

"That way I can help keep an eye on you, sweetheart."

She could hear his voice even now as she lay in bed and uttered one last prayer before falling asleep. "Thank You, Lord, for all You've brought me through. And please tell my dad — wherever he is up there and whatever he's doing — tell him I said hi." She paused.

"And tell him I miss him."

FOUR

The meeting took place at Alvin's because, other than the Jesus statue in Jericho Park, it was the most well-known landmark in all of Bethany. Despite the smattering of fast food places that had sprung up along Highway 40, Alvin's had continued to thrive. It was the only place in town where you could still get a burger, fries, and Coke for less than three dollars and not go away hungry.

At a quiet table for six in the back corner of the diner, Joshua met Mayor Frank, three of the city councilmen, and an attorney who handled general matters for the people of Bethany. The men exchanged pleasantries, talked about how big the trout were this time of year and the number of weeks until football season started. Then a silence fell over the table, and Frank cleared his throat.

"I'd like to explain the situation to Joshua." Frank's face was a mask of somber lines, and Joshua felt his heartbeat quicken.

What could be this serious?

"Go ahead, Frank." One of the councilmen nodded, and the others moved their heads in agreement.

Frank sighed. "You've heard of the HOUR group, right?"

Joshua's mind raced, trying to remember. "They're opposed to religious freedom . . . I'm trying to remember." This was Bob's expertise, not his. He felt a sense of panic as the others waited for him to place the group. "Wait a minute, I know. Humanity Organized and United in Responsibility."

Frank nodded. "Exactly."

A waitress appeared and took their order. When she was gone, Frank continued. "I have a connection in New York who called me yesterday. He told me on Monday morning someone from HOUR is planning to file suit against the town of Bethany."

Joshua's heartbeat accelerated. He looked from Frank to the other men and back again. File a lawsuit against Bethany? The town was too quiet, too small to ruffle the political feathers of a group such as HOUR. "Why would they do that?"

The men at the table exchanged glances, and just when Joshua thought he couldn't take the suspense any longer, Frank spoke up. "They want the Jesus statue."

For a moment Joshua was confused. The Jesus statue? What would a group such as HOUR want with Bethany's Jesus statue? "I'm not sure I understand."

Frank leaned closer. "They want it down, Joshua. Removed from the park. It's a Christian symbol standing on public property, exactly the kind of thing HOUR loves to go after."

A tingling sensation began in Joshua's fingers and made its way up through his arms and down his spine. HOUR wanted to remove the Jesus statue? Immediately his mind kicked into gear. "This is big . . ."

Frank sat back in his chair. "Exactly." He looked at the others. "Joshua, we've had a meeting and this is a battle we don't want to lose. We need more than general attorney wisdom this time." The general attorney in the group raised his eyebrows and took a sip of orange juice. Frank obviously was not worried about hurting the man's pride. "We'll have to wait until they file suit, but if they do . . . we've all agreed we want you to be our primary counsel on the case."

HOUR wanted to remove a monument that had stood as the single, most well-loved landmark in town for more than a hundred years? The story was bound to gain state-wide attention — even nationwide. Joshua had a sudden sense of panic.

This was too big for him. He needed Bob for this kind of thing.

As I was with Bob Moses so I will be with you.

But this is serious, Lord. It'll take more than me —

Joshua, I will never leave you nor forsake you.

Frank was looking at him. "I'm assuming you want the job." He paused, his gaze leveled at Joshua. "It'll be the biggest case you've handled since you and Bob opened shop."

"Right, I know." *Be strong and courageous* . . . "Of course . . . I'd be honored. The statue has to stay, it's that simple."

"Off the cuff, could you . . . I mean, you know, if you had to make a guess at it now . . . do you think they could force us to take it down?" Frank's usual eloquence had fled in light of all that was at stake.

Joshua swallowed hard. "Depends on how much precedent they pull."

"Precedent?" Frank's eyes narrowed. "Isn't the law clear cut?"

"Not usually." This from the general attorney, who cast a look at Joshua. "My understanding is that case precedent works against us this time, am I right?"

Joshua nodded. "Right. HOUR prides itself on eliminating the aspects of American culture they feel violate the separation of church and state. The Jesus statue is the perfect target."

There was silence as Frank crossed his arms, his teeth clenched. "That statue's part of this town. They don't have the right to come in here and —"

"We'll have to find a loophole, a way to outsmart them." Joshua hung his head for a moment and then looked at the others again. "I have to be honest, with Bob gone it won't be easy."

"You'll have our support, whatever we can do." The general attorney tapped his pencil. "It isn't a matter of the religious right or separation of church and state. That statue belongs to the people of Bethany, and my guess is there's not a person within a hundred miles offended by it."

"Save that." Joshua smiled. "We might need it for closing arguments —"

Frank broke in. "None of it matters unless they actually file suit. And we won't know that until Monday."

The men agreed to keep the issue to themselves unless it became a reality. In that case, they'd need all the favorable media contacts they could get. Joshua thought of

Faith Evans and hoped it wouldn't have to involve her. She'd been through enough without adding this.

The meeting was over, and the men went their own ways — all but Frank and Joshua. They talked about the possibilities as they wandered toward the parking lot. "I'll do whatever I can to help you." Frank shoved his hands in his pockets. "Be ready."

Be ready . . . be ready . . . The same words he'd felt God laying on his heart the day before. *Be strong . . . be ready . . . I'll go before you.* Yes, though the situation might seem impossible, the Lord had His hand in it.

Frank drove away and Joshua followed. But instead of heading home to Helen, he turned right and then right again on Main Street . . . half a block down to Jericho Park. It was a small place, really. Not like those built by newer communities, with tennis courts and indoor swimming pools and play equipment stretching half an acre. On the left stood a double swing set and two slides — set in sand. Also in the play area were two teeter-totters and an old metal merry-go-round, the kind kids powered by running alongside. Ancient maple trees edged the park on both sides, and a cement walkway meandered along the entire perimeter.

Across from the play yard was less than two acres of neatly manicured mature grass.

And standing proudly in the center of the grass was the Jesus statue.

Joshua climbed out of his car and walked toward it, remembering all the times he'd worked or played or loved or laughed in the shadow of that chiseled, ten-foot piece of stone. A few years ago the Bethany *Chronicle* ran a story about the statue, detailing the history of the piece. Created by a local artist, it was donated to the city before the turn of the twentieth century. Of course, back then Bible lessons were taught in public schools and the Ten Commandments hung in every classroom. The townsfolk received the statue gratefully, in awe of the artist's ability to capture Christ's expression of compassion.

Over the decades stories had risen and become part of the town's folklore — stories of people passing through town, spotting the Jesus statue, and being so moved they gave their lives to the Lord then and there. Or of people who'd been to the park a hundred times suddenly seeing something about the eyes of the sculpture that caused them to come clean with God and pray for a fresh start.

Joshua moved closer to the statue. It was

no surprise.

The statue depicted Jesus, arms outstretched, palms up, beckoning those with hurts or fears or pain to come to Him. There was something about the eyes . . . something steeped in love and peace and grace and forgiveness. Something that showed the way Christ would always yearn for the return of His people.

Joshua was at the foot of the statue now and he read the placard engraved at its base: "Come to me, all you who are weary and heavy burdened, and I will give you rest . . . Take my yoke upon you and learn from me, for I am gentle and humble in heart, and you will find rest for your souls. Jesus."

That was it. A person could actually feel his soul resting in the presence of Christ's words, in the shadow of His image. Not that the statue itself held any power, it simply directed one to consider the greatness of God, the peace one might experience if only he took Jesus up on His offer.

Certainly in light of the political climate and in light of the persecution promised in Scripture, it was understandable that some might find the statue offensive. But remove it from the park? Joshua thought about other public places he'd visited, parks with statues of famous generals, influential Native American leaders, or great men and women in the Civil Rights movement. If those statues were allowed, what right did HOUR have to remove one that depicted Jesus Christ?

Regardless of whether people took Him at His word, Christ was real. He lived and died and made a tremendous impact on people, both in His day and in the present. That alone should be justification for keeping the statue up. Christ was an historical figure.

But Jesus was so much more than that. And Joshua was willing to bet the people at HOUR knew this. Certainly they were aware that no other man in history had affected mankind as much as Christ. No other had demonstrated the power to instill such deep emotions and widely varying reactions from people. His presence was life-changing for some while it filled others with violent hate. There was no one else who evoked such a dramatic response from all who came to know of Him.

But then no other man was the Son of God.

Joshua sighed, studying the statue's eyes. They seemed so lifelike. So full of love, of compassion.

Joshua closed his eyes. *Don't let them file suit against us, God. What if we lose? What*

73

of the cost to the people of Bethany if the statue is forced to go?

Joshua blinked and turned his back to the statue. Gazing into the blue sky over Bethany he begged God again to keep HOUR from filing, painfully aware that the law was on their side, not his.

Be strong and courageous, Joshua. I will go before you.

The holy whispers resonated in Joshua's soul, bringing a sense of peace he hadn't felt since Bob died. Somehow he knew that whatever might happen Monday, God would see him through. He rested in that thought for a moment. *Okay, Lord . . . I'll trust You.*

After all, what choice did he have? Outside of God's intervention, if HOUR filed suit against Bethany on Monday the situation would be hopeless.

Whether Joshua was strong and courageous or not.

FIVE

Jordan drove to Bethany Sunday afternoon and by ten o'clock that night had checked into a local motel. Normally, seven hours in the car would give him time to review his caseload, strategize about upcoming lawsuits, and work on closing arguments for those in progress. This time, though, he'd been plagued by unwanted images, memories that had propelled him into an exhausting inner battle. Every few moments he was drawn to remember the past, to walk through it and touch it and savor life the way it had been. But just as quickly would come his determination to keep such thoughts at bay. He was a survivor, not a sentimentalist. He refused to live in yesterday's time zone.

If that wasn't enough, he was burdened by the uncomfortable feeling that his life's work was somehow flawed. His opponents were defenseless types, such as the New

York schoolteacher or pastors or youth group leaders. Was there really victory in winning cases against such people? People who certainly had never intended to cause harm? Shouldn't he have been using his legal talent to rid the streets of real criminals?

Of course, anyone who encouraged public expression of religion was a criminal in Jordan's mind. But still the feeling remained.

In the end he blamed his confusing thoughts on overwork and a lack of sleep. When he reached the hotel, he put away his things, brushed his teeth, and dropped into bed, where he immediately fell asleep.

When he awoke Monday he fairly sprang out of bed, showered, shaved, and had a cup of coffee two hours before he needed to be up. He had three very special visits to make. How they went would determine his final decision about filing suit against Bethany. His boss would agree with him either way. If Jordan called and said he'd changed his mind, that the statue was not as offensive as he remembered it to be, Hawkins would never mention it again.

Fifteen minutes later, he drove up in front of the Bethany courthouse and found a parking space. As he made his way up the steps, Jordan caught his reflection in the mirror. He prided himself on looking nice and today was no exception. A professional wardrobe should make a statement and his consisted of Armani suits, starched buttoned-downs, and soft leather dress shoes.

He cursed himself for not driving to Bethany and doing this sooner. Five years sooner. Back when the clerks at the courthouse had first refused to find his sister's file. He'd made more than twenty calls in the months and years since then, but always the answer was the same: "The records are sealed, sir. No one can get that information."

Jordan's heart beat hard in anticipation. He'd learned a few tricks since 1995. The only way past the fortress of red tape was to show up in person. He walked up to a counter labeled Records and waited his turn. Would this be it? In the next few minutes would he actually find out where they'd sent his sister?

"Next." A stout woman barked the word and cast an impatient glance at Jordan. He clutched his briefcase to his side as he moved up against the counter and smiled at the woman. Her name tag read Olivia.

Often women were moved to do what

Jordan wanted simply because of his looks. Olivia scowled at him, waiting for him to speak. Somehow he feared this was not one of those times. "Hi. I'm an attorney working on a local case." He smiled as though that were all the explanation he needed to provide. "I need to check out a file."

She scrutinized him, her face a twist of wrinkles and bad attitude. "You new around here?"

Jordan tried to look unaffected by her frigid tone. "Actually, I'm from New York. One of your citizens in Bethany asked me to consult on a matter. Can I give you the file name?"

Olivia shifted her weight, her lips a single line of distrust. "What local citizen?"

There was a beat while Jordan's mind raced for an answer. "He asked me not to mention his name. The lawsuit is highly confidential."

"You got ID?"

Jordan pulled out his wallet and flashed her several pieces, including his Bar Association membership card. Finally he tossed her a business card. Jordan Riley, attorney at law. *Come on, lady, what d'ya want?* When he could think of nothing else to hand her, he smiled again and waited.

Olivia released a heavy sigh. "All right,

what file do you need?"

Did all the clerks at the courthouse have Olivia's charming demeanor or was he just lucky? He cleared his throat. "It's a Social Services file. Mother died, two kids were sent to different foster homes. Should be two files, actually. I need the one under the daughter's name — Heidi Riley. No relation."

He hadn't spoken his sister's name for years. The pounding of his heart was so loud within him he figured everyone in the room could easily hear it. He watched Olivia write down the information and waited for her to turn around and head into the archives room for the file.

Instead she shook her head and set down her pen, like a judge rapping his gavel on the bench. "Social Services cases are closed to the public."

Jordan forced a chuckle to cover up his frustration. "I told you, I'm an attorney. I need the file for a case I'm working on."

Olivia planted her hands on her hips. "I don't care who you are, or what high-falutin' big city you're from. You're not getting a Social Services file. Cases where children are placed with foster families are of the utmost privacy in the state of Pennsylvania."

Panic replaced frustration as Jordan saw his opportunity slipping away. "Listen, I can see the file if I want to. But all I really need is one piece of information. Maybe you could check it yourself and give me that detail."

Olivia stared at him, not answering one way or another.

"I need to know where the girl, Heidi, was placed. Who she was placed with." *Give me a break, here, lady . . .*

Olivia's eyes grew wide and she laughed out loud. "That's exactly what the state wants kept private." She thought a moment. "How old did you say the case was?"

Jordan's shoulders fell. "Sixteen years." Would he never find Heidi? Was there no way to see the file?

A deep chuckle rang from behind the counter again as Olivia shook her head. "A case that old wouldn't be at this courthouse anyway. Those files are at the state's microfilm library. You'd have to petition them if you want a chance to be heard. Even then, I've never heard of opening a placement case. Only the person whose file it is has a right to see those records."

"Fine, I'll try the microfilm library." Jordan smiled, wondering if it hid the pain that racked his heart. *Heidi, don't give up on me . . . I'm trying to find you.*

"You know —" Olivia's expression softened, as though what she was about to say might actually help Jordan feel better about his wasted effort — "after sixteen years she wouldn't be at the same foster home anymore. She's probably married and living halfway across the country."

"Yeah." A hundred knives pierced Jordan's heart as he stared at the woman. "Thanks."

He was in his car in five minutes, driving to his second visit. As he navigated the streets of Bethany the memories came again. He and his mother and sister riding bikes through the shady roads near their home.

"I'll race you, Jordan . . ."

Heidi's voice echoed in the hallways of his memory, sounding as alive today as it had all those years ago.

Stop! Jordan ordered himself to remain in the present. Three more turns, and he was on Oak Street, the place where he and his family had lived for what seemed his entire childhood. He slowed the car, struck by how small and crowded the houses looked. *We thought we lived in a castle back then.* He kept driving, searching for signs of the house he still knew better than any other, the only place he'd ever felt at home.

81

Finally he saw it. It was beige now instead of white, with chocolate brown shutters instead of the blue his mother had painted the summer he was six or seven. It seemed to be about half the size he remembered, but otherwise it looked the same. He thought about walking up to the door and asking for a look around. Then he changed his mind. It would be one thing to walk once more through the rooms where they'd been a happy family. But there would be no avoiding his mother's room, the place where she'd spent most of her time in the months before her death.

Jordan felt tears in his eyes and blinked them back. That was years ago. He had moved on, and now there was just one reason for driving through the old neighborhood. His gaze shifted to the house next door, where the Moses family had lived. Was it possible they still lived there? That maybe — just maybe — after all the years that had passed . . . Faith was right here in Bethany?

He parked the car and walked up the sidewalk to the place where he had spent so many of his boyhood days. He knocked on the door, then took a step back, running a hand over his suit, smoothing the wrinkles. If Faith didn't live here, maybe the new owners remembered the Moses family.

The door opened and a man in his sixties — a man Jordan had never seen before — looked at him curiously. "Can I help you?"

His heart sank. "Yes, I'm looking for the Bob Moses family. They . . . uh, they used to live here."

The man smiled, but it didn't hide his guarded expression. "You a friend of the Moses family?"

Jordan nodded and remembered his small-town manners. "Yes, sir. Lived next door when I was a boy. I live in New York now, just passing through."

"You haven't heard then?"

Heard what? Had something happened to Faith? Jordan fought the urge to turn and run before his memories could be altered by whatever the man was about to share. "No, sir. Last I knew, they were still living here."

The man swept his palm over the top of his white hair. "I'm sorry to be the bearer of bad news, but Bob Moses died not too long ago. Let's see, it's been about a month now. Had a heart attack at his law office here in town."

Jordan could think of nothing to say. Bob Moses had been the only father figure he'd ever known, a man who personified everything good and honorable and trustworthy.

Even if he had lied to him. And now he was gone. A thickness in Jordan's throat made it difficult for him to talk. "The . . . the rest of the family? They moved, I guess?"

The stranger waved his hand as though he were chasing off flies. "Oh, they moved years back, bought a nice place in the country five miles out of town."

What about Faith? The question perched on his lips ready to take wing, but Jordan contained it. He'd had enough bad news for one day. He reached out and shook the older man's hand. "I'm Jordan Riley, I should have introduced myself."

"Joe Cooper." The man's handshake was firm and strong despite his years. "Good to know you."

Jordan took another step back. "Well, I guess I'll be going. I'm . . . I'm sorry about Mr. Moses."

"All of us were. Whole town showed up at his funeral. Never saw two young women cry harder than those girls of his."

Faith! Maybe she did live somewhere nearby. "Girls?"

"Bob's girls. Faith and Sarah. You musta known 'em if you lived next door."

"Yes, sir, I did. Do they . . . are they still in the area?"

"Sarah married herself a chemist and

moved a few hours away, I believe. And Faith . . . well, son, everyone knows about Faith."

Again Jordan fought to keep control. He loosed a quick laugh. "Like I said I've been away for a while now. Lost touch, I'm afraid."

Joe's eyebrows lifted. "Faith's a local star. Does the eleven o'clock news every week-night. I think she married some football hero, but don't hold me to it. Not sure where she lives, either, but it must be close."

Jordan fought the urge to race for his car and drive to the news station. So what if she was married? With everything they'd shared as kids he was sure she'd want to see him now. He jingled the keys in his pocket. He had come this far . . .

Suddenly he wanted to find Faith so badly he could barely stand to wait another moment. "What station is she with?"

The man cocked his head back and squinted. "I believe it's WKZN." He leveled his gaze at Jordan. "Yeah, that's it. WKZN."

Jordan backed up another two steps. "Listen, I gotta run, but thanks for the tip. Maybe I can find her before I leave town."

Joe waved and let his hand hang in the air. "Nice meetin' you, Jordan. Now don't go and get yourself lost in that big city of yours."

Jordan waved one last time and climbed in his car. Maybe Faith would know what happened to Heidi. He was out of the neighborhood and on Main Street before he realized that Faith wouldn't be at the station yet. It was only ten thirty in the morning. Besides, Jordan had one more visit to pay. Even if it was the hardest one he'd make all day, he had no choice but to go. He stopped at a local florist, purchased a dozen long-stem yellow roses — his mother's favorites — and headed for the cemetery.

He had only been to the place where his mother was buried three times. Once on the day they buried her and twice after that — in the weeks before Social Services stepped in — when he had needed her strength and had ridden his bike to the cemetery to sit by her simple grave, marked by a flat, square stone supplied by the state. Jordan had promised himself he'd replace the marker with a proper tombstone when he had the money, but he hadn't been back to Bethany to take care of it. Now the idea seemed to belong to another person.

Carrying the roses, Jordan tried to remember where his mother's plot lay. His eyes fell on a grave that looked newer than the rest, with tiny blades of grass just starting to poke through a fresh mound of dirt. Jordan meandered toward it and saw a large, bronze plaque at the base of the plot. "Robert Samuel Moses, 1944–2001, Lover of Betty, Sarah, Faith, and Jesus, most of all. Religious freedom fighter."

What?

Jordan's gut recoiled at those last words. Religious freedom fighter? Bob Moses? Hadn't he worked corporate law back when their houses were next door to each other? If he was a religious freedom fighter, that meant . . .

Jordan hunched down near the stone and hung his head. It meant he and Bob Moses had been waging battle on opposite sides of the war. They could even have wound up in court against each other. The reality cut Jordan to the core. How disappointed would Mr. Moses be if he knew the truth about Jordan's occupation? Especially after the Moses family had done so much for Jordan, his mother, and his sister . . .

Jordan studied the tombstone again. *Jesus, most of all . . . Jesus, most of all . . . Jesus, most of all . . .*

His mind flooded with images of his dying mother, of Heidi driving off with the social worker — and Jordan's heart steeled itself again with determination. What good had Jesus done for his mother? For him or his sister? For that matter, what good had He done for the Moses family? Faith and her parents and sister had lived for God, trusted in Him, depended on Him, and where had it gotten them? Bob Moses was buried just as deep underground as Jordan's mother. Two people who loved God more than life, yet here they were. Their lives cut short by the very same God they'd spent a lifetime serving.

He stared at the roses in his hands and scanned the burial grounds. The image of a willow tree appeared in his mind and he looked over one shoulder, then the other until he saw it. There, at the back of the cemetery . . . the pauper's section, where they buried people with little money. People forgotten over time. Jordan clenched his teeth and strode in that direction, not stopping until he found it. The white marker was dirty, dulled by the years and neglected. Weeds — though cut back — grew around the plot.

Tears stung at Jordan's eyes. *Mom . . .*

He knelt and laid the flowers on the ground, noticing how they dwarfed the small stone. "Evelyn S. Riley, mother." That was it; all that was left to remember her by.

Jordan ran his fingers over the rough marker and ached to have her at his side again, yearned once more to be the boy who would run home from school and share his day with her, feel the validation of her hug.

Jordan pictured her, pretty and petite, a brown-haired woman whose hardships in life he'd known nothing about because she'd never once complained about them. Jordan's father had abandoned them before he and Heidi were out of diapers. Two years later police notified his mother that Earl Riley had been killed in a head-on collision with a cement wall. Drunk and out of work, behind the wheel of a stolen car. Jordan's mother had been careful to spare him and Heidi the sordid details, but after she died — when Social Services stepped in and took them — the facts were repeated before judges and social workers a number of times.

"Jesus will take care of us, kids . . . don't you worry about us . . ."

His mother's words rang simply, sweetly through the whispering fronds of the willow tree, as though she were still speaking them now. A teardrop rolled off Jordan's cheek and landed on the grave marker and he rubbed it with his fist, cleaning off some of the dirt.

Jesus. Jordan released a short laugh. Yes, lot of good He'd done. Left Jordan's mother to raise two kids alone, then sat back and watched while she died of cancer. What kind of God would let that happen?

"I'm going home, Jordan . . . this isn't my home and it isn't yours, either. Cling to Jesus, son . . . Don't let walls grow around your heart because I'm sick . . . because I'm sick . . . because I'm sick."

His mother's words ran across his heart again and again. His poor, sweet, gullible mother. There was no God and no heaven. Only lonely, old cemeteries where people such as Evelyn Riley and Bob Moses lay rotting beneath the earth's surface.

"Jesus loves you, son."

Right. Jordan wiped his cheeks, stood up, and stared once more at his mother's tombstone. "I miss you, Mom." His voice came out in a strained whisper, which was all he could manage under the burden of his emotions. "If you can hear me, if you can see me . . . I miss you." A sob lodged in his throat and he swallowed it back. "I'm trying to find Heidi, but I'm not sure how. I wish . . ."

He couldn't finish the sentence. Couldn't bring himself to say that he wished the God she had so strongly believed in had been real after all, and that if He were real, He might have cared about them as much as his mother believed. If He were, if He had . . . maybe she could ask Him to help find Heidi.

But it was all a batch of fanciful stories and groundless traditions. Jordan bent down and touched the stone once more. "Goodbye, Mom. I still love you."

He turned and made his way out of the cemetery, back toward his motel . . . back to consider whether he would file a lawsuit against Bethany that afternoon. He would lock himself in his room, lay out the briefs he'd written, and make a decision, once and for all.

He drove back along Main Street and —

Jordan slammed on his brakes, nearly causing a pileup. Waving his apology at three drivers, he pulled to the side of the road and stared. There it was — a block from the old neighborhood — Jericho Park and the infamous Jesus statue.

He climbed out of his car, crossed the street, and found the bench he'd been so familiar with sixteen years ago. A bench just five feet from the statue. As he sat, his eyes were drawn to the lifelike expression in the carved eyes. Powerless against the pull, Jordan felt himself drifting back in time.

He could see his mother, stirring a pot of soup on the stove and smiling at him. "You know what?" The memory of his mother's voice rang in his heart. "My favorite place in town is Jericho Park and the Jesus statue."

The Jesus statue . . . the Jesus statue . . . the Jesus statue. Jordan closed his eyes and pictured himself a ruddy-cheeked teenage boy riding his bike to this spot, this very bench . . . night after night after night . . . to his mother's favorite spot.

Begging God to let his mother live.

He blinked and saw the statue the way he had as a boy, the arms beckoning him, the eyes seeming to know his pain. And suddenly it wasn't one memory or two, but a whole flood of scenes and voices all taking Jordan back in time to the days when he had actually believed they would all live happily ever after.

Six

The house had belonged to Earl Riley's family. Otherwise there would have been no way Evelyn Riley and her two children could have afforded to live on Oak Street. They'd lived in a one-bedroom apartment until word came that Jordan's father was dead. Jordan was five at the time and though he didn't remember Earl or the policemen who came to the door that afternoon, he remembered what happened next.

There was a party — at least it had seemed like a party — and everyone was paying special attention to him and Heidi. A fancy lady with a feathered hat spent much of that day bawling and fussing over his mother, saying things like, "You poor dear" and "I had no idea Earl wasn't taking care of you."

Back then Jordan hadn't been sure what it all meant, but a little while later he and his mother and Heidi moved into the house on Oak Street. "It's a gift from your grandma," was all his mother would say. Often Jordan wondered why his grandma had given them a house but never came to see them or stay for dinner.

It all made sense now, of course.

Jordan blinked and felt the chill of a breeze against the back of his neck. His father had been the black sheep, the boy-gone-bad from a wealthy, upper-crust family in Philadelphia. His father's father had died in his fifties of a stroke, and Jordan guessed that his grandmother hadn't known a thing about him or Heidi or their mother until the accident. Then — so her grandchildren would always have a place to live — the old woman had paid cash for the small house on Oak Street and given it to his mother. That done, she'd washed her hands of the three of them.

"I want the lady with the pretty hat to come see us again," Heidi had said one night while they were cuddled on their mother's lap for a bedtime story.

"The pretty lady is busy, sweetheart. But I'll tell her you'd like her to come and maybe one day . . ."

Another memory came into focus. Jordan was eight years old — maybe nine — and he and Heidi and Faith had walked home from school. When they came inside, they

94

found his mother at the kitchen table, her hands over her face.

He and Heidi were at her side immediately, while Faith stood close by, her pretty face shadowed with concern.

"Mom, what happened? What's wrong?"

His mother had sniffled once and wiped her eyes with her fingertips. "Nothing, kids. I'm fine." She smiled at them, her cheeks swollen from crying. "You remember the nice old lady? The one who gave us this house?"

Jordan and Heidi nodded.

Their mother sniffled again. "Someone called today and told me she . . . she died."

At the time Jordan remembered feeling relief. It was too bad for the old lady, but at least there wasn't something wrong with his mother. Strange, he'd thought, that she would be so upset over the death of someone she barely knew.

A flutter of action brought Jordan back to the present, and he watched a bird land on the Jesus statue. He narrowed his eyes as though trying to see into the past. His mother's tears were easier to understand now, in light of thirty years of life experience. She must have felt so alone, so abandoned. First by his father, then by the old woman. True, she had given them a house.

But she had never extended her friendship, her seal of approval that Jordan and Heidi and their mother were worthy of her time and attention. That afternoon, hearing that she was dead, must have ended his mother's dreams of someday being close to the only family she had left.

It had been another reminder that all they had in the world was each other.

Jordan could see himself throwing his arms around his mother's neck and comforting her that day. "It's okay, Mom. You don't need anyone but me and Heidi."

And that was true, until the year Jordan turned ten.

Everything about his childhood seemed to crystallize that year — his relationship with Heidi, with his mother, with God Himself. That was the year Jordan knew without a doubt that everything would work out for them. And that belief started because of his growing friendship with Faith Moses.

For the first five years of living on Oak Street, Jordan saw Faith as little more than a nuisance. She was a yucky girl who happened to live next door, someone to talk to and walk home from school with, a big sister figure for Heidi, but nothing more. Faith hung around the house after school sometimes, and once in a while he and Heidi would go to her house. But the summer he turned ten, it was as though someone flipped a light switch and he could see Faith for the first time. She was beautiful, even back then, possessed of a combination of joy and grace that gave her the air of a princess. Not that she ever acted that way. It was simply who she was.

One night she and Jordan played checkers after school while Heidi stayed home with their mother. The afternoon gave way to evening and just before dark a big man with an even bigger smile burst through the door and shouted. "Hey, family, the happiest man in the world is home!"

Jordan had never been formally introduced to Faith's father until that evening. "And who do we have here?" The man wore a neatly trimmed beard and the light from his blue eyes seemed to fill the room.

Faith jumped up and ran into her father's arms. "This is Jordan from next door, Daddy. You've seen him before." Even now Jordan could remember the pang of jealousy he'd felt seeing Faith and her father that way.

Jordan blinked back the wetness in his eyes as the image faded. What would it have been like to be hugged by his dad, to be loved that way by a father? The little boy inside still wanted the experience, but Jordan had no more understanding of that kind of love than he'd had twenty years earlier. But even twenty years hadn't dimmed the memory of the smile on Bob Moses' face when he and Jordan met.

"Jordan, welcome to our home. This is the place where Jesus lives!" The man was so happy, so sure of himself that at first Jordan had taken the statement literally. It seemed true enough, for at Faith's house people were always laughing or dancing or praising God about something. If Jesus had to live somewhere, chances were he lived with the Moses family.

Jordan stayed for dinner that night and every now and then his eyes would meet Faith's and they would giggle. When he went home that evening he made an announcement to his mother. "I'm going to marry Faith Moses one day."

His mother smiled at him and pulled him close, the way she always did when he came through the door. "Are you now?"

Jordan nodded. "Yep. I like her, Mom. Jesus lives at her house."

Jesus lives at her house?

The memory was more than a little startling, and Jordan shifted, gazing at the tops of the trees along the park's edge. Was *he* the one who introduced Jesus to his family? He'd always assumed it was Faith's mother, Betty, who'd led them to the Lord. But that wasn't how he was remembering it now . . .

An arrow of regret pierced his heart. If he'd been the one, he was deeply sorry. There was no reason to believe Jesus was alive — not back then or today. Yet somehow his mother had fallen completely in love with Jesus Christ. And it had happened sometime after he'd come home from Faith's that night.

Another picture came into view of Heidi and him watching television with Faith in the den while their mothers talked quietly in the next room. The women had their Bibles out, as they did several times a week when Faith's mother came to visit. A few weeks later he and Heidi and their mother started attending church with the Moses family. And Jordan still remembered the highlight of their Sunday outings: As they walked from the car to the church building, Mr. Moses would put his arm around Jordan's shoulders and ask him questions.

"Did you have a good week, Jordan? Been talking to Jesus much?"

Jordan didn't remember his answers or even all the things Mr. Moses asked. Just the feeling of the man's arms around him.

Two months later, his mother got baptized at church, and after that there was something different about her eyes. She'd always been kind and gentle, quick with a hug and a kiss for him and Heidi. But that day she pulled them aside and told them what happened. "I gave my life to Jesus, kids. And one day I want you to do the same thing. He loves us all very much . . . and I love Him more than anything."

Jordan had bristled just a bit at that. More than *anything?* More than Heidi and him? His worries didn't last long, because whatever loving Jesus meant, it seemed to only make their mother more wonderful, as though it had accomplished something deep and lasting within her. There was a peace in her eyes, a joy that remained whether the welfare check came on time each month or not.

It was a joy that was still there two years later when she began to have a strange cough that wouldn't go away.

Jordan was twelve that year, Heidi just nine. Still his little sister picked up on their mother's condition and shared her fears with Jordan. "I'm worried about Mama," she told him one night. Their mother had gone to bed early, pale and tired, and Jordan was in charge of doing the dishes and making sure they were both in bed by nine. He pulled Heidi into a hug. "I know. Me too."

"You think we should pray to Jesus?" Heidi stared at him, her brown eyes glistening with sincerity.

Jordan thought of the way his mother loved God, the way she talked about Jesus as though he no longer lived only at Faith's house but at their house too. "Okay, let's do it."

Then Jordan and Heidi held hands and talked to Jesus as though He was right there with them, part of their circle. Jordan remembered keeping his eyes closed, wondering if he opened his eyes whether Jesus would really be standing there with them. "Mama loves you, Jesus. So make her better quick, okay? And thank you for giving us each other."

It was something he'd heard his mother pray and it seemed appropriate that night. Over the next few weeks she had several doctor's appointments and for a while the cough seemed to go away. It came back in the springtime when Jordan was thirteen, and this time she seemed worse than before.

One afternoon Jordan and Faith were walking home from the local junior high when he stopped and sat on the edge of the curb. His feelings were all jumbled that day.

He'd seen Faith talking to another boy at school, and though they were too young to date, he couldn't fight the uncomfortable feelings squaring off in his heart. If he hadn't known better he'd have thought he was actually jealous. But it wasn't just Faith. He was worried about his mother, too. She seemed to be getting thinner, wasting away a little more each day. The combination of feelings was simply too much and as Jordan sat on the curb, he hung his head and choked back a sob as two teardrops fell to the ground.

"Jordan, what's wrong?" Faith was immediately at his side, her arm around his shoulders. "Are you sick? What?"

Worried as he was about his mother, his heart suddenly overflowed with thoughts of Faith. He sniffed once and studied her eyes. "Am I your best friend?"

She was so pretty, her pale blond hair framing her face as she nodded. "You know you are."

"Then why were you with Scott Milton today at lunch?" Jordan could still hear himself, hear the way his voice sounded as he asked the question. Not angry or accusatory, but wounded.

Faith's eyes danced. "Jordan Riley, you mean you're jealous of old Scott Milton?"

She giggled and removed her arm from his back, punching him playfully in the shoulder. "I thought you and me were only friends." She raised her chin a notch. "Besides, everyone says you like Lorianne Wilcox."

It was Jordan's turn to laugh, and he bumped her playfully with his shoulder. "Don't believe everything you hear."

"It's true, isn't it?" She was teasing him, and he loved the way she made him feel. Even back then, when he was too young to know what it all meant.

"No, it isn't true. Lorianne has a big nose."

A knowing look filled Faith's eyes. "I'll be sure to remember that." She pretended she was taking notes on an invisible piece of paper. "Jordan Riley . . . doesn't like . . . big noses."

Jordan stopped laughing and his smile fell. Faith stared sadly at him, clouds dimming the twinkling in her eyes. "What is it? What's wrong?"

Jordan knew she was the only one he could talk to about his fears. Heidi was too young and he didn't want to scare her. Of course he could never tell his mother; she would be devastated to know his true feelings. "I think . . . I think my mom's dying."

Faith's eyes flew open and she shook her head. "No, Jordan. Don't say that. She's just sick. Remember, it happened last year, too?"

Jordan hung his head again. "I know, but this time it's different. Like she's not ever going to get better again."

Faith was adamant in her response. "Then we need to pray. Right away so Jesus knows what you're feeling."

Jordan nodded and waited for Faith to take the initiative. She reached out and held his hand in hers. "Father God, we come before You knowing that You hear us when we pray . . . please, Jesus, make Jordan's mom get better. He and Heidi need her so much. And please help Jordan trust You so he won't be afraid." She said some other things too, but Jordan didn't remember them. He was torn between trying to focus on the prayer and enjoying the way her hand felt in his.

When they were finished they looked up at each other, and Jordan realized all the other kids had made their way inside already. It was just he and Faith alone on the curb, a spring breeze washing over them. Without giving it another thought, Jordan leaned forward and kissed her on the lips. A simple kiss that was neither lingering nor rushed. The kind of kiss that meant they were more than friends, but still too young for anything serious. Faith's cheeks grew flushed, and for once she had nothing to say.

Jordan looked through her eyes straight to her heart that afternoon. "I'm going to marry you one day, Faith." He grinned and poked her in the ribs to lighten the mood. "So don't go spending too much time with Scott Milton."

There was a new shyness in Faith's eyes as she smiled at him. "Okay. And don't forget to pray about your mom. Jesus'll help her, Jordan. I just know it."

Looking back now Jordan wasn't sure if it was Faith's words that afternoon or his deepening sense that something was terribly wrong with his mother that had spurred him to start riding his bike to Jericho Park. He would sit on the very bench he occupied now and pray to Jesus about the thoughts that filled his heart. Usually his trips to the park were at night, after he and Heidi had finished their homework, after the two of them had cleaned dinner dishes and he was sure his mother was sleeping comfortably. Then he'd tuck Heidi into bed, jump on his old bicycle and head for the Jesus statue.

Jordan had no idea how often he'd visited

Jericho Park during that time of his life. The only person who knew what he was doing was Faith, but even she didn't know the range of thoughts he brought before the Lord at the foot of the statue. He prayed for his family and his grades and his baseball game. Money was scarce and he wanted a scholarship to play baseball in college so he could get a good job and make a decent living. That way they could afford the best doctors for his mother. He even prayed about Faith, knowing that somehow the two of them would be together one day.

But most of all he prayed for his mother.

Faith had asked him about the statue before. "It's not like that's really Jesus. You know that, right?"

Jordan had laughed. "Of course I know that. It's just a good place to pray. It makes me remember Jesus is real, not just some imaginary person, you know?"

Faith grinned. "I know. I feel the same way. I'm glad we have the statue here. It must make Jesus happy that it's right there on Main Street for everyone to see."

As his mother's health worsened that summer, Jordan began making the trip to Jericho Park every night. Sometimes Faith would come with him and they'd sit on the bench together, holding hands as they prayed for Jordan's mother. Once in a while they'd share a brief kiss or two, but nothing more. When school started that fall, Jordan and Faith privately knew that they shared a relationship, but they also understood they were too young to make their commitment public. Whereas they'd held hands innocently in their younger, childish years, now they were careful to only do so when they were alone.

On several occasions, Heidi had caught them that way, hands linked as they talked outside on the curb. Once in a while she'd tease them, but most of the time she understood.

"You still love me too, right?" Heidi asked him one night before they went to sleep.

"Of course, silly. You're both my best friends."

By the time the leaves changed in October that year, Jordan's mother was at the doctor every other day for some kind of appointment, and she wore a scarf all the time. *Chemotherapy.* He understood now, but at the time he'd had no idea what that meant. Only that she looked worse all the time and with each passing day his fears grew stronger than ever. He began listening in to her conversations with Faith's mother. One afternoon he overheard her say something about telling the kids, choosing the right time. That night he found her alone in her room and knelt by her bedside.

"What do you want to tell us, Mom?" He whispered the words so he wouldn't startle her, and she turned her head weakly in his direction.

A smile filled her thin face. "Oh, hi, Jordan. Wasn't it a beautiful day?"

Panic worked its way through Jordan's young body. "Mom, I don't want to talk about the day. I want to talk about you. What did you want to tell us? You said something to Faith's mother about talking to Heidi and me. About what?"

Tears welled in his mother's eyes, and she breathed out for a long time. "I guess it's time you know." She hesitated as though she would have done anything in the world to keep from having to tell him this news. "I have cancer, Jordan." She swallowed and for several moments couldn't speak. "Do . . . do you know what that is?"

Jordan had the feeling he'd been plunged under a twenty-foot tidal wave. He felt the same way he'd felt when Jimmy Julep hit him in the stomach with a fast pitch back in fifth grade. He clutched his sides and nodded. "Faith's grandpa died of cancer."

His mother smiled. "Right." She struggled

to catch her breath and wound up coughing for several seconds. "I have it in my lungs, honey. The doctors say that Jesus might be calling me home."

"No!" Jordan had to work to keep from shouting as anger and fear fought for position in his heart. "I've been talking to Jesus every day about you, Mom. You're going to get better!"

She reached out and took his hand in hers. Even now Jordan remembered how weak her grip was. "I want you to take care of Heidi, okay? And one day we'll all be together again . . . in heaven."

Jordan shook his head, raw terror strangling him as he fought the truth with every breath in his body. "No, Mom! God wouldn't do that. You're going to be fine."

"Jordan, it's time you knew the —"

"No!" He was on his feet, angry with her for reasons he didn't even understand. "Don't talk that way, Mom."

Without waiting for her response, he ran outside and climbed on his bike. Five minutes later he was on his knees, weeping at the foot of the Jesus statue. "Don't take her away from us, Lord, please. I'll do anything You want. I'll quit baseball or stop spending time with Faith. I'll do more chores and get better grades in school.

Please, Lord . . . just let her live, please!"

Faith must have heard the same thing from her mother that night because she went looking for him. Thirty minutes later she showed up at the park and gently fell on the ground beside him. She wrapped her fingers around his and hung her head, sobbing softly alongside him. There were no words between them that night, only tears as they both raised their silent voices to God and begged Him to save Jordan's mother's life.

A wave of nausea came over Jordan now as he remembered how bad things had gotten after that, how terrified Heidi became at the thought of losing their mother, how she'd started to stutter because of the fear that welled within her. And most of all how their mother had suffered . . .

Suddenly the memories were more than Jordan could take. He took a deep breath and let go of all the images except one . . . him and Faith in this very park, fingers linked as they prayed for his mother.

What do you think of your Jesus now, Faith?

The thought filled his mind and anchored there. What could she possibly feel but disillusionment? Jesus had taken his mother, her father . . . and left Jordan and Faith grieving for the people they loved. He tried to picture Faith, wondering what she might look like now, what hand life had dealt her. And whether sometimes, when the leaves turned in the fall as they were about to do in a few weeks, she remembered kneeling beside him at Jericho Park and holding hands with a boy who was her very closest friend.

He stared at the statue, the outstretched arms and passionate eyes, and he was filled with an overwhelming, growing sense of purpose. Coming to see the statue, praying to Jesus every night . . . none of it had done any good. Not for Jordan or his mother. The words on the inscription, the statue's very presence, all of it implied promises that had nothing to do with reality. If there was a God, then He'd let Jordan down in his greatest hour of need. Certainly the same had to be true for other children in Bethany, children who had grown up in the shadow of this stone memorial to deception.

Well . . . no more. This was a public park, after all. A place where people had the right to laugh and run and play without being confronted with a fairy-tale Jesus who only pretended to care.

Jordan stood and made his way back to his car. He didn't need to look over the briefs. He knew the legalities so well he could recite them in his sleep. Before he pulled away, he saw three children skip toward the statue and stop near its base. In obvious wonder they stared up at the stony face, pointing and talking amongst each other.

He wanted to shout at them, warn them against putting their faith in a God who would take away everything that mattered in a boy's life — his closest friend, his sister, and his mother. Jordan worked the muscles in his jaw as he checked traffic, pulled onto Main Street, and headed toward the courthouse.

It was just before two o'clock; there was no time to waste. The lawsuit had to be filed before another hour passed.

The statue had to go.

SEVEN

At just after two o'clock that day, Charles and Heidi Benson pulled up in front of Jericho Park and killed the engine. "There it is." Heidi stared across the grass at the old play area and scanned the grounds until her eyes fell on the Jesus statue. "We used to play here every day."

Charles glanced at the clock and shrugged. "We have time. Wanna walk for a bit?"

"Good idea." Heidi patted her rounded abdomen. "It'll be a long drive home and the last thing I need is leg cramps."

They climbed out and Charles came up alongside her, tenderly taking her hand in his as they started walking. "So . . . do you think you could live here again?"

Heidi gazed out across the park. They'd taken the day off so Charles could interview at a medical clinic in the newest part of Bethany. He'd been working out of a busy office near downtown Philadelphia for two years — ever since finishing medical school. Now, with the baby on the way, they'd agreed it would be nice to get out of the city.

But Bethany . . .

Heidi sighed. "I have mixed feelings."

Charles was quiet as they walked, allowing Heidi to remember life the way it had been when she last lived in this same small town. She'd told him how she and Jordan and their mother had shared a house not far from the park, how the days before their mother got sick were little more than a happy blur. It was what happened afterward that made it hard to come back, hard to walk in the very park where they'd played back when each day seemed more charmed than the last.

Their mother died when Heidi was ten, and afterward someone from the state stepped in. Heidi held the memories at bay and watched a boy about twelve years old pushing his little sister on the swings. The two laughed as only children can . . .

That had been Jordan and her back then, hadn't it? Happy and sure that their time together would never end?

"You okay?" Charles bent his head so she could hear his words, soft and filled with concern.

"Just thinking . . ." She looked up, conveying with her eyes the fact that she needed this time, needed to remember again what had happened that year. At first she and Jordan had lived alone with the help of their neighbors . . . Mosely or Moss . . . Moses . . . something like that. But after a few weeks the state intervened, and she and Jordan were sent to separate foster homes.

She could still hear her brother's voice, see him standing there before her, tears streaming down his face as the people from Social Services waited to take them away in two different cars. "We won't be apart for long, Heidi, I promise. Just until they can find us a home where we can live together . . ."

There was no forgetting the way she'd clung to him that day, knowing he was all she had left in the world.

"Don't let me go, Jordan. Please!"

He had shaken his head, placing his finger to her lips. "Shh . . . it's okay. You can call me whenever you need me. We'll be together soon, you have to believe that."

But it hadn't turned out that way. She stayed in one foster home for a week and then was transferred to another. Even now she remembered asking about her brother but getting only vague answers in response.

"It's difficult to place siblings your age," one social worker told her. "We're doing our best."

Then one day she overheard her foster parents talking. Something about Jordan running away and getting locked up at a boys' camp. Before they could finish Heidi burst into the room, screaming. "I want to see Jordan! He doesn't belong in a camp, he belongs with *me*."

She was so upset at the thought of losing her brother that she threw a tantrum, screaming at the top of her lungs, her fists flailing. The next day she was transferred to a foster home across the state. Four weeks later her foster parents, the Morands, sat her down.

"There's been an accident at the camp where Jordan lives." Mr. Morand took her hands in his. Heidi remembered liking the Morands from the beginning. They were kind and gentle and somehow in their presence the tragedies she'd suffered seemed bearable.

Now though, her young heart raced with fear. "An accident?"

Mrs. Morand nodded. "An underground cavern collapsed and many of the boys were killed, Heidi."

She shook her head, her eyes wide with

fear. Not Jordan . . . not her brother . . . "What . . . what about Jordan?"

"Honey, I'm sorry. He was one of the ones inside and he —"

"No! He would have gotten out. He's bigger than other boys and strong. He never would have died in there!"

The Morands held her close and let her sob away her grief long into the night as they stroked her hair and comforted her. Something Mrs. Morand said that night stuck with Heidi even to this day. "He's with your mother now . . . taking care of her in heaven until you can all be there together."

Now Heidi stared sadly at the Jesus statue. Once her family had come to believe in Christ, the statue had always been a beacon of hope. Her foster mother's words had been true; they had to be. And they were the only reason she survived that time at all.

A year later, the Morands adopted Heidi and raised her in a suburb north of Pittsburgh, where over time she was finally able to put the tragedies of her childhood behind her. The Morands loved her as if she were their own daughter, and in their care Heidi flourished. She was active in high school — involved in tennis and track. Her senior year at her church's fall kickoff she met Charles, a new boy whose family had just moved to town.

She and Charles dated through college and married before he started med school. Now they wanted a quiet place where Charles could practice medicine and they could raise their family. A place not too far from the Morands. When Charles got word that the clinic in Bethany was looking to hire a pediatrician, the two of them scheduled a day trip and he arranged an interview.

"They want me," Charles had told her when he found her in the hospital cafeteria after the interview.

She threw her arms around his neck and squealed. "I knew it."

"I can start November 1."

"Honey, I'm so proud of you." It was true. Charles was everything she'd ever dreamed of in a man. He took care of her the way . . . well, the way Jordan had when she was a little girl. She could hardly wait to have their baby and set up house wherever he got a job. Even in the town that harbored all her childhood memories.

Charles interrupted her thoughts. "Everything looks good to me, the offer, the hospital . . . the community." He slowed his steps and faced her. "I guess it's up to you. Whether you can be happy here or not."

Tears clouded Heidi's vision and she swallowed hard. "It makes me wish Jordan had lived. That we could have stayed close and somehow . . . I don't know . . . maybe been adopted together." She walked a few more steps, and he fell in beside her, silent, waiting for her to continue.

"My parents told me they would have adopted Jordan too. If he hadn't . . ." Even after so many years it was hard for her to picture her strapping brother, buried beneath tons of earth in the camp accident. Wouldn't he have found a way out? Couldn't he have heard it coming and run for daylight before it was too late? But her thoughts went unspoken.

"I like to think of him the way your adoptive mom does . . . up there in heaven taking care of your mother until you can all be together again." Charles put his arm around her shoulders and held her close.

A single tear made its way down Heidi's cheeks. "Me too. But I still miss him."

There were questions in Charles's eyes and Heidi understood. If she felt this way now, just walking near the Jesus statue, would it be impossible for her to live in Bethany? To walk the streets daily where she and Jordan once lived? To take their children to Jericho Park — a place where she and her brother once played?

Heidi sighed. "It's in the past, Charles." Her voice was quiet, choked by emotion. "I have you now . . . our life is everything I've ever wanted." She hugged him again. "I can do this. I can live here, raise our family here." She kissed him as two more tears fell onto her cheeks. "Call them and tell them yes."

EIGHT

The Monday night newscast was always busier than most because with it came the weekend wrap-up, stories that covered not only that day's events but also any loose ends from Saturday and Sunday. By the time Faith left the soundstage at just before midnight, she was exhausted in more ways than one.

She'd called the Social Services department earlier that day, and though the piece on Rosa had appeared several times during daytime broadcasts, not a single person had called about her. *Is there no one for her, God?*

I have appointed you for this, my daughter.

Faith made her way through the station's back corridors toward the rear parking lot. What had God appointed her for? Getting the news out about Rosa? If that was the case, why hadn't anyone called? At age six, she was a sweet-natured child, but give her three or four more years in foster care and Rosa was bound to grow jaded. The innocent faith that lit up her countenance would certainly grow cold in light of the truth that no one wanted her.

I'd adopt her myself if I wasn't single. The thought simmered in Faith's heart like an overcooked vegetable. It was true, wasn't it? She'd go through the process, work with the system and make Rosa her own daughter if only her personal life wasn't so uncertain. But Rosa needed a father, too . . . a real family.

I will supply all your needs. Wait for the appointed time.

Faith had no idea what *that* meant but she was sure of the message, felt it resonate deep within her soul. And for reasons she didn't understand, the holy whispers sent a ray of hope through her. If God said it would all work out, then somehow — against the odds — it would. For Rosa and for herself.

She pushed the heavy metal door open and was met by an icy wind. The parking lot was dark and she moved quickly, pulling her jacket close as she stared into the starry sky. Fall had arrived, all right. And with it the promise of colder days ahead. Football weather, really. Her father's favorite time of year.

"Faith . . ."

The male voice came at her from across the parking lot and it stopped her in her tracks. She backed up a few steps toward the building, staring into the darkness until she saw the shape of a man about twenty yards away. Her heart pounded. Was it a fan? A stalker? She didn't recognize the voice — and suddenly realized how vulnerable she was.

"Who is it?" She continued taking steps back toward the station door, determined to alert security before she became the victim of an attack. "Come into the light."

"Don't be afraid, Faith." The man took three slow steps into a circle of brightness that came from one of the station windows. "It's me. Jordan."

Faith felt her knees go weak. It couldn't be . . . "Jordan who?"

Step by step he moved closer, and Faith's breath caught in her throat as she made out his face. It wasn't possible, but it was him; her childhood friend . . . the boy who'd asked her to marry him the summer they were just thirteen. He was a man now, tall and dark with looks that likely stopped women in their tracks. His designer suit suggested he had done well for himself, and

Faith was flooded with feelings she couldn't quite decipher. Whatever they were, she was glad for the darkness, glad he couldn't see the heat she felt in her cheeks. "Jordan Riley? How in the world did you find me?"

"I was in town . . . on business." He smiled, and there it was. The same eyes and grin he'd had as a teenager. It was Jordan, all right. Without giving it another thought, she came to him and hugged him.

"I can't believe it's you." She pulled back and looked at him. "Who told you I was here?"

"I went to your old house. A Mr. Joe Cooper told me you were a big star now doing the news for WKZN." Jordan grinned again, his eyes twinkling. "You looked beautiful tonight, Faith."

"You saw me?" Was she dreaming? Was this really Jordan Riley standing here, talking to her after so many years? To think he'd come into town and seen her on the news that night . . .

"I watched you for five minutes and I knew I had to see you in person. I have a few meetings tomorrow, then it's back to New York, so tonight was my only chance. I thought I'd surprise you."

How long had it been? What was he doing now? Was he married? And what had happened to his sister, Heidi? A hundred questions shouted for Faith's attention, and she tried to think of which was most important. "So, tell me about yourself . . . what've you been doing?"

Jordan put his hands in his pockets and studied her. "It's so good to see you, Faith. You have no idea . . ." He hesitated, glancing around. "Can we get coffee somewhere, sit and talk a bit?"

Faith shrugged. "Sure. My mom's visiting her sister in Chicago, so she won't notice if I'm late."

Jordan looked at her strangely. "Your mom? I thought . . . aren't you married?"

A short laugh escaped Faith's freezing lips. "Definitely not."

He tossed his hands in the air and laughed. "Well, me, neither. I guess that means it's a date."

Faith's heart soared at Jordan's words and she stepped back, surprised at herself. What was she feeling, an attraction? To Jordan? After so many years had gone by? She chided herself for letting her imagination get away with her. They'd been kids back then, after all. This was nothing more than an old friend checking up on her.

He angled his head, his eyes locked on hers. "So . . . not married, huh?"

"Nope."

"Long story?"

"Very."

Jordan took a few steps back toward his car. "I'll follow you."

Faith led him to a twenty-four-hour diner in the heart of Bethany, a place for people who worked the night shift or needed a quiet moment alone in the still of the early morning hours. When they were seated at a booth, Faith again felt the familiar draw to him. Just as she'd felt it all those years ago . . .

The waitress brought them coffee, and Faith studied him over the brim of her cup. "How long's it been?"

He smiled. "You mean since I kissed you and asked you to be my wife?"

They both laughed, and he took a swig of his coffee. "I was trying to figure it out on the way over here. Sixteen years I think. They took me away right after my mother died and that was just before Christmas 1985."

The mention of his mother put a deep sadness in the air between them. "Whatever happened to Heidi?"

Pain flashed in Jordan's eyes, and he looked down at his hands. "I don't know. We lost track of each other. That was part of what I wanted to do this week, but the records are sealed. I've been trying to find her since I graduated from law school."

Faith felt sick to her stomach. Jordan and Heidi had lost track of each other? Sixteen years ago? She pictured how Jordan had been with his sister, how he'd looked after her and played with her even though she was younger than his friends. "That's awful, Jordan. There must be someone who knows where she is."

He shrugged and when he looked at her this time it was as though walls had been erected around his heart. What had been transparent a moment earlier was now guarded, hidden behind a fortress of stone. "I haven't found anyone yet. The clerk today told me I could register a petition with the state's Social Services, but only people directly involved had the right to see the files."

"But that's you . . . you're as involved as you could be. For goodness sake, they took you out of your own house and separated you from her without giving either of you a choice."

Jordan smiled, but the gesture looked forced. "Those things happen. I'll look for her till the day I die, but I've accepted the fact that I may never find her."

"So what happened when you left here? Where did you go?"

"At first I was at a foster home. But one day I overheard the social worker say there was no way the state could keep Heidi and me together. So I ran away, tried to find the house where she was staying but wound up getting in trouble instead. I was thirteen and they figured I was unstable. Incorrigible, I believe they said. They sent me to a boys' camp in the foothills about six hours from here. Southridge, it was called."

"A boys' camp?" Faith could feel the blood draining from her face as a memory began to take shape in her mind. "But . . . weren't my parents thinking of adopting you both?"

"I don't know. No one ever said anything to me." His eyes locked onto hers and she saw concern there. "Faith, I'm sorry about your dad. He was a great man." Jordan's eyes grew wet. "He was the only father I ever knew . . ."

Faith blinked back sudden tears. "I miss him so much."

"I bet." Jordan hesitated. "He was practicing law in town, is that right?"

She nodded. "He and his friend Joshua Nunn opened a law office and took on religious freedom cases. They'd gotten off to a great start when Dad had his heart attack."

They fell silent, and Faith shook her head. "Imagine how different things might have been if you'd lived with us, if we'd adopted you and Heidi."

Now that she had remembered it, she could hear a conversation playing in her mind, one between her parents a few nights after Jordan and Heidi were taken from their home. "It's the only thing we can do, Betty . . ."

"I know, but I worry about Jordan. It might not be good to have a boy Faith's same age living under one roof."

Her father had been adamant. "It'll work out. God will see us through."

Yes, she was sure of it now. Her parents had contacted Jordan's social worker and asked about adopting both Heidi and him. "The more I think about it the more I'm sure. They wanted to adopt you both."

His eyes grew wide. "You're serious? Your family was really going to do that?" Awe and regret seemed to play out across his face simultaneously.

"I remember them calling about it." She studied him, frowning. "Did you ever hear anything?"

Jordan shook his head, his eyes a well of

sadness. "They probably told your parents I was a risk. By that point they'd already moved me to the boys' camp."

How awful that Jordan had been sent to a camp for delinquent boys when all he'd wanted was a chance to be with his sister. "I'm so sorry, Jordan."

He drew a deep breath and smiled — but the smile didn't seem genuine. It had a polished, practiced look about it — as though he were familiar with masking his real feelings. "Enough about me, what about you?" He reached across the table and squeezed her hands gently before pulling back and finishing his coffee. The feel of his fingers against hers sent electrical currents up her arms and down her spine. "What's the long story behind not being married?"

Faith was completely flustered. The touch of Jordan's hands on hers had brought back feelings for him she hadn't known still existed. Logic told her that at twelve, thirteen years old one wasn't wise enough to understand love. But the reality lay in the feelings assaulting her heart. She had cared for Jordan deeply, with a wholehearted in-nocent devotion that is possible only for young people. Indeed she had loved him at a time when life was most impressionable. Now that they were adults, the memory of those earlier feelings — combined with the heady closeness of sitting across from him — left her unsure what to say or do next. *Help me get a grip here, God. . . .*

He was waiting for her response. "Okay, but tell me if you get bored." She grinned at him and the way he looked at her made her cheeks grow hot again.

"Trust me, Faith, nothing you say could bore me."

She inhaled and forced her heart to beat normally. Then she told him how she'd studied journalism in college and started as a sports reporter. Two years later she fell hard for a professional football player.

Faith hesitated and Jordan raised an eyebrow. "Anyone I'd know?"

Everyone knew Mike, but Faith wasn't ready to go into details about her relationship with him. Even now it was too hard to share over a casual cup of coffee. Especially with Jordan Riley. "It isn't important."

The warmth in his expression told her he understood.

"Then I had my accident."

Concern fell across Jordan's face. "Accident?"

She nodded. "Three years ago. I was driving home from work and a little boy ran out in front of me. I swerved and missed him, but hit a power pole. Wrapped the car around it. They pried me from the wreck, and I was in a coma for two weeks."

"Two weeks?" He ran his hand over his hair. "Faith, you're lucky you lived."

Faith pictured the people who had filled her room the day she came to, people who had been holding vigil since the accident. "Not lucky, blessed. I had people praying for me around the clock, Jordan." She hesitated, surprised at how emotional she still felt when she thought back to that time in her life. "My dad put together a prayer chain, and for two weeks people took half hour shifts praying for me. Not a moment went by when someone wasn't praying."

"Hmm." The muscles in Jordan's jaw flexed. "That's nice." Something hard flashed in his eyes, and Faith couldn't decide what it was — but she had the oddest feeling that she'd offended him somehow. Strange. Jordan was a believer; certainly he wouldn't have been put off by prayer.

"The doctors said it was a miracle. It took nearly a year of operations and therapy for me to learn how to eat and walk and be independent again. When I got out of the hospital, I moved back in with my parents, and two years ago I finally felt good as new.

That's when I took the job at WKZN."

Jordan eased himself forward as they both accepted coffee refills from the waitress. "Lots of people are never the same after an accident like that."

"All credit goes to God. Without His help I wouldn't have made it. That's for sure."

"Right."

An awkward silence filled the distance between them, and Faith studied him closely. There it was again, a flicker of distaste or anxiety, as though she kept touching a sore spot somewhere near his heart.

"You okay?" Faith uttered the question before she could stop herself. Jordan was a man now, someone she barely knew. What right did she have to probe into the private places of his emotions?

Surprise filled his face but he glanced down at his coffee cup as the corners of his mouth lifted. "Yeah, sure."

He wasn't going to elaborate so Faith tried another tact. "How 'bout you? You left the camp at some point, obviously. What's God been doing in your life?"

She stretched out her legs and felt their feet touch. Without saying anything she discreetly moved hers to one side. He looked up at her again, and though his smile was back, the discomfort in his eyes remained. "I stayed at camp till I graduated from high school. Spent most of my time playing baseball and wound up with a scholarship to play at New Jersey State."

Finally some good news. Faith clapped her hands. "Jordan, that's wonderful. You always dreamed about playing ball in college. You have to tell me all about it."

He chuckled at her enthusiasm and spent the next half hour regaling her with stories of his playing days. She remembered then that he'd mentioned something about law school. "So after college you became a lawyer?"

He nodded and signaled for the check. "I should let you get some sleep; it's one-thirty."

Faith didn't care how late it was, she didn't want the night to end. It felt so good to share a few hours with him after all the years that had passed without him, without knowing what had happened to him. "What kind of law do you practice?"

Jordan let his gaze fall for a moment and then flashed her a smile plucked from their early days together. "This and that. Civil rights stuff. Nothing interesting."

"If you'd lived with us I bet you'd have been working right there alongside Dad.

Don't you think?"

The walls in Jordan's eyes grew thicker, impenetrable. "It's late, Faith." There it was again. That artificial smile. "I have to go. I have a long drive tomorrow." He laid a five-dollar bill on the table and stood to help her with her jacket. As their arms touched Faith caught her breath at the jolt that went through her. What was wrong with her? She pulled her jacket on the rest of the way. Probably just adolescent memories playing tricks on her emotions.

Whatever the reason, she was strongly aware of Jordan beside her as they left the diner and headed for their cars. Before they said good-bye, Jordan pulled her into a hug then looked intently into her eyes. "It was good seeing you again, Faith." He ran his thumb along her eyebrow. "I thought I'd lost you forever."

Her heart skipped a beat, but she held his gaze. Was he going to kiss her? Here in the diner parking lot? He brought his face closer to hers and whispered against her face. "I never stopped thinking about you."

A floating sensation came over her, and she nuzzled her face against his. "I thought about you, too." She pulled away, wanting to ask him but not knowing how to word it without sounding blunt. "Want my phone number? So you can call me from New York?"

In response he brought his lips to hers and kissed her gently, tenderly — but this wasn't a young boy kissing a girl for the first time. It was the kiss of a man. A man who Faith knew for certain was as attracted to her as she was to him. They drew nearer to each other as the kiss continued, but before it could become more passionate, Jordan drew back. "I have to go. I'll call you."

A dozen emotions assaulted Faith and she searched his eyes. If he could kiss her like that, then he must still care for her. But if he was interested in her, he certainly hadn't said so. *Why are you doing this, Jordan? What's going on in your head?* She kept her concerns to herself, all but one. "You don't have my number."

"I'll call you at the station."

Then, in what seemed a poorly scripted ending to a wonderful evening, Jordan opened her car door and ushered her inside. "Good-bye, Faith." He bent down and their lips briefly came together once more.

He climbed into his black sports car and before she could turn the key, he drove away.

Jordan's entire body trembled as he pulled out of the diner parking lot. It had been heaven spending an evening with Faith, seeing her again, feeling her in his arms. She was more beautiful than he could have imagined, more intuitive to his feelings. He hadn't planned to kiss her, but after their hug, there was nothing he could do to stop himself. In all his life nothing had felt so right as having her in his arms, kissing her.

But it had been deeply wrong and he was furious at himself for letting his emotions get the better of him.

What right did he have listening to Faith talk about the miracle of her healing and the ways people had prayed for her? As though he still shared that same belief system? He had planned to tell her that he no longer bought into the stories about Jesus loving him and God having a plan for his life, but somehow the words hadn't come.

He eased up on the pedal and drove slowly back to his motel room. If only things had been different, if her parents had gotten word to his social worker earlier about their intention to adopt Heidi and him. Jordan couldn't imagine how things might have turned out, but they would definitely have been different. Maybe Faith was right. Maybe he would have wound up working alongside Bob Moses on the other side of the battle for religious rights.

But none of that mattered now.

He'd already made his decision, already filed the lawsuit. He'd taken a public stand against the very things Faith held dear, the things her father had devoted his final days defending. Jordan let out a strangled huff. Of course he hadn't asked Faith for her phone number. Angry tears stung his eyes as he let himself into his motel room. Faith represented everything good and pure and clean about life; ideals he knew nothing about and didn't believe in, anyway.

There would never be another date between them, never another kiss.

After tomorrow, Faith would learn what he'd done. What he'd become. Then he'd no longer be her old friend, a man who'd captured her heart in the parking lot of a Bethany diner.

He'd be her enemy.

NINE

One of the benefits of doing the eleven o'clock news was that unless Faith was working on a *Wednesday's Child* segment, she had her days to herself. When she awoke that Tuesday morning, after a night consumed with thoughts of Jordan, Faith knew there was only one way she could right her perspective.

By spending a day with Rosa.

Since the interview there had been one other time when Faith had contacted Rosa's social worker to arrange an afternoon with her. Over the weekend they'd seen the latest Disney movie and today . . . well, today Faith wanted to take her back to Jericho Park. Rosa had been drawn to the Jesus statue, and Faith couldn't think of any place she'd rather spend a few hours to sort through her emotions.

Faith planned to pick the child up at her foster home just before lunch. She brought a picnic and found the girl ready and waiting.

"You came!" Rosa ran down the sidewalk, her hair bouncing behind her, and flew into Faith's arms. "Did you see me on TV again?"

"I sure did." The girl's hair felt smooth beneath Faith's fingertips, and she and Rosa locked hands as they made their way to the car. Rosa's words rang in Faith's heart. *You came . . . you came . . . you came . . .* How many times had the child been let down if Faith's simple commitment — the mere act of showing up as she'd promised — meant so much?

"You sure looked pretty."

Faith pulled into traffic and headed for the park as Rosa grinned at her, her eyes huge and full of expectation. "Did my new mommy and daddy call yet?"

An ache settled around the base of Faith's heart and she swallowed a sigh. "Not yet, sweetheart, but that doesn't mean anything. Jesus has a plan, remember?"

Rosa's smile faded some and she settled back into her seat. "Uh-huh. My forever parents will come for me in His timing. Right? That's what my foster mom says and you too."

"Right, baby . . . that's right. Jesus has

someone planned for you and one of these days you'll meet them and it'll feel as if they were there all along."

"One of these days . . ." Rosa sighed and stared out the windshield. There was nothing cynical or defeated in the little girl's tone. Only a resignation that as of yet there were still no parents for her, no one to call her own. *You know I'd take her if I could, Lord . . .*

Silence.

Faith felt the beginning of tears and forced herself to be cheerful. It wouldn't help Rosa if she were sad this afternoon. This was a day for playing and laughing and enjoying their time together. They arrived at the park and shared a peanut butter sandwich and homemade cookies. Faith was pushing the child on the swing, when she noticed the way two little girls nearby whispered about Rosa's missing fingers. Faith slowed the swing down and tickled Rosa.

"Okay, sweetcakes, get off."

Rosa grinned at her and slid down to the ground. Once the swing was empty, Faith sat down and pulled Rosa onto her lap.

"Hold on!" Faith waited until the child had a tight grip on the chains, then covering the girl's deformed hand with her own, Faith pumped the swing higher and higher, savoring Rosa's little-girl laughter.

Something about Faith's acceptance of her seemed to convince the other little girls that Rosa was okay. After a few minutes the two of them came and stood nearby. "Can she play with us?"

Faith felt a surge of hope as she slowed the swing, breathless from the cool fall air and the thrill of the ride. She leaned close and spoke softly in Rosa's ear. "Wanna play with them?"

Rosa bobbed her head up and down. "Yes, please . . ." And with that she and the other girls ran off to the merry-go-round. The tears were back as Faith silently celebrated the victory. *She needs a mom, Lord . . . someone who can help her win those battles every day of her life.*

No words of wisdom echoed in Faith's soul as she made her way to a nearby bench. She watched the children play and gradually her mind wandered once more to the night before.

Jordan Riley.

Was his return some part of God's plan? Faith thought about that and decided it could be. After all, they were both still single and whatever attraction had been there for them as kids had obviously lasted over the years. She sighed and tried to imagine what might have happened if Jordan hadn't disappeared for sixteen years of her life. There would have been no Mike Dillan to forget about, no broken heart.

What had she been thinking to date a man such as Mike Dillan anyway? Faith sighed and crossed her legs, enjoying the way the sun felt on her shoulders. Becoming Mike's girlfriend wasn't something she'd planned; it had just sort of happened. Faith hadn't let herself remember that time in her life for years, but now, watching Rosa play with her new friends, still basking in the memory of Jordan's kiss from the night before, Faith felt herself drifting back.

For years after Jordan left, Faith waited for him, asking her parents where he lived and imagining ways she might find him again. Through junior high and even high school she never had a boyfriend, because every time one of her peers was interested she compared him to Jordan. *Someday,* she'd tell herself, *someday God will bring us back together.* It was a sentiment she wrote in her journals and carried with her straight into college.

Her four years at Penn State were a blur of busyness and activities led by her involvement with the school newspaper and broadcast department. There was little time for boyfriends, but every now and then she'd spend a weekend at home and wind up at Jericho Park, on the bench near the Jesus statue where she and Jordan had spent their last days together. *Where is he, Lord?* She'd let her imagination run wild. Maybe he'd moved on to another state or another country . . . maybe he'd gone to college and was spending all his free time trying to find her. Wherever he was, he wasn't in Bethany, and the chance that Faith would ever see him again was practically nonexistent.

Faith stared at the Jesus statue now and tried to remember herself as she'd been back then, a senior in college, working as a broadcast intern for a small student-run station not far from campus. She'd been too busy to do much more than keep to her schedule and once in a rare while think about Jordan and what might have been.

Mike had come into the picture two years later when her internship led to a full-time sports reporting position at the Philadelphia CBS affiliate. Mike was a tight end with the Eagles, and from the first day Faith was assigned to do sidebar stories on the team, he'd made his presence known.

He had come up to her after the game, when her interviews were over and she was making her way to the car. "Hey, gorgeous."

Faith remembered not being sure how to answer him. He was good-looking, but she was on the job and determined not to date players. She wound up waving to him as though she hadn't heard his comment, relieved when he waved back but went his own way. *Good . . . keep him far away from me, Lord . . . pro athletes are nothing but trouble.*

That had been only the beginning. As she got to know the personalities on the team better she learned that Mike was a devoted Christian who gave both his time and money to local charities and churches. After her first five weeks covering the team, he began asking her out.

She would smile and change the subject, sticking to her professional list of questions and assignment objectives. "I don't date players."

"I'm not a *player*," he'd grin at her. "Players hang out with different girls every week. I'm a professional athlete, and you're a professional reporter . . ."

His relentless pursuit of her chipped away at her resistance with one fine-sounding argument after another.

One sunny afternoon before practice, it was: "What are you afraid of, Faith? I don't bite."

Or after a game, when the locker room had cleared: "Why won't you go out with me? I think we have a lot in common."

And in the parking lot a week later: "We're adults, Faith. When are you going to take me seriously?"

After a month of saying no, Faith finally agreed to have dinner with him following a home game. They went to a little-known Italian restaurant, and six weeks later, Faith had fallen hard for him. They became expert at keeping their relationship a secret, sure that it would cast a questionable light on Faith's reporting if word got out.

Faith squinted and let her gaze settle on Rosa, enjoying the way she laughed and ran as she played tag with her two new friends. If only things hadn't gotten so serious between Mike and her. She would have been okay with a casual friendship, a dating situation with long-term potential. Instead, on their first-year anniversary they went to the same Italian restaurant and Mike tenderly took her hands in his.

"Faith, I've never loved anyone like I love you." There had been unshed tears in his eyes, tears that at the time seemed utterly genuine. He let go with one hand and reached into his coat pocket, pulling out a velvet box. As though he'd practiced for the moment, he opened it in a single move. There inside lay a diamond ring bigger than any Faith had ever seen. "Marry me, Faith."

The memory faded, and she gritted her teeth, noticing that her hands were clenched. Even now, when she was glad for not having made the mistake of marrying him, the anger and hurt he'd caused her still lay in the open places of her heart. If only she'd seen it coming back then.

Rosa caught her gaze and waved at her. "Hi, Faith!"

Faith's love for the child made her heart swell. "Hi, sweetie!"

Confident that Faith was there for her, watching her, Rosa returned to her play. Faith glanced down at her hands, remembering how she'd gone home a week after Mike proposed and shown the diamond ring to her parents. They'd met Mike by then, and though her mother was thrilled with the idea of their engagement, her father had been wary.

"Something about him doesn't ring true." Her father had stroked his beard thoughtfully. "I can't put my finger on it, but it makes me worried for you, Faith. I have to be honest."

She'd only given her father a teasing smile and a quick kiss on the cheek. "Would any man ever be good enough, Daddy?"

There was just one aspect of their relationship that caused Faith any private doubt. Mike hadn't wanted to set a wedding date. She could still hear his weak excuses. "I need to focus on my career right now, Faith. It'd be impossible to be married and keep up my performance as an athlete." He'd weave his fingers through her hair and pull her close, kissing her. "You understand, right?"

And she had. After all, he'd been a perfect gentleman, respecting her determination to stay pure, at least respecting it until his marriage offer. Faith had her own apartment, and certainly they'd had their moments of temptation, but always he found his way to the front door before midnight and without putting any pressure on her. They prayed together, attended church together, and talked of having a godly marriage, one that the Lord Himself would bless for all time.

Faith uttered a sad laugh.

In the end, her father's doubts had been more genuine than anything Mike had promised. The changes came after the engagement, and though they were subtle, they were persistent. "We're practically married, Faith . . ." he'd whisper as he kissed her neck, running his hands along her sides.

"Do you really think God would care if I stayed the night? Just this once."

Week after week Faith could feel her resolve wearing thin, but still she refused his attempts. "We've waited this long, Mike. It's important to me. To both of us, right?"

"Please, Faith . . . just one time . . ."

Three months after getting engaged, when they were alone in her apartment well after midnight, she couldn't find the words to tell him no, couldn't hold back from welcoming his embrace and finally giving in to the physical love they'd both been resisting. Six weeks later a home pregnancy test confirmed what she already knew.

She was a Christian sportscaster carrying the baby of one of the players on the team she covered.

Faith felt nauseous as she remembered what happened next. She'd told Mike about the baby and suggested they set a quick wedding date, but he was distant and vague, careful not to make promises. *Why didn't I see it coming, Lord?* Faith's unspoken question hung in the rafters of her mind even now. It was behind her; it had to be. Forgotten as though it had never happened . . .

The sun was shifting and a chill passed over her. It was almost time to get Rosa back to her foster home. She blinked and tried to forget the way the story ended but there was no getting around it. For the next month Mike seemed always too busy to return her phone calls.

It wasn't until she saw a newspaper photo of him with one of the team cheerleaders that she figured it out.

She'd broken down and cried when he finally called her a week later. "How *could* you?"

"Listen, Faith, you're too serious for me. I'm not ready to settle down."

She had been so distraught she'd spent the afternoon fighting violent bouts of nausea and anxiety. The bleeding started later that night, and by the next morning she had lost everything that might remind her of Mike Dillan. At the end of the month she took his diamond ring to a pawnshop and hocked it to pay her hospital bills.

The only person who ever knew about the baby was her father, and his support had been exactly what Faith had expected. "I'm sorry, honey." He held her, stroked her hair and comforted her as he'd done when she was little, back when having an argument with a girlfriend was the worst thing that happened to her. No snide remarks or reminders about how he'd seen it coming, no chastisements on how she should have known better than to date a professional athlete. No digs about Mike's supposed belief in God and how that had turned out to be nothing more than good public relations for his high profile persona.

Only understanding and grace.

The same grace God Himself had extended her when the ordeal was over. Faith's throat was thick with the memories, and she swallowed back a wave of tears. God had never turned His back on her. Not then, and not years later when she had her accident. Not even when her father died.

No, God had been there through it all.

She thought about Jordan, how she had long since given up the idea that she'd ever see him again and somehow she knew the Lord had His hand in that too. Had she ever felt so at ease with another man? She knew she hadn't. Though she'd been attracted to Mike, she'd been cautious from the beginning. First because of their professional conflicts, then because of her father's concerns. Her subtle fears about Mike had been easy to bury, but now, in light of her time with Jordan, the difference was striking.

No one had ever made her feel the way Jordan did. Maybe because she had loved him back when they were so young.

Faith noticed the sun making its way

toward the horizon and she locked her attention on Rosa. Poor, girl. *Lord, give her a family, please . . .*

She cupped her hands around her mouth. "Rosa, let's go, honey."

The little girl jumped up and waved at her new friends. Then she ran up and circled her arms around Faith's neck. "Is it time to go?"

Faith's heart felt as though it had slipped through a hole in her left sock. "Yes, sweetie pie. Your foster mom's expecting you back."

Rosa stared across the park toward the Jesus statue. "Know what I asked Jesus for today?" She angled her head in Faith's direction and grinned, her eyes filled with light.

"What?"

"I asked Him to let *you* be my mommy."

There was a choking feeling at the back of Faith's throat as she fought more tears. *What's this feeling I have, Lord? I can't be her mother, You know that. I can barely take care of myself.*

Be strong and courageous, my daughter. Life is not lived within the safety of walls.

Faith gulped back a sob as she knelt and hugged Rosa. After a moment she drew back, looking straight into the child's soul.

152

"Oh, honey, I would love to be your mommy. There couldn't be any better daughter for me than you."

Rosa's eyes glowed with hope. "You mean you'll do it then? You'll take me home to live with you?"

"Sweetheart . . . I don't know." There was nothing she could do about the tears and Faith held the girl close once more so she wouldn't see them. Why was she feeling this way — as though she'd been born to love this little girl? Faith wiped her cheeks and looked at Rosa again. "I'll ask Him the same thing, okay?"

Rosa's smile took up most of her face as she tucked her small hand into Faith's. "My Sunday school teacher says that Jesus always hears us, even when we don't get the answer we want."

Discreetly, Faith wiped away another release of tears. "That's right, honey."

Rosa stared across the park again. "Know why I like the Jesus statue?"

"Why?" They walked without any sense of purpose, both reluctant to see the afternoon end.

"Because it makes me know how big Jesus is." Rosa released her grip on Faith's hand and stretched her arms as far as they could go in either direction. "Bigger than anything in the whole wide world."

Faith caught the girl's fingers again and squeezed them gently. "Don't you ever forget it, honey. Don't ever forget it."

Rosa's words still played in Faith's mind that evening as she got ready for work. The news didn't start until eleven, but she had to be there four hours early to write and edit her newscast. Ultimately Dick Baker had final editorial say over what aired, but Faith liked to think she played some role in shaping the flavor of Philadelphia's news.

I'd come in six *hours early if they'd give me a little more influence . . .*

She pulled a navy rayon blouse from her closet and slipped it on. Her bedroom was smaller now that she'd moved back into her parents' house, but it had been the smartest thing she could do at the time. Besides, she and her mom were agreeable roommates, and with Dad gone now and Sarah married, it made no sense for Faith to live across town alone.

Faith wished her mother were here now, but she'd gone to Chicago for eight weeks to help her sister recover from ankle surgery. Faith's mother had planned the trip months before her father's death, and they'd both felt the trip might actually do her some good, get her out of the house.

But her absence left the house too quiet.

Faith had located matching slacks and was about to slip them on when the phone rang. Maybe it would be Rosa's social worker calling to say that they found her a family . . .

Faith grabbed the receiver on her bedside table. "Hello . . ."

"Faith, it's me, Joshua." There was a pause and Faith sat on the edge of the bed. Why would her father's former law partner be calling her? "We've got a problem. I wanted you to know before you got to work and found out."

Her heart rate quickened in response. "What happened?"

Joshua drew a deep breath. "You've heard of the legal group HOUR?"

Faith searched her memory bank, but came up empty. "It sounds familiar . . ."

"Stands for Humanity Organized and United in Responsibility. They make their mark with religious freedom cases, you know — hassling churches, forcing Scout troops to act in violation of their guidelines, making sure nativity scenes don't crop up in public places — that kind of thing."

"Okay." Faith felt her shoulders drop as her body relaxed. Whatever it was, it didn't involve her.

"Anyway, yesterday afternoon they filed a

lawsuit against the town of Bethany."

Faith could feel the blood draining from her face. "What for?"

Joshua's voice was thick with emotion. "They want the Jesus statue torn down."

Anger released into her veins like a dose of adrenaline. "What? Why would they want that?"

"It's a religious symbol in a public park. Precedence says they probably have a valid point, and Frank's asked me to work on the case. Could be the biggest I've done."

"Frank Furlong? Mayor Frank Furlong?"

"Right."

"He's worried about it?"

"Faith, we're all worried about it. HOUR sent an attorney to Bethany yesterday, and by this morning we were already fielding calls from three major newspapers and all the network affiliates."

"Even WKZN?" Faith was stunned. What would cause an outsider to drive to Bethany and attack the statue in Jericho Park? It wasn't hurting anyone; in fact it was part of the town's history, its heritage. Faith felt her anger rise another notch.

"It'll be one of your top stories." He hesitated. "I wanted you to hear it from me first. I know you're on . . . well, I know the station's watching you."

The realization of what Joshua had done finally dawned on her. Here he was, about to be thrust in the limelight of a case that would be the most controversial Bethany had seen in decades, and the thing he felt compelled to do was call her. Joshua was more than her father's friend and partner, he was her friend, too. And with her father gone, it meant everything to Faith to know that he'd chosen to look out for her.

You're so good, God . . . first seeing Jordan last night and now this. "Thanks, Joshua."

"It's what your dad would have done."

"So what happens next? When's the hearing?" The anger had turned to something altogether different, a sense of justice, of fighting for what was right. It resonated in Faith with a strength that was foreign to her, and she suddenly had to know more details, find out where she fit into the picture and how she could be part of the solution.

"The judge assigned us a date, four weeks from tomorrow. The last Wednesday in September." He paused. "The guy from HOUR tried to talk us into taking the statue down without a fight, met with us yesterday afternoon. When we told him no, he filed suit and headed back to New York."

New York? Faith's fingers began to

tremble. *"I have to get back to New York . . .
New York . . . New York. . . ."*

It couldn't be. He would never have been
involved with an organization such as
HOUR, not in a million years. Still, how
many other New York attorneys had passed
through town yesterday? Her throat was
suddenly dry and she had to work to find
her voice. "Did you get the guy's name? The
attorney, I mean?"

"From HOUR?"

"Yeah, the man from New York?" Faith
held her breath as she heard Joshua shuffling through papers.

"Yeah, just a minute." There was a pause,
and Faith didn't think she could stand the
suspense. Even if she was right, if it was
Jordan, she had no intention of telling
Joshua she knew him. It was all too much
of a shock.

"Okay, here we go . . . just a minute . . .
let's see . . . it's right here."

No, don't let it be . . . it can't be . . .

"His name is Jordan Riley."

Ten

At five minutes before eleven Jordan tuned his satellite receiver to a channel he'd never watched before his brief visit to Bethany: WKZN out of Philadelphia. Since Philadelphia was a major market, it made sense that Jordan's satellite service would carry it, but he was surprised all the same.

Since seeing Faith the night before, feeling how she worked magic on his heart and soul, he'd been plagued by more doubts than he cared to admit. He had never experienced a connection that strong to any woman, never had the unexplainable urge to take a woman home right then and marry her . . .

Of course his feelings didn't matter. What mattered was that he and Faith had grown into adults who stood on opposite sides of a religious Grand Canyon. As strong as their opposing views were, he knew there would be no bridges to build, no earthly way to span the distance between them. Any chance that may have existed would be demolished after Faith learned the truth.

No, he'd never hold her again, never have the chance to tell her that he would remember last night as long as he lived . . . but he still had her news show. Once he found the channel, he sat stone still and waited for the broadcast to begin.

The music came first, then a gradual close-in on Faith and her coanchor. The man spoke first. "A second victim in last week's local gun battle is dead today as police continue looking for the suspect."

It was Faith's turn. "And in Bethany, a powerful law firm takes aim at the city's favorite landmark."

Jordan searched her beautiful eyes for any sign that the story had hit her personally, but he saw none. He could only imagine what sort of emotional turmoil was going on just beneath her polished veneer. He studied her eyes, her hands. *Don't hate me Faith . . . this has nothing to do with you.*

"Good evening everyone, I'm Ron Leonard . . ."

"And I'm Faith Evans, welcome to tonight's edition of WKZN's *Nightly News*."

Leonard talked a few minutes on the gun battle story; then the camera fixed on Faith.

"An attorney from Humanity Organized and United in Responsibility filed suit yesterday against Bethany claiming that the nearly hundred-year-old Jesus statue violates the Constitution's call for a separation of church and state." Faith kept talking but the camera cut away to a shot of the Jesus statue, with young children playing nearby. "For nearly a century the Jesus statue has stood as a landmark in Bethany, Pennsylvania, without a single complaint waged against it."

Jordan watched, his palms sweaty. Did she know he was the attorney?

"But all that changed yesterday when Jordan Riley, an attorney with the HOUR organization, filed suit asking that the statue be removed."

Well, that answered that. A strange sadness settled over Jordan. After spending more than a decade wondering about Faith, looking for her, they'd lost each other again in less than twenty-four hours. The camera cut back to her.

"There'll be a hearing on the matter Wednesday at which point Judge Randall Webster is expected to make a decision. Hundreds of citizens from Bethany and surrounding communities are expected to attend."

Oh, they are, are they? Jordan raised a single eyebrow. Despite his boss's warning that this case could gain national attention, Jordan hadn't really expected a fight. Case precedent on such matters was clear: Whenever a city had chosen to erect a religious display or statue, almost without exception the city had been made to take it down. Jordan wondered if maybe Faith was talking about herself or if she knew for a fact that citizens had already rallied against him.

Faith turned to her partner. "Quite a case, huh?"

Ron shook his head. "Bound to be in the news for a while."

The camera hadn't focused back in on her, but still Faith continued the conversation with her coworker. "I'm from Bethany as you know, and all I can say is that this Jordan Riley — whoever he is — doesn't know what he's getting himself into."

Jordan felt as though he'd been stepped on by an elephant. *Whoever he is?* Faith — his childhood best friend, the woman he'd kissed so gently the other night — had referred to him on East Coast television as *whoever he is?* She must be furious with him. The knowledge of that truth cast another strange layer of grief over him. What was wrong with him? Was he surprised that she was angry? He should have expected it the moment he realized she still lived in Bethany.

No, there was nothing shocking about Faith's reaction. After all, Jordan had always known how she loved Jericho Park and the Jesus statue in particular. But somehow he'd hoped she might understand, that she might see how God had let him down, how He'd taken his mother, his sister . . . even his chance at a relationship with Faith. Jordan wasn't the bad guy here, couldn't she see that? Jesus was.

The lawsuit was an act of mercy, really. No city in America should have a statue honoring such a cruel God.

The minute the newscast was over, Dick Baker marched across the soundstage, the capillaries in his temples purplish and threatening to burst through his skin. He pointed his finger at Faith's partner. "Leonard, out!" Dick's bellow echoed off the stage's fiberboard sets.

Faith gulped. *If he fires me, Lord, let me get out of here without crying.* Ron Leonard, his hair and stage makeup still perfect, scowled at their boss, looking as if he might argue the station manager's approach. But instead he gathered his things and stormed off the stage. When he was gone, Dick turned to her.

"I warned you, Evans. What you did out there tonight was over the top. I mean completely unprofessional." He was breathing hard, his face almost as red as the veins in his neck. "The story didn't call for you to talk about the citizens of Bethany. What . . . were you out taking a private poll this morning?" He barely paused to grab another mouthful of air before he answered himself. "Of course you weren't. You said hundreds of citizens from Bethany and other towns were expected to be at the hearing and that is simply a lie. A complete fabrication of the facts."

There were knots in Faith's gut but it was too late to back down now. She'd made the decision to express her opinion on the air because it was the least she could do. If people knew that Faith Evans didn't want the Jesus statue moved, they'd likely side with her. She had that kind of following. The elderly saw her as a pretty daughter they needed to protect. Women related to her freshness and lack of guile, and men, well, it had never been difficult for Faith to gain the support of men. Not since she was ten years old and won a beauty pageant at the county fair.

He was waiting for an answer, and Faith

met his gaze head on. *Okay, God, give me the strength . . .*

"I live in Bethany, Dick. I know the way people think there. It'll probably be more like a thousand people. That's how much they love that statue."

"*No* one —" he shouted the words and then gritted his teeth as he struggled to tone his voice down — "no one at this station is free to present his or her own news without some kind of outside research. Otherwise we're reduced to a group of op-ed mouth-pieces spewing *our* thoughts and *our* ideas and *our* take on the news as it relates to *us!*" He paced two steps out and then back again, his hand raised for emphasis. "And what was that ad-lib thing you did? The camera wasn't anywhere near you! It was Ron's turn to speak, and all of a sudden we hear little Miss Opinionated talking about how this attorney from HOUR doesn't know what he's gotten himself into?" Dick massaged his temples with his thumb and forefinger, then he peered over the top of his hand and his eyes locked on hers. "Who in the world gave you permission to make such a statement?"

Faith didn't blink. "Ad-libbing is part of the job. It sounds conversational and approachable and friendly. It makes viewers tune back in tomorrow. Remember, Dick? Those were your words from last month's editorial meeting."

Dick glared at her and slammed his raised hand down on the countertop between Faith and him. She started from the ferocity of it. "You know darn well what I meant in that meeting! I was talking about scripted ad-libs. The kind that bridge us from news to weather, and weather to sports. Not a free-for-all, utterly biased conversation where all of Philadelphia gets to hear Faith Evans's opinion of HOUR."

Faith sighed. "Listen, Dick, I'm sorry. I didn't think it was out of line."

The station manager threw his hands in the air. "Sometimes I can't believe the networks are considering you for a national spot. I mean, don't get me wrong, Evans. You're beautiful and bright and you connect with our viewers like no other female anchor in the last decade." He moved closer and the corners of his eyes narrowed. "But the network has made it clear that I'll lose my job if I let you or anyone else use airtime for their own agenda. I cannot — *will* not — tolerate your Christian posturing on my news program." He was so upset his hand shook and he drew it back. "I could fire you, Evans, you know that?"

She knew he was right. Her contract included a promise of no biased reporting, which meant that even though it might look to the public like religious discrimination if she was let go, the truth was it would be perfectly legal.

Do not be dismayed, daughter, I am with you ...

The sudden silent reminder of God's presence in her heart caused a warm calming feeling to spread out from her gut. Baker was waiting for an answer, and Faith forced herself to reply. "Yes, sir. I know."

"You will take tomorrow off without pay and you're to see me before going on the air Thursday."

Thursday? That meant she wouldn't be there for the *Wednesday's Child* segment. If she didn't do it, no one would. She had planned on running the segment on Rosa again in hopes that someone, somewhere would fall as quickly in love with the precious child as Faith had. Making her miss Wednesday was the worst punishment her boss could have meted out. *Lord, see what happens when I try to stand up for my beliefs? What good did it do?* There were no words in response, only images. A candle under a bushel, a buried coin, and walls around something Faith couldn't quite make out. It didn't matter, the message was the same: God wanted her to be bold, no matter the cost.

Dick's voice was so loud Faith was sure most everyone at the station could hear him. "Tomorrow I'll write up a probation form, which we will both sign . . . and the next time you pull a stunt like this, Evans, you're fired. It's that simple. You can forget about any help from the network. The big boys like your talent, but pretty mouthpieces are a dime a dozen. If I don't keep the executives happy they'll have both of us gone before the weekend." He lowered his face so that he could stare straight at her. "Have I made myself clear?"

There was no point arguing. "Yes, sir."

Dick spun and walked away. Faith watched him go and knew she should have felt discouraged, and she was — about missing *Wednesday's Child* the following day. But as she left the station she felt strangely inspired, uplifted — as though she'd taken the first step toward a life that God had been calling her to for years. It was a small step, but it was in the right direction, and though her job hung in the balance, Faith was curiously unconcerned.

By walking the narrow path ahead of her she somehow knew she would be safer and more secure than at any other time in her life. Faith paused as regret hit her over one fact: Jordan had become an enemy over-night, someone attacking her home, and she wondered for the hundredth time since Joshua's call why her long-ago friend had filed the lawsuit in the first place.

And how he'd had the nerve to hide the fact from her that night at the diner — and later in the parking lot. He had filed suit that very day . . . he must have known she would be upset by it. Otherwise he wouldn't have been so evasive when she asked him why he was in town.

The thought of it turned Faith's stomach.

Had he only wanted to trick her, use her for a night of reminiscing? And what did he have against Jericho Park and the Jesus statue? Faith had no answers, but there was someone who did. As she climbed into her car that night she made a plan to get Jordan's phone number and call him.

Even if it was the last time the two of them ever talked.

The easiest way to find him, Faith knew, was to call the HOUR organization in New York, so at two o'clock in the afternoon the next day from her mother's kitchen she did just that. Once Faith had Jordan's number from the operator, she was connected to his secretary in less than a minute.

"Jordan Riley, please." Faith put on her professional voice, hoping to ward off any censoring by the woman.

There was silence for a beat. "Who may I say is calling?"

"Faith Evans. It's about a case we're working on."

Again there was a hesitation. "Just a moment, please . . ."

Faith sat back in the kitchen chair and forced herself to be calm. *I can't believe it's true, Jordan . . . you've sold out to the other side, given up the precious faith you and your mother and your —*

"Hello?" The voice at the other end lacked any of the warmth it had held the other night, back when he'd wrapped her in his arms and . . .

"It's Faith." She could hear ice in her own voice as well and she felt as though she were lying, as though the role of enemy didn't quite fit yet.

"Faith, I was going to call you tom—"

"Don't lie to me, Jordan." She was maintaining her cool exterior, not showing too much emotion. "You knew you weren't going to call from the moment you saw me at the station."

He was silent and Faith took the cue.

"Listen, obviously you're upset and mixed up. You must have personal reasons for wanting our statue down, for suing Bethany over the Jesus statue . . . but I meant what I said."

"Which was?" He, too, sounded dry and businesslike. Gone was the man she'd connected with, the one whose voice had been heavy with years of memories and longing.

"The whole town will turn out." She was careful with her words. "I think you're making a huge mistake."

A laugh void of any humor came at her in response. "You really don't get it, do you, Faith?"

She hated his condescending tone. "No, I really don't. The Jordan Riley I knew would have loved God too much to attack Him in court."

"I've changed since then. Grown up. I thought you could see it that night . . . when we were together."

Faith felt her stomach tighten. "The man I was with was not someone different. He was the same boy I loved as a kid."

"The same —" Jordan's voice was softer this time, but he cut himself short. When he spoke again it was with fire. "I prayed to Jesus, Faith. The same Jesus honored by that stupid statue. And what did it ever get me?

My mother died, my sister was sent off to live with strangers, and I never heard from her again. I never heard from you, either. I lost everything that mattered to me that year, Faith. And the reason it hurt so bad was because of the Jesus statue."

In the silence that followed, a light began to dawn in the shadowy places of Faith's heart. Jordan blamed God for the losses in his life. And now he was trying to get rid of the Jesus statue as his way of exacting revenge. "Why the statue?"

"Because —" his words were like bullets spewing from a semiautomatic — "because there's no such thing as a Jesus like the one in the statue. A Jesus with open arms, welcoming those around Him to come, to bring their troubles and lay them at His feet so that He might make things right again. God — if there *is* a God — is a hands-off, mad scientist. Someone who set the world in motion and then stood back to watch it self-destruct."

Faith leaned forward, physically ill at Jordan's anger toward the God they had once worshiped side by side in church and Sunday school. *Lord, how did this happen? How had Jordan missed the point that God didn't promise a trouble-free life, just peace and joy and friendship through the troubles?*

"I'm sorry, Jordan. I . . . I didn't know you felt that way."

"Well I do, and you ought to feel the same way." He huffed. "The Lord took your dad, He took away your relationship with that football player, and because of the accident He took a year of your life. How can you defend a God like that?"

What struck Faith most was that Jordan honestly had no answers for himself. "I can defend Him because He loves me. He loves you too, Jordan."

"Wake up, Faith. He couldn't care less about either of us."

She sighed. "I don't want to get into a theological debate. I just want to warn you. The Jesus statue belongs to the people of Bethany, and any battle you wage there is one you'll ultimately lose."

"Then I guess I'll see you and the rest of the town in court." His voice was sharp and cool, lacking even the anger it had held earlier. "Good-bye, Faith."

Jordan hung up before she could say anything else, and her own anger rose in her defense — then an image filled her head. Jordan Riley, thirteen years old, kneeling on damp grass in the freezing still of night a few feet from the Jesus statue, begging God to let his mother live.

Faith closed her eyes and felt tears spill onto her cheeks. She bowed her head and prayed for her father's old law partner, Joshua, and the people of Bethany, that they might have strength to fight the battle of Jericho Park. Then, with a full and broken heart, she prayed for the boy she had grown up with, the one she had once dreamed of marrying, the one who had lost so much the winter of his thirteenth year.

And for the bitter man he'd become.

ELEVEN

Heidi and Charles were stretched out on their living room sofa enjoying the opportunity to chat about their move to Bethany. Charles had given notice at the hospital, and for the most part everything was in order. Heidi watched him now, the love in his eyes, the way he cared so much about her happiness. He put his hand on her belly and smiled.

"It's getting bigger."

She pushed her fist into his shoulder and giggled. "Not *it*, silly. *Her.*"

"Ah, another princess in the house!" He laughed. "Ultrasounds can be wrong, remember. Happens at the clinic every day."

"Not this time. I have a feeling about her." Heidi placed a protective hand over her abdomen. "She's our little sweetheart." Her eyes lifted to his and her heart felt light as air. "I can actually picture her."

The baby kicked, and a grin spread across

Charles's face. "*Must* be a girl. She's feisty, just like her mother."

He snuggled in close to her, his arm around her midsection as though he were cradling them both. "You don't mind moving in November . . . right after the baby's born?"

She chuckled and ran her fingers through his hair. "As long as I've got you and God on my side, I can do anything."

There was a comfortable silence between them and Heidi stared out the window at the gold and maroon leaves on the tree. Fall was her favorite time of year. Summer's last hurrah — its shout that life is, and life will come again. It was the time of year her mother had gotten sick, a time when Jordan had been her greatest strength, her pillar of hope that God would work through their mother's illness no matter what happened. Even after their mother died Jordan had been strong for her, holding her, assuring her that one day they'd all be together in heaven.

Heidi sighed. Days like this it was easy to picture Jordan as he'd been back then, dark-haired and muscle bound, eyes glowing with sincerity. What if he hadn't been in the cave that terrible afternoon at the boys' camp? What if the state had kept them together instead of separating them?

"You okay?" Charles brushed her bangs to the side and looked into her eyes. "Feels like you're a million miles away."

"I am." She snuggled against his shoulder and resumed her study of autumn out their living room window. "Just thinking about Mom and Jordan."

Charles exhaled through pursed lips, and she could feel his concern for her. He understood the place in her heart that would always remember, always yearn for the people of her childhood days, for her mother and brother. An idea occurred to her and she turned her attention back to Charles. "What if we name her Jordan Lee?"

Charles cocked his head thoughtfully and then drew near and kissed her. "I like it."

"Really? You do?" Her mood soared with the possibility that her little girl might carry on her brother's name. The name of an uncle her daughter would never know.

"From everything you've told me about Jordan, he was kind and strong and loving. He cared deeply about God and his family. Our little girl couldn't have a better name."

Heidi buried her head in Charles's shoulder again. "I love you so much. Thanks for understanding."

He squeezed her once. "You make it easy."

A few minutes passed and he grabbed the remote control. "I want to see what the president said in his address last night."

They watched the opening story and after a few minutes Heidi stood up. "I'll get dinner." She moved behind Charles and massaged his neck and shoulders.

"Mmm." He closed his eyes and the corners of his mouth lifted. "Can't we just skip dinner?"

She laughed and gave him a final squeeze. "You might not need it, but I'm eating for two." She ducked her head in front of him, kissed him on the cheek, and left the room.

Charles craned his neck and watched her go. How did he get so lucky, anyway? Married to the perfect woman and about to be a first-time father? He turned his attention back to the television. It was good to see Heidi smile. Too often this time of the year she was lost in thought, remembering ghosts from her past. He sighed and flicked the channel. If there was one thing he was anxious to ask God, it was why He'd taken Jordan Riley so young. Hadn't it been enough to call Heidi's mother home without taking her brother too? A news program played on but Charles was too lost in thought to hear it.

He wasn't angry with the Lord, just curious.

It didn't matter that he'd never met Jordan. Charles had heard enough about him to feel like family, as though he could easily recognize him if he passed him on the street. Clearly Heidi had been crazy about her brother, and every fall her feelings for him came back stronger than ever. The reason was simple: During the hardest time in Heidi's life, Jordan had meant everything to her.

The news program moved onto another story, and Charles focused on what was being said. Something about a park in Bethany and a lawsuit to remove a statue. He tried to make sense of the story, but he'd already missed too many details. He wondered if Heidi knew about the case. Probably. He leaned back into the couch and yawned. Maybe he'd talk to her about it over dinner. His thoughts shifted to the playoffs and whether the National League had a team worthy of the World Series. For that matter, where the big games would be held that year and whether he'd have a chance to take in any baseball action before the move.

By the time Heidi called him for dinner, he'd completely forgotten about Jericho

Park and the obscure news item regarding a legal fight over some statue, or the fact that he'd ever intended to bring up the story to Heidi in the first place.

TWELVE

In the small law office in Bethany, the weeks passed in a blur of case study and preparation for Joshua Nunn. But when the day of the hearing arrived, he felt no more prepared than the day he'd been given the case, the day he'd had the strange dream.

"You ready to beat this guy?" Frank had asked in a phone call that morning.

Joshua hadn't been sure how to answer him. Frank was the mayor after all, the one who had put such faith in Joshua's abilities in the first place. From the beginning he had known it would be a tough case to win. Now that he'd had a chance to study case precedent, he was fairly sure it was impossible.

A pain took root in his gut. "I'll give it my best."

"Don't worry about a thing, old friend. We've got the Lord on our side."

That much was sure, Joshua knew. Twice

in the past week various churches had held prayer rallies at Jericho Park with as many as three hundred people — singing and agreeing with each other that the Jesus statue was part of who they were, a key facet of their town's history and personality. The gatherings had done a great job of making the townspeople heard. All three local network affiliates had carried stories about the public outcry on their nightly news, making Faith Evans look like a prophet.

"Think there'll be a group at the courthouse?"

Frank chuckled. "If you call a thousand people gathered on the courthouse lawn a group."

Joshua gulped. "A thousand people?" *Lord, I'm not up to this. I need Bob . . .*

Be strong and courageous . . . I will go before you.

The silent words reassured him, easing the kinks in Joshua's belly.

"At least that many. People are outraged over this. Lot of nerve that HOUR group has, messing with our statue. That's the message the people want to convey and I'm betting they actually get heard today." Frank offered a few more words of encouragement then wrapped up the conversation. "Gotta run if I want a good seat. See you there."

Joshua rubbed the back of his neck and leaned forward in his chair. "See ya."

If Bob were there they'd have had an early morning prayer time, bowed their heads together, and taken the issue straight to the throne room of God. Since that wasn't possible, Joshua was left with only one option: pray alone. The image of Bob's daughter came to mind, and suddenly he knew he would not be praying alone that morning. Wherever she was, Bob's daughter would be lifting her voice as well, asking God, even begging Him, to have mercy on the people of Bethany, Pennsylvania.

Even if case precedent and HOUR and everything else were against them.

Joshua folded his hands, stared for a moment at the photo of Bob Moses on the office wall, closed his eyes, and hung his head. "Okay, God, here it is: You know the situation . . ."

Faith pulled into a nearly full lot across the street from the courthouse, parked her car, and instructed herself to calm down. Her heart pounded as though it were trying to break free from her body and start a life of its own.

"God help us," she whispered as she climbed out of her car and locked the door.

She'd gotten up earlier than usual that morning and prayed for nearly an hour, but still peace eluded her. In the weeks since speaking to Jordan, since hearing the determination in his voice, Faith's confidence that the city would win the case had eroded like beach property in winter. Now that the morning of the hearing had arrived she was more nervous than ever.

She wasn't covering the story for the station, but she'd be recognized all the same. Days earlier she'd been warned to stay out of the camera's view — keep her distance if she wanted to keep her job.

"You're recognized everywhere you go," Dick Baker told her. "No anchor of mine will be taking sides on a political issue like this one."

His words echoed in Faith's mind as she made her way past a peaceful demonstration on the front lawn, nodding at several people who waved in her direction. She entered the courtroom and found a seat near the back. The courthouse was located just outside Bethany in a newly renovated area designated for state government buildings. Judge Randall Webster would preside, and Faith was not at all comforted by the fact. Prior to taking the position as a jurist for the state of Pennsylvania, Judge Webster had been a defense attorney who earned a reputation for getting his clients the lightest possible sentences. He was a liberal man who'd made it abundantly clear he saw no place in society for religious icons, the Ten Commandments, or any mention of God whatsoever. Faith felt certain that if it had been up to Judge Webster, the dollar bill would say, "In us we trust." And that philosophy pervaded everything he said from the bench.

Faith spotted her father's partner across the courtroom and their eyes met. She smiled and discreetly pointed upward, mouthing the word, "Believe." Joshua nodded, his eyes filled with warmth even though uncertainty controlled his face. He returned his attention to his notes, and Faith shifted her gaze to the other side of the room.

Her breath caught in her throat as she spotted Jordan Riley. He moved easily from one end of the table to the other, his chiseled face masked in concentration, shoulders filling out his dark designer suit. She berated herself for being attracted to him. *God, help me remember he's on the wrong side.*

He moved toward what looked to be a team of attorneys, and they surrounded him the way athletes do in the final moments before a game. Clearly Jordan was in control of the meeting. He spoke commands to several of the men, and one at a time they peeled away and took their seats, either at the plaintiff's table or in the first row behind it.

She looked at him, hoping he would meet her gaze, but he was too caught up in his preparation. *God's on our side, Jordan . . . besides, nothing will bring back your mother.*

Faith saw that every seat in the courtroom was taken, but still people continued to stream in, lining two and three deep along the walls. Finally, security guards blocked the entrance and began turning people away.

Judge Webster entered the room and a hush fell over the crowd. He studied the mass of people, looked from perfectly dressed Jordan to the older Joshua and gently rapped his gavel. "Order . . . court is in session." His voice was deep and gravelly and carried with it an authority that sent a shiver down Faith's spine.

Please, God, be with us . . .

"This court will now hear the matter of Humanity Organized and United for Responsibility versus the city of Bethany, Pennsylvania."

Joshua watched as the judge lifted his chin and stared down the bridge of his nose. "I understand there are —" he made no effort to hide his sarcasm — "a few people interested in the outcome of this case." His voice boomed out from the bench. "Let's make one thing clear up front. No intimidation will take place in my courtroom. People are welcome to have an opinion." He gestured toward the window that overlooked the courthouse greens. "They are even invited to line up twenty deep across the lawn." He paused and glared at Joshua. "But nothing they say or do will influence the rulings I make in my courthouse now or at any other time. Is that clear?"

Joshua felt every eye in the room on him. "Yes, Your Honor, of course not."

The judge glared at Jordan next. "That goes for you, too."

Jordan Riley grinned at the judge as though the man were a favorite uncle. "Absolutely, Your Honor."

Judge Webster sat back in his seat. "In that case, let's begin. We'll hear from the plaintiff first." He motioned at the audience. "The rest of you may be seated."

Those who had seats did as the judge directed, and Jordan took the floor. He paced slowly in front of the tables, holding his notes as though if he studied them long enough he might remember what to say.

Joshua knew that wasn't the case. He'd done his research on Riley. The man's memory was one of the best in the business. The notes in his hands were merely for appearances, a device intended to give the impression that everything he said — from his opening argument to his closing remarks — was strictly from case law and researched material. That way he wouldn't come across as having a personal vendetta against the people of Bethany or their Jesus statue. Rather he was simply a legal servant of society, doing his best to maintain the line between church and state.

Joshua wondered if he was the only one in the room who saw through the ploy.

"Your Honor, the HOUR organization has filed suit against the people of Bethany for what is clearly a violation of state law. In the center of Bethany is a park — owned and operated by the city. And at the center of the park stands a ten-foot-high statue of Jesus Christ." Jordan paused as though he might rest his case on that note alone. "We believe the statue represents a conflict between church and state and is therefore a violation of the Constitution." He stopped pacing and stood with his legs shoulder-width apart, the folder held at his side. "The law is clear that no state government shall endorse or suggest or force any religion on its constituents. Clearly Jesus Christ is the universal symbol for Christianity. And since the Jesus statue stands on public property, its presence suggests a religion that is not only government-sponsored and endorsed, but quite possibly mandated."

Jordan shrugged his shoulders and cast an easy smile at Judge Webster. "Very simply, we want the statue removed as soon as possible."

The judge nodded. The lines on his face had eased considerably. "Go on, Counsel."

Jordan nodded and resumed his meandering pace across the front of the courtroom, his eyes on his notes once more. Joshua watched him and was caught off guard by something in the young man's eyes. His face was familiar in an eerie sort of way . . .

"In addition to the law — which is clearly on our side — we believe we have ample precedent to prove our point. With us today we have research from dozens of past cases, both from the state and Supreme Court level. If it pleases Your Honor, I'll give a summary of that research at this time."

Judge Webster gestured toward Jordan in a way that was just short of rude. "Continue."

Across the room Joshua tried to read the

feeling coming from the bench. Anyone who knew the judge knew where he likely stood on the issue of church and state. But Joshua knew the man also prided himself on not being biased. Joshua prayed that pride would work in their favor.

Jordan set his things down on the plaintiff's table and sorted through them for a few seconds before apparently finding what he was looking for. "Here we are . . ." And with that, Jordan neatly and succinctly cited exactly fourteen sources that were similar in nature, cases where a nativity scene or a Christian fish symbol or a cross was eliminated from the landscape of any place even remotely public. For good measure, he included two examples where private establishments were ordered to remove their Christian symbols as well.

After talking for less than an hour, Jordan set his notes down and looked at the judge. "That's all for now, Your Honor." A warm smile filled his face. "We are not looking to punish or in any way penalize the people of Bethany. We merely want the good citizens of this country to feel free to live and work around public areas without being forced to adhere to a specific religion. In essence —" he gestured toward his team of attorneys, and again Joshua had the strange feeling he'd seen the young attorney somewhere before — "we want to preserve the rights of the people to live free from the burden of state-sponsored religion. Now and as long as this great nation might stand. Thank you, Your Honor."

Jordan took his seat, and Joshua gathered his notes. He was certain his opponent had reams more of case precedent to support the idea that religious icons and displays ought not to be left standing on public property. That was fine. Joshua had prepared as well. He smiled to himself and felt a peaceful confidence come over him. God had promised to fight the battle, to go before him. Surely that meant victory, right? He stood up and headed toward the center of the floor, six feet from the judge's chair, praying for the right words.

"Your Honor, I appreciate the comments and concerns presented by the plaintiff. But I disagree that this is a case of the HOUR organization looking out for the rights of the people." He glanced at his notes and allowed a measured pause. The last thing he wanted was to appear rushed and flustered, as though he had to work to defend the city's position.

He took a steadying breath and continued. "The statue in question was given to the city of Bethany as a gift nearly a hundred years ago." Joshua squared up before the bench and met the judge's eyes straight on. "If the city had received a statue of Pocahontas or Christopher Columbus or Martin Luther King Jr., certainly no one would object to having it placed at the center of the city's oldest park. Like Columbus or King, Jesus Christ is a person of great historical significance, both in our United States history as well as the history of the world. Removing the statue of Him now is, in this city's opinion, a violation of the citizens' rights to cherish this gift, to look upon its considerable beauty and expression, to consider the historical significance of the man it represents." He made his way to the defense table and sorted through a series of files. If his opponent could look loaded with precedent, so could he. "I'd like to share some case law supporting that opinion."

The reality was Joshua had been able to find only two cases that even remotely upheld the idea that the Jesus statue should remain standing in Jericho Park, but he played them for all they were worth. One case involved a cross anchored on a hill that was — technically — part of the Texas state park system. It was also, however, a landmark by which those traveling the interstate could determine how far they'd traveled and how much time remained on their journey. Ultimately it was deemed more of a landmark than a religious icon, and the courts allowed it to stand.

The other case centered on the town of Camp Verde, Arizona, and an annual Christmas parade that culminated in a float depicting a living nativity scene. The parade entry included Mary, Joseph, an actual baby playing the part of Jesus, and an assortment of donkeys and sheep being tended along the parade route by Boy Scouts in shepherd garb. Since the parade was sponsored by the city, someone cried foul one year and filed a lawsuit requesting that the religious parade entry be excluded from the procession. After much bantering back and forth, a state court judge ruled that the parade was — in nature — organized around a Christmas theme, and that Christmas was, inherently, a celebration of Jesus Christ's birth. Therefore it was within the city's legal bounds to include in its Christmas parade the nativity scene, and the float was allowed to stay, right down to the babe in swaddling clothes.

Joshua did his best to make these cases look similar to the one involving Jericho

Park. He played up the fact that government groups were involved in both cases and remained intentionally vague on his comparisons that a landmark and a Christmas float were almost exactly the same thing as having a Jesus statue in the center of a public park.

But as he spoke, even Joshua could hear the gaping holes in his argument. It was one thing to have a directional landmark or a holiday-themed parade entry. Joshua simply had no precedent demonstrating a city's right to maintain a religious presence on public property for no apparent reason. The landmark case was the most similar and the night before he'd decided to hammer on that one more than the other. Now as he neared the end of his remarks, that's exactly what he did.

"Your Honor, the people of Bethany use the Jesus statue as a meeting spot. They talk about it as though it were part of the town's landscape. Generations of Bethany citizens have held annual picnics around the base of the statue and found comfort in the fact that though things change with time, the statue remains. It stands regardless."

He set his notes down and faced the judge again. "It is our opinion that the Jesus statue is as much a landmark as the cross that stood in the publicly owned hills of Texas. We ask that you make a decision allowing it to stand. Thank you, Your Honor."

Joshua caught Faith's weak smile as he sat down. Was his case that lacking? *Come on, God . . . make it happen.* He winked at Faith, turned and took his seat.

The judge looked from Joshua's table to that of the plaintiff and leaned forward. "This court will recess for ten minutes while I consider both arguments. We will meet back here at ten-fifteen at which time I will give my decision."

Frank Furlong and several members of Bethany's city council surrounded Joshua, patting him on the back and assuring him he'd done a fantastic job. But Joshua thought their remarks seemed canned, contrived — as though they were trying to convince themselves of something that suddenly seemed almost impossible.

A noise began to build outside, and Joshua turned toward the window. People covered the grounds below, some of them carrying signs that read, Stay out of our park and It's HOUR statue. Many of them marched peacefully, while others formed prayer circles. Joshua watched, and the pressure he felt nearly suffocated him. He shuddered and turned back to the others. "You were right." He looked at Frank. "At least a thousand."

Frank and the others joined Joshua at the window, and the men watched as the group formed a single line and began marching around the lawn, singing what sounded like a hymn. Frank flipped a lock on the window frame and lifted the glass so they could hear more clearly. Immediately their song became audible, the words ringing over the voices in the courtroom, stopping conversations and gradually causing some people to join in the song.

"Great is Thy faithfulness, oh God my Father. There is no shadow of turning with Thee. Thou changest not, Thy compassions they fail not . . . as Thou has been Thou forever will be. . . ."

Joshua felt tears stinging at his eyes and he blinked them back. The people were united in this, that much was sure. They didn't know what the outcome would be but they agreed on one thing: God would be faithful. Suddenly the pressure he'd felt a moment earlier lifted. It wasn't Joshua who would deliver victory to the people, but God. And whichever way the case went, He was in control. Faithful as He always had been, always would be.

The song grew louder as more voices

joined from among those in the audience. "Great is Thy faithfulness, great is Thy faithfulness, morning by morning new mercies I see. All I have needed, Thy hand hath provided. Great is Thy faithfulness . . . great is Thy faithfulness . . . great is Thy —"

"Shut the window!"

Joshua started and turned to find Judge Webster standing near the bench.

"And stop singing! I will not stand for this type of disruption in my courtroom." He sat down and fanned his robe around him in a huff of anger as the voices around him died off one by one.

Joshua hurried back to his seat, certain deep in his gut that he'd lost the case.

Back at the window, Frank hesitated long enough to show his frustration toward the judge. Then in an angry motion Frank slammed the window shut, silencing the voices of the crowd midrefrain. He took his seat with the others from Bethany as Joshua prayed that the people outside — people protesting with praise — would not blame him or the mayor for the decision that was about to be made.

The redness in Judge Webster's cheeks lightened some, and he settled back in his chair. "That's better." He looked at the younger attorney and managed a crooked smile. "I have heard a variety of cases in my courtroom over the years, but I must say I've rarely seen one as clear-cut and simple as this one." His eyebrows lowered as he gazed across the room at Joshua. "I've had time to go over the case precedent cited by both parties and I have but one choice."

He sifted through several sheets of paper. "Our country ought to be grateful for organizations such as HOUR who come along and help us find balance in the public places of our national life." Judge Webster stared at Joshua. "To think that a public park has had a Jesus statue standing at its center for nearly a hundred years is appalling. It suggests that Christianity is the religion of the day and that Jesus Christ is to be worshiped and adored among the people. It is no better than the statues built back in Communist Russia or in Red China today, where public artwork represents a government-mandated mind-set. A mind-set that is inherently dangerous and in direct opposition to the freedoms for which this country stands."

In his peripheral vision, Joshua could see an HOUR attorney lean over and whisper something to Jordan. Both attorneys then looked across the room at Joshua and exchanged a smile.

We've lost . . . O God, we've lost.

You will not have to fight this battle, Joshua. The battle belongs to the Lord . . .

Okay, God, but we're running out of time . . .

Be strong and courageous.

He swallowed hard, keeping his eyes on Judge Webster. Waiting for what he knew was coming.

The judge was going on about the value of separation of church and state. Finally he paused and cleared his throat. "For that reason, it is my decision to side with the plaintiffs in this case and to order the Jesus statue removed at the expense of the city of Bethany." He narrowed his eyes and looked directly at Joshua.

Father, I know You're in control, but I don't understand this . . .

The judge continued. "You, Mr. Nunn, will instruct the city officials that they have thirty days to remove the statue. A hundred-dollar penalty will be exacted on the city for every day it continues to stand past the deadline." He motioned toward the crowd. "I will expect you to conduct yourself with decorum after court is adjourned. Anyone who protests in an unsuitable manner —" he peered over his wire-framed glasses — "and that includes singing — will be arrested and held in contempt of court." The judge hesitated only a moment. "Court is adjourned."

Immediately there was a rustling of whispers and people began moving about the courtroom. In the confusion, Joshua looked across the table and saw Jordan Riley staring straight at him, his eyes filled with a strange mixture of victory and sadness.

Joshua's heart skipped a beat as the pieces fell into place. He met Jordan's gaze and held it, studying the eyes of the man who had claimed victory over Joshua, the Jesus statue, and the people of Bethany. Suddenly he knew why the young attorney looked so familiar.

His was the face in the dream, the one he'd had the day he was packing Bob Moses' things at the office. When Bob's face had disappeared from the framed photograph hanging on the office wall, it had been replaced by the image of a younger man with angry eyes and a handsome, chiseled face. A face Joshua had never seen.

Until now.

The face of Jordan Riley, chief counsel for the HOUR organization.

THIRTEEN

Nearly two weeks had passed since the ruling, and Faith knew from Joshua that the Bethany city council had held several emergency meetings in recent days. There wasn't much to discuss. Since the judge had ordered the Jesus statue removed, there was little they could do but decide on a ceremonial way to watch it go. A farewell party perhaps, or a designated day where the town could gather at the park for a picnic and hear a few words from key members in the community. There was talk of selling the statue to J. T. Enley, a retired stockbroker who had made millions in the market in the late nineties. Or perhaps donating it to a museum in Philadelphia. They also talked about selling the statue in an auction and donating the proceeds to a local charity.

Still, a deep and angry sadness remained, a sense of astonishment that a single attorney could breeze through town, file a lawsuit, and summarily have a town treasure eliminated. The story had made headlines in both local papers and was easily the biggest item in the newscast for three nights after the ruling. Tonight would be more of the same. According to Joshua, reporters had attended the latest council meeting earlier that day.

Faith finished applying her makeup and pinned her hair up, certain she'd feel the smirks of several station employees tonight as much as she'd felt them for the past fourteen days. She'd made her views public and she'd lost. The statue was coming down, and there was nothing she could do to stop it.

She slumped back against the wall in the boxy dressing room and stared at herself. Her father would never have let the statue be removed. Not that Joshua hadn't done his best in court; he had. But Bob Moses was a man who refused to let life get the best of him. Faith didn't know how, but her father would have found a way to keep the statue standing.

So what did that say about her?

What good had she ever brought to the world around her? She woke up at her parents' house, washed and cleaned and shopped for her mother, and on occasion spent a day with Rosa Lee. Every night on the air she dressed the same and smiled the same and used the same polished voice to deliver news that people could have gotten from a dozen different sources. Newspapers, other networks, the Internet.

Her job didn't really matter to anyone.

Mike Dillan continued breaking hearts in every town he played, Rosa went without a family, the Jesus statue was ordered down. Through it all, she'd been little more than a meaningless bystander. A weak-willed, passive participant with none of the gumption and determination that had been the benchmark of her father's life.

"Evans, let's go!" The voice on the other side of the door snapped her out of her reverie, demanding her attention for yet another newscast, another series of stories she would read for the cameras. Faith Evans, expert mouthpiece.

Lord, make me a light . . . help me bring about change.

As if in response, an idea came to mind. A brilliantly simple, amazing idea that took shape in Faith's mind in less time than it took her to grab the door handle and turn it. She hesitated for a moment, staring at the wooden door as a smile filled her face. The idea was so solid, so sound, Faith knew it had to have come from the Lord.

And as she breezed out of the dressing room and headed for her place on the soundstage she knew something else as well.

It just might work.

The next morning Sandy Dirk, Rosa Lee's social worker, got a phone call from a man who said he was from WKZN. His conversation was quick and to the point: "Our Internet site isn't receiving nearly the hits we'd like it to get."

She rolled her eyes, reached for a pencil and began doodling on a notepad. Sandy had seen so many down-and-out kids come through her foster home that she'd lost track of the number. Rosa was destined for the long-term facilities. She was too old to draw the attention of a couple looking for a baby, and though Sandy loved the children in her own way, she no longer got sucked into relationships with them. Hers was merely a stopping ground, a place for children no one wanted until the state could figure out something else. Often the only thing better was a group home, and Sandy had never known a child yet who hadn't been hardened beyond recognition after spending a year in such a place.

There was nothing quite like the pain of

watching officials from Social Services — and on some occasions even police officers — show up at the house, take a child and all her belongings, and haul her off to live at a group home for an indeterminate amount of time. Whatever a child's demeanor was when he or she left for group care, inevitably it would be worse six months later. People who knew Sandy understood that her gruff voice and no-nonsense approach was merely a front to prevent children from getting too comfortable in her care. And to keep herself from getting too comfortable with them.

Now as the man on the other end spoke, Sandy jotted the words *Internet site* and coughed into the receiver. "Okay, I heard ya. What's your point?"

The man drew a breath deep enough to hear over the phone lines. "We have advertisers, Mrs. Dirk. People who want to buy space on our Web site — especially the *Wednesday's Child* page."

"What's that have to do with me?" Sandy peered out the back window to make sure Rosa Lee was still playing outside with the other children.

"We're taking Rosa's picture off the site. To make room for other kids."

A flicker of understanding passed across

Sandy's mind. "You mean because she isn't cute enough? What with her missing fingers and Asian blood, is that it, Mr. Baker?"

Sandy chuckled twice, though it sounded more like an exaggerated huff. She'd been against the *Wednesday's Child* program from the beginning, convinced it would do nothing to increase Rosa Lee's chances for adoption and would most likely wind up hurting her in the process.

"The children who are getting attention from online users are younger than Rosa." The man sounded as though his patience was running low, as though it was demeaning to talk to a woman of Sandy's stature. "The fact is, Mrs. Dirk, no one's even asking about Rosa. She'll be off the Web site as of tomorrow morning. I thought you'd like to know."

Sandy thought for a moment. "Does Faith Evans know about this?"

There was a long pause on the other end. Apparently her question had hit its mark.

"No . . . the *Wednesday's Child* Web site has nothing to do with the program anchor. Unless you have other questions, Mrs. Dirk, I have appointments to keep."

Sandy hung up the phone and stared at it a moment, knowing that after tomorrow, getting Rosa Lee adopted would be virtually impossible.

In fact, it would be nothing short of a miracle.

Dick Baker hung up the station phone and buzzed Laura Wade, the young woman who manned the station's Web site. She was twenty-three, possessed a Microsoft certificate and a brain that seemed even quicker than the station's lightning-fast computers. Normally he had little to do with the Web site, but this was something special. Three days earlier, an anonymous caller had asked for him by name, offering to pay ten thousand dollars for a spot on the site under one condition: Baker had to keep Faith Evans from making any more opinionated outbursts.

At first Dick had balked at the request, assuming the caller was a nutcake. But after further questioning him, Dick learned that the man was from HOUR — the same group that had won the lawsuit against the town of Bethany. "Any suggestions?"

There was a pause. "*Wednesday's child.* That's Evans's project, isn't it?"

Baker was impressed. The man had done his homework. "Okay . . . so?"

"Remove the photos of one or two kids she's particularly fond of. That ought to get her attention."

A strange rumbling began in the pit of Baker's stomach. "How do I justify removing a child? They all need homes. The staff'll ask questions."

The caller chuckled. "That's up to you."

Baker thought about the ad money and his mind raced. Certainly he could remove the little Asian girl's photo. The other featured children were younger, healthier. Not biracial. Certainly he could make a case that they would adopt easier. Besides, the Asian girl belonged on a Web site for special-needs kids, not in a showcase position such as WKZN offered.

"All right. I can take care of that." Dick informed the man that the cost for the ad space was only seven thousand dollars per month. What he learned next cinched the deal.

"We'll be sending out two checks. One for the first month and a three thousand dollar check made out to you. For . . . administrative expenses."

Dick hadn't needed any more information than that. He imagined the cruise he and his wife could take with the bonus. There'd even be enough for gambling money . . . souvenirs . . . time off.

The checks had arrived the day before, and he'd already spoken with Laura, the

Webmaster, about the ad. HOUR's insignia and hot line number had been displayed prominently at the top of the *Wednesday's Child* Web page since last night.

Getting the Asian girl's picture removed had been another thing altogether.

The station's standard permissions form for children who appeared on the *Wednesday's Child* program and Web site stated that a child's guardian had to be contacted before his or her picture could be removed from the Internet page. Dick hated having to contact Rosa Lee's social worker, but there'd been no other way. At least he hadn't lied to the woman. The fact was, there *were* younger, more desirable children whose pictures belonged on the Web site. Rosa Lee was something of a distraction, a misfit. Dick held his breath as the phone rang in the station's computer lab.

"Yes?" Laura's voice was robotic, as though she'd spent too many years in the company of a computer.

"Baker here. I notified the social worker. Pull the photo of Rosa Lee."

Baker heard a series of clicking sounds as the woman's fingers raced over the keyboard. "Okay. She's gone."

As he hung up the phone he smiled to himself — but even as he did, Baker felt a twinge of regret. What heartless person at HOUR had sent in the request that Faith's favorite child or favorite children be removed from the site? He let the thought pass. The benefits far outweighed any damage to his conscience over the issue. WKZN would come off looking like it approved of HOUR, a fact that would help balance the conservative on-air views Faith Evans continually spouted. Baker could use HOUR to maintain an unbiased position, thereby pleasing the network executives in Philadelphia. His station had picked up an extra seven thousand dollars and he'd made a tidy bonus in the process.

Satisfaction filtered through Baker's veins. There was one other benefit, the icing on the cake, really. If the HOUR group was intent on pressuring Faith Evans to quiet her religious views, then that would take the burden off him.

In the end, it was a win-win situation for everyone.

At just past eleven that morning Faith sat by the fireplace in her parents' house sipping hot, steamed milk and second-guessing herself. She stared at the dancing flames, and though the warmth from the fire spread over her body, an icy wind resonated in her heart. The idea that had seemed so perfect the night before now felt impulsive and shallow and more than a little dangerous.

Faith curled her legs beneath her and considered the outcome if she went ahead with her plan. Certainly it could cost her a chunk of her savings — as well as any pretense of impartiality she might still have among her coworkers. She drew a deep breath and sank further back in her chair, her lips pursed together.

She had to be realistic about it . . . it could mean losing her job.

The image of Rosa Lee filled her mind, and she picked up the phone. Maybe an afternoon with the little girl would make Faith's decision more clear, help settle her priorities into place. She dialed a number she had long since memorized and waited while the phone rang.

"Yup." As far as Faith could tell, Sandy was an upbeat woman who dearly loved the children she cared for. The fact that she wasn't as tender or soft-spoken as Faith might have been didn't make her any less valuable in the lives of the kids. It merely underlined the fact that Rosa and the other children needed families.

"Hi, Sandy, it's Faith. Any calls for Rosa yet?" Faith held her breath. It was the same question she asked every time she called, praying all the while that someone had seen the Web site, a mom or dad who wanted to make Rosa their daughter.

"Nope, and it don't look like it'll happen any time soon."

Faith clenched her teeth and felt her heart sink halfway to her knees. *Poor Rosa. Why, God? Why isn't there someone for her?*

Silence.

There was no time to question the lack of holy reassurance. Sandy sounded more discouraged than usual, and a strange sense of alarm rippled through Faith. "Did something happen?"

"Yeah, something happened. That boss of yours down at the station called this morning and said they were pulling Rosa's picture from the Web site." Sandy paused, and Faith felt as though the fire had spread straight to her soul. "Something about her being too old."

Faith's hands began to tremble and her mouth went dry. "Dick Baker called you?"

"He's the one." Sandy's voice rang with cynicism. "Get the little girl's hopes up and then pull the rug out from underneath her. Don't tell me Rosa Lee's too old. If she were a white girl with a normal hand she'd be on the Web site as long as it took her to find a home."

Faith's mind was reeling. Why hadn't anyone from the station called to tell her about the decision? How come she hadn't known they were looking to keep older children off the site? "I'm sorry, Sandy. I'll see what I can find out and I'll give you a call back."

Five minutes later she had Dick Baker on the phone. "Why didn't you tell me you were pulling Rosa's picture?" She didn't bother masking her anger.

"Nothing says I have to contact you first." Baker sounded flip and unyielding. "I'm too busy to get involved with matters such as this."

Faith could feel her heart pounding in her throat. "Not too busy to call Rosa's social worker earlier today and get the child's picture removed. Why would the station manager have to take care of something like that? Isn't that the Webmaster's job?"

"Listen, *your* job's on thin ice as it is, Evans. I don't need some two-bit anchor questioning my decisions." His anger came like a sudden storm and she felt her heart rate quicken in response. "Not that I have to tell you this, but it wasn't my call. We had complaints from advertisers, and honestly they had valid points."

"Complaints?" Faith pressed her fingers up along her scalp and let her forehead settle in her hands. "About Rosa?"

Mr. Baker sighed as though he could barely tolerate her. "About her age. She belongs on a special-needs Web site; not the WKZN *Wednesday's Child* page."

A dozen questions jockeyed for position and Faith tried to articulate the most important. "What advertiser could have possibly cared about that?"

"This conversation is over. I'll expect you in at the regular time this evening and I don't want to hear another word about the matter. It's your job to locate orphaned children; it's our job to manage the Web page." He might have been a rabid bear for the way he growled at her, but this time Faith's fear dissolved, leaving in its place a growing determination as foreign to her as the idea of arguing with her boss.

"Do I make myself clear?"

"Yes." Faith gulped silently, considering her options. She had to know who the advertiser was, what company would single out a lonely child such as Rosa and have her picture removed from the Web site. "I'll see you at the station."

Faith moved across the room to the computer and accessed the Internet. Typing in the correct address she pulled up WKZN's home page and clicked onto the *Wednesday's Child* link. What she saw made her sit back in her chair, her heart hurting as though it were bound and gagged.

Across the top of the page was a banner advertisement for HOUR.

The realization took nearly a minute to sink in. Clearly Jordan Riley had placed the ad, but why? Was this how he'd chosen to pay her back for her televised animosity toward him and his group? Faith felt the enormity of their differences more sharply than ever. To think he'd take out his anger on a little child — a child as desperately lonely as he himself had once been. Faith had the strong desire to call him at work and tell him how she felt. Instead she reached into the cupboard and pulled down the phone book. Flipping to the list of government offices her eyes searched the page until she found what she was looking for.

Mayor Furlong answered on the third ring.

"Hey, Frank, it's Faith Evans." Her body tingled from the adrenaline racing through her system. There'd be serious repercussions, no doubt, but nothing could stop her now. This call was for the people of Bethany, in memory of her father. It was for little

Rosa Lee, and most of all it was for Faith herself.

She had lived in the shadows long enough; this time her mind was made up.

Suddenly she knew that this feeling — the odd sensation that her heart was in her throat, the way her body pulsed with conviction — this was what her father had lived for.

It was a feeling that what was about to be done was inherently right.

No matter the cost.

"Hello, Faith. What can I do for you?"

Faith cleared her throat. "I'm interested in buying a piece of property from the city."

FOURTEEN

The meeting took place after hours in a spacious, well-appointed office on the top floor of the headquarters for HOUR. In attendance were all three partners, as well as five of the firm's top lawyers.

The notable exception was Jordan Riley, whose case against the town of Bethany was causing more than a little concern.

A silence fell over the room, and Peter T. Hawkins, the oldest and most intimidating partner, rose from his seat and leaned against the wall. "Morris, tell 'em about the phone call."

T. J. Morris stood and slid his hands in his pockets. This was the year he'd been hoping to make partner and he knew he had no choice but to play the part asked of him in the Bethany case. There was the other detail as well . . . the bonus money.

What would Jordan think if he knew they were meeting behind his back? That they'd resorted to blackmail to make sure the press portrayed HOUR in a favorable light? He restrained a grimace, but not the thought that came with it: *What have I become?*

For a fleeting instant his thoughts nearly got the better of him. But with each man in the room waiting for him to speak, he had no time to answer his own question — and no answers, even if he'd had the time.

He stared at his notes and then lifted his eyes to meet those of his peers. "We received a phone call this afternoon from a reporter in Bethany. Apparently the city council held another of its emergency meetings today, and the reporter caught wind of something he thought we'd find interesting."

T. J. raised a piece of paper so he could see his notes more clearly. Beneath his shirt he could feel the perspiration building along his collarbone. The Bethany case was supposed to have been a natural winner, a simple, open-shut situation. Now he was at the center of what could wind up being a public relations nightmare. He exhaled slowly.

"Apparently a private citizen came forward yesterday and offered to purchase part of Jericho Park." He glanced at the stone-cold faces around him. "The piece where the Jesus statue sits."

There was a shifting of legs and glances about the room, and two of the partners whispered something to each other. T. J. waited until they were quiet again. "The city council chose not to inform the people of Bethany about the offer. Instead, they accepted it without question."

Steve Nelson sat forward in his chair. "What was the offer?"

"Ten thousand dollars." T. J. glanced at his notes again. "That includes the statue. Joshua Nunn, the attorney for the city, has requested a hearing for early next week, at which time we expect him to ask Judge Webster to throw out the case against Bethany. By that time the statue will no longer belong to the city, but to the private citizen, so there is no way a judge can rule separation of church and state." He looked at the others and tossed his notes onto the table.

Hawkins had stood throughout T. J.'s announcement and now he stepped out to the front of the room. "Tell them who bought it."

T. J. felt a drop of sweat roll down his right side underneath his dress shirt. "Faith Evans, the WKZN newscaster for the Philadelphia affiliate. Pretty girl with the whole town on her side."

Everyone spoke at once.

"That's a conflict of interest . . ."

"Reporters can't get involved that way . . ."

"Does the station know what she's done?"

Hawkins slammed his fist on a nearby desk and the room fell silent again. "HOUR simply will not stand for this debacle of justice. We cannot have it. The press will have a field day with us. Outsmarted by a bunch of bungling townspeople and some . . . some religious fanatic reporter!"

T. J. cleared his throat, and the attention shifted back to him. "Obviously Jordan Riley needs to know about this development. But for now —" he glanced at Hawkins — "we thought it was best to discuss this without him."

Hawkins's face contorted into a frustrated mass of wrinkles. "Jordan's got —" he waved his hand in the air — "a personal interest in this case. I think we all know that. He wanted the statue gone in the first place." Hawkins looked as though he'd swallowed something that was still moving in his stomach. "But he let something slip the other day in a conversation with T. J. It seems back when he was a boy he was in love with the very same girl who's giving us fits."

One of the other partners lurched forward, his face pale. "Faith Evans?"

"Yes." Hawkins spit the word as though he had a bug in his mouth. "Faith Evans." Hawkins shifted his gaze back to T. J. "I assume you took care of that little item I requested."

T. J. nodded. "Of course." He was still having trouble sleeping at night, wondering when HOUR had stooped to using orphans as pawns, but he kept that to himself. "I placed an ad on the WKZN Web site, paid off the station director, and got the photo of a young girl removed from the *Wednesday's Child* page. Apparently, the orphan was Faith Evans's favorite, and by now she knows HOUR was responsible for the child's removal."

"Excellent." He looked at the others. "I have nothing against this Evans woman personally, you understand. But she's taken up the wrong battle. In cases such as this, intimidation can make for superb warfare when the battle gets intense. And this figures to get downright ugly before it's all over." Hawkins looked at T. J. "Tomorrow I want you to call the news station and talk to Dick Baker; he's the station manager. Tell him you have something that might interest him. Then ask if he knows that his nighttime anchorwoman has purchased a piece of Jericho Park to help the town of

Bethany sidestep Judge Webster's ruling." Hawkins chuckled and scanned the room again. "Something tells me there'll be an opening for an anchor on the WKZN eleven o'clock news by tomorrow night." He nodded at T. J. "Give us the rundown on the plan from here."

T. J. took a step forward, hoping he looked more together than he felt. *I'm only being a friend . . . it's for Jordan's good . . .* But the party lines felt as comfortable as thumbtacks in his gut and he cleared his throat. "We'll work on a solution tonight and then tomorrow get the information to Jordan, who will then file a secondary suit at the same time the city asks for a reprieve. That way the media will be less likely to focus on the people's defensive move — the sale of the park land — and more likely to highlight our next stage of attack." He looked at the eyes of the men and saw they were tracking with him. He raised his chin and his voice grew steady.

"In other words, we don't want the story to be the sale of the park land. Not for a single day. Obviously it'll be an aspect of the story, but the main point of interest must be whatever move *we* choose to make."

Hawkins stepped forward and waved his hand at the others. "That's where you all come in. No one, and I mean not one of you, will leave this room until an action based on case precedent has been decided on. At that point, T. J. will write up the plan as a single brief and give it to Jordan tomorrow."

T. J. blinked. He could just imagine Jordan's reaction when he learned he had not been one of the first to hear Bethany had sold the land to Faith Evans. Or when he found out that T. J., one of his best friends, had been part of the plan to leave him out. But then, business had to come first. And if Hawkins was being level with him, his work on the Bethany case could mean he'd make partner that much sooner.

Hawkins sat down and leaned back in his chair. "Jordan Riley must never know about this meeting, is that understood?"

The men around the room nodded, and three of them agreed out loud. As they began tossing out ideas and jotting down notes, T. J. tried to convince himself that such meetings were a necessary part of being a lawyer. That blackmailing reporters, getting an orphan's photo pulled from a Web site, and holding clandestine meetings behind the back of a coworker and friend were an understandable price to pay in the fight for human rights.

He tried to believe it was all in Jordan's best interest. Just a way of ensuring his friend's heart didn't get too involved — which would only render him ineffective.

But for the first time since T. J. took the job at HOUR he could only convince himself of one thing: This time he and his coworkers were going too far.

Hawkins waited until the others had filed out of his office before returning the call. The message had come in just before the meeting. An advisor to one of the top politicians in the state of Pennsylvania wanted to talk to him.

Hawkins felt his heart beat hard against his chest. Whatever this was, it ought to be interesting. He dialed the number and waited for the man to take the call.

"Hello, sir. Peter Hawkins here. With the HOUR organization."

There was a pause as the man switched off his speakerphone. "Thank you for calling me back." He hesitated and lowered his voice some. "I have some people interested in funding your Jesus statue case."

Hawkins sat up straighter in his chair. "Funding it?"

"Yes." The man chuckled quietly. "We've gotten wind that the statue's been purchased by a private citizen. Some of our . . . friends thought this might mean complications to the case." He paused. "I'm talking about an awful lot of money, Mr. Hawkins. But there's one catch . . ."

Hawkins's throat felt suddenly dry. Funding? From a political office? "What?" He grabbed a notepad and a pencil and poised himself, ready to write.

"You have to win the case. We want that statue down, regardless of the cost. Am I making myself clear?"

Hawkins doodled the word *clear* on his notepad. "Yes, sir, you are. You mind if I ask why your office is interested?"

"That should be obvious." The man's voice was so soft Hawkins had to strain to hear him. "Election year is coming up. Who wouldn't want to claim such a victory before hitting the campaign trail? The special interest campaign trail, that is." The man's voice grew serious. "As I said, we're talking about a lot of money."

Hawkins could no longer help himself. "How much?" He drew a dollar sign on the notepad and waited.

The man rattled off a figure, and Hawkins dropped his pencil, his breath trapped somewhere deep inside his throat. "I'm listening."

"Very well —" the caller chuckled again — "here's what we want to do . . ."

Jordan Riley paced his office like a caged jaguar trying to warm himself on a December morning in New York City. "Explain it to me again, T. J., because it doesn't make sense. I'm out of the office for one day researching some innocuous Bible club, and Hawkins asks you to write a brief on *my* case? A case that's been over for weeks?"

It was just after noon on Friday, the week before the Jesus statue would be down for good and suddenly everything certain about the case had dissolved in the time it took T. J. to sit him down and close the door. And why did his friend look so nervous? Something about this newest twist in the situation didn't ring true to Jordan and he was operating under a barely controlled rage.

"I told you. Hawkins got word that a private citizen bought the Jesus statue and the land where it sits. Joshua Nunn requested a hearing for next week, and Hawkins thought you could use some help. He asked me to write a brief and meet with you this afternoon." T. J. uttered an empty laugh. "What, no thanks? A guy spends a day writing a brief for his friend, and this is

226

the appreciation I get?"

Jordan stalked from his desk to the large picture window behind it and stared outside, his back to T. J. "Who bought the land?"

"I told you, we're not sure."

Jordan whipped around. "You expect me to believe that? Hawkins doesn't know? He used to be an investigator before he turned lawyer, remember?" Jordan huffed and returned his gaze to the window. He wanted to ask his friend to leave so he could take a minute and collect his thoughts. Why wouldn't this case go away? He'd have to go back to Bethany now, which meant he might well run into Faith again. He hated the thought of facing those innocent, warm eyes of hers . . . of standing up under her questioning, accusing gaze.

Her words filled his mind, as they had often in the past weeks. *"The Jesus statue belongs to the people of Bethany and any battle you wage there is one you'll ultimately lose . . . one you'll ultimately lose . . . one you'll ultimately lose . . ."*

How many times since the lawsuit had he wished he could call off the whole thing, run back to Faith, and tell her he hadn't changed after all? That he really was the same boy she'd been in love with all those years ago.

But he couldn't. He wasn't. It was that simple.

The person he was now could not be undone because of a jumble of teenage memories. He had taken his stand — armed himself for war — and there would be no going back, no convincing himself that Jesus was real or that the court battle he'd waged was not worth giving his life for.

No matter what Faith had done to his heart that night in the parking lot.

Jordan turned back to his desk and sat down, holding his conflicting emotions at bay. He had no idea why T. J. had been brought into this, but it was time to make sure Faith's words didn't turn out prophetic. And whether T. J. would be sent to Bethany with him or not, he needed a game plan. Even if it wasn't one of his own making.

"Okay." Jordan gritted his teeth as he leaned forward and met his friend's gaze straight on. "Tell me about your brief."

Fifteen

It was Monday morning, twenty-four hours before the Jesus statue was legally required to be removed from Jericho Park. The morning of the hearing that would end the case once and for all. Rain beat a steady pattern against the courthouse roof and a blustery wind howled through the trees on the lawn.

As always, the wet weather made Joshua's knees ache. A reminder of his cross-country days. Still, as he walked the hallways toward Judge Webster's courtroom, there was a definite spring in his step.

In fact, he hadn't felt so good since before Bob Moses died.

God had promised to go before him, promised His faithfulness, and indeed, it was coming to pass. The goodness and steadfastness of the Lord. To think that Faith would purchase the piece of Jericho Park where the statue stood. It was a move her father would have made, but not Joshua. Not in a dozen years of studying law briefs.

He rounded a corner and headed through the double doors of the courtroom to an inconspicuous spot in the back. He was glad he was the first to arrive. *How could I ever have doubted You, Lord?* He thought again of Faith, of her brilliant move and the change in her over the past few days. As though she'd somehow found the drive and determination of her father. Of course, if the station management discovered that *she* was the one who'd bought the land with the statue, the fallout would be devastating to her career.

Joshua glanced at his watch — he had forty minutes before the hearing began. Good. He'd need at least that long to pray for Faith, for the case, for a dozen other needs . . .

Finally he prayed for Jordan Riley — something he'd felt compelled to do every day since the last hearing, since he realized Jordan's was the face he'd seen in his dream. Joshua still had no idea what it all meant, but he was sure of one thing. The young man needed prayer.

Suddenly, Joshua's silent pleadings were interrupted by the sound of several people and a clanking of equipment making its way toward him. As the entourage rounded the bend and headed his way, Joshua felt the blood leave his face. What was this? Reporters? For a simple hearing? How had they gotten wind of the story?

And what would their presence mean for Faith?

The minutes passed slowly while the camera crews took up their positions. Jordan Riley appeared, followed by another dapper-looking attorney wearing a dark suit as expensive and tailored as Jordan's. Immediately the reporters were on Jordan, pumping him with questions, cameras running.

"Is it true you have a response for whatever happens today in court, Mr. Riley?"

"Can you tell us the details?"

"Who purchased the land, Mr. Riley, can you tell us?"

Joshua gritted his teeth. So they knew about the land . . . *Help Faith, Lord . . . please.*

Joshua's opponent exuded cool assurance as he answered their questions. Yes, he had a response; no, he couldn't discuss the details until the hearing was over; no, he had no idea who purchased the land.

"I'm assuming the city will reveal that information today." Jordan nodded politely and excused himself as he and the other HOUR attorney made their way to the plaintiff's table.

Joshua listened to them and chill bumps rose on his arms. As he stood to take his place at the defense table, the reporters turned their questions on him.

"Mr. Nunn . . . Mr. Nunn . . . Tell us, who purchased the land from the city?"

"Did the town have a vote in the sale of the statue?"

"Was this a ploy by the town of Bethany to circumvent Judge Webster's mandate?"

They acted like a pack of rabid dogs. Joshua held his hand up and repeatedly told them he was unable to comment until after the hearing. He took his seat near the front of the courtroom, his mind racing in silent prayer.

There was no time to think about the outcome. Judge Webster appeared from behind closed doors and took his place at the bench. He surveyed the reporters and cameramen and raised an eyebrow at Jordan. "Well, Mr. Riley, it seems whenever you come to town the local press is intent on capturing every detail."

Jordan nodded politely and allowed the slightest grin. "Yes, Your Honor."

Judge Webster banged his gavel once.

"Court is now in session." He stared strangely at Joshua. "Will the counsel for both sides please rise?" He waited until they were standing, then he addressed Joshua. "I understand you come with new information regarding the case of the HOUR organization against the city of Bethany, Pennsylvania. Is that correct?"

"Yes, Your Honor."

"And you —" the judge looked at Jordan — "will be filing another suit in response, is that right?"

Joshua steadied himself against the news. What other suit was the judge talking about? There was no way Jordan Riley could have come prepared to file a counter-suit unless . . .

He closed his eyes briefly. Unless he'd been tipped off about the details of the hearing.

Be strong and courageous, Joshua . . . I will go before you always.

The holy whisperings still infused him with peace, but Joshua definitely could not see God's plan unfolding.

"Mr. Riley, you may be seated." Judge Webster leaned back in his chair and waved toward Joshua. "Present your brief, Counselor."

Joshua straightened his tie. *Give me the*

words, Lord . . . I can't do this alone . . . He walked up to the bench and raised the document in his hand. "Your Honor, in the weeks since our last hearing, the situation at Jericho Park has changed considerably. It is my intention to inform you of those changes and then — once you understand them — I will request that you throw out your earlier decision."

Judge Webster raised a single eyebrow and shifted his lower jaw to one side. "Continue."

Joshua studied his notes for a moment and then looked at the judge. "Last week, a private citizen came forward and offered to purchase the piece of park property where the Jesus statue currently stands." Joshua moved to the second page. *Make him open to the idea, Lord . . .* "That citizen paid a substantial amount, the price of which is detailed in the brief I'll provide you. The price included not only the land, but the statue as well."

The judge leaned forward. "And so . . ."

Joshua nodded politely and continued. "Now that the land and statue in question no longer belong to the city, there is no conflict with the separation of church and state law. Therefore, we request that you throw out your earlier decision, since such a decision cannot be enacted on a private citizen."

There was a pause while Judge Webster stroked his chin and studied Joshua. He seemed less antagonistic than he'd been back when they'd had the first hearing, but something about the man's eyes — a knowing look, or perhaps a smugness — left Joshua anxious and uncertain.

He had the feeling the judge had known all along what this second hearing was about and was merely going through the motions.

"Mr. Nunn, I'd like the name of the private citizen, please."

Joshua's heart skipped a beat. *No, not with the press here . . .* "The private citizen?"

Webster raised both eyebrows this time. "Yes, Mr. Nunn. The private citizen who purchased the park property. I need a name, please."

Out of the corner of his eye Joshua saw reporters whispering to one another, their pencils poised, faces awash with anticipation. If the judge pushed, Joshua knew he'd have no choice but to present the documents that showed Faith as the buyer. Real estate dealings were public record. "Well, Your Honor. The citizen desires to remain anonymous. The city has chosen to honor that desire."

A ripple of slow laughter escaped Judge Webster's throat. Then just as quickly it faded, and he raised his eyebrows at Joshua. "It isn't optional, Counsel. Either you tell me the name of the citizen, or I'll have to assume this is nothing more than political posturing, a trick devised by the city of Bethany to avoid carrying out my order. You give me the name, or I'll hold you in contempt of court and have the statue removed anyway." He looked at his watch. "At this point you'd have less than twenty-four hours to get it down."

Joshua worked his jaw, desperately searching for a trick door or an open window, any way out of the jam he was in. But there was no escape . . .

There was an odd light in the judge's eyes, and Joshua wondered again if the man didn't already know the answer, if he was playing with Joshua, drawing out the hearing in anticipation of watching the press's reaction. Because finding out that Faith Evans had bought the property was definitely going to be news.

Just last night he'd spoken to her about this very thing — about the possibility that he'd have to give her name in court. She'd been adamant: "It doesn't matter what happens, Joshua. If you need to tell them it was me, then tell them. I want the statue to stand. If I lose my job, so be it. God'll take care of me. I'm not worried."

Joshua loved the girl for her attitude, and he knew her father would be proud. But it didn't make this moment any easier. He clenched his teeth and released them. "Very well, Your Honor. The citizen is Faith Evans."

A roar went up around the courtroom as reporters reacted to the news. Joshua closed his eyes for a moment and heard Faith's name uttered over and over, heard the whispered comments . . .

"Faith Evans? The nighttime anchor for WKZN?"

"*She's* the citizen who'd purchased the park property?"

"Faith Evans helped the city of Bethany avoid a ruling by a state judge?"

While Joshua felt certain someone had leaked the information to the judge, clearly the news took the press by surprise. He glanced at his opponent and thought Jordan looked paler than before. His eyes were glazed over, as though the revelation of Faith's name had sent him spiraling to some far away place.

Did Jordan even know who Faith was?

Joshua didn't think so. After all, the young attorney lived in New York, too far to recognize Faith as a WKZN news anchor. Besides, why would Jordan care who had bought the property? Joshua couldn't quite place the expression on Jordan's face, but it wasn't simple anger or aggression or the desire to win. It was all of those things, but Joshua could swear there was also regret.

Judge Webster banged his gavel twice and waited for the uproar to die down. "Order. I will not tolerate another outbreak. If you people —" he motioned toward the reporters — "can't keep quiet I'll have you all charged with contempt." He turned his attention back to Joshua. "So you're telling me that the land has been purchased by Faith Evans — the same Faith Evans who does the WKZN *Nightly News?*"

Joshua's chin dropped several inches. "Yes, Your Honor."

There was a moment of silence while the judge considered this new information. "Very well, then. You have a point, Mr. Nunn. Since the property now belongs to a private citizen, there is nothing I can do to enforce the removal of the statue." He glanced at the others in the courtroom. "I hereby dismiss the earlier judgment against the city of Bethany and will no longer require officials of that city to remove the statue of Jesus, which now stands on private property." He cast a calculated look at Joshua. "You may be seated." His gaze shifted to Jordan. "If you have something to add, Counselor, please take the floor."

Jordan undid the lower button on his jacket and stood, approaching the bench with a practiced ease. Joshua watched him with a mixture of admiration and regret. *What an impact this young man would have made if he'd been fighting for Your side, Lord . . .*

"On behalf of the HOUR organization, I'd like to share with you details of another lawsuit filed this morning and brought up as an emergency matter before you today."

The judge nodded to Jordan. "Go ahead, Mr. Riley."

"It is our opinion that the spirit of the law in this case has been evaded. Yes, the people of Bethany seemed to have found a loophole by selling the public property in question to . . ."

Jordan stopped short of saying Faith's name, and Joshua was sure there was more to the story than he knew.

"To a private citizen." Jordan took several steps toward the judge but spoke loud enough for the reporters in the back to hear.

"But Your Honor, we fear as a result that justice has not been served. In response, the new lawsuit names the city of Bethany as being responsible for subjecting park-goers to a blatantly Christian display — whether on private property or not. In the suit we are asking for a remedy, which we believe is reasonable and would serve the same purpose as Your Honor's original judgment. We will expect Mr. Nunn to have some type of response, of course, but not until we make our requests clear."

Jordan's jacket hung beautifully on his lanky, athletic frame, and Joshua had the sickening feeling that somehow — regardless of Faith's effort to put herself, her job, her reputation on the line — the HOUR organization was going to win. *I know You're here, Lord. Make Yourself known . . . please . . .*

Judge Webster nodded and motioned for Jordan to continue. "Explain the remedy you're seeking."

Jordan reached for a document and flipped past several pages. "Okay, here it is. HOUR is asking that Your Honor order the city of Bethany to build a wall around the statue. Since the statue is ten feet high, the wall would also be ten feet."

Joshua's heart ached at the thought. Was

it possible? Would a judge really order a wall to be put up around the statue? He began scribbling notes, listening to every word the judge said.

"Hmm. A wall, is that correct?" Judge Webster actually smiled, as though he wished he'd thought of the idea.

Joshua let his gaze fall to his hands. So much for taking pride in being objective.

"Yes. It is our opinion — and quite obviously your opinion based on the earlier ruling — that the people who visit Jericho Park should not be subjected to the Jesus statue. We understand that although a small piece of property — along with the statue —'now belong to a private citizen, there is still the problem of the statue seeming to be supported by the city of Bethany. In summary, that is our case and the remedy we seek."

The judge looked comfortable and happy, like a man enjoying a favorite movie for the fourth time. He shifted his attention to Joshua. "Mr. Nunn, normally I would postpone making such a decision, but since it's so closely linked to the previous matter, I will ask you to state the city of Bethany's position."

Joshua rose and locked eyes with the judge. "Your Honor, erecting a ten-foot-high fence around the base of the Jesus statue is a ludicrous suggestion. Not only would it be wrong to leave a private citizen with no access to her property, but it would also create an eyesore in a park that has been beautiful, generation after generation. A park in existence for more than a century."

For the better part of an hour, the two men debated the issue until finally the judge had heard enough. "I will take a brief recess and return in a moment with my decision on this new action."

Joshua buried his attention in the notes at his table and across the courtroom he could see Jordan doing the same thing. Joshua had expected him to use the time to entertain the reporters, to talk up the fact that Faith Evans had started this mess by purchasing the property. But Jordan was easily as intent on his notes as Joshua. The minutes flew by, and finally Judge Webster returned.

Once he was seated at the bench, the judge glanced at a sheet of paper in front of him and rapped his gavel a single time. "Court is back in session. I have made two decisions while in my chambers, both of which will affect all parties concerned in this case. First, I want to agree that Mr. Riley has a valid point about the people who happen to visit the park. It is wrong to assume the public will know that part of the park — the place where the Jesus statue stands — belongs to a private person. For that reason, most park-goers will believe the statue is supported and maintained by the city of Bethany."

His glasses fell a notch lower on his nose and he looked hard at Joshua. "My understanding on the ruling that separates church and state is very simple: We cannot have a city park giving the appearance of having sided with one religion over any other. For that reason there must be a wall erected around the statue."

Joshua thought about his short-lived victory and his stomach settled somewhere around his ankles. *God, where is this going? Faith put her job and reputation on the line, but for what? What victory is there with a fence around the statue?* There was no time for holy answers. The judge was moving on to his second point.

"However —" the judge shot a gaze at Jordan — "I've made another decision as well. I'm not sure that the statue requires a ten-foot high wall. That, Mr. Riley, I will leave up to you."

The man beside Jordan pointed to something in a file on their desk, and Jordan nodded. He stood and faced the judge. "Your

Honor, it is the opinion of the HOUR organization that nothing short of a ten-foot high fence will successfully hide the statue in Jericho Park." He glanced at his associate, then back at the judge. "We don't feel we need thirty days to make that decision."

Joshua felt more like a silent bystander than a part of the proceedings, but he knew if he didn't say something now he might not have another chance. "Your Honor, may I interject?"

Judge Webster shot him a surprised look and seemed to consider Joshua's request for several seconds. "Very well, go ahead."

"Since the property now involves a private party, I believe another hearing — between that person, myself, and Mr. Riley — is essential. Certainly we cannot come up with a final decision without consulting the person who now owns that property." Joshua stepped back and resisted a smile. He hadn't planned on making that argument; the words could only have come from God. *Thank You, Lord . . .* He blinked and waited for the judge to respond.

The muscles in Judge Webster's jaw tightened and relaxed three times before he spoke. "We do have an unusual situation here, I'm afraid. Mr. Nunn is correct — we must involve the private citizen before I make a permanent ruling." He checked his notes. "At the same time, I have already stated that the people must no longer be subject to a statue of Jesus Christ in the center of a public park." He leaned his forearms on the bench and frowned. "For that reason I am ordering that a temporary ten-foot-high plywood wall be erected around the statue for thirty days, until our next hearing. At that time I will hear from Ms. —" he looked at his notes again — "Ms. Faith Evans, along with the plaintiff and defendant in the case. Only then will I make a permanent ruling." He leveled his gaze at Joshua. "You will inform the Bethany city council that they have seventy-two hours to build the wall around the statue, and that the city is to incur the cost of building it."

"Yes, Your Honor." Joshua did his best to hide his disappointment. At least the ruling was only temporary. Still . . . he was heart-sick at the ground they'd lost. He'd come to court that morning certain the judge would throw out his earlier ruling, sure that Faith's decision to purchase the park land had been God's way of handing them a victory. Instead the city was now party to yet another lawsuit and in three short days the Jesus statue would be surrounded by a ten-foot wall.

The hearing was over and the reporters moved in with their questions, most of them directed toward Jordan Riley.

"Are you happy with the judge's ruling?"

"Do you think the wall will become permanent?"

"Is it right for a newscaster to get involved in something this political?"

The air of tension in the courtroom lifted as Jordan smiled at the cameras. "We won't be completely happy until the ruling is permanent, but it's the best we could hope for at this point."

"What type of wall are you going to request at the next hearing?"

He glanced at his friend and flashed another smile for the reporters. "Brick."

"Do you feel justice was served today?"

Jordan hesitated, and from where Joshua was gathering his legal files several feet away, he could see the air of professionalism in the way Jordan angled his head, his eyes suddenly serious again. "Justice will be served when we don't have to go to court to see that the Constitution is honored. There are still hundreds of thousands of citizens across America who hold to a dangerous belief that the government should advocate a state religion — Christianity, to be specific." He shifted his attention to another camera. "We attorneys at HOUR refuse to rest until that belief has been eradicated from the public conscience of these great United States."

Across the room, Joshua resisted the urge to roll his eyes. Jordan couldn't have sounded more polished if he'd been running for office. The reporters seemed to be finished with the plaintiff's point of view and the group of them migrated across the courtroom and fell in around Joshua. But whereas they'd smiled and bantered easily with Jordan, they seemed to have just one question for Joshua Nunn and the Religious Freedom Institute:

"How can we get in touch with Faith Evans?"

SIXTEEN

Jordan hadn't expected to be back in Bethany so soon, but now that he was there he planned to spend the night and return to New York in the morning. When the press had finished with him, he dismissed T. J., explaining he had to take care of paperwork at the local courthouse.

"I'll take a room next to yours," T. J. said as they made their way to the parking lot. The men had driven to Bethany in separate cars since T. J. needed to finish a case he was working on before driving up. "You never know, you might need help. Besides, that way we can find some all-night Italian diner and catch up on the other half of life — you know, the hours we actually spend at home."

Jordan looked at his friend, convinced again that something wasn't right. Without a doubt Jordan and his assistants could have handled today's hearing on their own.

Dozens of times he'd handled more demanding hearings without the help of an associate. And now — instead of heading back to New York to be with his wife and baby daughter — T. J. wanted to spend the night in Bethany?

They walked in silence and arrived at their cars, parked side by side at the back of the lot. Jordan leaned back on his and faced his friend. "What's up, T. J.?"

Jordan had known T. J. for years. They were hired at the same time and had spent at least one Saturday a month fishing the rivers and lakes outside the city. They'd double-dated on occasion. In all of New York, T. J. was Jordan's best friend.

So why wouldn't his best friend make eye contact?

"Nothing's up. I mean, why hurry back to the office?"

T. J.'s voice lacked conviction, and Jordan felt a fluttering in his gut. What *was* this?

Jordan slid his hands in his pocket, leaned harder against his car, and crossed his ankles. "Level with me, buddy. I'm serious." He positioned his head so he could see T. J.'s eyes.

Even above the occasional gusts of wind in the maple trees that lined the parking lot, Jordan could hear the heaviness in T. J.'s sigh. "Hawkins asked me to stay."

Jordan felt the ground beneath him give way. "What do you mean? Why would he do that?"

T. J. shrugged. "I'm not sure anymore, Jordan." He looked up, his gaze level. "Maybe you should ask him." T. J. turned his head and stared across the parking lot, as though watching invisible monsters closing in. "Sometimes . . . I think we're losing our focus."

"What d'ya mean, buddy?" Jordan's voice was softer than before, and he searched his friend's face. What wasn't T. J. telling him?

T. J. gave a few quick shakes of his head and looked at Jordan again. "Nothing." He forced a laugh. "It's been a long couple days." He glanced at his watch. "Tell you what, you stay here and take care of business and I'll head home." The corners of his mouth lifted and he winked once at Jordan. "She misses me when I'm gone more than one night."

Without saying another word, T. J. fished his keys from his pocket and climbed into his car. Jordan was torn between relief that he had some time to himself and concern about whatever it was T. J. wasn't saying. "Wait a minute —" he grabbed hold of his friend's open car door and stooped down

— "what aren't you telling me?"

T. J. looked at him, then pursed his lips and angled his head. "It's all for a good cause, isn't it, Riley? Isn't that what they tell us?"

A ripple of panic shot through Jordan. "*What's* for a good cause? You're losing me here, Teej."

"The whole thing." He motioned toward the courtroom. "The fight for human rights. Battling the little guys. It's all for a good cause." He put his hand on the steering wheel. "Look, I gotta get going or I'll never make it home for dinner."

Jordan got the message. He let his hand fall from T. J.'s car door and stepped back. He nodded at his friend as he turned the key and backed out of the spot. Maybe Jordan had been looking too deeply into things. Maybe Hawkins merely wanted to make sure they won the case. But something about that thought felt as comfortable as bad seafood in his gut. Jordan blinked, trying to see the bigger picture. Whatever it was, he knew he could count on T. J. If something was eating at him, Jordan would find out sooner or later. "Drive safe."

Not until T. J.'s car turned out of the parking lot and disappeared down a narrow side street toward the freeway did Jordan release the air that had been building up in him since the old lawyer's revelation. Faith Evans had purchased the park property? How was that possible?

He stared at the scant leaves still clinging to the branches above him. Why would Faith make so bold a move now, when she held a prestigious position with WKZN and sat poised on what could be a move to national television? He remembered something Faith had said back when they were kids, back when Jordan had spent every evening praying at Jericho Park: *That statue isn't Jesus, you know that, right? It's just a picture of Him . . .*"

Surely she felt the same way today. So why the fight? What did it matter if the statue came down? He thought about all she could lose, the way she would likely be mocked and held up for ridicule before the public eye after today's hearing.

"Ah, Faith . . ." Her whispered name took to the wind like one more dead leaf. He'd spent sixteen years searching for some sign of his past, some remnant that would help him connect those early days with the life he was living now. His mother was gone; Heidi too. And until that fall, Faith had been little more than a distant memory, a symbol from a time when everything was as it should have been.

Before God had pulled the rug out from underneath him.

And now that he'd found Faith, there was more distance between them than ever before.

Jordan squinted and tried to see through the barren branches to the sky beyond. Was He there, that mighty God, the one Faith clung to so blindly? Did He know that the lovely Faith Moses was about to take a fall, about to be the sacrificial lamb in a media event that was far from played out?

Another breath eased its way through Jordan's clenched teeth, and he slid into his car. He was an attorney at the top of his game, a man who after tonight's news would be credited with single-handedly foiling the plans of an entire city. A human rights advocate to be reckoned with and admired in legal circles around the country.

But for all that, as Jordan drove out of the parking lot he had to fight an urge that made no sense whatsoever. An urge he could barely acknowledge and would certainly never voice. The urge to call the judge and drop the case. Then to find Faith, gather her in his arms, and love her the way he'd wanted to do since that magical, long-ago fall. Back when his mother was well, and Heidi was there, and everything good in life seemed to center around one very special girl.

Faith was at the station all of two minutes when she realized there was a problem. Cameramen and stage hands omitted their usual greeting and scurried out of the way when she entered the building. Before she even had time to hang her coat in the dressing room, there was a knock at the door.

"Yes . . ." She had no reason to be fearful. After all, she'd survived two newscasts since buying the property and still no one had said a word about it at the station. By now she'd decided that maybe they wouldn't find out; maybe she had the right to buy property like any other citizen. So what if she was an anchor for the nightly news?

Her certainty fell away like a poorly built house of cards when she saw Dick Baker's secretary at the door. "Mr. Baker wants a word with you." Normally the older woman was friendly, but this time her tone was curt and after delivering the message, she left quickly.

Faith made her way down the hallway and found the door marked Station Manager. The moment she knocked, Mr. Baker's voice boomed from behind the door. "Come in!"

Faith's stomach felt like it was being trampled by a herd of cattle. She crossed her arms tightly, gripping her sides with the tips of her fingers. "You wanted to see me?"

She expected him to be mad, but his face lacked any expression whatsoever. *Someone's told him. Dear God, give me strength. You promised You'd get me through this . . .* Faith froze, unblinking, waiting for her boss to speak.

Mr. Baker leveled his gaze at her, and Faith saw that his features were hard and cold as steel in wintertime. "It came to my attention a few days ago that you'd done something incredibly stupid, something I hoped wasn't true." He paused, and she saw another emotion filter across his eyes. Disgust . . . even disdain. "As I told you before, the network has talked of bringing you up, giving you a reporter position on a national level. A move like that would have looked good for us, given the network moguls a reason to keep their eyes on the Philadelphia station."

Faith's knees felt weak and she shifted her weight. *Help me be calm, Lord . . . I can do all things through Christ who gives me strength . . . I can do all things through Christ who —*

"Today, however, I learned from several reporters — including ours — that the information I'd heard the other day was true." The man made *true* sound like profanity. Faith could see he was working to remain calm and though she was tempted to join the conversation to defend herself, she kept silent. There was no doubt in her mind that he'd found out about the Jesus statue. She kept her chin up, her eyes on his, and waited for him to continue. *I can do all things through —*

Mr. Baker suddenly stood and began pacing near his desk, rubbing the back of his head as he spoke. "When I hired you, Faith, I warned you that being an anchor would require your unbiased attention. That there was no room here for your religious views. You signed the contract promising as much." He stopped and pointed at her. "You're a public figure as long as your face is on television every night. I made that clear to you from the beginning."

He resumed his pacing, staring at his feet as he walked. "Our reporters must be intelligent, law-abiding citizens who, though they cover the news, must steer clear of ever *being* the news." He glanced up at her. "You understood that when I hired you, am I right?"

"Yes." Faith could feel God's peace working its way through her being, could feel God's promise for strength being fulfilled.

I can do all things through Christ who gives me strength . . .

The verse she'd relied on since her breakup with Mike had never felt more real than at this moment. Certainly this was not the worst situation a believer ever faced . . . How had John the Baptist felt when he was called in and asked to lay his neck across King Herod's dinner plate? And how about the martyr, Stephen, who refused to answer even one complaint lodged against him, not even when the rocks started to fly?

Of course, the greatest example of all was Jesus . . . called in and questioned about His identity, knowing full well the deadly fate that awaited Him before the weekend was through.

No, whatever Dick Baker might say or do, it couldn't compare to any of that. Faith steadied herself and waited for what was coming.

Her boss spun around and faced her. "The story I hear is that you bought the land where that Jesus statue stands. You contacted Bethany officials and paid ten thousand dollars for it so the city could avoid following the judge's order." His chuckle was bitter and filled with sarcasm. "Believe me, I'd like to look each of those reporters in the face and tell them they were wrong. Tell them there's no way any anchor of mine would do a foolhardy thing like that. Especially when I'd already told her not to do anything of the sort." He raised his voice. "But in this case, I had nothing to tell them."

The man walked four slow steps toward her, his eyes never leaving hers. "Did you do it, Faith? Is it true?" He stopped in front of her and crossed his arms, his glare boring into her like a drill bit.

"Yes . . . it's true." Her voice was kind but firm as she felt the Scripture continue to work its way through her heart and soul. "I am an anchorwoman, and yes, I promised to be unbiased. But I'm a Christian first, and a citizen second. I have a right to purchase property like anyone else."

Anger burned in Baker's eyes, but he neither shouted nor stormed about the office as Faith had seen him do on other occasions. Instead he jerked his head up, sucked in a deep breath through his nose, and studied the ceiling. When he looked back at her, his words were matter-of-fact. "Very well. And now I have the right to fire you."

I can do all things through Christ who gives me strength . . . I can do all things through . . . She forced herself to exhale so she wouldn't pass out. *Help me, God. See me through.* Faith knew there was no debating him on the issue. Instead, she endured the five minutes of paperwork in silence. Dick Baker gave her a final paycheck, then shook his head. "You could have been something special, Faith. The stars were all lined up in your favor."

She could feel tears in her eyes, but it didn't matter. Because in a part of her mind so close she could almost touch it, she could see her father's face, hear him telling her, "Well done, honey. Well done."

She gathered her dismissal documents and shook Mr. Baker's hand. Meeting his gaze, she let a smile tug at the corners of her mouth. "My life isn't guided by the stars, sir. It's guided by the One who made them. And whatever happens from here, He's got it perfectly in control." She hesitated for a moment. "I'm sorry about all this."

Her boss didn't seem to know how to take that, and Faith wondered what he'd expected. He scratched the back of his head and shrugged. "I have someone else filling in for you tonight. We'll hire a new anchor

259

within the week." He seemed to be searching for the right words. "Good luck, Faith."

Fifteen minutes later she was on the doorstep of Joshua Nunn's office, the same office he had shared with her father. Joshua appeared in his suit jacket, and Faith guessed he'd been on his way home. It was after six, after all, so she was surprised to catch him there at all.

"Faith, what is it?" There was a pained look in his eyes, and almost immediately realization settled over his face. "The station found out?"

It was a moment her father would have understood perfectly, but in his absence, Faith felt as though she had nowhere else to turn. Joshua held out his arms, and she took a single step forward, collapsing against him and giving way to the sobs that had been building since she'd first gotten to work.

"There, there, honey, it's okay . . ." Joshua stroked her hair as he pulled her into the office and closed the door. "Did they fire you?"

Faith took three quick breaths and tried to control her tears. "Y-yes. I want so badly to be strong, Joshua. But it's too hard. I'm not as g-good at it as Dad and you."

The feel of Joshua's strong arms around her reminded her of her father, and Faith felt her tears start to subside.

"Sweetheart, there are times when I don't feel good enough, either." He smoothed her hair off her face. "But the truth is neither of us has to be like your dad. We can just be us, the way God made us to be. That's enough, understand?"

Faith swallowed hard. "I hated being passive, sitting by while bad things happened around me." She drew a steadying breath and wiped her cheeks with the back of her hand. "That's why I bought the land. It was something I could do, something I believed in." She eased herself into a nearby chair, and Joshua took the one opposite her. "You know why I did it, right? It isn't that the Jesus statue has some kind of magic powers or anything. It's just a piece of rock, really. But it *stands* for something, for the freedom of the people of Bethany. Freedom to have a statue of Jesus Christ in our public park, freedom to worship Jesus and talk about Him and not have to live in fear that the government will one day take away our right to do so." She lifted her chin and felt her strength returning. "Know what I mean?"

Joshua leaned forward and planted his elbows on his knees, his eyes filled with compassion. "I know exactly what you mean." He uttered a quiet laugh. "Faith, my dear, you're more like your father than you think."

She sniffed again and smiled. "My father was never unemployed."

"No, but he would gladly have given up a job if it meant standing up for what was right."

Faith studied Joshua for a moment and decided it was time he knew. "You know the attorney for HOUR, Jordan Riley?"

Joshua worked the muscles in his jaw. "I know him."

Faith sighed and shook her head, running her fingers up through her bangs. "We were friends as kids." She looked up again. "I thought you might want to know."

Understanding passed over Joshua's features. "Very interesting. I had a dream before I got this case . . ." He pointed to the photos on the wall, one of himself and one of Faith's father. "In the dream my picture was still on the wall, but your father's was missing. In its place was a picture of an angry young man — a man who looked exactly like Jordan Riley." Joshua eased back into his chair and stroked his day-old beard. "I've been praying for the young man, Faith. Why don't you tell me about him? Maybe this is the answer I've been waiting for."

Her eyes closed as she allowed herself to

drift, allowed the hands of time to unwind, to take her back to the days when she and Jordan were barely teenagers, to the winter his mother got sick. As the images took shape, she told the story for the first time in more than a decade.

"Jordan was the kindest boy I'd ever known." She smiled. "A grown-up in a thirteen-year-old's body. He never knew his father, but he had the instincts of a dad, especially after his mother became ill. He made sure his sister, Heidi, was in before dark, helped her with her homework, and cooked dinner for their family."

She opened her eyes and blinked back fresh tears. "He was a wonderful boy, really."

He smiled. "It sounds like it."

Emotion filled her throat. "We were best friends, and when his mother got sick we spent hours talking on the porch, sitting side by side, sharing our feelings. That was when I told him about Jesus. Before long, Jordan and Heidi and their mom began attending church with us. They read the Bibles Mom and Dad gave them." She swallowed, letting her head fall back against the chair. "Oh, Joshua, in those early days — before we knew Jordan's mother was dying — it seemed like new life had been breathed into him . . . into his home."

Faith wiped at a trail of tears on her right cheek. "I always knew he wanted a father. But until Jesus became part of his life, Jordan's world revolved around his mother and Heidi and me. After finding that faith in God, it was almost like his life was complete. He had the three women he loved and a Father who would never leave him, never give up on him. A Father who would love him into eternity."

Faith hesitated. Should she tell Joshua about Jordan wanting to marry her? Immediately, she knew the answer. Telling Joshua would be like telling her own father. Besides, she needed to talk. She'd talked with her mother on the phone, of course, and Mom had been very supportive when Faith explained that she'd been fired from the station. They'd prayed and even cried together, and her mother told her how proud her father would be of the stand she was taking. And yet . . . for all that the call had helped, she needed to talk to someone face to face.

"Jordan wanted to marry me." She smiled through her tears and made a sound that was part sob, part laugh.

Joshua's eyebrows raised. "Jordan *Riley?*"

"We were so young back then. I think we

both thought we'd live next door to each other and go to church together and grow up that way forever. It seemed only natural that at some point we'd get married. We —" she swallowed back another sob — "we had very strong feelings for each other."

She shared in detail the terrifying day she'd found out Jordan's mother was dying. How she'd overheard her parents talking and crept closer to the wall, still out of sight, so she could pick up every word.

"She isn't going to make it, Bob. The doctors told her this morning." It was Faith's mother's voice — and she was crying.

Faith's father had taken a long time to respond. "We need to pray for a miracle. That's all we can do."

Her mother wept then, her voice strained with sadness. "But . . . if she doesn't make it . . . what'll happen to those kids, Bob? It isn't right."

Most of the time Faith's father was upbeat, full of life and enthusiasm and had an answer for every dilemma. But that afternoon he released a heavy sigh, one Faith could still hear to this day. "We can't let them be separated, even if it means we take them in to live with us."

The whole conversation had scared Faith to death. Why Jordan and Heidi? Why their mother, when she was all those kids had? And what if she did die? Did that mean God wasn't listening to them? That He hadn't heard their prayers? Would Jordan and Heidi really come and live with Faith and her family? How would that make Jordan feel? He loved his mother with all his heart . . .

Faith sat back in her chair, the memory of those feelings making her uncomfortable and more than a little confused. As strong as her beliefs were, as devoted as she was to Scripture, as strongly as she loved her God, a God she related with personally, the questions remained. There were no more answers today than there had been back when she'd first felt them rise up in her heart.

"Jordan rode out to that statue every day. Every single day." Faith felt the sting of tears again and gazed out the window, remembering how Jordan had been singly determined to pray his mother back to health. "He'd ride his bike out to Jericho Park and fall to his knees, face flat to the ground on behalf of his mother. He'd pray and pray and . . . sometimes I'd join him. I'd kneel down in the wet grass beside him and hold his hand, and we'd pray together. Begging God to spare his mother."

Joshua shifted his position and leaned his elbows on the arms of the chair. "She didn't make it?"

Faith reached for a tissue from the desk that had been her father's and headed off the streams of tears making their way down both sides of her face. "No. She died before Christmas."

At the service, Heidi had grabbed onto the casket and wailed for her mother. Only Jordan had been able to pull her away, wrapping his arms around her and comforting her so the minister could carry on with the eulogy. As far as Faith could remember, Jordan never broke down in front of his sister. He saved that for his time with Faith.

"What happened to Jordan and his sister?"

At Joshua's question, Faith frowned. "They lived alone in the house next door for a while, maybe two weeks or so. No, it had to be less time than that. Three days, maybe four. Anyway, every evening following the funeral, I'd sit beside Jordan on his front porch and let him talk."

She could still hear his agonized cries today. "Why, Faith . . . why'd He let her die? Doesn't He love me? How can I look after Heidi on my own?"

Faith remembered struggling for the right words and usually failing. The best she could do was offer him her hand and once in a while her arm around his shoulders when the questions grew too great and there was nothing left but the quiet sobs of a brokenhearted teenage boy. A boy she had come to love.

But that wasn't the worst of it.

"I was outside the day the state workers came to the house . . ." Faith sucked in a deep breath. "They came in two cars, and I stood off in the distance while the first worker explained the situation. Jordan and Heidi were to pack their things in separate suitcases. Clothes, a few toys, special pictures. Anything they wanted to save. They would be going to different foster homes —" her voice caught, and she cleared her throat — "until the courts could find a way to get them back together."

Joshua stared at her, his stunned expression mirroring her remembered emotions. "They separated them?"

She nodded. "But not without a fight. Heidi panicked. She kept crying, refusing to go with them, to leave her brother." The way the girl had screamed and thrown her arms around Jordan's waist was as vivid a picture in Faith's mind today as it had been that fall so many years ago. Heidi's agonized words echoed through her again.

No. I won't leave him! Mama wants him to stay with me. We have to be together . . . No!

Nooooo!"

Faith closed her eyes and pushed her wet tissue against the bridge of her nose. She took several seconds to compose herself before continuing the story. "My parents weren't home when the social workers came. Maybe, if they had been, things would have been different somehow. I don't know." She swallowed hard. "In the end, Heidi's crying didn't change anything."

Left with no choice, Jordan and Heidi had done as they were told. They filled a couple of suitcases with all the belongings they would ever have from the place that had been their home. The social workers promised them that soon, very soon, they could come back home and people would help them get their other things — their beds and books, belongings that wouldn't fit in a suitcase.

"When they finished packing, they stood on the front yard clinging to each other, waiting while the workers whispered together. I crept up behind the adults and came alongside Jordan." She'd known from the look on his face that Jordan wanted to hug her, to pull her aside and ask her to pray for him or to promise her that he'd be back. But Heidi needed him, and all he said was, "This is only for now. We'll get it all straightened out, I know it."

Faith had nodded and kept her distance, giving Heidi the time she needed with her brother. After a few minutes, the first worker turned to them and held out his hand. "Heidi, why don't you come with me? We'll get you settled tonight, and by tomorrow we'll probably have the whole thing figured out."

"No!" Heidi had screamed at the man, clinging to Jordan, sobbing, much as she'd done at her mother's funeral. "I won't leave him!"

Faith remembered Jordan's pale face, how he'd looked decades older than his thirteen years. He seemed too terrified to cry, too shocked to do anything more than respond as an adult, the way he'd been responding ever since his mother had gotten sick. "Heidi, it's okay." He put his face close to hers and forced her to look at him. "It's just for a few days. They'll bring you to me as soon as they find a place for both of us."

Her screaming subsided, and she studied his face, her eyes wide with fear, her fingers clutching tightly to the sleeves of his sweater. "I d-d-don't want to go, Jordan. I need you."

Jordan had pulled her close, running his hand along her back. "Shh, Heidi, it's okay. Pray to Jesus . . . ask Him to work it out so we'll be back together soon."

The sound of Heidi's sobbing changed then and even at that age Faith could tell the fear was gone. In its place was a sadness that could simply not be measured. "I'm going to m-m-miss you, Jordan. I love you so much . . ."

The memories were devastating, and Faith fell silent, not even wiping away the tears coursing down her cheeks.

"Faith, are you all right?"

She met Joshua's concerned gaze and nodded, grateful for his care. "I'm fine. It was just a terrible time. Even the social workers were crying before it was over. Jordan kissed Heidi on the top of her head and on both her cheeks and promised, no matter what, that they would be together again. In the end, he had to walk her to the worker's car and hold her hand through the open window, clinging to her fingers until the car began to pull away and their hands came apart."

Faith closed her eyes and she could see them as clearly now as she had back then. Jordan, sobs jerking his shoulders as he reached out to his sister; Heidi, her arm still sticking out, reaching back to her brother, tearstained face pressed against the back window as the car drove out of sight.

"It was one of the most awful things I've ever seen." Faith opened her eyes and stared sadly at Joshua. "Something I'll remember as long as I live."

"What happened to Jordan?"

"After Heidi was gone, he fell against me, and I almost believed he might die from the grief. He kept asking me, over and over, if I believed they'd let Heidi and him be back together."

"What did you say?"

Faith shrugged. "The only thing I could say. I told him to pray that God would bring Heidi back to him. He just had to trust and pray."

She gazed at Joshua through another wave of tears. "You know what, though?"

Joshua bit his lip, and Faith saw that his eyes were wet too. "No one ever brought her back?"

Faith shook her head and glanced out the window once more. "He never saw her again, not once." Her eyes found Joshua's. "That boy prayed for his mother to live — I mean he *prayed,* like I've never seen before or since, Joshua. He prayed, and she died anyway." She swallowed hard. "He prayed that way for Heidi, too . . . that'd he'd see her again, grow up with her, and look after her the way he'd promised his mother. But to this day he has no idea where she is or if she's even still alive."

She clenched her fists. "Maybe that'll help you understand Jordan Riley a little better."

Joshua seemed to consider his next words carefully. "You've seen him, haven't you?"

The memory of their kiss flashed across the surface of Faith's heart. "Yes."

"He must have been very special to you back when he was a boy . . ."

Faith angled her face in Joshua's direction. "Honestly, I think I loved him. We were just kids, I know, and our feelings for each other were innocent enough. But they ran deep all the same."

Joshua let that sink in, and Faith's gaze fell to her hands. "When he came to town that first time, back in the fall, he told me he'd changed, but I didn't know what he meant until I saw him in court. He's so angry at God . . . he doesn't know who he is anymore."

"Does he . . ." Joshua squirmed in his chair, as though he weren't sure he should continue.

"It's okay, ask. I'll tell you what I know."

"Does Jordan still have feelings for you, Faith?"

Sadness settled over Faith's shoulders like a lead blanket. "That first night I think we realized we both still have feelings for each other. But now . . ." She lifted her shoulders, wishing she could ease the tension that seemed to grip her neck. "It's like we're on opposite sides of the ocean."

She eased herself from the chair, stood, and stretched. "You need to get home."

"You'll be expected to speak at the next hearing, you know."

Faith nodded. "I'm organizing a prayer rally at the park the morning the wall goes up. Let's meet in your office after that."

Joshua agreed and walked her to the door. "I'm sorry about your job, Faith."

"God has a plan, right, Joshua? Isn't that what my father always said?" She leaned up and kissed the older man's cheek. "Even in this."

SEVENTEEN

Something was wrong.

Heidi knew it as surely as she knew the personality of the baby inside her. The pains were coming every five minutes now, and she was certain this was not another false alarm. They'd been to the hospital twice in the past three days and each time doctors had checked her and sent her home. But this was different. Something deep inside, where intuition mingled with holy whisperings, told Heidi there was trouble. She hadn't felt the baby move in nearly ten hours.

With shaking hands she picked up the phone and dialed Charles's number at the clinic.

"Heidi, honey, what is it? My nurse said you were crying."

"I'm scared —" Heidi's voice broke — "I can't feel the baby."

Charles had always been a rock, but in

that moment he was silent. When he finally spoke, he had just one piece of advice. "Pray, Heidi. I'll get there as soon as I can. But until then, pray."

Heidi wrapped her hands around her abdomen and rocked as another pain seized her midsection. Minutes passed and she lay huddled on the couch. *Hurry, Charles . . .* Then she remembered what he told her. *God, You know I love You . . . hear me, now. Save my baby, Father. Please don't let her die.*

There was the sound of tires screeching around the corner, tearing into their driveway. Heidi struggled to her feet, stooped halfway over, and met her husband at the door.

"Honey, what happened? When did it get like this?" He swept her into his arms and hurried her out to the car. "We all agreed it could be two more days."

A string of sobs lodged in her throat as another pain sliced through her. "I n-n-need to go . . ."

Heidi's bag was already in the car, and in ten minutes they were at the hospital, where she was whisked by stretcher up an elevator to an operating room, Charles close by her side. Heidi clutched her husband's hand, and suddenly she could see Jordan's image.

She'd lost her brother and now she was about to lose her firstborn. "No, God . . . please . . . let her live . . ."

Heidi's voice was barely a whisper but Charles heard it and lowered his head close to hers. "God, we beg You . . . be with our baby."

A technician worked furiously, taking Heidi's blood pressure and inserting an intravenous line into her wrist as a doctor hooked up a fetal monitor. Everyone seemed to be working faster than usual, and their serious faces only made Heidi more afraid. She craned her head up from the pillow and searched out the doctor's face. If only Charles were her doctor . . . "Is her heartbeat okay?"

Charles squeezed her hand and looked at the doctor in charge. "Heidi told me in the car that she hasn't felt the baby move in ten hours."

The doctor worked the sensors expertly around Heidi's belly. "I can't find anything yet." He met Heidi's eyes first and then Charles's. "That doesn't mean there's a problem, but I'm concerned enough to get her into surgery. I think the best course of action is to do a caesarean section and get that baby out."

"Dear God, no . . ." Heidi began to cry

again, one hand firmly tucked in Charles's, the other gripped around her protruding stomach. "She can't die . . ."

The doctor was talking to Charles about anesthetic and epidurals and the process of a C-section delivery when Heidi began seeing black spots. They grew larger and larger until they took up most of the scope of her vision. The effect left her feeling as though she were floating above the gurney. The pain faded considerably . . . but an alarm sounded in Heidi's soul.

Something isn't right . . . get their attention . . .

The strange, silent warning demanded her response, and she used all that remained of her strength to find her voice.

"Help . . . me . . ."

Her cry was so faint the others in the room almost missed it.

"Get a line in! Her blood pressure's dropping! Quick, start the infusion, get a fluid bag and —"

"Heidi, hang on, baby. Jesus'll save you, honey! Don't go to sleep until you —"

"Get her into the operating room stat and let's get the —"

The voices jumbled together, making no sense. The black spots joined up, and she couldn't decipher the faces of the people around her, couldn't feel the baby or the pain or anything but a few gentle prods here and there.

The floating sensation grew stronger, and suddenly Heidi could see herself on the stretcher some three feet below. Charles was off to the side, his head buried in his hands, his shoulders shaking while a roomful of doctors and nurses worked on her.

I'm here, can't you see me? What's wrong with everyone?

The questions passed through her mind, but she couldn't seem to make them come from her mouth. In the place where she found herself, hovering above the room, the pain had stopped entirely and she could no longer hear the voices of the others.

Beyond them, beyond anything earthly, was a glow that grew brighter with every breath she took. Or was she breathing? Maybe she wasn't breathing at all, but rather existing in some other dimension, separate from any of the trappings of the body on the gurney below. Heidi was drawn to the light and she prayed for direction. *Lord . . . is that You?*

The voices in the hospital room grew barely loud enough to understand and again Heidi strained to make them out.

"We're losing her! Grab the paddles!"

"Let's get the baby, now!"

What about Charles? Heidi couldn't see him anymore . . . and there was something else, some reason why she was at the hospital in the first place . . .

An otherworldly peace came over her, and she realized why she was there. For the baby, of course. A sweet little girl, their firstborn. But where was she, and why was Heidi looking down at herself when she should have been breathing and pushing and helping in the delivery?

The light grew brighter.

Help me, Lord . . . I want to see my baby . . .

For I know the plans I have for you, daughter.

Heidi's head began to swirl, and her vision grew blurred. The light faded. *Father, help me . . . I'm afraid . . . I need Charles and my baby . . . my baby girl, Lord, let her live . . . please . . .*

The light grew brighter and brighter until it was all she could see. Then suddenly there was nothing but empty, quiet darkness.

She woke slowly, her eyelids feeling as though they were taped shut, and for the first few seconds Heidi thought she was alone. There were no sounds of hurried doctors, no desperate demands for fluids or blood pressure readings or assistance.

No babies crying.

"Charles?"

The voice that came from within her sounded like it belonged to someone else, like maybe she had cotton stuck to the inside of her mouth. Her hand rushed to her stomach and felt the flattened place where the baby had been just yesterday . . . or was it today?

"Charles!" Where was he? Where was the baby, and why was she alone in this hospital room?

"Honey, I'm here." Charles was at her side in an instant, and she forced her eyes open.

"Where were you?" Tears spilled onto her cheeks, and she searched his face, willing him to tell her the truth. "Where's the baby?"

He leaned over her, holding her close, his tears mingling with her own. "Thank God . . . thank God, Heidi. I thought I'd lost you. You've been in a coma for two days."

A coma? For two days? An urgency began to build in her heart, and she pulled away so she could meet his gaze. "What happened to her, Charles? Where is she?"

A smile filled his face, and his eyes glowed with a warmth she'd never seen before. "She's fine, sweetheart. She's down the hall in the nursery."

Heidi's tears came harder now, and she clung to him, giving way to the sobs that had been building in her heart. "I thought I'd lost her . . ."

"No, honey, she's perfect. Wait'll you see her." He nuzzled his face against hers and wove his fingers through her hair.

Odd images filtered through Heidi's mind. "I had the strangest dream . . . just as the baby came, like I was watching the whole thing from above."

Charles sat up straighter, his mouth open as he searched her face. "You were bleeding, Heidi. They lost your pulse, your blood pressure, everything. Clinically, you were dead." He searched for the right words. "It was God, Heidi. He brought you back, sweetheart. It was a miracle."

Charles took her hands in his and bowed his head. "Thank You, Lord. I will never forget this. Never." He kissed her tenderly and pulled back, his eyes dancing even under the glare of hospital lights. "You see a lot of amazing things as a doctor, but I've never seen anything like this. It's a miracle that either of you lived."

There was a sound at the door, and a nurse appeared pushing a small clear bassinet. As she drew closer, Heidi searched for her daughter's face — and what she saw made her eyes fill with fresh tears. The baby was more beautiful than any she'd ever seen. Charles moved to the small bed and carefully lifted the infant, shifting her straight to Heidi's waiting arms. The nurse smiled and left them alone to share the moment.

"Oh, Charles, she's perfect." A tear fell onto the baby's cheek, and Heidi laughed, wiping first her own face, then that of her tiny daughter. She took hold of Charles's hand with her free one and squeezed it. "She *is* a miracle. God is so good."

They admired the infant snuggled between them, trying not to imagine how different this day might have been if not for the grace of God and the second chance at life they'd been given. Charles broke the silence first. "So did we decide on a name?"

"Remember that day? The name I had then?"

Charles nodded, his eyes twinkling. "I wanted to make sure you hadn't changed your mind."

Heidi stared at her daughter again and smiled. "I haven't changed my mind. I've always known what I wanted to call her." Her heart felt like it might burst from joy as her eyes stayed fixed on her little girl's delicate features.

"Well, that settles it then." Charles tickled the baby's chin. "Your name is Jordan Lee — after your uncle Jordan."

Heidi smiled and ran a finger over the baby's eyebrows. "Hi, little Jordan Lee."

"Jordan Lee . . ." Charles's arm was around Heidi then, holding her close and whispering the baby's name over and over in a way that told Heidi he absolutely understood.

"It fits her, sweetheart."

She swallowed back a wave of sobs as she nodded. The moment was perfect except for one thing.

Jordan Lee would never have the chance to know the one for whom she was named.

Another two days passed and Jordan Lee was thriving beyond anyone's expectations. Heidi understood now what had happened. A tear in her placenta had caused internal bleeding, which in turn nearly killed her and the baby. Throughout her hospital stay, doctors who'd had nothing to do with her delivery made their way in and introduced themselves, curious to see Dr. Benson's wife and baby, a pair who'd literally come back from the dead. Heidi spent her time holding her daughter and reveling in the infant's sweetness and good health, and the intensity of her own feelings.

Charles had been right, their daughter's name fit her. She had Jordan's dark hair, his chiseled face. She was beautiful, and it grieved Heidi in a way she hadn't felt in years to know that this side of heaven Jordan would never see her.

It was after noon and the television played in the background as Heidi and Charles cooed and marveled over their little girl. There was a chance they could go home later that afternoon and they hoped the doctor might stop by any moment with Heidi's discharge papers.

She eased back onto a stack of pillows as her eyes fell on the TV screen. "Nothing but news . . ."

A reporter's voice was saying, "In other news a shocking development in the case of the Jesus —"

"I can't wait to get home." Charles smiled at her. "And know that both of you are right there with me where you belong."

Heidi smiled at him. "For a few days, anyway, until we pack up."

In the silence between them the newscaster continued. ". . . private citizen Faith Evans purchased the property from the city in what some people say is a conniving attempt at obstructing justice. The attorney for HOUR, Jor—"

"You mean the move?" Heidi groaned as a grin worked its way across Charles's face. "Just think, three weeks from today we'll be moved in, unpacked, and ready to put down roots."

She chuckled. "That's my Charles. The eternal optimist." She adjusted Jordan Lee so the tiny girl was nestled between the two of them. "Right now I can barely put my feet on the floor, honey. Putting down roots might take more than three weeks."

"True." They both smiled and glanced back at the television.

"Another hearing in less than a month to determine what type of wall would make the best permanent barrier. And in other news, the president told the public this morning —"

"What wall?" Heidi lowered her eyebrows.

Charles smoothed her bangs off her forehead. "I wasn't listening. It's a slow news day. Most of the stories are just filler."

Heidi reached for the clicker dangling on the side of her hospital bed and turned off the television. "I've got you and Jordan Lee and a new home waiting for me in Bethany, Pennsylvania . . ." She leaned up toward her husband's face and their lips met. The kiss lingered, and when he pulled away she knew she'd never been happier in all her life. "The last thing I need is filler."

EIGHTEEN

It was just after seven o'clock in the morning and a thin layer of fog hung over the town of Bethany as Faith arrived at Jericho Park. She positioned her car so she could see the Jesus statue. In a few hours, ten-foot-high plywood walls would surround it, and Faith wanted to be there early, wanted to mingle with the locals as they arrived by van and bus for the prayer rally. They'd decided to march around the park, singing hymns and stopping every ten minutes to pray. This would go on throughout the construction of the wall, and Faith was certain their peaceful protest would make all the local news shows.

She leaned back against the headrest. How had things gotten so crazy? Her father's face came to mind, and she smiled even as she released a heavy sigh. "Dad, you wouldn't recognize me . . ." She gave a short, soft laugh. "Mom says I'm trying to take your place, but you know me, Dad." Her smile faded and tears filled her eyes. "I'm scared to death."

Memories drifted in on the fog and filled her heart with images from days gone by. A sunny afternoon began to take shape, the year she and her sister, Sarah, were seven and thirteen years old, and had been ordered not to play catch in the house. Their mother was in the backyard working in the garden when Sarah found a softball and grinned at Faith. Sarah was on a park-league softball team that year and was always looking for someone to play catch with.

"Let's pretend we're trying out for the World Series."

Faith could see her own little pixie face contorted in grave concern. "Outside. Mom says we have to play outside."

Sarah peered around the wall and gazed into the backyard. "Mom won't know. Besides, it's too hot out there. Come on, don't be a baby."

Faith remembered her stomach hurting from the conflict. Stay inside and risk getting in trouble, or refuse to play with her big sister and be labeled a baby. Finally Faith gulped back her fears and nodded. "Okay, but be careful."

Sarah grinned and grabbed the ball, tossing it at Faith. Her heart beating wildly in her little girl chest, Faith snagged it from the air and smiled. "Good throw." She remembered feeling better about the game after that. It wasn't so bad, throwing the ball in the house. What was their mother worried about, anyway?

They played that way for five minutes, but then Sarah caught the ball and held it. "Let's pretend I'm the pitcher and you're the catcher, okay?"

Faith shrugged. "Okay. I'm the catcher."

Sarah wound up like a mountain lion ready to spring and fired the ball straight at Faith's nose. In a split-second decision, Faith fell to the ground, missing the ball — and the spray of glass that exploded in her direction as the ball soared straight through the window.

The timing couldn't have been worse, for at that moment a key turned in the front door and their father walked in. At almost exactly the same time, their mother entered the house from the backyard and peeled off her work gloves. "Hi, honey, how was your day?" Her smile lasted only until she made her way into the front room and found the girls and their father staring at the pile of glass and a jagged, gaping hole in the window.

Their mother stepped around the broken pieces and stared outside. "What happened?"

"I was just asking that question myself." Their father set his things down, his face stricken with disappointment.

"Obviously they were playing ball in the house." She looked from Faith — still cowering on the floor — to Sarah, huddled against the opposite wall. "Whose idea was this?"

Faith looked at Sarah and waited, expecting her to come clean with the story. Instead, her sister was staring at her shoes as though she had no intention of saying anything. Their father was not a man who raised his voice except with laughter when he was playing cowboy or horsie games with them. But that afternoon he came close. He ordered Sarah and Faith to the sofa and stared at them long and hard.

"In this life we all make mistakes," he began, his voice a low growl. "But I did not raise my daughters to be liars. Someone better tell me what happened or you'll both be punished."

For three minutes — three whole minutes — he stood there, hands on his hips, his eyes shooting invisible guilt rays down upon

Faith and her sister. They were quite possibly the longest minutes of Faith's childhood, and she remembered feeling like she might be sick all over the clean carpet. She was about to open her mouth when her father pointed a finger at Sarah. "Young lady, you're the oldest and I'll have to assume this is your fault. Now why don't you tell me what —"

"No, Daddy." Faith was on her feet and she threw her arms around her father, her eyes squeezed shut as though she couldn't stand his anger for one more minute. "It was my fault. I told Sarah we could play catch and I didn't catch the ball. Don't be mad at her, please, Daddy. Please . . ."

The memory made Faith chuckle under her breath as she wrapped her jacket tighter around her shoulders. She thought back to how Sarah had cast her a surprised glance, but it didn't matter. Their father's face relaxed, and he patted Faith's hair, running his hand down the back of her head and onto her back. "Thatta girl, Faith. Thanks for being honest. Now you know the rules, and I'm still going to have to punish you. You'll spend the rest of the day in your room, but you told the truth and that should make you feel good about yourself."

Faith wasn't sure she'd told the truth, but

she certainly remembered feeling better. Much better than sitting on the sofa squirming beneath her father's angry gaze. She gladly took the punishment, content because no one was mad at her anymore.

It had been that way as far back as Faith could remember. She hated conflict, couldn't tolerate people being angry with her or anyone else for that matter.

Another memory came to mind. Her father ran in fairly influential political circles and once in a while he'd have friends with opposing views over for dinner. Faith recalled several times when after the meal they'd gather in the living room over hot coffee and even hotter conversation.

"Aw, Bob, you lean so far to the right you'd make a minister look liberal."

Her father would raise his hand. "Now, wait a minute, don't forget about that tax you people invented to cover the —"

The longer they talked, the louder they grew. Faith understood now that the banter was all in good fun, and that her father's visitors left the house with their friendships intact. But back then, from her childish perspective, the discussions had made her worse than nervous. Typically she'd work her way into a corner of the kitchen and sit on the floor, her knees pulled up to her chin until her mother found her that way.

"Faith, honey, what're you doing?" She'd stoop down and place the back of her hand against Faith's forehead. "Are you sick?"

Generally Sarah would be helping with the dishes and she'd toss out a sarcastic comment about Faith finding any excuse to get out of doing chores. But that wasn't it at all. Faith finally explained herself one evening later that year when the conversation between her father and his friends again grew heated. That night, Faith ran from her spot in the kitchen to her bedroom upstairs, tears streaming down her face.

Minutes later her mother found her in bed, the covers pulled up over her head. "Honey, whatever is the matter? Is it something you ate? Don't you like it when Daddy has his friends over?"

Faith pulled the covers down a few inches so that only her eyes and the top of her head were showing. "It scares me . . ."

Mom pulled the blankets down further and looked at Faith's arms and neck. "Why, sweetie, I think you're having an allergic reaction. You have hives all over your body."

Immediately she summoned a doctor who confirmed the thing Faith understood better now. "It's nerves, Mrs. Moses. Is there something happening in the home, something that might be upsetting her?"

By that time, her father's friends had gone home, and Daddy stood alongside her bed, frowning his concern at both the doctor and her. "I can't think of anything; Faith's a very happy little girl, doctor."

But after the doctor was gone, her parents sat down with her and drew out the truth. "It scares me when Daddy and his friends fight."

Her father looked at her and then put his hand over his mouth. Just when she thought he might burst out laughing, his eyes grew sad and dark, like the deep places of the river that ran outside of town. "Honey, those men and I like talking about things we don't agree on." He cast his gaze at the ceiling as though he was searching for the right words. Then he looked at her once more. "We might sound like we're fighting, but we're only sharing our different views."

Mom stood off to the side, her chin lowered just so, a crooked smile on her face as her father leaned over and snuggled Faith close to his chest. "I'm sorry we upset you, honey. You should have told me a long time ago."

Faith knew he was right, but the idea of approaching her father and complaining about his conversations with his friends was almost as frightening as the visits themselves. After that her mother made a point of keeping Faith and Sarah busy when her father had friends over, and she never again remembered hearing them talk that way.

There were other situations — her relationship with Mike Dillan, her refusal to stand up to Dick Baker at the station, her inability to confront the HOUR organization over their request that Rosa Lee be removed from the Web site . . .

She had always managed to find the easy route, the path of least resistance, the road that might keep life calm and even keeled.

Several cars pulled into the parking lot, and people she recognized began piling out, forming a circle on the grass in front of the statue. Faith shook her head. How was it, considering her determination to avoid conflict, that God had her here, in the middle of a political hurricane? Her, the weak-willed Faith Evans Moses?

As the crowd began to build she found herself sliding down in her seat. *I can't do it, God. They think I'm their leader, and I'm not. I want to go home and hide under the covers . . .*

Be strong and courageous, daughter. You will not fight this battle alone. I will go before you . . . the battle belongs to

the Lord.

The words washed over her, giving her a strength that was not her own. She drew a deep breath and sat up straighter. It was true. She would not fight the battle alone. She had God and Joshua and a thousand friends across the city. In the end, God's will would prevail, whether the statue remained fenced or not. All He wanted of her was loyalty and obedience. Suddenly her father's words came back to her, words he'd spoken days before he died. He and Joshua had been hired to take a case involving prayer in a public school and the media involvement figured to be considerable.

"If it doesn't go our way it could break us," Dad told her and Mom at dinner that night. His eyes shone with sincerity as he continued. "But you know I've learned something over the years of walking with the Lord. My best successes come when I am at my absolute weakest."

His words had seemed strange, incongruous, as though her father couldn't possibly have uttered them. He had never been weak, at least not as far as Faith knew. But he'd gone on.

"When I am weak, my God can be strong. And it's the battles He fights for me that end up being my greatest victories of all."

In the end, the school district in question had agreed to settle out of court, fearing they faced a losing battle. Her father had celebrated the news with them the day before his heart attack.

"See?" His cheerful voice filled their home with life. "I couldn't do it, so God went before me and look what happened. They dropped the case! Those students can go on praying, and the Lord wins a victory all because we were willing to step out on His behalf."

Her father's words soothed the restless places in her heart, and Faith sucked in as much breath as she could muster. She climbed out of her car and headed toward the crowd as dozens of people turned and motioned for her to join them. Across the park she saw a construction crew and cringed as two of them nailed the first piece of plywood around the base of the statue.

The battle had begun.

It was time to meet the people, time to acknowledge that she was out of ideas, out of options, and fully incapable of fighting.

Most of all, it was time to do whatever it was God had for her to do. Even if it put her squarely in the middle of the greatest conflict of her life.

■ ■ ■ ■

Rosa Lee was putting together a puzzle on the kitchen table in the minutes before school started when she remembered something. "Faith told me I could see her today. Is she coming for me?"

Her social worker wiped her hands on a dishtowel and walked closer, smiling at the puzzle. "Nice job, Rosa. You're almost done."

Rosa brought her lips together and did a huffy breath. "Excuse me, ma'am, did you hear me? Is Faith coming to get me this afternoon?"

Sandy Dirk sat down at the table and looked sad for a minute. "Rosa, Faith's very busy today —" She stopped the way grownups do sometimes, and then kept talking. "Did Faith tell you about the Jesus statue, honey?"

Rosa's heart lit up and she could feel her face change into a giant smile. "Oh, I love the Jesus statue. Faith took me to the park lots of times and we looked at the statue and talked about it." Rosa felt a little worried for Miss Dirk, in case she didn't understand. "It's not really Jesus, you know that, right?"

Miss Dirk seemed to rub a smile off her face, and she squeezed Rosa's shoulder real soft like. "Of course."

Rosa nodded, glad Miss Dirk knew the truth. "It's just a reminder of Jesus. Sort of like when I draw a picture of Him in Sunday school." Her smile was back again. "I think it's the bestest picture in the whole world, Miss Dirk. Because my Jesus —" she held out her arms so that her hands were stretched out toward heaven — "my Jesus is even bigger than the trees. And He always has His arms open for me to hug Him anytime I want."

Miss Dirk's eyes looked kind of wet and shiny, but she smiled. "Yes, honey, that's right. Anytime you want."

"Like when I'm thinking about having a mommy and a daddy and wondering when God's going to bring them to meet me. That's when it's really nice to remember just how big my Jesus is."

Miss Dirk blinked at Rosa. "Some sad people are trying to take the Jesus statue down. Did Miss Faith tell you that?"

A sick feeling filled up Rosa's tummy and she dropped the puzzle piece in her hand. "Take it down? You mean like take it away so it isn't in the park anymore?"

"Yes, honey." Miss Dirk covered Rosa's

hand with her own. Rosa made herself think as hard as she could, but no reasons came to her. Why would anyone want to take the Jesus statue down? Then she got an idea, and her heart grew kind of jumpy. "Is Faith going to stop them? She likes the Jesus statue, too."

"Well, that's just it, Rosa. That's what Faith's doing today. She's meeting with a lot of people from the town who like the statue, and they're going to pray for the sad people who want to take it down. That's why she can't come and play with you today."

What? Faith would be praying for the sad people? Rosa sat up straighter and pulled her knees beneath her. "Then I need to be there, Miss Dirk. It's my statue too. Faith would want me there, praying with her, I know she would."

Her social worker smiled, and Rosa knew the answer was no. "You have school today. I can't keep you home so you can pray with Faith."

As soon as she said the words, Miss Dirk's face looked the same way it had one night when she burned the squash and ate a whole bite of it anyway. Rosa leaned closer. "But Faith told me there's nothing more important than praying. It's the whole reason we're here on earth."

Miss Dirk put her elbows on the table and slumped over a little. She stayed that way for a long time and finally she looked at Rosa, her lips squished together. "Oh, all right. What could it hurt?"

Rosa jumped from her seat, clapped her hands, and danced about the kitchen floor. She spun and twirled her way in front of Miss Dirk and stopped only long enough to get more information. "When can we go, huh? Is Faith already there?"

Miss Dirk looked at the big clock on the wall and nodded. "Probably." She tugged on Rosa's shirt, straightening out the wrinkles. "Go get your sweater, and I'll take you there now."

Rosa clapped some more and hurried her feet up the stairs to the closet she shared with two older girls. She grabbed her sweater, pulled it around her shoulders, and checked the mirror. A piece of her hair was sticking out above her ears, and Rosa tucked it in neatly and smiled at herself. Faith was right. Jesus had made her a very pretty girl. She waved at herself real quick and skipped back down the stairs.

If Faith was going to pray for the sad people who wanted to take the statue down, then Rosa was sure everything would work out just fine. God would see to that. She waited by the door for Miss Dirk to get her coat and keys and grinned quietly to herself. Even if it wasn't sunny outside, it was going to be a wonderful day after all. She was going to spend it talking with her two favorite people in all the world.

Faith Evans and her best friend, Jesus.

The six o'clock news used the protest at the Jesus statue as their lead story, and Joshua watched it closely in his living room, his wife at his side. Two of the three major networks chose to play Faith as the primary local angle, saying things like, "Former WKZN newscaster Faith Evans — who lost her job because of her role in the fight to keep the Jesus statue standing — led the protest at Jericho Park this morning . . ." and "The battle has already been costly to local residents, especially Faith Evans, who was removed from her position as anchor for WKZN because of her role in the fight to keep the Jesus statue . . ."

Joshua watched for many reasons.

First, he wanted to see the way the statue looked with walls around it. He hadn't been able to bring himself to drive by the park that afternoon, hadn't wanted to stomach the sight of the statue walled up with plywood, so the pictures on the news were his first chance to see the effects of the judge's ruling.

Also he wanted to get a feel for the residents' heart on the issue, whether they were tired of the battle or willing to go the distance to see their statue standing proudly the way it had stood for a hundred years prior.

Two minutes into the newscast, he could see that none of the city's supporters were losing their fervor. If anything, their numbers had grown, making the crowd a considerable force as they marched around the park while workers erected the plywood wall. Every station carried several sound bites from Faith and featured her in much of the taped footage. In several shots Joshua saw a little Asian girl at Faith's side, a child no older than five or six who looked at Faith with wide, adoring eyes. He tried to remember where he'd seen her before and it hit him.

She was the little girl featured a few weeks back on the *Wednesday's Child* program, the one Faith had hosted. Obviously Faith's love for the girl went beyond her role as an interested reporter. He watched as Faith's face filled the screen and a reporter asked her whether the battle of Jericho Park was worth losing her job over.

"Recently I've come to understand that there's nothing more important, more sacred than your convictions." She smiled in a way that was contagious among the reporters, disarming them, Joshua noticed, before they might realize what was happening. "I believe the people have a right to their statue . . . our statue. Even if it does depict the central figure in the Christian faith. This is the kind of battle that's worth fighting." She smiled again, a smile void of animosity. "My father taught me that."

There was something about Faith's open-hearted smile that touched Joshua deeply. As though she held no anger toward the people at HOUR or the station manager who had fired her, but rather a deep compassion. It was not something that could be faked, and Joshua knew it was the same love for people her father had carried in his heart during his days battling for religious freedom.

The camera moved in on Faith once more as she bent to give the little girl a hug, and suddenly Joshua was struck by Faith's beauty. *Oh, Bob, if you could see her now . . . Lord if You could let him know . . .* How proud his old partner would have been of his daughter. Little Faith, all grown up. Joshua thought back and in his mind he saw her as a girl, running across the backyard with the other kids during a family barbecue. Now she was poised and confident, filled with a peace that Joshua knew could only come from one source.

The segment drew to a close, but the image of Faith remained in Joshua's heart.

She was simply breathtaking, both in appearance and in the purity of her convictions. He leaned back into the sofa and wondered if somewhere in New York City, Jordan Riley was watching the same newscast. And whether the attorney's desire to see the Jesus statue removed could possibly be stronger than the feelings he must be having for the very special young woman who'd once been his friend.

A woman who had risked everything to see the statue remain standing.

NINETEEN

Jordan flipped off the television and stretched out on his leather sofa, his hands folded beneath his head. The newscast had clearly favored Faith, and that surprised him. Normally the media would take HOUR's side and make a woman like Faith look fanatic. Instead they'd given her ample time to share her point of view and done nothing to contradict it. The fact that the local networks had footage of the wall going up only made Faith look more like the persecuted victim.

The overall effect was that justice had been thwarted, not meted out on the public's behalf.

Jordan replayed the images of Faith again in his mind and felt a smile tug at the corners of his mouth. He knew he should be angry. What right did the people of Bethany have to demand a statue of Jesus Christ remain standing in a public park? A ripple of frustration worked its way down his spine, but only a ripple. Normally he'd be furious with the way the story was handled, ready to hold a press conference the next day with the walled-up statue in the background, and slam every angle Faith had chosen to discuss.

Instead the only reason he wanted to go back to Bethany was to find Faith and tell her what a great job she'd done, how successfully she'd managed to articulate her point of view without looking like a religious fundamentalist. He caught himself grinning again at the memory of her poise, of the beauty that seemed to come from somewhere deep inside. What was it about her that had worked its way so thoroughly into his heart? And why was it happening now, when they were on opposite sides of a national legal battle?

The phone rang, and Jordan blinked back the images of Faith. It was nearly seven o'clock and he'd been so caught up in the newscast he hadn't even considered fixing dinner.

"Hello."

"Jordan, it's T. J." His friend sounded nervous, and an alarm sounded in the sensory panel of Jordan's mind. Ever since the hearing the week before things had been strange at the office, as though people were carrying around some kind of secret and Jordan was the only one not in the loop. He'd tried to dismiss the feelings, chock it up to the fact that he had a lot going on. But the signs that something wasn't right continued.

He sat up. "What's up?"

"I'm at the office still and . . . well, a bunch of us saw the Philadelphia news a few minutes ago."

A bunch of them? "What, Teej, a party and I wasn't invited?" He did his best to sound casual, but his concern rose a notch. Why were they so interested in his case? And why hadn't they included him?

T. J.'s brief laugh sounded hollow. "Not a party, just a chance to see how the local media's playing the story."

"Let me guess . . . there aren't a lot of smiles in the room." Jordan intentionally kept his tone light, not wanting to validate T. J's seriousness.

"Well . . . uh, Mr. Hawkins is here, and the other partners. They wanted me to call and see if you'd watched it."

"Yeah, I watched it. So what do they want me to do? Put a contract on the girl?"

There was silence on the other end. "They're not laughing, Jordan." T. J. had lowered his voice, and Jordan figured the others in the room had resumed talking. "The coverage was bad."

Jordan sighed, raking the fingers of his free hand over his knee. "I saw it, remember? I know it was bad. How does that involve me?"

Voices in the background grew louder and for a moment there was no one on the other line. Then, "Riley, this is Hawkins."

Jordan hung his head. Why were they so relentless this time around? Wasn't it like any other issue HOUR battled? Jordan's insides squirmed as though he'd developed an ant farm deep in his gut. Something just didn't add up . . . "Hey, Mr. Hawkins, I guess you saw the news?"

"That girl is killing us, Riley. She must be stopped."

Jordan released a sound that was part exasperation, part chuckle. "She has a right to be interviewed by the press, sir. You understand that, right?"

"So where's our presence, Riley? Why're you back here in New York while those religious do-gooders take up the entire six o'clock news?"

Jordan stood and paced toward a large window that overlooked swarming city streets far below. His stomach churned and he realized he'd lost his appetite. "Have you checked my caseload, sir? The Jesus statue isn't the only case I'm working on."

There was a pause. "Well, it is now. I'll get someone else on your other matters. Starting tomorrow I want you in Bethany, Pennsylvania, making yourself available to the media and seeing that this thing gets turned around." Hawkins's voice was a study in controlled fury, and again Jordan was struck by a sense of incongruity.

What did they want? There were walls around the statue, weren't there? Besides, HOUR would carry on whether the Jesus statue stood or not. After all, *he* was the one who'd found it in the first place. How had it suddenly taken top precedence at the firm? "Fine. I'll pack tonight and leave first thing in the morning."

Hawkins seemed only slightly appeased by Jordan's answer. "We want a press conference tomorrow afternoon, a victory statement, something the rest of us can identify with."

Jordan leaned his forehead against the cool glass of the window. Why had he ever become an attorney in the first place? He should have been a fireman like his buddy Chip from the boys' camp. Fighting fires *had* to be less stressful than this. "Yes, sir

. . . I'll schedule it as soon as I'm in town."

Hawkins uttered what Jordan figured was supposed to be a sigh, but it sounded more like the hiss of a snake. "You won't let us down, will you, Riley?"

No one had ever asked him that before, ever doubted that he gave everything to his work. Jordan felt his face contort as he tried to make sense of Hawkins's comment. "Of course not, sir. I'm the one who found this case, remember?"

"That's true." Finally there was a degree of confidence in Hawkins's tone. "And when it's over there'll be a bonus in it for you, Riley. Keep that in mind."

"A bonus?" The partners got healthy bonuses at the end of every year, and now and then a productive attorney, one who billed out more hours than his peers, might see a small bonus as well. But no one he knew had ever been offered a bonus for a single case.

"Ten thousand dollars, Riley. You get a permanent wall, ten feet high, around that statue and you earn yourself ten grand." He paused while the figures sank in. "Have I made myself clear?"

Jordan straightened and felt the blood drain from his face. Whatever had happened, it apparently involved a third party.

A very wealthy, very influential third party. One that wanted the Jesus statue gone as badly as every attorney at the HOUR organization.

Jordan dismissed his earlier thoughts of Faith and pondered what Hawkins said. His eyes closed as he imagined what sort of deal might be hinging on this case. Bonus or not, he had to give everything to the battle now. The fight was more fierce than ever, and he was directly at the center of it. He nodded his head slowly, as though trying to convince himself of the words he was about to say.

"Yes, sir. Perfectly clear."

"Very good. Then you won't let us down." It wasn't a question.

Ten thousand dollars? Jordan opened his eyes, a new determination pulsing through him. "No, sir, I won't let you down."

In the executive offices of HOUR, Hawkins hung up the phone and smiled at the others. "I think I've convinced him."

One of the older men wrinkled his eyebrows together and shook his head. "Riley's nothing but a boy. We've got ourselves national interest in this case, and I think you men know what I'm talking about. It's time to hand it over to T. J."

T. J. uncrossed his legs and leaned forward in his seat. "Jordan's my friend . . . I could help him and not make him too suspicious."

Hawkins sat on the edge of the desk and considered that. "Everyone in this room knows what we're talking about. A million dollars, gentlemen. That's a hundred thousand for each of the partners, twenty grand for T. J." He stared at his feet for a moment then back at the others. "The problem is Faith Evans. Without her, the people have no voice, no sense of organization." He swore under his breath. "She's the one who bought the statue, after all." His gaze shifted and he studied each of the men around him. "We need to silence her; it's that simple."

T. J. shifted in his seat and blinked. "Meaning?"

"Meaning I need you here. Let Jordan handle the matter in Bethany. I have friends at the national network level. I'll put you in touch with them. See if there's any interest in bringing her up to the network, get someone to call her. Maybe we can lure her away from this ridiculous park situation."

T. J.'s eyes were wide, but he nodded. "Yes, sir, first thing in the morning."

"And if that doesn't work . . . well, there are other ways." Hawkins reached for a pencil and tapped it rapidly on the desk. "Find out who the little girl was. Maybe she's the key to Evans's conscience."

"The little girl?"

Hawkins felt his lips curl ever so slightly. "It's time to do whatever it takes." He glared at the others. "I will not have another public display of sympathy like we saw today. That statue is ours, am I making myself clear?"

There was a chorus of "yes, sirs" and a round of head nods.

They'd do as he said, Hawkins was sure. There was too much money riding on their success this time. And something else that only the partners would ever know about, something all the money in the world couldn't buy.

A four-year commitment of support from a primary team of very influential advisors. Advisors to a politician with more political power than anyone at HOUR had ever dreamed of having.

There was no way one crusading woman was going to cost them that.

Jordan finished packing and set his suitcase out in the hallway. It was a cool night, bordering on cold, and Jordan found his old parka, the one he used to use when he and his college buddies would go camping in upstate New York. It felt good on his arms, lighter and less confining than the suit jackets. He took the stairs down and welcomed the burst of fresh air as he strode out onto Twelfth Street and headed toward Second Avenue.

The air might not have been country fresh, but it was better than the boxy feeling he was getting in his apartment. The conversation with Hawkins, his promises and implied threats, played over again and again in Jordan's head, but after five minutes of walking the images changed. In their place Faith's face returned to haunt him. It was a sure bet her nights weren't spent walking city streets . . . How had she been fortunate enough to land a career that kept her in Bethany?

Then like a brick it hit him: Because of him, she no longer had a job. The thought settled like week-old pizza in his stomach, and he quickened his pace.

All around him the city hummed with activity, and Jordan suddenly longed for the nights when he would ride his bike to Jericho Park. Nights when the only sound was the whirring of his spoked wheels and the wind in the giant maple trees. Sometimes it had been so quiet at the park he could have sworn he heard the moon rising in the sky above him.

If only his mother hadn't died.

He thought of her now, her gentle spirit and loving touch. The way she had imparted to him her sense of wonder over a waxing crescent moon or a singing blue jay in flight or the distinctly vibrant colors in a monarch butterfly. It was no wonder there were times when Jordan thought he might suffocate if he lived another day in the city. With his mother, every day had a magical quality, a sort of expectancy that something small and ordinary would become a miracle. Jordan kept his pace steady and turned the corner, heading down another endless street, stepping over the occasional drunk passed out against the side of a building. The city air had a pungent smell to it, a mixture of rotten garbage, exhaust fumes, and air pollution that never went away. It made him miss the freshness of small-town air in a way he hadn't for years.

Jordan stared up at the sliver of sky between the converging buildings. When Faith's family had told them about Jesus, it had been as though everything in life finally made sense. Jesus had created everything, from the small wonders to the magnificent landscapes, all of it for their enjoyment. But there was more; He'd created them as well and best of all, He had a plan for them to spend eternity with Him. All of it had been so believable.

Jordan stuffed his hands in the pockets of the parka and continued down the street. How blissfully peaceful those early days had been, back when it not only made sense to believe that way, but the Jesus rhetoric actually seemed true. A city park appeared in the distance, and Jordan headed for it. It wasn't grand like Central Park, or anything even close to resembling the quaint ambiance of Jericho Park. But it was a patch of grass with trees that might, for a few hours, help Jordan forget he was trapped in a city where butterflies and crescent moons didn't seem to exist.

He made his way across the street and found a bench. In the recesses of his mind he knew it wasn't the safest thing — hanging out in a park at this late hour in the heart of New York City — but he didn't care. Besides, the way he felt inside, his face was bound to scare away any unwanted company. He settled into the bench and stared straight ahead at a sickly tree struggling skyward. As gentle and loving as his mother had been, the end had been awful. A nightmare that no matter how many years passed Jordan couldn't forget.

Eventually the cancer moved to her lungs. As a thirteen-year-old boy he hadn't understood what was happening, but it made sense now. It started in her breast, moved into her lymph system, and wound up killing her when it took over her lungs. That was the only way he could explain her cough. Those last two weeks before she died, his mother coughed in a way that still sickened him today.

He and Heidi would be doing their homework at the kitchen table and they'd hear their mother wake up in her bedroom upstairs. At first she'd cough lightly, a few times, then a few more. After a minute or so, she'd be hacking so hard Jordan remembered fearing for her life. He'd jump from his chair, grab a cup of water, and rush to her room.

"Mom, are you okay?"

There she'd be, perched on the edge of the bed, little more than a skeleton. Her hair gathered in one hand, the other over her mouth, she'd cough with a convulsing force that sent her nose almost crashing into her knees. "Yes, Jordan . . . I'm okay . . . don't . . . worry about me."

He'd step from side to side, helpless, watching her, wanting to do something but knowing there was nothing he could do. Then she'd point to the floor. Her bowl. She wanted her bowl. He'd grab it as quickly as he could and hand it to her and although she'd eaten no dinner, although she'd probably eaten nothing all day, her coughing would turn to dry heaves.

"It's okay, Mom, I'm here." He'd stand beside her, rubbing her back and hiding the tears that made their way down his face. Once in a while Heidi would appear at the door, her eyes wide with fear.

He'd hold his finger to his lips, knowing that their mother was unaware of Heidi's presence. "Shh . . . it's okay," he'd mouth the words to his sister. "Go back downstairs."

No matter how long the spasmodic episode lasted, Jordan would stay there, putting his fingers over hers, helping her hold the hair off her face. When it was over, when her body finally released her to lie back down, Jordan would hurry to the bathroom and get a cool cloth for her forehead. "It's okay, Mom. It's all over. You're going to be all right."

How many times had he said those words? Every day, every hour? Jordan knew now, much as he'd known then, that the words were more for himself than anyone else. His mother had known the truth from the beginning. *"God's calling me home, Jordan . . . He's calling me home."*

But Jordan and Heidi weren't ready for her to go. Hadn't God known that? Hadn't He cared?

He pulled the parka tighter, grateful he was the only person at the park that night. His mother's illness had gotten worse with each day until finally — the last day of her life — he hadn't bothered to ride to Jericho Park. He no longer wanted to spend time talking to Jesus; he wanted to be with his mother. Wanted to cling to her and stay by her side, to will the life back into her and love the cancer out of her body.

Faith's family was with them every day, nearly all day long that last week. Faith's mother would bring dinner and her father would sit by Mom, praying for her, talking to her. Not until sometime around eight o'clock, when his mother seemed able to sleep, would the Moses family go home. After that Jordan often led Heidi to her room and prayed with her. When she was asleep he would spend an hour or so at Jericho Park, then come home and creep into his mother's room, taking her hand, kissing it as his tears fell onto the dirty knees of his jeans.

"Don't go, Mom. Stay with us. Please . . ."

A few times Faith had stayed with him, having been given a reprieve on her normal curfew in light of Jordan's mother's condition.

"Can she hear you?" Faith whispered one night.

Jordan remembered feeling angry at her question. "Of course she can hear me. She's sick, but she's going to make it, Faith. God's going to heal her."

Even after Faith had gone home, Jordan stayed at his mother's side, finally falling asleep on the floor, his hand clinging tightly to hers. He and Heidi had skipped school every day that last week, and time lost all meaning.

The morning of his mother's last day, he got up early and had a feeling she was already awake. He sat straight up on her bedroom floor and rose to his knees, peering over the top of the bed, making sure she was still breathing. When he saw that she was, he gently took her thin, bruised hand in his and smoothed his fingers over the top.

Her eyes opened and moved slowly in his direction and the shadow of a smile crossed her face. "Jordan . . ."

Heidi must have felt something different that morning, too, because she appeared at the bedroom door, and Jordan motioned her inside. His sister knelt beside him and he put his free arm around her as she reached over and linked her fingers between those of Jordan's and their mother's. "Hi, Mom . . . how're you feeling?"

Jordan had no trouble remembering his mother's face that morning, but the image of Heidi was less clear. Had she been fearful or sad or unaware? Had she known, like him, that their mother's time was running short? Did he take the time to tell her, to explain to his sister what was happening?

Jordan thought about that for a moment and decided he hadn't. Why would he have? Until that last day, he'd thought for sure God would heal her. But that morning there was a different look in his mother's eyes, a sadness and joy that Jordan still couldn't explain. As though she was about to take a much-anticipated journey and her only regret was having to say good-bye.

"Heidi . . ." Their mother's voice was clearer that morning. For days she would cough violently every time she tried to speak, but this time she was comfortable, at peace. "Heidi, you're so beautiful . . . you must . . . put Jesus first . . . always."

Heidi threw herself over her mother and hugged her, weeping and wailing over the prospect of what was happening. In that moment it must have been obvious to both Jordan and Heidi: They were saying good-bye to their mother. "Don't go, Mommy, please . . . I love you too much."

Heidi carried on for a long while, and Jordan could do nothing but rub her back with one hand and their mother's hand with the other while quiet tears coursed down his face. After a while Heidi sat up again and leaned into Jordan. There was silence while their mother seemed to summon what little strength remained. Jordan pulled Heidi more tightly to himself as they watched, waiting for their mother's next words.

"I love you, Jordan . . . you're such a good boy . . . so . . . kind."

The memory of the moment was more vivid now than it had been since that awful morning, and Jordan felt the sting of tears in his eyes. He had cried so much that year, the year he lost his mother and Heidi and Faith. But tears had not touched him once in the time since then. Not since his move to the New Jersey boys' camp. He was a survivor, a loner, really. A smart and lonely kid who'd found a way to make it on his own.

But here, now — the memory of that last day with his mother so real he could almost touch her again — tears filled his eyes and spilled onto his cheeks. His eyelids closed and he saw her as she'd looked that day, so frail and weak her skin was practically translucent. She stayed very still in the bed, but her eyes darted between Heidi and Jordan. "Jesus . . . Jesus wants you to know . . . He loves you, Jordan. Keep praying, please. And one day . . . when you come home . . . I'll be waiting for you. Just like I used to wait for you here."

When you come home . . . when you come home . . . when you come home . . .

Why hadn't he remembered those words until now? The last thing his mother had said to him, the last thing that made sense amid her frenetic coughing and drug-induced incoherency was an invitation. When it was his turn to go home, she'd be waiting for him. Just like she'd always waited for him when he was a boy.

The thought was sadder than anything Jordan had considered for a very long time. To think she'd been so certain of God and heaven and eternity that it really had been like going home. In her mind, the cozy house they had on Oak Street wasn't home at all, but rather a temporary stopping ground. Heaven. That was home to his mother, and her last morning on earth had been spent trying to convince Jordan of the same.

Her words rang in his heart. *When you*

come home . . . when you come home . . .

He wouldn't have struggled with the idea back then, back when his blossoming faith had been the only life preserver in a raging sea of tragedy. Had his mother known, somehow? Back then, with death mere hours away, had she known he would grow up to be an angry, cynical man who scoffed at the mere idea of a higher power and summarily dismissed the thought of eternity? Had she known?

The memories faded as Jordan caught something moving behind him, off to the side. He turned and saw three shabbily dressed teenagers heading his way. *Just try and mess with me tonight, punks.* They laughed and poked each other in the ribs as they came closer and stood in front of him, half-circling the bench.

"Okay, rich boy, what ya got for us?" The kid was tall and skinny, with ratlike eyes and bushy hair.

Jordan chuckled and let his eyes run the length of the boy and his friends. "Isn't it past your bedtime, children?"

A short boy with pants that sagged nearly to his knees kicked Jordan's shoe. "Bet we could get a couple ten spots for those leathers, what ya think?"

His redheaded, squatty companion yanked

at Jordan's coat sleeve. "And a couple more for this." He looked at his friends, and they all burst into laughter.

Jordan felt his patience waning, but just as he was about to tell them to leave a glint of light reflected on a sizable knife in the skinny kid's back pocket. Just as Jordan had known his mother was going to die that morning sixteen years ago, he knew without a doubt what was about to happen.

He was going to be murdered.

They would rob him, maybe strip him of his coat and shoes, and stab him right there in the park. His lip curled. *So, God, is this Your way of showing You love me?* For a split second he wondered if there was time to reconsider, to analyze whether God's alleged promises might be true after all. *If You're there, God, now's the time to show me.* He sat up straighter and stared at the teens. "Get lost."

The skinny one moved in closer, and his eyes narrowed, the pupils black as flint. "Don't tell us what to do." He reached back toward the knife.

Jordan's mind raced in search of a plan, but all he came up with was a plea. *God, if You're really there, keep me safe. I'm not . . . I'm not ready to go home.*

"You're pretty stupid, rich guy." The teen's

bushy hair shook as he jerked the knife from his pocket and pointed it at Jordan's throat.

The sirens came at that exact instant.

They couldn't have been more than a block away by the sound of them. The kid glared at him and shoved his knife back in his pocket. Then he and the others took off, running across the street, away from Jordan and the park. Before they could get to the other side of the road, several police cars converged on the area, and officers sprang from the cars, guns drawn. Using a megaphone, one of them shouted at the boys, "Police! Drop your weapons and freeze."

For a moment it looked as though the teens might try to outrun the officers, but then they came to a strange stop, almost as though their feet had gotten stuck in wet cement. No, that wasn't it. Almost as if someone unseen had grabbed them by their ankles. Jordan gawked at the unfolding scene as, one at a time, the teenagers dropped to the ground, their hands spread out in front of them. One of the policemen found the skinny kid's knife and tossed it to his partner. There were knives in the pockets of the other boys as well. In a matter of minutes, all three teens were whisked away in the police cars, leaving Jordan to absorb what had happened.

He had prayed to God for help . . . and for what felt like the first time in his life, the Lord had answered. He really and truly had answered his prayer. Not in a way that might be confused with coincidence or good vibrations or a strangely timed bout of luck. No, the teenagers being arrested seconds before they might have attacked him was something else altogether.

Even for a nonbeliever like Jordan, there was only one possibility. God had worked a miracle right before his eyes.

He began walking, and fifteen minutes later he was back at his apartment, assailed by doubts and doing his best to ignore whatever strange thing had happened back at the park. He must not be getting enough sleep. The teens were just punky kids. They weren't really going to harm him, were they? And if there was a God, He wouldn't have answered a prayer from someone like him. It was all just a strange set of coincidences . . .

Jordan put on a pair of sweats, flipped on his favorite sports channel, and sank into his leather recliner. Whatever had happened back at the park didn't matter. He was determined to make good on his word to Hawkins. He had a job to do in Bethany, a ten-thousand dollar job.

And regardless of whether angels or God Himself had intervened on Jordan's behalf, he intended to do it.

TWENTY

The walls around the Jesus statue had been up for two full days and the outcry against HOUR was building across the city with each passing moment. It was nine o'clock at night when Faith returned home exhausted from another prayer vigil. She gazed around the empty kitchen.

Another night alone.

If only Mom were here . . .

Faith understood, of course. Aunt Fran's recovery required her to stay off her feet at least eight weeks, and since she lived alone, Faith's mother had been adamant about going to stay with her sister. No doubt about it, Mom was where she needed to be.

Faith tossed her coat on a chair, made herself a cup of tea, and sat at the kitchen table. As she sipped the warm liquid, she closed her eyes, remembering the conversation she'd had with her mother about the legal fight and the loss of her job.

"You have to do what God's telling you, Faith. I'm completely behind you."

Her mother had been shocked and then distraught to learn that Faith's opponent in the battle was Jordan Riley. She remembered him fondly as the boy who had been their neighbor all those years ago. "The walls around the statue are nothing to the walls that must stand around that boy's heart. I'm so sorry I'm not there with all this going on, dear."

"It's okay, Mom," Faith had assured her, though she wished her mother could be with her. Especially to talk through her feelings about Jordan.

Her mother had asked about how it felt to have Jordan as an adversary. "It hurt at first," Faith told her. "But I understand him better now. He's in too much pain to see what he's doing."

Faith cupped her steaming mug in her hands. It was true. She held no animosity toward Jordan, just a deep sadness that the tragedies in his life had caused him to think of God as an enemy.

Father, am I doing the right thing? Is the Jesus statue worth all this?

I will fight the battle, daughter . . . Go forward in My strength, not yours . . .

At the reminder, Faith drew a calming

breath. She had no choice but to heed the words she continued to hear deep in her heart. The battle had grown more heated than ever. There were times she felt as if the expectations of the entire town rested on her shoulders, while she herself was balanced precariously on a tightrope two miles above the city. And if that hadn't been enough to consume her mind . . .

Jordan was back in town.

He'd held a press conference the day before, stationing himself in front of the walled-in statue and apparently inviting every member of the media within a three-state radius. Based on the number of vehicles that had congregated around the park for Jordan's statements, Faith was sure he considered the conference a success.

She took another sip of tea and spread the newspaper out on the table in front of her.

Like the first time she'd seen it earlier that morning, she couldn't help but laugh, even just a little. The photo on the front page was taken barely twenty-four hours after the wall went up, but citizens had begun to show their dislike for it by spray painting sentiments across the plywood. The photographer had captured Jordan speaking into a dozen microphones, the walled-up statue in the background. Taking up nearly half the photo were these words written across the wall: "God rules."

Faith stared at the picture and marveled at the goodness of the Lord. Obviously Jordan's press conference had been in direct response to the media coverage she'd received the day before. Even the daily paper captured the fact that the public loved Faith. "Media Darling Sides with People of Bethany," one headline read. Faith had expected to be persecuted, berated, and mocked for her stance. Instead the Lord seemed to be using her to bring the people together, to shed light on the public's right to keep the statue.

The night before, she'd watched the news segment on Jordan's press conference and winced when he made comments that seemed directed at her. "I won't smile and tell you a litany of lies intended to pacify the people." His face had been stern. Strikingly handsome, Faith had to admit, but stern. "The truth is this: People have a right to separation of church and state." He'd pointed to the walled statue behind him. "That wall is proof that every man, woman, and child in this country has rights, and that among those is the right to choose your own religion. Buddhists and Baptists — both are welcome in the United States and both should be welcome at Jericho Park. I can only imagine the outcry if, for instance, I donated a statue of Buddha to the people of Bethany. If a statue like that stood in the park, people would be lining up across the city to have it removed."

Jordan's voice rang with sincerity. "That's because there's a sentiment in this land that Christianity should be endorsed by the government." He paused — for effect — Faith was sure. "Tolerance toward this type of public Christianity leads to an endorsement. And an endorsement will one day lead to a mandated, state-sponsored religion." Jordan raised his voice. "We must preserve our freedom of religion . . . our freedom to choose. That's why HOUR is here in Bethany, fighting for every citizen in this country. Fighting to save us all from the tyranny of a state-sponsored religion."

Faith had watched the entire segment and sighed at the sadness in her heart as she turned off the television. Could Jordan really be that far gone? Was her childhood friend really the same man speaking out against God at a press conference? She studied Jordan's newspaper photograph, looking for anything remotely familiar — the earnest eyes, gentle heart, or dimpled smile. But there was nothing except the shape of his face, chiseled chin, and cheek-bones.

Otherwise he looked like a stranger.

Images from the prayer vigil came to mind, and Faith considered the commitment of the townspeople who'd come that night. It had been obvious by their kindness that they were there as much to support her as to support the Jesus statue. If their favorite daughter were involved in the cause, then by golly they'd be involved too. Faith smiled at the memory. With each gathering the numbers grew, and people often asked what they could do to help. She thanked those who spoke with her, but the truth was frighteningly simple: They could gather the support of everyone in the state, but the decision would still be up to the judge.

Faith held her cup of tea closer to her face and let the steam warm her cheeks. It felt like days since she'd had a moment alone, time to talk with the Lord and seek His direction. She'd wanted to stay at Jericho Park after everyone was gone, to pray as she'd done when she was a young girl, back when she and Jordan would go there together. But dozens of people obviously planned to stay until she left.

She checked her watch and saw that a half hour had flown by. Surely the last of the prayer warriors had left the park by now. Faith considered the idea, pictured having the park all to herself and the chance to sit on her favorite bench and pray. Yes, it was just what she needed. The temperatures were expected to hit freezing that night so she bundled up in a full-length wool coat, gloves, and a scarf. Satisfied that she'd be warm enough she made her way out to her car. In five minutes she was back at Jericho Park.

She scouted the area before getting out of her car and found it empty. Without hesitating another moment she made her way across the familiar path toward the bench, the one closest to the Jesus statue. Her statue.

Faith sat down and pulled the coat tightly around her body. She thought about how busy she'd been earlier with the crowd gathered around. So busy she hadn't taken time to really look at the walled-in statue. In some ways it felt like some sort of bizarre dream, a surreal image of a fantasy future world where all signs of God might be forcibly eradicated from the public landscape. Faith stared at the plywood and half expected to look around the city and see churches boarded up as well. To think her father had devoted his final years to preserving religious freedom only to die months before the fight showed up on his own doorstep.

That was what coming to the park at ten o'clock was all about, really. Taking time to remember her father. "Dad . . ." Tears filled her eyes as she studied the covered statue. "You wouldn't believe the battle we're fighting." She uttered a sad laugh. "It's ridiculous."

She closed her eyes and imagined her father still alive, imagined him sitting beside her, holding her hand. Felt the way he would sympathize with her for losing a job she'd dreamed about all her life over the battle at Jericho Park. *Daddy, I need you here. Joshua needs you. God, how can You let us fight this battle without him?*

Faith tried to hear the Lord's answer, but the only sound was the faint rustling of a handful of stubborn leaves that hadn't yet fallen from the trees above. It didn't matter. She knew the answer already. God was with them; He'd go before them.

But at what cost?

The question whispered through her, much like the wind through the leaves. She hesitated. Would she ever find another job as an anchorwoman now that she'd become a key figure in a national legal battle? And what about Jordan? Win or lose, he'd wind up back in New York, never making peace with his mother's death or finding Heidi. Without any of the answers that might have restored his trust in God.

The tears that had been gathering spilled over and flowed steadily down her cheeks. As they did, Faith realized she'd been too caught up in the moment to grieve the changes that had happened around her, too busy to let down her guard and weep over all that had transpired in the days since her father's death. What she wouldn't give to be eight or ten again, running with Sarah and her father in the backyard of their home on Oak Street, certain that life would go on that way forever.

Faith allowed the tears, doing nothing to stop them, or the sadness that gripped her heart. With the Jesus statue walled up everything about her life seemed uncertain and hopeless. Yes, the town of Bethany supported her, but the people couldn't force the judge to make the right decision at tomorrow's hearing . . . they couldn't get her a job . . . or transform Jordan into the boy he'd once been.

And they couldn't bring back the man who had always been bigger than life, the man who had given everything for his convictions.

"Daddy, I'm here. I miss you . . ." Her words took wing and blended with a chorus of whistling wind gusts. Faith looked up and stared hard at the stars, dancing in the clear, cold, late-night sky. "God, please, tell Daddy I love him."

Jordan wasn't sure what he was supposed to do in Bethany for three days, but based on the media coverage and the size of the demonstrations against what he was trying to do, he knew one thing: He wasn't a popular figure. For that reason he holed up in his hotel room most of the day, aware that his photograph was on the front page of the paper. He'd spoken to Hawkins earlier and somehow the firm had seen a copy of the article.

"What's this, 'God rules' garbage?" Hawkins had blasted the question across the phone line, and Jordan had to ease away from the receiver to protect his ears. "Was that the only place you could set up a press conference? You might as well have been talking for the other side."

"I had no control over the photographer's angle." Jordan had never felt more insecure about his job. He'd figured out that the ten thousand dollars must have been only a fraction of the bonus money. Otherwise the partners would never have been so interested in the Bethany case. But none of that changed the fact that it was up to him to make sure public opinion was at least balanced in these final days before the hearing.

Hawkins had ended the conversation by asking Jordan the strangest question. "You haven't seen the girl, have you?"

"The girl?"

"The girl. Faith Evans. Have you seen her?"

For the tenth time in as many days Jordan felt as though his entire existence was founded on shifting sand. Why would Hawkins care about that? And why would he ask in the first place? Jordan hadn't told anyone about his childhood friendship with Faith Evans. No one but T. J., and Teej was his best friend. No way he'd say anything.

Before Jordan could muster an answer, Hawkins barked the question again.

"No, sir, I haven't seen her."

"Good. She's the enemy, Jordan. Don't forget it." He paused. "Don't let us down, we're counting on you."

Six hours had passed since then, and just after dark Jordan managed to sneak out for a bucket of fried chicken. Now that was gone, and he felt restless again. His time at the city park in New York had been cut short by the close encounter with the street thugs and besides, nothing in the city could compare with what Bethany offered. As he paced the boxy motel room he realized the only place he really wanted to go was Jericho Park. He'd allowed himself to journey down almost all the roads of his past, but there were a few he hadn't yet traveled and there would be no place like Jericho Park to allow the years to fade away.

He dug through his suitcase and came up with an old New York State sweatshirt and a Mets baseball cap. He slipped on a pair of tennis shoes and the parka he'd worn the other night, pulling it up close to his neck. Locking the motel door behind him, he set out on foot.

He realized there was no reason to walk fast — no sirens in the distance, no men with knives looking for solitary prey. Just the simple sleepy streets and suburban homes that made up the neighborhoods a mile from downtown. He took in every detail as he made his way closer to the park, noticing how little the area had changed in sixteen years. For a moment he pretended he was thirteen again, making his way home from Benjamin's Market with a quart of milk and a loaf of bread, confident that his mother and sister were waiting for him behind their nicely painted front door.

Jordan sighed and continued down the familiar streets.

That was the hardest part of being in Bethany. On the outside it all looked the same, felt the same. Even the cool early winter air was the same. But beneath the surface everything was different. It was the same feeling he'd had looking at his mother lying in a coffin. The shell of the woman was there, but none of what mattered most.

Jericho Park lay ahead of him, and he crossed Main, avoiding the circles of light from the street lamps. He was fifty yards from the bench when he saw a woman sitting alone, staring at the walled-up statue.

Fine. The other side of the park's as good as this one. He veered to the right, careful not to attract the woman's attention as he padded along a narrow strip of grass between the sidewalk and the curb. At the far end of the park, he turned left and walked in the darkest shadows until he reached a different bench. He sat down and allowed his eyes to adjust to the lack of light as he surveyed the park. The plywood around the statue stood out like a rusted Chevy on a neatly manicured lawn. He'd ask for brick, of course. Ten feet of dark brick, with a plaque explaining how the public had a right to choose. A nice touch to make the walls less of an eyesore, more of a message for the children of future generations.

Jordan let the words play in his mind and heard himself sigh. Who was he trying to kid? There were no cameras rolling now, no political posturing needed for the quiet hours of the night. The wall looked ridiculous and would look equally so made of wood or straw or the highest quality dark brick. He leaned back and stretched his feet out in front of him. Faith was right. The statue belonged to the people and they had a right to keep it standing — visible for all the world to see.

Staring at the strange-looking walls, he found himself missing the Jesus statue, the way the arms stretched out, the Scripture verse inscribed below. *Come to me all you who are weary and I will . . .*

Jordan blinked. What was he doing? How could he miss something that had played a part in the greatest deception of his childhood? He'd had more faith than all the people in the New Testament combined and *still* his mother died, still his sister had been taken away. He remembered the way his mother spoke so clearly to Heidi and him that last day, as though she'd known she had only hours to live.

He closed his eyes . . . feeling again his desperation as that awful day wore on and his mother's weakness returned. She coughed and gasped for breath, frightening them until finally Jordan ran next door and summoned Faith's family. Immediately Faith, her sister, and their parents took up their places at the Riley home, helping his mom and comforting Jordan and Heidi. Faith's parents took turns sitting beside his mother, while Jordan stood stiffly in the hallway outside and Heidi wept in the arms of one of the other adults. Jordan remembered staring at his mother through the open door, willing her to sit up. *Come on, Mom . . . get up. Talk to us . . .*

For a while she seemed to get better. Her coughing episodes grew less frequent and Jordan dared to believe that maybe . . . just maybe . . . a miracle was taking place before his eyes. "Mr. Moses —" Jordan had been hopeful as he came up behind Faith's large father and tugged on his sleeve — "I think the cough's going away. Maybe she's coming around some."

Mr. Moses clenched his jaw and led Jordan out of the room. Then, in quiet tones, he explained the situation. "She's coughing less because she has less air. Her breathing is slower and she's drifting in and out of our world here. Sort of like she's halfway to heaven, Jordan."

Jordan must have looked confused because Faith's father put a hand on his shoulder and stared deeply into his eyes. "It won't be long, Jordan. Your mother is dying, son."

As awful as the news was, Jordan remembered feeling some comfort in the way Mr. Moses had called him *son.* As though every shred of support and security wasn't slipping away from him and that even if his mother did die, he and Heidi wouldn't be alone in the world. Jordan nodded and looked around the man at his mother. "Should we . . . should we tell her good-bye?"

Faith's father had tears in his eyes. "Heidi said you already did. I guess your mother had a chance to talk to you earlier today, is that right?"

Jordan nodded, his eyes trained on the form of his mother in the next room. "We had a real nice talk."

Mr. Moses squeezed his shoulder again and pulled him close, hugging him the way Jordan had always imagined a father might. "I'm glad, Jordan. Really, I am."

Then, even though she could no longer hear them, Jordan and Heidi returned to the bedroom and sat on either side of the bed, holding their mother's hands and talking to her in quiet tones. Heidi was not ashamed to cry and she wept throughout the day, occasionally throwing herself across her mother and holding her close despite the fact that their mother was no longer able to respond. "Don't leave us, Mommy."

Jordan hadn't felt the same freedom. His world was changing with each passing hour, and any moment he was about to be the head of the household, the only person who could look after Heidi. He kept his back straight and his lower lip stiff as he squeezed his mother's hand again and again, praying for some sort of response. He had tears, for sure, but they were quiet tears. Tears that coursed down his face and made wet marks on the legs of his jeans. Now and then Heidi would come up behind him and take hold of his shoulders, resting her head against his back as she sobbed silently.

They stayed that way for hours, Heidi and Jordan on the bed with their dying mother. Finally, just before six o'clock that evening, she made three quick gasping sounds and then exhaled long and slow. Even now Jordan remembered the sound. It was the same sound his bicycle tire had made back when he was twelve and had run over a pop bottle on the way home from school. A long, slow hiss that seemed to last forever until there was no air left.

"Mom!" Jordan shook her so she might draw another breath, but as he watched, her features relaxed and a tranquillity came over her. One moment she'd been there, fighting for her life, and the next she was simply gone, leaving nothing but the shell of the body she'd once occupied. He remembered being sure she'd gone to heaven. Since then, though, he'd convinced himself that heaven didn't exist. The peace on his mother's face after drawing her last breath was merely death taking another victim. Heidi's reaction had caused an ache deep in his heart, like a bruise that never healed even to this day.

His sister realized what was happening at the same time Jordan did and she screamed, dropping their mother's hand and running across the room to Faith's mother, clinging first to her and then moving alongside the bed back to Jordan. "Bring her back, Jordan, make her come back!"

He winced and eased himself out of the memory. Heidi had been terrified of being alone, living without their mother. Only Jordan's presence in her life had given her the security she'd needed to survive that day and the ones that followed.

He felt tears stinging at his eyes and wondered how long it had been since he'd grieved the loss of his mother and sister. Of course, back then he hadn't imagined he'd lose Heidi the same week. Somehow he'd figured he could raise her by himself, that they might continue to share the house on Oak Street, eating an occasional meal with Faith's family and getting themselves off to school on time each day. He'd had no understanding of utility bills and food costs or that there might be a law against children living alone.

They'd been taking care of themselves for months, ever since their mother got sick. Why should that change now that she was gone? As they got through the next few days, it wasn't a problem either of them considered. Faith's mother was over often, taking them to the funeral home and helping them understand what was happening. Looking back, Jordan realized the church or Faith's family must have paid for his mom's funeral, the casket, and burial plot, because certainly his mother had no money. Once when he was old enough to search the records he looked into what had happened to their house. According to his file — which lacked any specific detail — the house was sold to pay his mother's medical bills.

Jordan guessed that the government took the rest.

The days after his mother's death were as much a blur now as they were sixteen years ago, but in the still and quiet darkness of Jericho Park, Jordan did his best to remember. They had worn their nicest church clothes for the funeral, and Heidi hadn't been able to pull herself away from him. She was so sad, so afraid at the loss of their mother that she wouldn't speak to anyone but Jordan. Especially the morning of the funeral service.

"She w-won't really be there, right Jordan? In the wooden box?" Heidi had found him in the bathroom that morning getting ready. She was so distraught she could barely speak. "Even though . . . even though her body will be there, right?" Tears filled her eyes, as they did all the time back then.

Jordan adjusted his white button-down shirt that the Moses family bought him and rubbed a dab of gel into his hair. It was the last time he'd see his mother and he wanted to look his best. "No, Heidi. She won't really be there. Having her body there is just a way of giving people a chance to say their good-byes."

"But . . . but she's already gone, right?

Like if I talk to her, she won't be able to hear me, right?" Heidi stood inches from him, waiting anxiously for his hand to be free so she could take hold of it.

Jordan set the tube of gel down and pulled her close. "She won't hear you, but God will. Remember what Mom said? Don't stop praying . . . and one day when we go to heaven she'll be waiting for us."

Jordan frowned into the cool dark air. Had those really been his words? Had he truly felt that confident in the hours before his mother's funeral? He wasn't sure. He just knew he'd vowed to take care of Heidi until she was grown. Other than Faith and her family, Heidi was all he had and clearly she needed him.

The air was getting colder and frost was appearing on the park grass. Jordan looked across the field and searched for the woman he'd seen earlier. Whoever she was, she'd gone home. Jordan knew he should do the same. The hearing was scheduled for ten o'clock the next morning. But somehow he didn't want to leave this place — or the memories of those days after his mother's death, the last days with Heidi. Jordan remembered making breakfast for her and doing laundry and making sure they got to bed on time. Faith's mother was there a lot, and so was her father. But most of the time Jordan had been in charge, and though they were still reeling from the loss of their mother, there was comfort that went beyond words in the fact that they had each other.

How long had that time lasted? Jordan used to think it was a week or so, but now it seemed more like two or three days at the most. Either way, it hadn't been long enough. Faith's father had pulled him aside and promised he'd do all he could to see that Jordan and Heidi stayed together. Certainly he hadn't contacted the state and reported them living alone. But somehow the office of Social Services got wind of their situation and one afternoon — the day they'd returned to school — two workers came and asked them to pack their things. Heidi had been terrified about going away, even for a night, but the state workers promised she'd be back with Jordan in a day or so.

Promises that meant nothing at all.

He remembered Heidi's cries and wide-eyed terror as one of the workers drove her away from their home. Jordan had watched her go, believing he would die from the separation and helplessness of that moment. He had promised to take care of her and suddenly in an hour's time she was gone.

His heart felt tight and trapped at the memory, awash in an ocean of pain that still hadn't even begun to subside. "Heidi, where are you?" Jordan stared out ahead of him and wondered what she might look like now. Heidi . . . his little sister . . . the one who had depended on him for everything that last year they were together.

Another onset of tears burned his eyes. Jordan rarely afforded himself the chance to miss her this way, but here, with visions of that terrible afternoon as real as they'd been in the months that followed, he felt as though his heart would break from missing Heidi. He should have done more to find her, searched for her, refused to give up. Instead he'd made a series of bad decisions, choices that only cost him whatever hope he'd had of getting them back together again.

There was a rustling behind him and he whipped around. First New York City, now Bethany. Wasn't any place safe from the crazies who roamed the night? He scanned the bushes and a movement caught his eye. It looked like the same woman who'd been at his bench earlier that night, and she was walking toward him. Before he could clearly see her face she spoke.

"Jordan, it's me . . . Faith."

His heart skipped a beat as a series of emotions washed over him. Shock at seeing her here at the park, seeking out solitude at the same hour he'd chosen; guilt and sadness, and as she came into the light, a desire he hadn't known before in his life. She was so beautiful, her heart so clearly like it had been when they were kids living next door on Oak Street. It was all he could do to keep from meeting her halfway, taking her in his arms and apologizing for everything that had happened over the past few months.

He read her eyes as easily as he had sixteen years ago. She cared for him still — regardless of the war they were waging against each other, she cared. Then he moved to one side of the bench and patted the empty place beside him.

There were a dozen things he could think to say to her, but instead he held her gaze and hoped she, too, could see beyond the battle lines.

Twenty-One

Faith was still quite a ways off when she recognized Jordan. Something in the way he stretched out and stared off in the distance — the tilt of his head and the long legs that refused to stay bunched up beneath him — the same as when he was a boy.

For a moment she stopped and considered turning back. What would she say to him? After all they were enemies now, weren't they? But in the quiet of the darkened park the trappings of their current situation seemed to fall away. Here, in the shadows of the walled-in Jesus statue, they were merely two grown-up kids who'd lost each other a very long time ago when life was its most impressionable.

Looking at Jordan she saw him as he'd been in his mother's room the day she died, the way he'd held his head high at her funeral, the way he'd clung to his sister the day she was taken from him. Rather than fight him or berate him for his political views, she wanted only to take him in her arms and soothe away the years of hurt and anger and bitterness.

Jordan . . . her long-ago best friend . . .

When he finally spotted her she knew that she'd been right that first night in the diner parking lot. No matter what words came out of his mouth when the cameras were rolling, he was the same Jordan Riley she'd loved as a girl. When he patted the empty place beside him on the bench, she came to him willingly.

"I thought it was you." She took the seat, careful to keep her distance, angling her body so she could see him. Although they sat in darkness, the stars cast enough light so she could make out his features.

"I must have walked right past you. Were you sitting on the bench over there?" His voice was quiet and kind, and Faith felt herself relax.

"Yeah. It's been kind of crazy lately." She stared across the expanse of frosty grass toward the towering plywood walls. "I guess I needed some time alone."

Jordan followed her gaze and waited a moment. "I know what you mean."

There was an uncomfortable silence, and Faith could sense him searching for something to say. Something that didn't involve the statue or the fact that common sense said they were crazy to be sitting on a bench in a hidden corner of the park in the middle of the night.

He turned to her and seemed to force a smile. "Tell me about the little Asian girl."

Her gaze fell, and she tried to still her racing heart. "Rosa Lee?"

"I don't know . . ." He changed positions so that he was closer than before. "She was by your side at the protest the other day. I saw her with you on the news."

Faith gulped and tried to concentrate. Something about being in his presence was making her feel thirteen again, like they were only pretending to be adults locked in a legal battle. "She's . . . she's a foster child. Sometimes she reminds me of you." Suddenly her heart soared at the chance to share her deepest feelings with him. "She wants me to adopt her."

Jordan's smile seemed more genuine this time. "That's wonderful. Will you? Adopt her, I mean?"

"Oh, I don't know." She felt the corners of her mouth lift some. "Actually, I'm praying about it." Faith thought of the little girl and how close they'd grown in the past weeks. "I keep waiting for a real family to show some interest. You know, with a mom and dad. I think she deserves that." She hesitated, not sure if she should tell him. "Besides, my next job might take me away . . ."

He searched her eyes. "Away?"

She nodded. "I got a call today from the station's competition. A national network. They're considering me for a spot."

Jordan's eyes lit up, and for the first time that night his grin reminded her of the boy he'd once been. "For the national news? Faith, that's great!" He reached for her hands and squeezed them, then as the moment faded he let go and crossed his arms tightly against his chest.

Faith couldn't bring herself to tell him the rest of the conversation. The network executive had acknowledged that Faith was embroiled in a national legal battle. "Be careful," he'd told her. "Don't do anything too extreme. And keep a low profile. I have to be honest with you, prayer rallies, protests, that kind of thing won't look good, Ms. Evans."

She and Jordan fell quiet, and an icy breeze kicked up a pile of long-dead leaves. Faith angled her head, studying Jordan. She wanted desperately to know the thoughts that filled his head. Was he here to strategize his next move? Or was he drawn to the past the way she was so often these days? *Talk to me, Jordan . . . like old times . . .* "What are you thinking?" Her voice was soft, allowing him the right to refuse to answer.

He shrugged and met her gaze. "About Heidi."

Faith's heart melted. He was the same; deep inside he was still the same. "I think about her a lot. Especially since . . ."

"I know," Jordan finished for her. Their voices were quiet, like the night around them. Even the breeze had stilled, and time seemed strangely suspended. "Since that night at the diner."

Faith nodded. "She loved you very much, Jordan."

He sighed and narrowed his eyes. "It was my fault what happened. I let her down."

Faith shook her head. "None of it was your fault. The state took you to separate homes and even if you'd —"

"No." His tone was gentle but insistent. "You don't know the whole story."

Faith thought about that for a moment and angled her head, trying to understand. For all the success Jordan had managed to achieve professionally, she suddenly knew he had no one to talk to, no friend like she'd been to him that year before he was taken from his home. She thought of a hundred things she could say. *Talk to me, Jordan. Share your heart with me. So what if we're enemies in the morning? Right now we're thirteen again, and you can tell me whatever's on your heart.* She swallowed hard and let her thoughts fade. "Tell me, Jordan. I have all night."

And to her surprise, he did.

Drawing a slow breath he stared straight ahead and talked as though the events were only just now happening, as though he could see them unfolding before his eyes the way they had that terrible year. "They put me in a foster home, and every hour I asked about Heidi. Two days passed, and then three, and I overheard the lady on the phone. I don't know who she was talking to, but she said she didn't think they could find a place for Heidi and me, for both of us. She said it could be weeks before I saw my sister again."

Jordan paused, and Faith allowed the silence. He closed his eyes as though the events of the past were settling into their proper order. Finally he looked at her and exhaled, his breath hanging in the air. "On the third day I set out on my own. The man of the house had told me where Heidi was staying — with a family on Birch Street. I figured I knew my way to Birch Street and even if I had to knock on every door I'd find her eventually." He released a frustrated huff. "I should have known better. One call to my social worker, and I might have had a visit with her that night. Maybe they didn't know how badly I needed to see her."

Without thinking, Faith reached out and took Jordan's hand in hers, wrapping her gloved fingers around his. "That's why you got sent to the boys' camp?"

Jordan gripped her hand, his gaze still straight ahead. "I wasn't gone an hour when the police came cruising up behind me. I'd almost made it to Birch; I was so close I could practically see Heidi waiting for me, calling my name. When the police asked me to get in the car, I ran the other direction." He released a sad laugh. "I was thirteen. What chance did I have at outrunning two police officers? They caught me, cuffed me, and tossed me in the squad car. That afternoon I was shipped thirty minutes away to the Southridge Boys' Camp."

Faith felt suddenly awkward holding Jordan's hand and she quietly pulled it back. "You can't blame yourself for that, Jordan. You were doing what you thought was best."

"I should have been patient. Who knows?" He turned and locked eyes with her. "Everything might have been different." He paused, his eyes more intense than they'd been all night. "Absolutely everything."

Faith thought she understood what he was saying. If he'd had the chance to grow up alongside Heidi he would not have held the anger he held today. He might not have become a human rights attorney, and perhaps . . . perhaps she and Jordan might even have stayed friends or . . . She refused to dwell on the possibilities. "Did you . . . at the camp, did they tell you anything about Heidi?"

"Not a thing." The muscles in Jordan's jaw flexed and he fell silent. He turned his attention to the spread of grass in front of him. "The camp was like a prison. Up at seven, chores till nine. A bowl of slop for breakfast each morning, lessons through the early afternoon, and four hours of hard labor before dinner."

Faith felt tears in her eyes. That was the type of life he'd been forced to live in the months after losing his mother? After losing Heidi? After losing his home and Faith's family and everything that had mattered to him? The reality of it tore at her heart, and she pictured Rosa Lee . . . stranded in the system, without a family. Where would she wind up when she got old enough to have a bad attitude? At a similar camp, fighting for her place among a houseful of angry young women? The thought made her shudder. "Oh, Jordan . . . I had no idea."

He nodded, his expression unchanged. "The boys at the camp were tougher than I was — serious hard-core kids. Most of them were drug addicts or thieves, guys destined for prison. I thought about Mom and Heidi —" he looked at her — "and you . . . every day, every hour. But there was nothing I could do about it. It took all my strength just to survive."

She always believed he'd remembered her, that he thought of her in those days after he was taken from his home. But this was the first time he'd said so, and a warmth made its way from Faith's heart out across her body. "You thought of me, Jordan? Really?"

He stared at her, and there were tears in his eyes. "Every day, Faith. I kept thinking . . ." He swallowed hard. "I kept thinking you and your parents would show up at the camp and take me home, rescue me from that awful place and help me find Heidi."

"We wanted to . . ." Her voice drifted. "I talked to my mom . . . she's in Chicago helping my aunt. She said they hadn't called social services because they were afraid once the state got involved it would be impossible to adopt you." She looked at the tops of the distant trees. "I guess my dad wanted to talk to an attorney friend of his about adopting both of you privately. But the state stepped in before he could do anything."

Jordan shook his head. "It doesn't matter. Things happened the way they did for a reason, right?"

Again she wanted to take him in her arms and hold him until the hurt faded from his heart. But she had a feeling it would take a lifetime, and they didn't have that. Morning was fast approaching. In six hours this strange time between them borrowed from a place where yesterday lived would be all but forgotten.

Come morning, they'd take up their places on opposite sides of the battle once more.

She decided to be honest with him. "Jordan . . ."

He turned to her and smiled sadly. "I'm sorry. It's late and cold. I'm sure you don't want to hear all this."

"No, I do . . . I just . . ." He was looking at her, waiting for her to finish. "I thought about you, too. Every day."

He searched her eyes. "I always wondered

if you heard about the accident. For a month after it happened I expected to see you and your family." He smiled and gazed up at the midnight sky. "I pictured your dad striding up to the front office, demanding they let me go, insisting that the camp wasn't a safe place for kids like me." He shook his head. "But the truth is you probably never even heard about it."

Faith's eyes grew wide. An accident? At the camp? "Wait a minute, I do remember something about it."

Jordan lowered his eyebrows and bit his lower lip, stuffing his hands deep into the pockets of his parka. "It was awful, Faith." Even in the shadows she could see heartache settle over his face. "There was a cave built into the side of a ravine, maybe a hundred yards from the main camp. Over the years people used it as a trash dump." He paused and released a long breath, gritting his teeth in a way that made his jaw more pronounced. "That afternoon . . . the owners of the camp decided it was time to clean it out."

Faith racked her brain, trying to remember where she'd heard these details before. She waited while Jordan found the strength to continue. "The cave was more of a tunnel . . . I don't know, maybe twenty feet straight into the side of the ravine. Trouble was it'd been raining for three weeks before they ordered the cleanup. We were an hour into the job when dirt began falling from the ceiling."

Jordan shook his head, and his features looked chalky white, even in the shadows. "I remember every horrifying detail." He paused and looked at her again. "Another boy and I were near the entrance. We barely got out. I mean, we had dirt on our backs and our legs were buried as the cave collapsed." He stared at the ground near his feet. "They used shovels and got me and the boy next to me out first. Then they started digging for the others. Seventeen boys. All of them trapped beneath tons of dirt."

He was silent for a moment, lost in the memory, and Faith barely noticed the tears that trickled onto her cheeks. *No wonder Jordan's so angry . . .* She wanted to ask the Lord why — why had He allowed the string of tragedies to happen to a boy so young, one so new in his belief? But something deep inside her lacked the confidence to even approach God with the issue. She shifted her attention back to Jordan. "I can't imagine."

Jordan nodded slowly, thoughtfully and

brought his eyes back up to hers. "For ten minutes we could hear the faint, muffled cries of the trapped boys. The camp owner dug as fast as he could, and after a few minutes firemen arrived and joined the effort." He shook his head, his eyes flat. "There was nothing they could do; it was too late."

Suddenly she could see the headlines, hear her parents talking about the accident. As she drifted back to that year, she gasped and her hand flew across her mouth. "I remember it now! The newspaper said you died!" She stared straight ahead, digging her fingers into the roots of her hair, searching her mind for details she hadn't remembered until now. Her eyes flew back to his. "My parents read the article and told me that night. They said they weren't sure it was true and the next day they made some calls and found out you were okay."

"The paper said I died?" Jordan's eyebrows lifted. "You're kidding?" He bit the inside of his lip and his eyes grew even wider. "Hey, what if Heidi heard the same thing?"

Faith caught his enthusiasm. "You know, you might be right. Maybe she thinks you're dead, and that's why she hasn't tried to find you."

"I've looked up her records, but never mine. What if somehow they got it mixed up and —" He stopped, and his shoulders slumped as he leaned back against the bench once more. Faith watched the despair settle over his face. "They wouldn't have gotten a thing like that wrong. The papers might have made a mistake, but not the state."

He looked at his hands. "I spent a night in the hospital while they looked me over. The next day I was moved to a boys' camp in New Jersey." He leaned his head back some and looked at Faith again. "I asked about Heidi every day for three months until finally the camp warden told me not to ask anymore." Jordan huffed, and Faith could see the bitterness in his tensed features. "He threatened to send me to a camp in Montana if I spoke her name again."

Faith pictured him, only months after losing his mother and sister, stuck at a camp so far from home with people who neither knew nor loved him. "I wish . . . I wish we could have found you, Jordan."

He shrugged, and she knew he was letting her see into the very depths of his heart. "I kept thinking they'd bring Heidi to me, find us a home together. But one year led to the next, and in no time I was finished with high school and playing college baseball. By that point I think I figured no one wanted to find me. I sort of had to let the old Jordan Riley die . . ." He studied Faith's eyes. "Know what I mean?"

She shook her head and felt her heart sink. This was his way of telling her he'd changed, at least from his perspective. But it wasn't true; the old Jordan hadn't died. She'd sat right next to him for the past half hour.

Jordan's heart raced deep within him at Faith's nearness, at the desire he felt for her. How had he gotten in this position? How had things gotten so mixed up, so far from what he wanted?

He wanted to pull her close and tell her the way he was feeling, but how could he? Nothing lasting could ever come from a relationship between them. They were complete opposites.

But, oh! What she did to him, sitting so close he could smell the subtle sweetness of her skin.

"What are you thinking?"

Jordan looked at her, and a flash of anger pierced his soul. What was he doing here, anyway? This was all about the court case. Faith didn't have feelings for him. "I know what you're trying to do."

She jerked back an inch or two and knit her eyebrows together as though he'd suddenly switched languages on her. "What's *that* supposed to mean?"

He expelled the air in his lungs and dug his elbows into his thighs. "I'm sorry. I'm not making sense."

Faith was quiet for a minute. Then in a voice soft as silk she whispered words that felt like balm to his empty heart: "The old Jordan isn't dead. He's right here."

Get up and leave! She's trying to change you, make you into something you're not! She's one of them, remember?

The silent, angry whispers pecked at his soul, but he ignored them. It didn't matter what her motives were, or what she was trying to do to him, or which side she was aligned with. He looked up and their eyes locked. Slowly she slid closer and slipped off her gloves. Then she lifted her hand to his face, framing his jaw with the most delicate touch he'd ever known. "He's not dead, Jordan."

He searched her eyes, painfully aware he was losing control at an alarming rate. His words slipped out before he could stop them. "Sometimes I think, maybe . . . maybe you're right."

Faith's eyes filled with tears, and suddenly

Jordan was sure beyond any doubt that the woman before him had no ulterior motives. Rather the two of them were caught in a time warp, transported back to that long-ago summer when they were two kids learning about love.

"Until tonight," she went on, "I thought it might be true, that the old you really had died. But now . . ."

He drew closer to her, savoring the feel of her hand on his face as she talked.

"Seeing you here, like this, I realized that somewhere inside of you the old Jordan Riley still remembers."

The night air was cold and oddly calm. Jordan looked into Faith's eyes, trying to memorize the moment and wondering if it wasn't all some kind of a dream. Finally, when he couldn't hold back another moment, he took her chin in his hands, allowing his fingers to caress the sides of her face. "I wanted to win this battle, Faith. For a long time I've wanted to win it. But I never meant to hurt you. I had no idea . . ."

Her eyes clouded over, and she turned her eyes toward the Jesus statue. Again there was quiet between them.

"What're you thinking about?" Jordan tucked the loose strands of her hair behind her ears. "You looked a million miles away for a minute there."

She looked back at him, and he wondered if she was as distracted by his nearness as he was by hers. It was all he could do to keep from taking her in his arms and . . .

If only there weren't an ocean of differences between us —

"It's cold."

At her words, Jordan nodded and closed the remaining gap between them, moving so close to her that his heightened senses took in every place where their bodies touched. The length of their arms, their legs . . . "Better?"

Faith hesitated, and Jordan knew she had to be waging an inner battle as well. But he felt her relax and snuggle close to him.

"Better." She positioned herself so she could look into his eyes again. "Remember what you said? About this case meaning a lot to you?"

He nodded, barely able to breathe for her nearness.

"It means a lot to me, too." The reality of her statement cut like a dagger, though it did nothing to stop the way he wanted her, the way he was sure he'd never loved anyone like he loved the woman at his side, the connection they shared. She was the only one he had ever been able to share his heart with.

"You have to be true to yourself, Faith."

Their eyes locked, their faces no more than an inch apart, and Jordan knew there was no turning back. Faith brought her cheek up alongside his and he nuzzled her face. "I will be . . . It's something I promised my father."

He eased his arm around her and pulled her against his chest. Finally, when he thought he'd die from anticipation, he whispered into her ear, "I still love you, Faith."

Sitting this close in the shadows of the park where they'd spent so many hours as kids . . . it was more than either of them could bear. The statue, the legal fight . . . none of it mattered with her so close he could feel her breath, smell her shampoo.

She cupped his face with both hands this time, her eyes full of questions. "Jordan, I . . ."

"Shh. Don't say anything." He could feel the early sting of tears. "We're different now, we look at life from opposite sides of the ocean. I just . . . I wanted you to know how I feel."

Her hands quivered against his face and he caught them in his own, protecting her from the freezing night.

Faith looked deeply into his eyes. "But you agreed with me. A part of you — who you used to be — still lives inside you. Isn't that right?"

Jordan let go of one of her hands, tracing her eyebrows with his thumbs. "If things had been different . . . who knows where we might be now." He warned himself not to do something he'd regret, but without paying heed he brought his lips closer to hers. This time he kept eye contact as he whispered the feelings that were flooding his heart. "I always loved you, Faith. What I felt for you was . . . I don't know, pure. Right. I never loved anyone the way I loved you. The way I still love you."

Certain they'd found a ride upstream in the river of time, he touched his lips to hers and kissed her until they were both breathless. When he pulled back, a breeze blew across them and he was struck by the insanity of their actions. What was he doing? Where could this possibly go?

A thought quickly took shape. Whatever their differences, this wasn't fair to either of them.

He searched her face, taking in the honesty and integrity and desire he saw there. The love. Tears pricked at his eyes again. "You're so beautiful, Faith. So good and right. But what we have between us is borrowed from yesterday." Before he could stop himself, he kissed her again, then drew back. "It isn't real."

Faith's eyes clouded. She lay her hand over his heart, and he knew she must feel the way he was trembling. "It is real. As real as the boy you used to be." She framed his face with her fingers again and kissed him with a passion that took him by surprise and was almost his undoing.

"Faith," he whispered when their lips came apart for a brief moment. "What you do to me . . ."

Again and again she moved her lips over his until he thought he might scream from the feelings welling up inside him. When they came up for air, she searched his eyes for a long moment, her voice barely a whisper. "You can't have your mother and Heidi back. But I'm still here, Jordan. That's proof that God loves you, isn't it?"

A single tear spilled onto his cheek, and he shook his head. "No. Tomorrow we'll be enemies again. I'll do whatever I can to see your Jesus statue walled up forever and you'll do everything in your power to stop me. Don't you understand, Faith? The God you love, the God you serve . . . He's my enemy. I spend all my time trying to have

Him eliminated from society."

She drew back from him, open-mouthed as though she'd been slapped. And in that instant a knife twisted in Jordan's heart — and he knew the moment they'd borrowed from time was gone.

Forever.

At Jordan's words, Faith felt like a bucket of ice water had been dumped down her back. *What am I doing here, God?*

She was still reeling from their kisses, convinced of the love she still had for him, but how could she stay when he talked about God being his enemy?

What should I do?

Go, daughter . . . I will be with Jordan.

Faith wrapped her arms tightly around herself and let her gaze fall to her lap. Though she ached for Jordan, she knew now she had no right falling for him. Not when he thought of God as his enemy. *Give me the words, God . . . restore him to You . . . please, Father.*

Words began filling her heart, and she looked at Jordan through wet, blurry eyes and began to speak. " 'For I am convinced that neither death nor life, neither angels nor demons, neither the present nor the future —' "

The light in his eyes disappeared as though

his heart had closed up shop. He began to shake his head. But still the words came and Faith could do nothing but speak them clearly, with all the love she felt in her heart. " 'Nor any powers, neither height nor depth, nor anything else in all creation, will be able to separate us from the love of God that is in Christ Jesus our —' "

"Stop it!" He put his hands on her shoulders and shook her. Not hard enough to hurt her, but hard enough to silence her. Anger flashed in his eyes, and it tore at Faith's heart like nothing she'd ever felt before. "I don't want to hear that, Faith. I'm serious. God is my enemy and nothing you can say will ever change that."

Her tears came harder and she pulled loose from his grip. "I'm not the one who doesn't get it, Jordan. You loved the Lord once, and that's something He doesn't forget." A sob escaped from deep within her, and she covered her mouth with the back of her hand. "No matter what you do . . . whether you put a wall around the Jesus statue or not . . . Jesus will still love you." She stood up and took three steps back. "And so will I."

With that she turned and began jogging back to her car, crying harder, not caring that the icy night air was stinging her face as she ran. What had she been doing, kissing Jordan like that? Was she crazy? Even worse, was Jordan right? Did the boy she loved no longer exist? Jordan seemed to have grown into a man determined to remain an enemy of her God. And yet . . .

His kiss still burned on her lips, and she was suddenly furious with herself. How could she feel so deeply for him when she knew what he stood for? Her tears came in torrents, both for herself and the way she'd betrayed God. *I'm sorry, Lord. Help me pull myself together . . . help me find the pieces of my heart.* She ran faster and before she could analyze her actions further she reached her car, climbed in, and drove away.

She glanced once more toward the bench where she and Jordan had been sitting but it was empty. *Lord, help me be strong next time I see him. How can he be so wonderful and warm one minute and so intensely angry and bitter the next? And how could I let myself kiss him? Oh, Lord . . . I need to keep my focus. Don't let me be distracted by my feelings, please, Father . . .*

I have loved Jordan with an everlasting love, daughter. Even now I am calling him . . .

The words washed over Faith with holy reassurance. She nodded, grateful. Let God work with him; it was too hard a task for her.

She would continue praying for Jordan's change of heart, but she knew she needed to pray for her own as well. Especially since the memory of his kiss, his touch, was stronger than she cared to admit. After all, she would see him again in ten hours.

When they'd face each other as public enemies in the Pennsylvania State Court.

Twenty-Two

When Jordan didn't answer his motel phone all night, T. J. knew he had no choice but to drive to Bethany. The hearing was at ten that morning, and the partners had made it exceedingly clear that they doubted Jordan's intentions.

"If he spends more than thirty minutes outside his hotel room I want to know about it. If he's in love with the girl, anything could happen." Hawkins had waved his hand in the air and pointed it at T. J. "You understand me, Morris?"

T. J. had nodded. "Yes, sir."

Hawkins crashed his hand down on his desk, knocking a stack of papers onto the floor. "The last thing we need is Jordan settling for some partial wall or even no wall at all just so he and the girl can pick up where they left off, wherever that was." He stared at the others. "With all that's riding on this case, his association with this woman is flat dangerous."

Hawkins's words echoed in T. J.'s mind as he set out before sunup for Bethany. Whatever the situation, he feared Hawkins was right. Friendship notwithstanding, when the phone in Jordan's motel room went unanswered until well after midnight, T. J. felt he had no choice but to go.

He would meet Jordan at court just before the hearing and tell him he'd come for moral support. Then all T. J. could do was hope Jordan wouldn't dare make an unexpected move with his best friend and co-worker watching over his shoulder.

At eight o'clock that morning the phone rang in Peter T. Hawkins's office. It was his hot line, the number he gave only to a handful of people, including his friends in influential political circles.

"Hawkins here." He sounded more confident than he felt. The blasted statue hearing was in two hours, and Morris had already called to inform him there was trouble. Jordan had been out all night, which only added to Hawkins's mounting doubts regarding the young attorney.

"Hello, Mr. Hawkins."

He sat straighter in his chair. The voice on the other end was one that would be recognized in many political circles. Had the statue case actually gained this type of attention? Hawkins had presumed the bonus money was something only the politician's advisors knew about, but apparently not. "Hello, sir. How are you this morning?"

"Good . . . and hoping to get better. I understand you have this Jesus statue case under control."

Hawkins gulped and struggled to find his voice. "That's right."

"Good, good." The man at the other end chuckled. Hawkins could only imagine the pressure this man must be under to make a deal like this with HOUR. He held his breath as the man began to speak. "People are watching this case, Mr. Hawkins. You and the crew at HOUR have always been our most powerful allies, but it's time to raise the bar." His voice grew less friendly. "We cannot have Jesus statues standing in our public parks. Not while I'm in office." He hesitated and his voice relaxed some. "You're aware of the bonus money?"

A thin layer of perspiration broke out on Hawkins's forehead, and he wiped it with his fingertips. "Yes. It's very generous, sir."

"There's more where that came from. Private money, you understand. Nothing illegal." He chuckled again. "Just make sure the wall goes up. We'll start with statues and work our way to the churches. Isn't that right, Mr. Hawkins?"

Hawkins forced a tight-lipped laugh. "Absolutely, sir. You can count on us."

"I always have. One of my advisors will be calling just before noon for an update. Make sure it's a good one."

"Yes, sir."

The phone call was over, and Hawkins felt several sharp pains in his left shoulder. Since when did political giants get involved in cases like this? The answer was simple: Since special interest groups had gained control of the man's office.

Hawkins kneaded his shoulder and the pains eased. It was all too complicated these days, too many people making deals and manipulating court cases behind the scenes.

The bonus money flashed across the checkbook in his mind. All one million dollars of it. Hawkins eased back into his chair. Maybe the job wasn't so complicated after all. Besides, the burden lay on Jordan Riley. If the walls fell in Jericho Park it would be Riley's fault. Certainly Hawkins had done everything in his power to see victory take place. He'd gotten the Evans girl fired and given her something to think about with the call from his friend at CBS. She had to know how much power the firm wielded.

They'd done as much as they could to eliminate Faith Evans as an obstacle — short of hiring a hit on her. Hawkins chuckled under his breath. Not that he'd ever be involved in something like that. HOUR *was* a human rights group, after all.

Besides, whoever was behind the money was interested in the firm long-term. Win this case, and there'd be plenty more "bonus" money down the road . . . that was the impression Hawkins had gotten.

He drew in a deep breath. They needed to win this case. Desperately. At the thought, his shoulder began to hurt again. For the first time in his life he found himself wishing the wacky religious freaks were right, that there actually was an almighty God. Because the way public opinion was tilting in Bethany, Pennsylvania, it was beginning to look like HOUR needed more than a little blackmail and string-pulling to pull this case off.

They needed a miracle.

The key players were gathered outside the courtroom — Jordan on one side of the hallway; Faith, Joshua, and the mayor of Bethany on the other — when the clerk found them and told them the news. Judge

Webster had the flu. The hearing had been postponed for one week. A reporter from ABC, who had arrived an hour earlier, immediately sent a wire preventing what figured to be as many as a hundred journalists from wasting a trip. In addition, a bulletin went out across local television and radio, so that only a few people who failed to hear the news had to be sent home.

Jordan felt his heart sink as the clerk explained the situation. Another week. He'd have to stay in Bethany, hold press conferences, and attempt to sway public opinion for another week — all the while avoiding the one woman he couldn't stop thinking about. It was like being sentenced to a torture chamber.

He shot a discreet look at Faith, admiring the angle of her head, the way her eyes danced with life when she spoke to the older attorney. The compassion and kindness she'd shown as a child were still very much a part of her . . . but she had more fire now. His eyes traveled the length of her, taking in the way her elegant skirt swished about her ankles and clung to all the right places, the way her blond hair fell from a simple knot halfway down her back. Everything about her called to him, beckoned him in a way he was barely able to withstand.

Jordan didn't know why he was surprised. She'd always been beautiful — but back when they were friends and neighbors, he'd taken her beauty for granted. Now . . . when there was no way to bridge the distance between them, when the memory of her kiss the night before was more pressing on his mind than anything else — including the fate of the Jesus statue — now the very sight of her left him with a sense of longing and urgency he knew he could never act upon.

He let his gaze linger a moment longer, then frowned. She was keeping to herself, refusing to even glance in his direction. He didn't blame her. The things he'd told her were as true now as they'd been last night: regardless of the attraction they obviously felt for each other, there wasn't enough common ground between them to build a sand castle let alone a life together.

Jordan sighed and reached in his suit pocket for his cell phone. As he moved down the hallway, he dialed Hawkins's private office number. He leaned against the wall as the line rang twice, but before it could ring a third time he heard footsteps.

Jordan looked up. "T. J.?" At the sight of his partner, he felt the blood leave his face. What possible reason would T. J. have for showing up at the hearing? *He must've left*

New York before sunup. His cheeks grew hot and anger like a mounting storm began to build. He disconnected the phone call and waited for an explanation.

"Hey, Jordan." T. J. looked around as he closed the distance between them, breathless from the walk. "Where's the crowd?"

Jordan's mind raced. One of two things had to be happening back at the office. Either the partners had suddenly lost confidence in him and sent T. J. to baby-sit, or there was a serious lack of communication between him and the others. Either option made Jordan's skin crawl.

One thing was certain: he had no intention of holding a conversation with T. J. in earshot of Faith and the others. He motioned to his friend and they found a place at the end of the hall, near a boxy windowsill. Both lawyers set their briefcases down as Jordan stared at T. J. and swore under his breath. "Here to take over?"

T. J.'s eyes were unnaturally wide and his smile looked painted on. "Of course not. Hawkins just thought you could use a little support. This is the big day, right?"

Jordan didn't blink. "It was postponed a week. Judge got sick." He paused, his eyes never leaving T. J's. "Don't lie to me, Teej. You didn't get in your car at four this morning and drive all the way to Bethany to wave at me from the back row. Tell me why you're here."

For the briefest moment it looked like T. J. was going to keep up the charade. He opened his mouth and was about to speak when his smile faded. Then, like a week-old helium balloon, his shoulders sagged and he thrust his hands in his pants pocket, shifting his gaze so that he stared out the window. "You weren't in your room last night." His voice was monotone, a statement of resignation more than anything else.

Jordan leaned in close, wondering just how much about this case was being discussed behind his back. "Teej, buddy, I didn't tell you where I was staying."

T. J. nodded, his eyes still locked on something outside the window, a faraway look on his face. "Hawkins told me."

Jordan felt like he was trapped in some strange dream. He hadn't told Hawkins where he was staying, either. Of course there were only three motels in Bethany, so Jordan wouldn't have been hard to find. But the idea of a partner at HOUR — one of the top legal talents in all the country — trailing him like some two-bit private investigator sent a chill down his spine. He grabbed T. J.'s arm, tightening his grip until his friend made eye contact with him. "You drove down here because I was out last night?" Jordan released a single chuckle as he let go of T. J. "Call me crazy, but I'm not seeing the connection."

"If you tell Hawkins I told you, we'll both be fired."

T. J.'s flat voice told Jordan his suspicions were right. Hawkins — and maybe the other partners — didn't trust him with the Bethany case. The truth made his blood boil, and he could feel his face growing hot.

He spoke in a barely contained whisper, sliding the words through lips tight with fury. "I'm waiting."

T. J. sighed and leaned against the windowsill. He was still having trouble making eye contact. "They want this case bad, Jordan. There's a lot of . . . *bonus money* at stake."

Jordan remembered the ten thousand dollars he'd been promised. "You know about it?"

"Yeah." T. J. huffed. "I know about it."

Jordan felt like a man in a foreign country trying to understand a language he'd never heard before. "Where's it coming from?"

"From the top, Jordan." T. J. narrowed his eyes, and Jordan could see his friend's reluctance to talk.

"Hawkins?"

"A lot higher than that."

"Meaning what? And how much is there? Why this case?" Jordan fired the questions as quickly as they came to mind. He glanced down the hallway and saw Faith and the others leaving, making their way toward the stairs. *Can't you even turn around and look at me, Faith?*

But she was caught up in a conversation with the mayor and never glanced his direction. When she was gone, Jordan turned his attention back to T. J. "I need answers, Teej. Tell me what you know."

His friend shrugged again and shook his head. "It's political."

"Political? You mean someone from the state?"

T. J. nodded. "Someone very high up the ladder."

Again there was no way Jordan could make sense of the situation. High up the ladder? What stake could anyone at the state level possibly have in the Jesus statue case? "Okay, give me the name."

"I don't know. Honest, Jordan." T. J. squirmed and shifted positions. "You gotta believe me."

Jordan exhaled slowly and gazed out the window before turning back to his friend.

"So you're saying the money came from an elected official?"

"I don't know how much HOUR's getting, but you have to win the case." He hesitated, and Jordan had the distinct feeling he was being lied to. "A permanent wall needs to go up around the Jesus statue or the whole thing's off."

"And that's why you're here?" His anger burned still hotter. If someone with significant political influence and financial backing felt it was important to win the Bethany case, Jordan should have been in meetings with Hawkins daily. It made no sense that T. J. was involved in those meetings instead. After all, the Jesus statue was Jordan's idea.

"Hawkins asked me to call you last night, but you were out. He got worried and told me to come. Wanted to make sure . . . you know, someone hadn't gotten to you."

Jordan's astonishment came out as another laugh. "You guys watch too many movies, Teej. This is a small-town case. I don't care how much national attention it gets, no one's hiring a hit on me." He crossed his arms. "What's the real reason? Hawkins didn't think I could pull out a victory?"

"No, Jordan. I swear. That wasn't it . . ." T. J. sounded like a bad actor, and Jordan was suddenly out of patience with him.

"Look, friend, why don't you get in your car and drive back to New York. Tell my boss that I've got things perfectly under control, thank you. And that I'm single and can stay out all night if I want to. Tell him if he thinks I need a backup he should say so to my face. If not, he should keep his nose out of my cases. The only reason I'm here at all is because he ordered it."

T. J. looked like he had pebbles in his shoes. "And . . . uh . . . what about the woman?"

Jordan lowered his eyebrows and felt the knot in his stomach grow. "Faith? The woman who bought the park property? The newscaster?"

His friend nodded. "Is she . . . you know, are the two of you seeing each other?"

A feeling of betrayal worked its way through Jordan's veins. "Is *that* what this is all about? Hawkins thinks I'm siding with the enemy?"

T. J. grimaced. "No, not at all. I was just asking. You told me you two used to be friends."

Jordan pictured himself kissing Faith in the park the night before. "Yeah, when we were thirteen. Obviously the word back at the office is that I'm caving in, lost in love, and suddenly inept at pulling off a simple separation case." He leveled his gaze at T. J. "Tell me something, Teej . . . how did Hawkins know about the girl? Because he asked me the same thing last week."

A knowing look took over his friend's features. "You don't think I . . . Jordan, I wouldn't have told him something like that. He must have guessed. Everyone knows you used to live here . . . Faith's a local girl . . . it wouldn't have been a stretch to think you might have known her."

Again Jordan had the strong sense T. J. was lying. He gestured toward the stairs. "Go home, Teej. And don't forget something . . ."

T. J. was already starting to retreat, taking small backward steps toward the stairs as though being around Jordan was more stress than he could handle. "What? Just say the word, buddy. Anything I can do for you . . ."

Jordan paused, assaulted by doubts, and studied T. J. one last time. "Don't forget you're supposed to be my friend."

Considering the way she'd come into the world, little Jordan Lee Benson turned out to be a sweet, content newborn, sleeping through the night almost from the beginning and giving Heidi's body time to recuperate from the traumatic delivery. She and Charles moved to Bethany on schedule, and Charles hired a housekeeper to help unpack the boxes and keep up the dishes and laundry. That Wednesday morning was the woman's first day off, and Heidi had decided to take it slow.

She'd already fed Jordan Lee, and the baby was down for her morning nap, giving Heidi a couple hours to herself. She sipped a cup of decaf and looked for something to read in yesterday's pile of mail. Junk mail . . . coupon flyers . . . advertisements . . . She scanned each item and tossed the stack in the trash. Then her eyes fell on the local paper. Photographers had been by Charles's office and taken pictures of him for a clinic ad announcing his arrival on staff. Wasn't that supposed to run on Wednesdays?

She slid the paper closer and tried to make sense of the photo on the front page. It looked like a construction site — some sort of partially finished building made of what looked like plywood. She found the headline and read it out loud: "Hearing on Jesus Statue Postponed."

She knit her eyebrows together and found the first paragraph. "A hearing to decide whether or not walls around the Jesus statue in Bethany's Jericho Park will become permanent was postponed yesterday. The hearing was rescheduled for Tuesday at which time court officials expect to have nearly a hundred members of the media and more than a thousand local residents in attendance for the final decision on what has become a case of national interest . . .”

Heidi sat up straighter in her chair. The Jesus statue had walls around it? Why hadn't she noticed? Who had put them up, and how had the case drawn national attention when she was only reading about it now? The answer was obvious. She hadn't so much as watched a news program or looked at a paper since having Jordan Lee.

Sadness like a dark storm cloud came over Heidi's morning. Was that what life had come to? A statue that had stood practically forever in a city park had to be removed because it depicted Jesus Christ? She thought about her brother, about how much time he'd spent at the park, staring at the statue. He would have been devastated to see it surrounded by plywood. She rested her head on her fingertips as she continued reading the article.

The information was both awful and fascinating. Joshua Nunn, a local attorney who headed up an organization called the Religious Freedom Institute was involved, as well as a former newscaster, Faith Evans. She had come forward and purchased the park land in an effort to keep the statue standing. The article said Faith had lost her job as a result of purchasing the land.

She thought about that. *Faith . . . Faith . . . Faith.* Hadn't Heidi and her family known a Faith back when they lived in Bethany? It began coming back to her, and she suddenly remembered. Faith Moses, that was it. She was the girl who lived next door, Jordan's friend. Heidi's eyes darted back to the place in the article where it listed the woman's last name and her heart sank. Faith Evans. It had to be someone different. Too many years had passed and besides, there were lots of women named Faith.

Heidi found her place in the article. The entire situation started because of a lawsuit filed by an attorney from the HOUR organization. Heidi rolled her eyes and huffed softly. The HOUR organization was always meddling in other people's business and calling it human rights. What *right* was it of theirs to come to Bethany and sue the city over something that had never involved them in the first place? She continued reading. The attorney's name was . . . was . . .

Heidi's breath caught in her throat. She felt as though she were free-falling from thirty thousand feet. It took ten seconds to remind herself to breathe, to assure herself that it was only some strange, twisted coincidence. Obviously it wasn't him. Her brother had been killed sixteen years earlier in the camp accident. But that didn't change the way her body reacted to what she was seeing in print before her.

The attorney who wanted the statue walled up was a man who worked for HOUR. A man named Jordan Riley.

Jordan Riley.

Heidi let her eyes settle on his name as the memories came back again, images of her brother sheltering her in his strong arms at their mother's funeral, of him holding her that awful afternoon on Oak Street when the state social workers took her away. Of the terrible moment when her foster father told her about the accident. She looked at the attorney's name again.

Jordan Riley.

Heidi blinked and looked away. It was an odd coincidence, but that was all. Her Jordan was dead. And if he *had* been alive, he would have been fighting alongside Faith Evans, whoever she was. He loved the Jesus statue as much as anyone in Bethany.

Besides, there was no way on earth Jordan would have represented a law firm like

HOUR. Not after the way he'd loved the Lord, the way he'd trusted in Him that last year they were together. Jordan's faith had been rock-solid, no doubt. It was something Heidi remembered most about her brother.

She finished reading the article, folded the newspaper, and bowed her head.

Lord, the people of Bethany need Your help. Please be with the judge as he has an important decision to make. Let him see with Your eyes, reason with Your heart at the hearing next week. And be with this Jordan Riley, whoever he is. Help him to know that You're real and that You love him. Most of all work in his heart so that —

Jordan Lee's hungry cry interrupted the prayer, and Heidi finished quickly as she headed toward the baby's room. Ten minutes later she was feeding her tiny daughter, cooing at her and reveling in the joy of their shared private moments. When the feeding was finished she changed the baby's diaper, did laundry, and fixed herself a chicken sandwich. By one o'clock, as Heidi finally fell into bed for a much-needed nap, the walled-in Jesus statue, the woman named Faith, and the confused young attorney named Jordan Riley, were the farthest things from her mind.

TWENTY-THREE

Rain beat a steady rhythm on the town of Bethany that Wednesday. With almost a week before the rescheduled hearing, Faith decided to take in an afternoon movie with Rosa. That left the morning with nothing to do but imagine how the next few weeks might play out. With any luck, the time would pass quickly. The peaceful protest wasn't scheduled until Friday night, when a dozen churches from the Philadelphia area had promised to join the people of Bethany in an effort to pray together about the judge's decision.

Things had been so crazy that Faith had found little time to read her Bible — something she'd enjoyed doing since childhood. Reading Scripture might be a chore for some people, a duty that went along with the calling to follow Christ. But for Faith it had always been more than that. The Bible was alive and active, and no matter what issue she faced, God's Word had something to say about it. She couldn't remember how many times as a little girl she'd run through the house looking for her father to show him some Scripture he'd probably seen a hundred times.

"Can you believe it, Daddy? Like Jesus wrote it there just for me!"

Faith's fervor hadn't diminished any during the years Jordan lived next door. In fact, until his mother got sick, Jordan seemed to share her enthusiasm. Faith could hear him still, commenting on various Bible stories while they sat side by side on her parents' sofa. "When I read the Bible it's like I have this calm feeling. Like God has everything in control."

Faith had already showered, and her damp hair hung loosely down her back. That was it really, wasn't it? God had it all under control. She thought about the sermon that past Sunday. They'd been reading in the book of Luke, the twenty-second chapter, where Judas made plans to betray Jesus and Jesus made plans to have the Last Supper with His disciples.

Faith settled into her father's favorite rocker and opened her Bible to that section of Scripture again. On the surface, it looked like everything was falling apart for Jesus.

Days earlier He'd come into town on the back of a donkey to the shouts of praise from hundreds of thousands of people. Crowds openly calling Him King and acknowledging Him for who He was. But now His entire ministry seemed to be unraveling. The devil — who had been looking for a chance to bring down the Savior since Jesus' birth thirty-three years earlier — saw a weak link in Judas Iscariot. And so, as Scripture taught, Satan caused Judas to accept a bribe from the chief priests in exchange for betraying his Teacher.

Faith loved the way Pastor Todd Pynch taught the story. He smiled often and even laughed on occasion, so that Faith and everyone in the small congregation felt as though they were there alongside Jesus, walking near the donkey, sitting across the table in the upper room.

Immediately after Judas's decision to betray Jesus, the Lord made plans with two of his trusted followers to prepare for the Passover meal. Faith smiled as she recalled Pastor Pynch's comments: "Notice how Judas was left out of the loop as they prepared that meal. Nothing happened that weekend that wasn't exactly as Jesus had planned it. His life wasn't taken from Him. He gave it up willingly."

The story brought Faith as much comfort now as it had last Sunday. Especially given her current situation. She was a marked woman, with no likely prospects for a television news job unless she was willing to somehow back out of the Jesus statue case — which she wasn't. There were no signs of potential adoptive parents for Rosa Lee, and Faith's childhood friend had not only turned on God, but because of his bitterness, was willing even to stand against her in court. Meanwhile a statue of Jesus Christ, her loving Lord, could very likely wind up hidden behind a brick wall.

Indeed, things seemed to be spinning in all the wrong directions.

But the truth was something altogether different. Something Joshua had tried to explain to her, the very point the minister had reiterated at church last Sunday.

God was in control.

Wherever there were people who loved Him, who lived according to His truth, God would continue to work all things to the good. Even in this.

Faith closed her Bible and stared outside at the garden her father had planted. Shrubs and rosebushes stood barren but for a few tenacious buds. *You were in control back when Jordan's mother died too, right, God?*

She flipped to the very last page in her Bible, the blank space after the concordance and maps and historical facts. The place for personal notes. Faith had gotten the Bible for her thirteenth birthday, and back then, back when the Lord didn't seem to be hearing Jordan, she'd written her thoughts on that last page.

It had been years since she'd read what was written there, but today, in the silence of her parents' house, she was drawn back the way a moth is drawn to a porch light. She was suddenly desperate to remember her little-girl heart and the way she'd felt when life was falling apart for Jordan Riley.

She'd written dates next to her earliest entries; her words scribbled in the smallest print possible. *Nov. 3, 1985 — Why is this happening, God? I told Jordan to read the verse that says, "Whatever you ask in my name, I will do it . . ." But his mom is still sick. Help me understand . . .*

And another entry six weeks later: *Jordan's mother died . . . his sister got taken away . . . Didn't we pray hard enough, Lord? Didn't You hear us?*

Faith let her eyes read over those entries again and again until tears clouded her vision. Suddenly she understood her own motive for waging battle on behalf of the Jesus statue. It was as clear as if someone had lit a match in the darkest cavern of her heart. The losses Jordan suffered that fall had changed her as much as they'd changed him. Indeed, they'd affected everything about their lives since then.

For Jordan, the unanswered questions and bitter seeds of doubt had sprouted into a full-blown war that raged in his heart to this day. He'd taken up his position, deciding that God either didn't exist or He was the enemy.

Faith's reaction had been the exact opposite.

At first, with no answers to anchor to, Faith had lived life with a lack of conviction. She spoke like a believer, attended church, and read her Bible, but her life choices bore out something altogether different. The hard decisions — what to do when Mike Dillon pressured her, when to take a stand in her role as television anchor, whether to adopt Rosa Lee — were decisions she made without seeking God. Instead they were decisions she made out of fear. Fear of losing Mike, losing her job, failing Rosa Lee.

And now, for the first time, she understood why.

Deep down in the hidden places of her

heart Faith had been afraid that if she depended on God, He would let her down . . . just as He'd let Jordan down the winter of 1985. Without consciously acknowledging it, she'd decided long ago it was better not to ask much of God. And she'd built her life around that philosophy . . . until the Jesus statue came under attack.

In light of her father's death and the judge's mandate that the statue be removed, Faith had unwittingly recognized it was time. Time to take God out of the closet and see what He might do in response to her prayers.

That was why this case meant so much to her. She desperately wanted to believe again, the way she'd believed in the days before Jordan's mother got sick. The Jesus statue wasn't the only thing with walls around it. Faith had put walls around God Himself. Protective walls, so that the Lord of her childhood might never be called upon to do anything miraculous, anything that might not come to pass and cause Faith to be disappointed. Anything that might put Him in a bad light.

The rain was coming harder now, and tears came from the depths of Faith's soul. She ran her fingers over her neatly written words, the painfully penned cries that had come from her childlike heart. She would never know this side of heaven why God had taken Jordan's mother, why life had been so hard on him back then. But she knew what Scripture taught. She closed her eyes and let the verse from John wash over her soul: "In this world you will have trouble. But take heart! I have overcome the world."

That was it, wasn't it?

Jesus had overcome the world. Regardless of how things turned out here and now, He was in control. Just like He'd been back when Judas agreed to betray Him. Nothing, not death or anger or lawsuits or lost jobs or homeless children, nothing could derail God's plans. The revelation felt like someone had lifted a truck from Faith's shoulders, and she desperately wished the same for Jordan.

A knock at the door pulled Faith back to reality. She closed her Bible, thanking God for letting her finally understand the fear that had eaten at her all her life, the poor decisions she'd made as a young adult, and her current determination to fight for what was right. She padded across the living room and opened the front door.

What she saw sent her heart spinning into her throat.

"Jordan . . ." He was so handsome, so much like the boy he'd been all those years ago. And this time the hard edges around his eyes were gone. She composed herself and held his gaze for a moment before speaking. *God, I don't know why You brought him here, but use me . . . give me the words to say so that maybe he could understand You better.* She swallowed hard and motioned toward the living room. "Come in."

Jordan had debated long and hard about making the trip to Faith's house, but in the end he knew he had no choice. With her skills as a reporter and her status as the town's most favorite person, she was possibly the only one who could help him find the files. And they needed to be found. Ever since their conversation the other day he'd wondered if somehow Heidi had gotten wrong information. If she believed — wherever she was — that he was dead, buried these past sixteen years. The visit would be purely informational, he'd told himself. He'd ask Faith for help, but avoid anything else.

Then she opened the door — and he had to order his emotions back into place. What kind of fool was he to fight against a woman like Faith Evans? Her eyes were so blue he felt sucked into them, and he struggled to remember why he'd come at all. She interrupted his thoughts with her invitation.

"Thanks." He wiped his feet on the outdoor mat and stepped inside. "Sorry to bug you at home."

Faith crossed her arms and lowered her head, her eyes lifted to his expectantly.

Jordan felt like a blushing schoolboy in her presence and he forced himself to speak. "I'm . . . sorry I didn't talk to you the other day at court."

She shrugged, her face still full of questions. Obviously he hadn't come to tell her that.

"Is your mother home?" Through all that had happened those past few months in Bethany he was sorry he hadn't seen Faith's mom, the woman who had been so helpful those last weeks before his own mother died.

"No." Faith's voice was quiet, guarded. "She's still in Chicago."

He nodded and studied his wet shoes as the tension between them grew. He wanted to take her in his arms and apologize for the other night, tell her that he needed her, and beg her not to hate him for his views against God. But he knew the idea was ridiculous. If he was going to get her help with the files, he'd better ask her now, before she kicked him out. He lifted his eyes to hers and held her gaze. "I need your help."

She stepped back and something in her features softened. "Take off your shoes." She leaned against the wall, her head angled in a way that reminded him of the young girl she'd been. "We can talk in the living room."

Jordan slipped off his loafers and followed her, waiting until she settled into the recliner before taking the chair beside her. "I want to see Heidi's file . . . in case the state gave her the wrong information."

"About the accident?" Faith's tone was hesitant, but at least she hadn't asked him to leave.

"Right. I've been to the courthouse and the records are sealed. I guess the file might even be at a different office now." He shrugged. "No one gives me a straight answer."

Faith nodded and shot a look at the ceiling. After a moment her gaze returned to his. "What about *your* file? Have you looked at that?"

Jordan settled back in his chair and stared at her. "Why my file? There wouldn't be anything there about Heidi."

"No, but there'd be information about you. Like whether the state thinks you died."

Jordan shook his head, trying to follow

her reasoning. "No, because the state sent me to the next boys' camp."

"Right, but it was in a different state. It's possible they opened a new file on you there and never corrected the one in Pennsylvania."

Jordan felt the smallest ray of hope pierce his heart. "I have nothing to do today or tomorrow and I thought . . ." He exhaled slowly and dropped his gaze to the floor. Why should she help him now, after he'd been so rude the other night, letting her run off without even trying to stop her.

Before he could voice his question, before he could excuse himself and tell her to forget he'd ever come, he felt her hand on his. He caught her look and saw a love he hadn't known since leaving Oak Street. A love for which he had no earthly explanation. "Jordan, I understand your political stance. I know we're public enemies at this point, but that doesn't change who I am inside. Or who you are." She smiled through eyes wet with tears. "I'll do whatever I can to help you."

They took his car and entered the courthouse thirty minutes later.

Faith was careful not to let her emotions get the upper hand, not to let Jordan too close. She did not want a repeat of the tender, stolen moments they'd exchanged the other night — not when she knew there was no future for Jordan and her. Not together, anyway.

As they parked the car, Jordan turned to her, and she could see the apology in his eyes. "This could be uncomfortable for you."

She understood. People would recognize them and wonder why they were together. Faith refused to acknowledge her concerns about the matter. "For you, too."

The muscles in his jaw tensed, and he caught her gaze and held it. "I couldn't care less what people think about me."

Faith wondered at the strength of his statement. She'd seen him talking to a man who was obviously a colleague the other day at court. Clearly the case held great significance to him both professionally and personally. But that wasn't her concern. She cast him a guarded smile and opened the car door. "Okay, let's go."

Jordan wore a sweatshirt, blue jeans, and a baseball cap, and Faith figured the lack of a suit would help hide his identity. He kept his gaze on the floor, the bill of his cap down as they made their way to the front desk. Faith recognized the woman at the counter and smiled. "Hey, Cheri, how're you doing?"

The woman's eyes instantly lit up, and she grinned at Faith. "I've seen you on TV and in the papers, Faith. Everyone's so proud of you . . . giving up your job and all." The woman leaned forward as though she had an important secret. "The whole town's rooting for you."

The woman's words warmed Faith's heart, and again she thought of the revelation she'd had earlier that morning. No matter how it looked, God was in control. "Thanks, Cheri."

The woman glanced at Jordan, who was standing a ways off looking at a pamphlet he'd picked up from the counter. Faith was quick to explain. "He's an old friend."

Apparently Cheri didn't recognize him, and she turned her attention back to Faith. "So what can I do for you?"

"Well . . ." Faith moved as close as she could against the counter. She didn't want one of the other clerks to hear her request. Cheri was an acquaintance from high school, and Faith was fairly certain the woman would get whatever files Faith needed. Even if it meant bending a rule or two. "I need to see a couple of foster care files. They might be sealed, but I'll only take a few minutes with them."

Nervousness flashed in Cheri's eyes, but she nodded. "Okay, I'll see what I can do. What're the names?"

Faith paused. "Heidi and Jordan Riley. They were brother and sister."

As soon as Faith said the names, Cheri's eyes opened wide. "The same Jordan Riley who's attacking our town?"

Faith had hoped the woman wouldn't ask, but now she had no choice but to be honest. She tried to sound confident. "Exactly."

Cheri's eyebrows bunched in the center of her forehead. "Does this have something to do with the Jesus statue case?"

Adrenaline flooded Faith's bloodstream as she searched for an honest answer. Did it have something to do with the case? Well, if the files helped Jordan find Heidi and if that, in turn, helped him get past his anger with God . . . then it would have everything to do with the case. "Yes." She nodded her head firmly. "Yes, it does."

That was all she needed to say. Cheri's eyes danced, and Faith could see she was grateful to be part of Faith's plans to outdo Bethany's enemy. "Two separate files, right? One for each of them?"

Faith nodded. "Right."

"Okay, wait here." She cast a glance at the workers stationed on either side of her and lowered her voice to a whisper. "I'll see what I can find."

Cheri disappeared, and Jordan was immediately at her side. "You asked for both?" He kept his gaze fixed on the voting brochure still in his hands but she could hear the disbelief and gratitude in his voice.

"Can't hurt." She nodded toward a counter with other pamphlets and information. "Keep busy. The last thing I want is her recognizing you."

Several minutes went by before Cheri returned. She had two folders tucked under her right arm. She approached the counter with a forced air of nonchalance and slipped them over to Faith as quickly as she could. "Twenty minutes, Faith." She gave Faith a wink. "The supervisor'll be back after that, and I need them put away. She'd have my head on a platter if she found out what I was doing."

"Thanks." Faith swept the folders up against her body and turned to leave. She didn't check to see if Jordan was behind her, but she could feel him there, a few steps back. As she made her way back outside she kept her face focused on the ground ahead of her. Now that she had the files, she wanted to avoid being recognized. Two minutes later she and Jordan were back in his car.

Jordan's features were pale. "I can't believe it was so easy. I've tried getting my hands on Heidi's file every year since I was twenty-two."

"Drive to the back of the side lot. No one parks there." Faith kept the files tightly on her lap while Jordan did as she said.

When they'd found a spot far from other cars, Jordan turned to her, his eyes filled with wonder. "No matter what these files contain . . . you'll never know how much this means to me, Faith."

She could feel her heart getting sucked into the moment and she steeled herself, giving him only a quick smile and pushing the folders into his hands. "Read them. We have less than twenty minutes."

Jordan looked at his file first. There were several entries beginning with the report from what appeared to be a neighbor. It stated that Jordan and Heidi were living alone after the death of their mother. He'd always wondered who'd reported them, but the man's name didn't look familiar. It didn't matter. The neighbor wasn't to blame; certainly he'd had good intentions. State officials would have figured it out eventually.

Jordan scanned the pages as quickly as he

could, flipping past the report detailing the day Jordan and Heidi were brought into care and the one that came a few days later: *"Jordan is a very unhappy boy. He talks about his sister constantly and threatens to run away. He appears to be a troublemaker."* For a brief instant, Jordan wanted to cry for the boy he'd been and the way the state officials had wrongly labeled him. There hadn't been a trace of troublemaker in him. Just a brokenhearted boy who had promised his dying mother he'd take care of his sister.

He flipped a few more pages and saw the entry when he'd finally made good on his threat to run away from the temporary foster home: *"Police say Jordan was belligerent and borderline violent. He kept insisting that his sister lived nearby and she needed him. Social worker says the girl is adjusting fine and that a visit will be arranged sometime in the next two weeks."*

"Anything good?" Faith's voice brought him back to reality, and Jordan shook his head. He'd almost forgotten she was still in the car.

"Not yet."

"Fifteen minutes, okay?"

"Okay." He skipped a few entries and found the one marked Accident Report. The hairs on his arms stood up as he searched the tiny fields of information looking for a sign, something to confirm that his condition had been wrongly reported. Finally, at the bottom of the document, he found what he was looking for. In a section marked Condition of Child was written one word: Deceased.

Deceased . . . deceased . . . deceased . . .

Jordan's eyes moved over the word again and again until he felt sick to his stomach. A note was attached after the report: *"Collapsed cave accident claimed the lives of numerous boys at the camp including Jordan Riley. State to investigate. Case closed."*

It was the last notation in the file.

"It's right here . . ." He pointed to the sheet and angled it so Faith could read the important parts. "They . . . they think I'm dead."

Faith stared at the report, her face a mask of concern. "Your active file must be in New Jersey." She sighed. "That happens sometimes. The system has too many files and when someone gets something wrong — especially if the subject moves out of state — sometimes the error is never found."

Jordan stared at the entry and his hands began to tremble. The real answers lay in the other folder — Heidi's file. He closed his own and handed it back to Faith. Then he did what he'd wanted to do for sixteen years — open the document that would give him a window to Heidi's other life, the one she had lived since that awful afternoon when the state worker took her away.

He drew a steadying breath and began reading. The reports were arranged in chronological order, stapled to the inside so that they could be read correctly. He saw entries similar to those in his file — a report from the neighbor stating that a brother and sister were living alone, the report when she was taken into custody, and a report from the first foster home where she'd been taken. Jordan read every word, soaking it in, desperate to know what had happened to her.

"Heidi is very cooperative. She is sad about the loss of her mother and talks of wanting to see her brother. But she has made great strides in getting along with her foster family. She is agreeable and despite her age would make an excellent candidate for adoption."

She was always such a good girl. Of course she'd been compliant. She'd been promised a reunion with Jordan, guaranteed that the two of them would be together again. She'd probably figured it would happen faster if she got along with her foster parents. Tears burned at Jordan's eyes and he blinked them back. He had no patience for blurred vision. Not now when he needed to see every stroke of the pen.

He scanned over three more similar reports and found one that coincided with the date he'd been sent to the boys' camp: *"Heidi's brother, Jordan Riley, was caught after running away from his foster home. He is considered unstable and a threat to his sister's security. He has been placed at Southridge Boys' Camp until further notice. This worker no longer recommends that Jordan have scheduled visits with his sister."*

Jordan gritted his teeth as a tear landed squarely on the report. How *dare* a stranger make a recommendation like that? What did a social worker know about Jordan or the relationship he and Heidi shared? He wished he could find the man today . . . he'd grab him by the collar and —

Jordan dismissed the thought. There wasn't time to waste hating people who no longer existed. This was about Heidi and him and no one else. He flipped the page and saw an entry marked Special Report. His heart thudded in his chest as he let his eyes work their way down the page. The report detailed how Heidi had been given the news that her brother had been in an accident at Southridge Boys' Camp: *"Heidi cried for several hours and asked if she could go to the hospital to see her brother. At this time Jordan Riley's status — whether he survived the accident or not — is unclear."*

Jordan turned the page, barely aware that he was holding his breath. The next page told him all he needed to know. It was another special report and it indicated that Heidi had been told the news: Her brother had been killed in a collapsed cave incident at Southridge Boys' Camp. *"Heidi is very upset and had to be sedated in order to sleep. State worker recommends extended counseling to deal with issues of grief and loss."*

The words seared Jordan's heart like a branding iron, filling in the places that had only been chasms of darkness and uncertainty. So it was true after all; so soon after losing their mother Heidi had been forced to deal with Jordan's death as well. Tears coursed down Jordan's face and he let his head hang for a moment. When he looked up again, he showed the report to Faith.

She read it and then looked up at him, her eyes wet too. "Jordan, it's awful. All this time —" She reached for his hand, much the way a friend might reach out in the face of bad news. "No wonder she hasn't looked for you."

The missing pieces of his past were filling

in quickly, but still there was a part Jordan wanted. "How much time?"

"Seven minutes."

Jordan nodded and flipped quickly through the reports, scanning the entries describing how well Heidi was responding to counseling, how she appeared to be bonding with her social worker, and how a placement had been suggested. Then abruptly he was at the last entry: *"Transfer was made to a permanent foster-adopt home. State workers believe Heidi will make a complete and successful adjustment and that adoption will be completed within the year."* In the place designated for the adoptive parents' names, there was just one word scribbled:

Morand.

"Morand?" Jordan practically shouted the word. He closed the file and smacked it against his thigh. "How is *that* supposed to help me find her?"

Faith squeezed his hand, released it, and folded her fingers together in her lap once more. "It isn't much to go on."

Jordan turned to the back of the file and scanned the last entry one more time. "No address, no phone number. For all I know they live at the other end of the state or halfway across the world." Frustration grabbed him like a vise grip and he felt like he was suffocating under a blanket-sized piece of plastic wrap. "That was fifteen years ago. There's no way I could find her now."

For all the answers the files provided, in some ways it was worse for Jordan than if he'd never seen them at all because now there truly was no hope. Heidi was gone from his life forever. Another wave of tears came, and he closed his eyes. Without warning, his mother's voice came back to him. *"Pray, Jordan . . . don't ever stop praying . . . don't ever stop praying."*

"Jordan —" Faith's voice interrupted his memories — "I know you don't believe in what I'm about to do, but it's all I know."

He opened his eyes and watched her bow her head, her heart and mind focused on a God he'd spent half his life fighting against. How had she known what he was thinking? That his mother's dying words on prayer had been rattling through his mind?

"Lord, we're out of options. You know Jordan's heart . . . the loss he's already suffered."

She paused, as though searching for the right words. The idea of Faith praying when it could not possibly do any good reminded Jordan of his mother again, her unwavering beliefs even on her deathbed.

Faith's voice rose a notch. "We have nowhere to turn now, no way to find Jordan's sister. Please, Father, bring them back together. I don't know how You're going to do it, Lord, but right here . . . right now . . . I thank You for what miracle You're working in this. No matter what happens, God, I trust You. And I'll always love you. In Jesus' name, amen."

She opened her eyes, and the light he saw there was too much for him. He shifted his attention to the folder in his hands. "I appreciate what you're trying to do, Faith, but there's no point."

Faith sighed hard and leaned back against the headrest, her eyes fixed somewhere on the ceiling of Jordan's car. "I don't understand why your mother died, Jordan. Or why Heidi was told you were killed in the accident. But I know the God I believe in is real." She was crying now, and the gentleness of a moment earlier was replaced by something Jordan couldn't quite identify. Anger maybe, or a deep, unquenchable fear. She stared at him, her eyes begging him to understand. "If I'm wrong about God, if your mom was wrong . . . what have we lost?" She let her question sink in. "But if you're wrong, Jordan . . ."

There was no need to finish her statement;

he'd heard it before both from high schoo and college acquaintances, and always he'c had an answer for them: *"I'd rather live ɛ truth that was doomed than a life of hope based on lies."*

This time, though, the words wouldn't come. It was as though the combination o: reading about Heidi and remembering his mother while sharing the intimate space of his car's front seat with Faith was too much for him. He handed Heidi's file back to Faith and gripped the steering wheel with both hands. Then he looked at Faith anc said the only thing he could think to say.

"Let's get the files back."

Twenty-Four

On the surface there wasn't any reason why Joshua Nunn should think the phone call strange. After all, Faith was at the center of one of the most fascinating religious rights cases ever. In fact, it wasn't so much the type of call or even the caller's voice that stuck with Joshua hours later.

It was the timing.

He'd been having a midday quiet time with God, alone in his office, wondering what more he could possibly do to convince the judge that a ten-foot high wall was unreasonable. The Scripture that day was from the book of Joshua, and it confirmed everything the Lord had been laying on his heart since he'd first heard about the case: "Be strong and courageous. God will go before you. You will not have to fight this battle . . . the place where you are standing is holy ground."

The verses all seemed to run together, lifting Joshua and taking away his fear. He had no idea how God was going to pull off a victory, but he believed with all his heart that somehow the Lord would come out a winner. Even if it didn't look that way to the public.

That afternoon he'd felt compelled to pray for wisdom. Like he'd done so many times in his life, he slid to his knees, closed his eyes, and raised his hands as high toward heaven as he could. "Lord, show me the way. I've done all I can do and still HOUR has the advantage. If there's something I'm missing, some way that victory might belong to You, Your people, show me now, Lord. I'm almost out of t—"

The phone rang before he could finish the word. Joshua did not immediately see the interruption as an answer to prayer, but rather as one in a series of distractions that were a regular part of his life lately. He quickly finished his talk with God and answered the phone.

"Religious Freedom Institute, Joshua Nunn."

"Uh . . . yes, I'm looking for Faith Evans." The woman seemed nervous, not sure of herself. "I got your number from information and thought maybe . . . is there some way you could get her a message?"

Joshua scooted onto the edge of his chair and forced himself to change gears. "Faith doesn't work here, if that's what you mean. But I can get a message to her."

"Are you the . . . the attorney representing the city of Bethany?"

The woman was obviously a fan of some kind, calling to wish them God's blessings or offer prayer support. Joshua inhaled slowly. "Yes, ma'am." He didn't want to seem rude but he had no time to waste on the phone. "Why don't you give me your name and number, and I'll give Faith the message?"

There was a pause and again Joshua had the sense the woman was uptight about something. "My name's Heidi Benson." She rattled off her phone number with what seemed like a sense of urgency. "I'd really like to talk to Faith about the case. I . . . I used to live in Bethany a long time ago and the statue meant a great deal to my mother."

Joshua's heart went out to the woman. 'I'll give her the message this afternoon."

Long after the phone call ended, Joshua was haunted by something in the woman's voice. It was a feeling that was completely unfounded, yet it remained. Joshua tried reaching Faith seven times before she finally answered the phone at just before five o'clock.

"Hello?" She sounded relaxed and upbeat, and Joshua was relieved. Faith had been under too much pressure lately, and he knew she was operating on sheer Holy Spirit power.

"You've been busy today." Joshua didn't want to question her about her absence. With everything going on, she deserved time to herself. "I've been calling you all afternoon."

"I took Rosa to the movies." She seemed breathless, as though she'd just come in the door. "It's snowing outside, Joshua. It'll be a perfect Thanksgiving."

The holiday was just eight days away and until Faith's mention of it, Joshua had barely considered how quickly it was approaching. He glanced out his office window and saw Main Street covered in an inch of powder. "Well, I'll be. First real snow of the season."

"Okay, what's so important?" Faith had caught her breath and sounded ready to chat.

"A woman called you. Wants to talk about the Jesus statue. She used to live here and the statue mattered a lot to her mother. I have her name and number for you."

"Just a minute." It wasn't the first time

such a conversation had transpired between the two of them, and after several seconds Faith returned with a pen and paper. "What is it?"

Joshua gave her the phone number and hesitated. "I don't know, Faith. Something about this one feels strange. The Lord kept putting it on my heart over and over again."

Faith chuckled. "You're just an old softie, Joshua. Now tell me her name so I can call her back."

"Her name? Oh, right." He looked at his notepad again. "Heidi . . . Heidi Benson."

When Joshua said the woman's first name, Faith about fell from her seat. But as she wrote down the last name she knew it couldn't be the same Heidi. By now Heidi Morand — or whoever she was — could have been anywhere. Besides, the phone number had a Bethany prefix. If Jordan's sister had lived in Bethany all this time she would have come forward a lot sooner, wouldn't she?

Faith thought back over the day and how Jordan had closed down after reading Heidi's file. Especially in light of her prayer that God help them find Heidi. They'd gone back to the courthouse, and she'd returned the file while Jordan waited in the car. After that he hadn't spoken much until he dropped her off.

"Like I said, I'll never forget this. You took a risk for me, Faith. It means a lot." Jordan's eyes were still teary, but he stopped short of hugging her or doing anything that could have been misconstrued.

After he was gone Faith was grateful for her plans with Rosa Lee. The time with Jordan had been hard on her heart and she needed a distraction. An old theater in town was showing reruns of favorite kids' movies throughout November, and they ended up seeing *The Prince of Egypt.*

Faith had to smile at the way God drilled a message home. First the sermon on Luke and Jesus' final days, then her realizations about her own life, and finally the animated movie. There the Israelites stood, toes in the water, enemies charging at their heels, and Moses did the only thing he could do: He raised his staff to heaven and begged God for a way out. He never would have asked God to part the Red Sea. It would have been beyond Moses' understanding. But God . . . ah, God didn't need Moses to figure it out. The answers belonged to the Lord all along. When things looked their worst — in fact, *especially* when they looked their worst — God was busy putting in overtime, making marvelous things happen.

Faith could feel it in her gut: He was going to do that in the Jesus-statue case as well.

She stared at the woman's name and phone number and decided to call her back. Faith could carry on a conversation while making dinner, and later she would call her mother and catch her up on all that had gone on in the past few days. Suddenly Faith remembered being with Jordan in the park the other night, the way he'd kissed her.

Well, most of what had gone on.

She dialed the number and waited while it rang several times. Finally there was a click and an answering machine came on. "Hi, this is Faith Evans calling for Heidi." She left her home number, confident that the woman wasn't a wacko. After all, she lived in Bethany and had a fondness for the Jesus statue.

The irony of the woman's name struck Faith again as she hung up. If only it *was* Jordan's sister. Wouldn't that be something?

Faith checked the boiling water and dropped in a handful of pasta. Even though the woman wasn't Heidi Morand, her name was a reminder that Faith still needed to pray.

While she stirred the spaghetti sauce she

spent the next fifteen minutes praying fervently for Jordan and his sister. That wherever Heidi was, she and Jordan might find each other again. The prayer brought about a freedom in Faith she hadn't felt in months.

The answer to the battle of Jericho Park wasn't strategies or case precedent or vigils in which they took turns talking about their rights. It was something Christ Himself had done, something she knew she must continue to do if there was any hope of seeing God glorified in the process. The very thing she'd been doing since seeing Jordan on her doorstep that morning.

Praying for her enemy.

Heidi was strangely energized when she and Charles got home at ten-thirty after their first date since the baby was born. With all the talk about feedings and diaper changes and nap schedules, they'd realized several days earlier that they needed adult conversation.

Together.

Charles's nurse at the office had baby-sat and in what seemed like a perfect ending to an already wonderful evening, Jordan Lee was sleeping peacefully in her bassinet and the house was cleaner than when they'd left.

"Wow . . ." Heidi wandered into the kitchen and found Charles digging through the cupboards for cereal. "What a great night."

He reached for a box of Grapenuts, set it on the counter, and pulled her into a lingering hug. "What I want to know is where that baby in the other room came from."

Heidi knit her brow together. Even after several years of marriage there were times when she wasn't sure if Charles was kidding. "What do you mean?"

His gaze wandered lazily over her green sweater and new black jeans. "There's no way that body of yours just had a baby. You look better than you did the day I met you."

After weeks of feeling tired and frumpy, Charles's comment made Heidi's heart soar. "Why, thank you, sir." She kissed him, nuzzling against his rough cheek, then rested her head on his shoulder, her eyes closed as she savored the feel of him. "I love you, Dr. Benson."

"Mmm. I love you, too."

She opened her eyes and noticed that the answering machine was blinking. "I wonder who called? No one knows us yet."

She made her way across the kitchen as Charles returned to his cereal. There was a click as Heidi pushed a button and stood back to hear the message. "Hi, this is Faith Evans calling for Heidi . . . I'm returning a call you made to my friend Joshua Nunn earlier today. Give me a call when you get a chance." Heidi scrambled for a piece of paper and scribbled the number as the caller rattled it off.

"Who was that?" Charles looked at Heidi from his place on the stool at the center island. He took another bite and waited for her answer.

She remembered then that she hadn't told him, hadn't even mentioned the story she'd seen in the newspaper earlier that day. She looked at her watch. The news was set to begin in five minutes. "We have to watch the news tonight. You won't believe what's happening in Bethany. It's big time, Charles. National news."

He was working on another mouthful of cereal. "You mean that whole mess about the statue at the park?"

Heidi let her mouth hang open. For a moment she considered telling him about the attorney for HOUR, how strange it had been to see her brother's name in print. But that wasn't the point of the story. "Yes. That's not just any statue, Charles. It was one of my mother's favorite places in town. My brother's, too."

"So who's Faith Evans?" He finished his cereal and set the bowl in the sink. "Her name sounds familiar."

"She was a newscaster at WKZN, but she was fired because she got involved in the Jesus-statue case."

Creases appeared on Charles's forehead. "They fired her for that?"

Heidi nodded. "I called the city's lawyer and asked him to give her the message to call me. I felt like she might need help."

Charles took Heidi's hand and led her into the den. "And what — my sweet, still-recuperating love — could you do to help?"

She knew he was teasing and she tilted her head, her gaze fixed on the ceiling as though she were trying to figure out a difficult mathematical formula. "Let's see, I could go door to door getting people involved, or stand at the park all day handing out flyers with one hand, feeding Jordan Lee with the other. I could . . ." She broke into a laugh and punched Charles lightly on the arm. "I'm not an invalid, you know."

He grinned and tickled her until she let out a light scream. Across the room Jordan Lee sighed and shifted positions. "There you go, wake up the baby . . ." he whispered. He was still chuckling, but a curiosity filled his eyes. "No, I'm serious, honey. What are you thinking of doing?"

Heidi stared at the television set. The news was just coming on, and she shot a knowing glance at her husband. "I could tell her I'm behind her 100 percent, and that we'll pray for her." Her shoulders lifted twice. She wasn't even sure why she'd called, just that she'd felt compelled to do it. "I don't know, Charles. I care about that statue. I had to do something."

"That's my little activist." He kissed her on the top of her head and stretched lazily. "I'll be in the shower if you need me. Let me know what I miss." He winked at her and disappeared up the stairs.

Heidi watched him go and thought, as she often did, how blessed she was. She turned her attention back to the television and the top story — a newsbreaking item about a banking crisis in Philadelphia. Heidi absently bit the nail on her forefinger as she waited. There was a reason she wanted more information, a reason she wasn't ready to admit even to herself. It had everything to do with the attorney's name.

Maybe they'd show his picture . . . maybe . . .

Heidi forced herself not to get worked up. Her brother was dead, the state had notified her foster parents, hadn't they? That wasn't a detail people got wrong.

Was it?

Since television news would have reported the postponement of the hearing the night before, Heidi wasn't sure they'd carry another story about the case. But sure enough, three items into the lineup a female anchor stared into the camera, her face serious. Heidi leaned forward in her seat. *Come on, give me something . . .*

"The countdown has begun for the people of Bethany, Pennsylvania, as they await the final hearing in a case that will decide whether ten-foot walls must remain standing around a statue of Jesus Christ." The reporter droned on, recapping details that even Heidi knew already. The story ended with an update on the attorney for HOUR. "Sources say Jordan Riley will remain in Bethany until the hearing, making himself available for press conferences and other media events involving the case." The anchor reminded viewers of Mr. Riley's press conference earlier in the week, and as she spoke, the station aired footage of a man talking before a dozen microphones and cameras.

Heidi was on her feet, her next breath forgotten. "Dear God. . . . it can't be . . ."

Though her blood ran cold and her head

was spinning, she moved trancelike across the room to the television screen. Falling to her knees, she touched the image of the man on the screen.

Jordan Riley.

"He's alive . . ." She whispered the words as the man's picture was replaced by the anchor. Then Heidi's voice became a shout. "He's *alive!* Charles, come here! He's alive!" She was overcome with a dozen different emotions, and she felt like she'd slipped into some far-too-real dream. The baby began to whimper, and Heidi held a hand up in her direction. "Shh, honey, it's okay." Heidi peered over the edge of the bassinet, relieved to see Jordan Lee's eyes closed. "I'll be right back."

Don't let it be a dream, God . . . please . . . He's alive! Jordan's alive! "Charles!" She darted upstairs as quickly as her feet could take her, into their bedroom and around the corner, where she found Charles wrapped in a towel, his hair still dripping from the shower. "Charles . . ." She froze in place, her knees knocking, heart stuck in a beat she didn't recognize. The tears came then, quickly and in rivers, warm with the mixture of pain and elation. "He's alive, I saw him!"

Her husband's blank expression told

Heidi he had no idea what she was talking about. "Who's alive?" He ran the towel across himself, slipped into a robe, and was at her side almost instantly. His damp fingers came up around the sides of her tear-soaked face as he searched her eyes. "Honey, what is it? What's wrong?"

Her voice was a whisper this time, and it was hard to draw a deep breath. "My brother . . . Jordan . . ." Spots danced before her eyes and she backed up. *Help me, Lord . . . I can't faint. Not now.*

Charles held her steady and eased her down onto the bed. Concern screamed from his eyes, as though he thought perhaps Heidi had lost her mind. "You're white as a sheet, baby, put your head between your knees." He kept hold of her shoulders as she followed his instructions. Though her body had no idea how to handle the shock of seeing Jordan alive, her husband did. And in Charles's presence, aware of his years of medical experience, she felt herself beginning to relax. *Thank You, God . . . help me get a grip . . .*

"I'm okay." The words sounded muffled as Heidi moved to sit up again.

"Slowly. Come up real slowly, babe." Again she did as she was told, grateful that Jordan Lee had slept through the ordeal.

When she was upright again, she felt another wave of tears, but this time when she spoke her voice was steady and certain.

"My brother's alive."

The sense of shock belonged to Charles now, and Heidi watched his eyes change from confusion to utter disbelief. He put a hand on her shoulder and sat beside her. "Honey, that's impossible. He's been dead more than fifteen years."

She shook her head and wiped her cheeks with the back of her hand. "I saw him on TV." There was no way she could convince Charles without an explanation. This time her lungs allowed her to breathe, and she inhaled deeply. "This morning when I read about the Jesus statue case I came across the name of the attorney from HOUR who started the whole thing, the man who sued the city of Bethany to have the statue removed." Heidi locked eyes with her husband. "His name is Jordan Riley."

It took a moment, but eventually a knowing expression filled Charles's face. "Honey, there are bound to be other —"

Heidi put her hand up to stop him. "I know that. I told myself the same thing." She pointed downstairs. "But a few minutes ago I was watching a news story about it, and they showed a picture of the attorney talking to a crowd at Jericho Park the other day." New tears pooled in her eyes and spilled over. "It was Jordan, Charles. I would have recognized him anywhere, case or no case."

The sadness in Charles's eyes told Heidi he wasn't convinced. "Sweetheart, Jordan was just a boy when he died. A lot of grown men might look the way he would have looked." He hesitated. "If he'd lived."

Heidi knew Charles didn't mean anything by his doubts, but they angered her all the same. After all these years she'd found her brother. He wasn't dead; he was alive! She pursed her lips and stood up. There was only one way to prove it to him. Without saying a word she headed out of the bedroom and toward the stairs.

Charles was on his feet, close behind her. "Where're you going?"

She glanced at him over her shoulder and saw in his hurried steps how deeply he cared for her. But she couldn't wait another moment to know she was right. "I have to make a phone call."

"But it's eleven-thir—"

Heidi was already dialing the number. A woman answered on the second ring, her voice wide awake. "Hello . . ."

"Did I wake you?"

"No . . . who is this?"

Charles came up behind her, wrapped his arms gently around her waist and drew her near, laying his head on her shoulder and waiting. There was a pause, and for a moment Heidi thought the woman was going to hang up on her. "I'm sorry, it's Heidi Benson. I shouldn't have called so late, but, well . . . is this Faith Evans?"

"Yes, it is, and don't worry about the hour. I stay up late." Heidi drew a breath. Certainly the woman would know the details about the attorney from HOUR. *Please, God . . . I need to know now . . .*

"You're calling about the Jesus statue case, right? I left a message with you earlier?"

Heidi could feel herself beginning to shake again and she willed her heart to remain calm. "Yes . . . I, uh . . . I have a question first, Mrs. Evans." She closed her eyes and pulled her fingers in tight against the palms of her hands. Charles still stood behind her, and she was suddenly desperate to know the truth. "What can you tell me about Jordan Riley, the attorney for HOUR?"

Faith paused. "What did you want to know?"

"Everything." Heidi said the word quickly to keep herself from screaming in frustration. "Whatever you can tell me . . . why

442

he's suing the city and whether he ever lived in Bethany?"

Again Faith was silent, then, "Yes, as a matter of fact, he did live in Bethany a long time ago. Back when he was a boy."

There was nothing Heidi could do to calm her heart now. "How old was he? When he lived here, I mean?"

Another pause. "I'm not sure I understand what this has to do with the case."

Heidi heard uneasiness in Faith's voice. *Let her hear my heart, Lord.* "It's very important. I think maybe I know the man." Heidi's voice broke. "Please, if you know anything about him, help me —"

"Are you . . . are you serious?" Faith's tone was suddenly as breathless and anxious as Heidi's.

"Yes, please . . ."

"Okay, Heidi. I'll tell you what I can." Faith's voice was kind, and Heidi knew instinctively she'd found an ally. She held her breath as Faith continued. "Jordan and I were friends . . . we lived next door to each other for several years before he moved away. He was thirteen that year."

The shock of Faith's words sent Heidi backward, against her husband. She lowered her head and was seized by a wave of sobs that had been building for fifteen years. Ever since she received the news that Jordan was dead. "Faith . . . then it's you?"

"I'm . . . I'm not sure I know what you mean. Look, Mrs. Benson —"

"Riley . . . I-I'm Heidi Riley."

Heidi heard the gasp on the other end. *What?* "I can't believe it . . . Heidi Riley . . . it's really you?"

A sound escaped Heidi that was part sob, part relieved laughter. "Yes, it's me. So my brother isn't dead?"

Faith was crying now as well. "No, Heidi. He's alive! He's alive and he's been looking for you ever since the state took you away. Where do you live?"

Heidi rattled off the address as she turned to Charles, grinning madly through her tears.

"Can you come over?" Faith sounded like she was crying too. "Right now? I think we have a lot to talk about."

Heidi agreed, and the two hung up. She grabbed her jacket from the back of a kitchen chair as Charles waited.

"What'd she say? Is it Jordan?"

She smiled through her tears. "You always wished you could have met Jordan, right?"

Charles nodded, his eyes glistening in stunned disbelief.

"Well —" she hugged him close, then

pulled back just enough to see his face —
"how 'bout this week?"

TWENTY-FIVE

Faith leaned against the wall to keep from collapsing. Heidi Benson was Jordan's sister? The shock jolted through her, making her feel she was in the very presence of God.

Stunned, she moved into the front room and sat on the edge of the sofa, watching and waiting. She was just about to get into bed when the phone rang. At first she'd thought it nervy that the woman had chosen to call so late, but when she heard the urgency in her voice, Faith had silently prayed for patience. Whatever Mrs. Benson had to say mattered deeply to the woman.

And now . . .

Faith shook her head. Now, she knew she'd been witness to a miracle.

Her father had loved moments like this, when it was blatantly obvious they were treading on holy ground. He would smile and say, "Looks like God has something up

His sleeve." There was a lump in Faith's throat and she swallowed hard as her thoughts drifted back to the last time she'd seen Heidi, the little girl's arm reaching desperately from a stranger's car as she was separated from her brother.

The noise of an engine snapped her out of the memory and Faith watched through the window as a car pulled up and a woman climbed out.

Heidi Riley . . . the very person she'd prayed for earlier that day in Jordan's car . . . *No one but You could have done this, God. No one but You.* Faith opened the door. Jordan's little sister had grown into a beautiful woman, with Jordan's striking features and hair — but that wasn't what made Faith's heart skip a beat.

Heidi Benson looked exactly like her mother.

There were no words needed as Heidi and Faith came together, eliminating the years between them in a single hug. Faith felt fresh tears sting her eyes and she laughed to keep from breaking down. "I can't believe it's you. It's too amazing."

"I read your name in the article, and I had the craziest feeling . . . but your name was wrong. So I knew you couldn't be the same Faith who'd lived next door to us."

Heidi pulled back and took Faith's hands in hers. "But here you are."

Faith led her inside, and they took seats next to each other in the living room. Normally she'd offer Heidi tea, but given the circumstances there was simply too much to talk about first. A smile lifted the corners of Heidi's lips. "You're so pretty, Faith. Just like I pictured you."

Faith laughed and dried her eyes. "And you look so much like your mother I could barely believe it wasn't her. Jordan's going to be amazed."

A look of raw pain flooded Heidi's face. "All these years . . . I thought . . . I thought he was dead."

"I know. We looked at the state foster care files today."

"Today?" Heidi's eyes grew wide. "You mean you were with him today? I thought with the . . . well, the two of you are on opposite sides of this thing." She stared at her hands. "I didn't think you'd be talking."

Faith saw a pink tinge shade her cheeks. Was she ashamed of her brother's involvement in the case? Compassion flooded Faith's heart.

"It's a long story." Faith's voice grew somber as Jordan's words flitted through her mind again. *"The God you serve is my enemy . . ."*

"Your brother's very hurt, Heidi. He spent most of his life looking for you. And after today . . ."

"What'd the files say?" Heidi's eyes grew dark.

"That Jordan was killed in the camp accident. There wasn't enough adoption information in yours for Jordan to have any hope of finding you." Faith could still see the sorrow on Jordan's face as he read the report. "After that he figured he was out of options."

Heidi's face twisted. She sat back in the chair, covered her face with her hands, and cried as though her heart were being ripped to shreds. She spoke through the spaces between her fingers, her voice was little more than a muffled cry. "All those years . . . thinking he was dead. We've lost so much time." She wept harder than before. "And now . . . he's not the person he was."

Faith dropped to her knees and embraced Heidi, smoothing her hand over the back of her head. "His views, his beliefs are different — but deep down, Jordan's still the same." She wanted to be honest, but Heidi had to believe there was hope. Faith remembered her night with Jordan at Jericho Park. "Sometimes when we've been together . . .

I've felt like he was exactly the same."

Heidi leaned back and reached for a tissue on the coffee table. She held the paper to her face, letting her head rest in her hands for several seconds. When she looked up she gave Faith a weak smile. "I'm sorry. I didn't plan to break down."

"Don't be sorry. It's right to grieve the years you've lost. You must have been devastated when you thought he was killed."

Lines of confusion appeared on Heidi's forehead. "So what happened? At the camp, I mean? How did they get it so mixed up?"

Faith exhaled and moved back to her chair, her eyes fixated on a crack in the ceiling. "A cave collapsed. Nineteen boys were working inside and Jordan was one of them. He could easily have been killed, Heidi. He and another boy were the only ones who got out alive." She met Heidi's questioning eyes. "He spent a day in the hospital, but he was fine." She paused, knowing the details wouldn't help Heidi with the fact that she'd been given wrong information. *Lord, give her strength . . . please . . .* "I don't know where the error came from — the camp officials or the hospital. But it doesn't matter now. Someone from the camp contacted another camp — out of state — and Jordan never returned to Southridge. My guess is his records are active somewhere in New Jersey."

"New Jersey?"

Faith's heart sank. She'd forgotten how much of Jordan's story Heidi didn't know. "Yes. He spent the rest of his school years in New Jersey. He went to college there on a baseball scholarship. He was never adopted but he did very well. He went to law school, passed the bar exam, and took a job with HOUR." Faith pursed her lips and glanced down. "He's one of their best attorneys."

"And you think it's because he's hurting, maybe even mad at the Lord?"

Faith looked at Heidi through a fresh layer of tears. "I know that's why. He told me so himself."

Heidi shook her head and closed her eyes. "I've been praying for him ever since you told me . . . the whole way over here."

Praying for him? A surge of hope worked its way through Faith. "So you're . . . you still . . ."

"Believe?" Heidi opened her eyes again. "My relationship with Christ pulled me through. Without Him . . ." Faith could see her struggling to control her emotions. Heidi swallowed hard and straightened. "I never would have made it."

The bond between them was growing, and Faith was glad. "I'm so glad for you . . . I hoped your love for God was strong. Something in the way you spoke, the light in your eyes . . ."

"My husband's the same way."

"Husband?" Faith realized there were still lots more details to be discussed.

"Oh, Faith, he's wonderful . . . my perfect match."

My perfect match. For some reason as Heidi said the words, Faith was surrounded by invisible images of Jordan. She saw him talking with her at the diner, sitting with her on the park bench, making her feel flustered and more connected to him than anyone in the world. Just like he'd made her feel that long-ago winter. She shook off the memories and the bittersweet feeling that wedged itself in her heart. While Heidi and her husband had been building their life together, she'd wasted years with Mike Dillan and spent months learning to walk again after her car accident.

Where's my perfect match, Lord? Obviously it isn't Jordan Riley. And where is Rosa Lee's match?

Be strong and courageous, daughter. I know the plans I have for you.

A sense of peace washed over Faith at the

silent reassurance, and she smiled at Heidi. "Tell me about him."

Her eyes sparkled, like a little girl about to describe her favorite birthday gift. "He's kind and loving and it breaks his heart that I lost my mother and Jordan when I was ten years old." Heidi's eyes grew softer. "We just moved to Bethany this fall. He's a pediatrician at the new clinic." Her eyes lit up. "Oh, and five weeks ago we had our first baby. A little girl."

"Five weeks!" Faith hadn't even considered the idea that Heidi might have a child or children, that Jordan was an uncle. "Wow, Heidi, you look great . . . you'd never know. What's her name?"

Heidi's eyes lifted to meet Faith's. "Jordan Lee."

More tears fell as both of them wept again, and something inside Faith swelled at the thought of seeing Jordan with his baby niece, an infant named after him. "Well, that settles it. You'll have to dress her up tomorrow."

"Why?" Heidi lowered her eyebrows.

"Because —" Faith grinned as she imagined the next day — "tomorrow's the day Jordan Lee gets to meet her uncle."

At nine o'clock the next morning Jordan

was lounging in bed, watching an old Western on cable. He had plans to join the local leader of a small, human-rights group for dinner — a meeting that would give him a window to the area's less popular viewpoint regarding the Jesus statue. Jordan remembered the conversation he'd had with the man — Wally Walters — after the last press conference.

"We've hated that statue as far back as I can remember. In fact, we wrote a petition asking the city to tax anyone who wanted to keep it standing." Walters had gone on describing his frustration in language littered with four-letter words.

Jordan had doubts about the productivity of such a dinner, and bigger doubts about the man himself. He was a lumbering hulk who towered six-five and had a tendency to spit when he talked. Jordan had wanted to know how many people were in Walter's local group and how many of those were opposed to the Jesus statue. The first three times Jordan asked, Wally avoided answering. Finally, when pressed for a specific number, Wally admitted he and a beer-drinking buddy of his were the group's only two official members. And both of them wanted the statue removed or walled up for good. "There are others, though, mark my words. They're just afraid to share their viewpoint what with the whole town ripe full of Jesus freaks."

Jordan rubbed his cheek, recalling the spray of saliva that had accompanied Walter's complaint. He stretched his legs to the end of the bed and yawned. What a waste of time. He thought of the cases he could be researching, the hours he could be billing back at the firm. The only good thing that had come from spending a week in Bethany was the fact that he finally knew the truth about Heidi.

For all the good it would do him.

He doubled the pillow behind his head and sat up straighter. Since reading his sister's file he'd made a decision. This time when he left Bethany — regardless of the outcome of the case — he was finished looking for her. After all, it wasn't as though Heidi was longing for him to turn up, searching for him, desperate to be reunited.

She thought he was dead.

Jordan pondered that and realized it wasn't far from the truth. The Jordan Riley she had known and loved had been dead since the day they took him to Southridge.

He flipped the channel to ESPN and stared at the screen absently, remembering Faith and her prayer that God help them find Heidi. He huffed under his breath and flipped back to the Western. How naive Faith still was after all these years. Couldn't she see it? God hadn't been there when that football player raked her over the coals . . . He hadn't been there when she gave up her safety for the life of a child and wound up in a coma for two months . . . He hadn't been there when her father died decades younger than he should have, and in the middle of doing God's work, no less. He chuckled lightly and shook his head.

Faith was a fool.

Oh, there was no denying the power she still held over him, the way her presence made him long to run off with her to a mountain retreat where politics and religion didn't exist. But that wasn't possible. If Faith was still able to cling to her beliefs after all she'd been through, all she'd watched Jordan go through, then nothing would make her let go. She'd be a believer to the day she died, and that counted Jordan out completely.

"Ah, Faith . . ."

He remembered the way he felt with her so close to him. "If only I could change your mind. You and I would be so good togeth—"

The phone rang, and Jordan stared at it strangely. Was it Hawkins again? Didn't the man ever rest? Jordan tried to decide whether his boss would be frustrated that he wasn't holding another press conference that morning or grateful he wasn't out fraternizing with the enemy. He picked up the phone, his mood suddenly sour. "Hello?"

The caller paused, and at first Jordan thought it was a wrong number. He was about to hang up when he heard her. "Hi . . . it's me, Faith."

Jordan closed his eyes and felt his body relax. Even if he never saw her again after this week, nothing would change the way she made him feel. "Hey, what's up?"

"I need to talk to you . . . today, say around one o'clock?" There was an urgency in her voice.

"Why?"

"Something's come up. I can't talk about it on the phone."

Jordan opened his eyes, sat up on the edge of the bed, and rested his elbows on his knees. As emotional as he'd been the past month it probably wasn't a good idea to spend time alone with her. Each time it was more difficult not to touch her face, to pull her close and . . .

He inhaled sharply. "It just so happens I have an opening at one."

She laughed, and the sound was like music from a favorite song he hadn't heard in years. "Okay, see you there."

"Wait . . ." A grin tugged at the corners of his mouth. "Where?"

"Oh, right." She was suddenly in a hurry. "Jericho Park, near the swings."

"Jericho Pa—" In the full-length mirror opposite the bed, Jordan watched his face grow dark. "If this is some kind of media event I need to know what's hap—"

There was a pause. "You should know me better than that." Hurt rang loud and clear in Faith's voice as she cut him off. "This has nothing to do with the case."

He felt his shoulders slump. "I'm sorry. It's just . . . there's been so much pressure from the office to stay on top of the media." He rubbed his forehead. "Why am I telling you this?"

There was silence for a moment. "Because deep down, where your heart lives, you still trust me."

He uttered a nearly silent laugh. *Faith, if only you knew . . . What I feel for you goes much deeper than trust and friendship.* "You think so, huh?"

She picked up on his teasing tone. "Yes and besides, I'm probably the only friend you have in town."

"That's not true." His grin was back. "I'm having dinner with Wally Walters."

"You and old Wally?" Faith laughed again, and Jordan felt warmed with relief that she wasn't mad at him for doubting her. "I didn't know they let him out at night."

"Very funny."

She was giggling harder now. "Let's just say your one o'clock appointment will make up for it."

"Okay." He stood up and wandered toward the closet area. The day looked a hundred times brighter than it had before her phone call. "But Faith . . ."

"What?"

"You'll have to prove it to me."

She didn't laugh. "I don't think that's going to be a problem."

Twenty-Six

Heidi's heart raced as she sat in the parking lot at Jericho Park and waited for Faith to show up. It was almost one, and Faith had promised she'd be there before Jordan. Heidi glanced at her baby daughter sleeping so peacefully in the backseat, and then at the driveway. She willed Faith's car to appear.

Come on . . . get here . . .

Her breaths came in short bursts, and her hands were sweaty against the steering wheel. She couldn't remember being this nervous about anything in her life. Conversations with the Lord had done nothing to ease her anxiety, and in the twelve hours since seeing Faith the night before, she'd had only a few moments of restless sleep. After crying herself to sleep weeks on end as a child and living with a hole in her heart since Jordan's supposed death, she could hardly believe she was about to see him again.

But there was a nagging doubt she couldn't quite shake. The last time she and Jordan were together, he'd been her hero, her protector. Now, he was the one hurting and they had moved miles apart in their walks with God.

What if Jordan didn't like her? What if all they had was surface talk and promises of Christmas cards? How would she handle that?

"And we know that in all things God works for the good of those who love him, who have been called according to his purpose." The words from the book of Romans played over and over in her mind . . . *those who love him, who have been called according to His purpose . . . called according to His purpose . . . called according to His purpose . . .*

Her heartbeat slowed, and she felt peace come over her like a protective shield. Jordan might be fighting God now, but the Bible was full of such men. Paul, for instance. Paul had overseen the killing of Christians, and yet God had still used him. Certainly Jordan had been called by God. He had given his heart to the Lord long before their mother got sick. Heidi leaned back in her seat and smiled.

Okay, God, I believe You . . . There's a plan in all this. But please . . . hurry up and show me.

Faith pulled into the driveway ten minutes before one and immediately found Heidi's car. Her heart soared as though it had wings. *Lord, You're so good. I can't believe this is happening.* Heidi and Jordan would want time alone, so Faith had decided to bring Rosa. School was out and the child loved spending an hour or two at Jericho Park. She shot a look back at Rosa Lee and grinned. "Honey, we're here. Get your coat."

Rosa did as she was told while Faith parked the car next to Heidi's, and climbed out. In the spot next to them, Heidi took Jordan Lee from her car seat and strapped her into a stroller. Faith held Rosa's hand, weaving her fingers between the child's. Then she led Rosa to the stroller where they peeked at the baby.

Tears filled Faith's eyes as she marveled over the infant's perfect peachy skin and dark hair. "Oh, Heidi, she's beautiful." Faith leaned in closer and ran her fingertips over the tiny girl's downy-soft forehead. The resemblance was striking. "She looks just like Jordan." Faith stood up and hugged Heidi. "I can't believe the two of you are really going to see each other . . . after all this time."

Heidi dabbed at her own tears. "I promised myself I wouldn't break down. Not yet." She uttered a cry that was part laugh. "I don't want mascara running down my face when he sees me."

"He's going to love you, Heidi. Stop worrying." Faith ran her thumb under Heidi's right eye. "There. No mascara." She grinned and looked down at the child beside her. "Rosa, I'd like you to meet Mrs. Benson. She's a friend of mine."

Rosa stuck out her good hand. "Nice to meet you, Mrs. Benson."

"What nice manners, Rosa." Heidi shook the child's hand and smiled, casting Faith a quick grin. "It's a pleasure to meet you, too."

The four of them made their way into the park and found a picnic table near the swings. Rosa was singing happy songs, soaring halfway to the trees in a matter of minutes.

"What a beautiful little girl. Is she family?"

Faith shifted her gaze to Rosa and sighed. "I'd like her to be, but no. She's a foster child up for adoption." Faith looked at Heidi once more. "I think I'm in love with her."

"I see that." Heidi smiled, and her eyes danced with the possibilities. "Is there a chance you'll . . . ?"

"Adopt her? I don't know." Faith could feel the tears again and she blinked them back. "I've prayed about it every day for weeks now, and it seems like God's telling me to wait." She glanced back at Rosa. "Deep in my heart I feel she deserves two parents — a mom *and* a dad." Faith felt the corners of her mouth droop a fraction. "And that's something I can't give her."

They were quiet for a moment as Heidi rocked the stroller back and forth and they watched Rosa swing.

"I wish we were sitting over there." Faith broke the silence and pointed to the bench closest to the walled-in Jesus statue. "That was Jordan's favorite spot when he was a boy." She let her gaze settle on the plywood walls and her heart felt heavier than before. The walls were starting to break away in a few places, no doubt pulled at by teenagers or people frustrated with the mandate. The whole situation was too sad for Faith. She turned back to Heidi. "But I promised Jordan this wasn't about the statue, and it isn't." She patted the wooden table. "This'll do fine."

Heidi was about to say something when a car pulled into the parking lot.

"That's him." Faith drew a deep breath and squeezed Heidi's hand. "I'll meet him halfway and explain what's happening."

She stood up just as Jordan climbed out of the car and shut the door. He wore casual dress slacks, a white button-down shirt, and a navy cardigan sweater. Even from fifty yards he was easily the most handsome man Faith had ever seen.

Jordan spotted Faith as soon as he pulled into the parking lot and felt a frown crease his brow as he slid from the vehicle.

Who was she talking to? Just his luck someone would see her there and cut into their time together. Faith knew just about everyone in town . . . and he was painfully aware that neither of them wanted people talking about their friendship.

He slowed his pace and waited for her.

As she came closer, he savored the sight of her and wished for the hundredth time she wasn't so dogmatic about her beliefs. Could the young woman before him really be his enemy? He dismissed the thought, forcing himself to keep a businesslike attitude. "Okay, this better be good." He slipped his hands in his pockets and smiled at her.

Her eyes lit up in response and she stopped a foot from him, crossing her arms and lowering her chin playfully. "It will be."

The woman Faith had been sitting with was watching them. "Should we find a better place?" He was serious now. It was important neither of them were seen together. "We can drive somewhere outside of town . . ."

Faith shook her head. "No. She's okay."

Jordan glanced at the woman again, then searched Faith's eyes. "Who is she?"

There was hesitation in Faith's face, as though she wasn't sure where to begin. Finally she drew a slow breath and locked onto his gaze. "Remember yesterday in your car when I prayed we'd find Heidi?"

He blinked. Why was Faith bringing that up now? "Okay, so . . ."

"Last night I got a call, Jordan. From a woman named Heidi Benson." She paused, and he felt as though his heart had taken leave of his body. He couldn't breathe. Couldn't think. All he could do was wait for her to continue. "At first I thought she was just another townsperson. You know, someone wanting to help keep the statue up."

"But . . ." Jordan forced the word through suddenly numb lips. His head was spinning. Nothing about the conversation fit neatly into any of his mind's file drawers.

"But . . . she wasn't. She saw you on television yesterday, Jordan. She lives right here in Bethany. Moved here a few weeks ago." Faith's eyes filled with tears, and they spilled onto her cheeks as she reached out and laid her fingers on his arm. "She came to my house last night. Jordan, it's her. Heidi."

He could feel the blood leaving his body — first his face, then his chest and arms. His legs trembled as he looked again at the woman sitting at the picnic table. "But . . . who is *she?*"

Faith's voice was little more than a whisper and her lip quivered as she spoke. "She's your sister, Jordan. And she wants to see you."

His gaze dropped to the ground and he clenched his teeth. When he looked up, he found Faith's eyes once more. "You're serious. You found her?" He gazed at the woman in the distance again. "That's . . . Heidi?"

"Yes, Heidi and her baby." Faith came to him then and hugged him, and he couldn't decide whether to run the distance between him and Heidi or fall to the ground and weep. It had been so long . . . and after finding her file he was sure he'd never see her again. Now . . .

"She . . . has a baby?" He folded his arms across his chest, squeezing his hands together in tight fists. "Faith, I can't believe it . . . I . . ." He looked at her, stunned, still not believing it was true, as tears welled in his eyes. "How can I ever thank you?"

"That's just it, Jordan." Faith leveled her gaze at him, her eyes unblinking. "God brought her back to you." She paused. "I had nothing to do with it. Remember that when you hit the pillow tonight."

Jordan nodded absently, and Faith moved her face inches closer to his. "I'm serious. You can't stay angry at God forever."

Her last remark left something unsettled deep in his gut, but he shifted his attention to Heidi. She was looking at the baby in her arms, and suddenly he needed to see her, hold her, be with her as desperately as he needed air. "Sure, Faith, okay." He hugged her again, truly grateful for her role in this. Finding Heidi had been nothing short of providence and good luck, mixed with Faith's kindness and determination. But it would only upset Faith to say so now. "Come with me?"

She shook her head. "I'm watching Rosa. I'll hang out with her while the two of you talk."

Jordan stared at his sister again, and this

time Heidi caught his look. She waved, though she was too far away for him to make out her face. "Hi . . ." He silently mouthed the word as he waved back.

"It's really her!" Jordan brushed away a tear and smiled. He began walking briskly toward Heidi, Faith still at his side. Dozens of images filled his mind . . . his sister walking home from school beside him . . . the two of them doing homework at the kitchen table . . . Heidi holding his hand as they crept into their mother's room in the days when her sickness first got bad . . . Heidi throwing herself over their mother the day she died and Jordan pulling her gently back, assuring her that no matter what, they'd have each other.

Heidi being torn from him that day in their front yard and begging to stay.

The look in her eyes as the car drove out of sight.

I promised I'd take care of her, Mom . . . but I never could because I couldn't find her. But now . . . I'll watch over her forever. Though his sister couldn't hear him yet, he talked to her anyway. "I'm coming Heidi. And I'm never, ever going to lose you again."

Heidi wanted to take Jordan Lee and race across the park to where her brother stood with Faith, but she couldn't do it, couldn't take her eyes off of him for fear he would disappear and everything about the past twenty-four hours would turn out to be nothing more than a haunting dream. She studied him, surprised at how tall he was, how he'd filled out. From the place where he stood, she couldn't tell if he looked the same, only that he'd become a man.

God, I'm not sure I'm ready for this . . . Please, heal him of his anger and bitterness . . . let my light, Faith's light, be enough to make him want to come home.

Do not be troubled, daughter . . . I know the plans I have for Jordan.

Heidi exhaled softly. "Okay, Lord. I'm ready."

Jordan slowed his pace as he neared her, and Faith veered off to the play area where Rosa was waiting for her. Heidi watched silently as her brother nearly stopped twenty feet from her. He looked like he was seeing a vision. Heidi understood exactly how he felt.

"Heidi . . ."

She nodded, and her words came out like trapped cries escaping the recesses of her very soul. "It's me, Jordan . . ." She set the baby down in her stroller and stood to face him.

There was no stopping him after that. He ran the remaining steps that separated them and swept her into his arms, lifting her off the ground and spinning her around in a full circle before setting her down. They hugged again, and he pressed his face against hers. "Heidi, I can't believe it's you."

She was sobbing and smiling all at the same time, and she took hold of his face, studying it through her tears. "You look the same." Her hand flew to her mouth, and she nearly fell from the power of her weeping. "I . . . th-th-thought you were dead."

Once more he pulled her close, wrapping her in his arms, and smoothing his hand over her back, her hair, just as he'd always done when they were kids. In the place where her memories lived, her brother had never died. Birthdays, special occasions, times when she remembered her mother . . . always Jordan was there. But now . . . to have him hold her like he'd done when she was ten years old . . .

It was more than she could take. "Don't let go, Jordan . . . please."

"Shh . . . it's okay, Heidi. I won't." His voice was a hoarse whisper, choked by the immensity of the moment. "I thought I'd never find you."

Heidi had no idea how long they stood

there, holding each other. It could have been hours or minutes. All she knew was she was transported back to the winter of 1985. No longer were they adults who'd spent half their lives apart, but a sister and brother certain that though the whole world might let them down, at least they had each other.

Eventually Heidi's sobbing eased, but she stayed in Jordan's arms all the same. How many times had she ached for his protection, cried for his loving assurance in the months and years after hearing about his accident?

And now . . . here he was. Alive.

She closed her eyes. "Thank You, Lord . . . oh, thank You . . . You're so good." She realized she'd whispered the prayer out loud, and pulled back some and grinned at him. "I told myself I wasn't going to cry." She laughed and caught two quick breaths. Her eyes were nearly swollen shut, but she smiled all the same. "I wanted you to think I was pretty."

Jordan searched her face and his fingers came up to frame her cheekbones. "You're beautiful, Heidi. And you're . . ." She saw that his eyes were red, his cheeks wet. "You're all grown up." He took in all of her and smiled even as more tears came. "The sister I lost was a little girl . . . but you . . . you look just like Mom did."

"That's what Faith said." Cooing sounds came from the place where Jordan Lee lay, and Heidi motioned with her head in that direction. "I have someone I'd like you to meet."

Her brother's eyes danced, and he linked arms with her, leading the way to the stroller.

She looked from her baby to her brother.

"Jordan, meet Jordan Lee." Heidi grinned at him as she saw the surprise in his eyes.

"You . . . you named her after . . ."

A sound that was part laugh, part cry came from Heidi. "Yes we wanted her to always know about her Uncle Jordan."

He looked at his niece for the first time his mouth opened and he stared at her, speechless. "Oh . . ." The last part of the word lingered in the cool November air. Several seconds passed and finally Jordan looked at Heidi, his face full of questions. "Can I . . . would you care if I held her?"

Heidi giggled, wiping an errant tear as she gently lifted the infant and set her in Jordan's arms. Again the resemblance was wonderfully clear. Heidi stood behind him and studied her daughter over Jordan's shoulder while he clutched the baby in a stiff embrace, holding his niece as though she might break in two.

"She looks just like you." Heidi put her arm around Jordan's back and pressed her cheek against his.

He turned and gave her a crooked grin. "Yeah, she does, doesn't she?" His eyes lit up. "Hey, you haven't told me about your husband." He gestured with his elbow at her wedding ring. "I saw it from the parking lot."

Heidi laughed again. "His name is Charles. He's wonderful and charming and he loves me more than life itself. He's a pediatrician at the local family clinic and he can't wait to meet you."

"You've told him about me?"

Heidi angled her head and locked eyes with him. "I never stopped talking about you, Jordan. He feels like he knows you."

They heard voices drawing near and they turned at the same time to see Faith and Rosa walking toward them. Heidi watched Jordan's reaction, noticed the way his eyes locked onto Faith's, and she had the sense that whatever it was the two of them shared, it was deep. Lasting. Heidi smiled as she remembered how Faith and Jordan had been as kids.

Whatever had gone on between the two of

hem since Jordan had been back, it hadn't
been all bad.

"I've gotta take Rosa home." Faith was
breathless from playing with the girl, her
cheeks red and striking, her smile all for
Jordan. No doubt about it, Heidi thought.
There was a definite attraction between
Faith and her brother . . .

Faith led Rosa up to Jordan. "Rosa, I'd
like you to meet someone else." Faith's eyes
lifted and connected once more with Jordan's. Without looking down, her face lit up
and she continued. "His name is Mr. Ri-
ey." Her eyes filled with warmth. "He's my
friend."

"Nice to meet you, Mr. Riley." Rosa held
out her hand.

For several seconds Jordan seemed unable
to break eye contact with Faith, then he
looked down and smiled. "Nice to meet
you, too. You're sure a pretty girl, Rosa."
Jordan did a little bow. "I understand you're
a foster child."

Rosa's dark, silky lashes moved up and
down as she blinked twice and looked from
Jordan to Faith and back to Jordan again.
"How'd you know?"

"I told him, honey." Faith stood behind
Rosa, her hands on the girl's shoulders.

Jordan nodded. "She wanted me to know

because I used to be a foster child, too . . a long time ago." He shot a glance at Faith and slipped his arm around Heidi. "Mrs. Benson is my sister."

Heidi leaned around Jordan and winked at Rosa. "We were both foster children."

Rosa's eyes grew wide. "Really? Wow . . ." Her expression seemed instantly infused with hope. "And you both found families, right?"

Heidi felt Jordan's pain at the child's comment as strongly as if they shared one heart. She resisted the urge to wince as Jordan struggled for the right words. "Everything worked out, if that's what you mean, sweetie."

Faith pulled Rosa gently back from the others. "Well, we've got to get going."

Rosa bid Heidi and Jordan good-bye, a grin still plastered across her face. She reached out for Jordan again but this time with a hand that was misshapen and missing fingers. As though realizing her error, the girl froze. Heidi forced her face to remain unmoved by the sight and watched while Jordan hid his reaction as well. At first Rosa seemed unsure what to do, her hand suspended in the space between her and Jordan, her eyes filled with questions.

Then carefully, tenderly, Jordan took her

hand in his. He held it, closing his strong fingers over her entire hand while he stooped closer to her. "Hope to see you again sometime, okay?"

Relief flooded Rosa's face and she nodded, her head angled sweetly. "Me too."

Without hesitating, Jordan leaned over and kissed her hand the way a king might kiss the hand of a princess. Heidi shot a glance at Faith and saw tears in her eyes. Something special was happening between the two of them.

No, she thought, studying the scene once more. It was something special between the *three* of them.

When Faith and Rosa were halfway back to the car, Heidi took a chance. "You're in love with her, aren't you?"

Jordan slid himself onto the top of the table and anchored his feet squarely on the bench beneath him. "Rosa? She's a little young for me . . ."

Heidi peeked at Jordan Lee and saw she was sleeping. Then she took her place on the table next to Jordan and linked her arm through his. "You know who. Faith Moses . . . Faith Evans, whatever. You're in love with her."

Jordan shrugged and cocked his head so he could see Heidi better. "It wouldn't matter if I was." His eyes grew sad, and Heidi sensed he didn't want to broach the next subject. Finally he sighed and stared back out in front of him. "If you saw me on the news you must know why I'm here."

Heidi held her breath. *Lord, give me the words . . .* "Yes. I know."

He studied her again and exhaled slowly. "Something tells me you're just like Faith and Mom and the other believers. You love God more than reason, right?"

"What makes you say that?" She tried to see into the depths of his soul.

Jordan sighed and gazed at a passing cloud. "I don't know. Something in your eyes. A glow or a warmth I can't really explain. I saw the same thing in the eyes of this teacher I came up against in court . . . and in Faith's eyes. It's what I remember seeing in Mom's eyes." He looked back at her and Heidi ached for him. "Am I right?"

She slid an arm around him, leaning her head on his shoulder like she'd done when she was little. "You are. I love God, I've never stopped. And deep inside, you haven't either." She paused. "Sometimes our walk with the Lord gets a little confusing, that's all."

Jordan uttered what sounded like a frustrated sigh, and Heidi felt his shoulder tense beneath her. "We have a lot to catch up on, Heidi. The whole religion thing isn't . . . I don't want to talk about it."

His reaction shook Heidi. *Lord, he's as bad off as Faith said. Maybe worse.* "Okay, fair enough. Let's catch up, then." She asked him about the accident at camp, his school days in New Jersey, and what it was like to play collegiate baseball. She even asked about his position at the HOUR organization. It broke her heart to imagine him sold out to a firm that was so obviously against the very beliefs the country was founded on, but she was careful not to share her feelings with Jordan. That was God's territory, not hers.

All she wanted to do was let him know he was loved — regardless of his opinions.

They were an hour into the conversation when she pulled an envelope from her pocket and held it out to Jordan. She noticed how time had yellowed it and made the creases sharp and pronounced, but the letter was still safely inside. Just as it had been that long-ago day. Scribbled across the front in their mother's handwriting was a single word: *Jordan.*

Heidi felt the tears again. "Here . . . it's for you." In all her life she hadn't imagined she'd get the chance to do this. But now that they were together, she wasn't about to wait another minute.

He looked at it. "What is it?"

"A letter. From Mom."

Jordan took it from her slowly, as though it were made of gold dust. For a long time he stared at the envelope, running his finger over his name. Then his eyes rose to meet Heidi's. As he spoke, his voice was thick with emotion. "How'd you get it?"

The answer was bound to make Jordan sad. After all, he'd never had a chance to come back to the house for any reason. "My social worker said I could go through my things and save what I wanted." Heidi paused, remembering the moment. "I checked my bedroom, and he went into Mom's room. He looked through the drawers and stuff. The letters were in her nightstand. Right on top. I always thought about opening yours, but I . . ."

He looked at her, his eyes wet again, too. "You what?"

She blinked and stared at her hands. "I guess a part of me always hoped I might find you again. Even after they told me you were dead."

Jordan drew her close and hugged her for a long time. When he pulled back he stared at the envelope and then at her. "You got one too?"

She sniffed once and nodded. "I've read it so often the folds are starting to wear out."

Jordan's eyes were flooded by what looked like an ocean of grief as he tucked the letter into his back pocket. "Thanks, Heidi." His voice was tender, his eyes even more so.

They heard someone approaching from behind. Heidi turned and saw Charles, his eyes full of questions. She nodded toward him, assuring him it was all right to come closer. He had told her that morning he might stop by sometime around two if they were still at the park.

Now here he was, and Heidi felt happy enough to float. She climbed down to meet him, hugging him and leading him by the hand to meet Jordan. Then she looked into her brother's eyes and spoke the words she'd only dreamed of speaking. "Jordan, this is my husband, Charles. Charles, my brother, Jordan."

The men shook hands, and Charles grinned. "You look pretty good for a dead guy."

All three of them laughed, and what little tension had existed dissipated like morning dew on a summer sidewalk.

They made small talk for a few minutes before Charles's beeper went off. He glanced at it. "Looks like my time's up." He reached for Jordan's hand again and for a brief instant caught Heidi's eye. "Listen, we'd love to have you come for Thanksgiving dinner if you can make it."

Even after all the years that had passed, Heidi knew Jordan well enough to know he was choked up. Too much so to speak. Instead he nodded, swallowing hard, his eyes focused at something on the ground.

Fresh tears nipped at Heidi's eyes and she slid an arm around both of them. "What he's trying to say is, 'Yes, thanks, I'd love to come.' "

Jordan looked up and shifted his gaze from Charles to Heidi and back to Charles again. "She's right." He grinned, though his eyes glistened with tears. "That's exactly what I'm trying to say."

Twenty-Seven

Joshua Nunn turned in early that night and almost immediately slipped into the strangest dream. He was in front of a crowd of supporters at Jericho Park, and everyone had an instrument of some kind. "We are here to represent God's people," he heard himself say. Then all at once instruments appeared in everyone's hands and they began to play. The sound was more beautiful than a hundred concert choirs, and not only that but someone was singing. Joshua gazed into the sky and saw hundreds of golden men circling above the park — just like the one who'd appeared to him that day in his office.

A voice boomed from the heavens, and Joshua fell to the ground. "See, Joshua, I have delivered Jericho Park into your hands . . ." The words faded, absorbed by the music of the people, who were now forming a line and looking to Joshua. *What do I tell them, Lord? I don't have the words.*

This time the voice was silent, echoing loudly within the chambers of his heart. *Be strong and courageous, Joshua. I will go before you. Tell the people to march around the walls.*

Joshua opened his mouth to give the command, but the people were already making their way around the perimeter of the park, playing music as they went.

"Can we shout?" a man yelled from the back of the line.

"Yeah, can we shout yet? Tell us when . . ."

"We want to shout . . ."

The voices grew into a chorus of grumbling that silenced the music. Joshua raised his hand high in the air. A surreal silence came over the park, and Joshua looked from person to person, realizing for the first time that he could see into their hearts . . . the condition of their souls.

"Do not give a war cry, do not raise your voices, do not say a word until the day I tell you to shout." Joshua smiled, for the hearts of the people were good. "Then . . . shout!"

The music resumed and the people began marching, only instead of their moving around the park, the park and its walled-up statue seemed to be revolving beneath them. At the end of one full rotation the sun disappeared and heaven's golden men shone like stars in the sky. Just as quickly, the sun returned and the people set out around the park again. This happened six times. On the seventh rotation, the sun remained in the sky and the people marched around the park seven times.

"Wait a minute, this isn't right." Joshua yelled out the words, but no one was listening. "This is the story of Joshua in the Bible. Stop! Can't you hear me? Stop! We need real answers here, not a bunch of people marching in place!"

Joshua's hands and legs trembled and suddenly he was falling to his knees, about to cry out to God for help, when there was the loudest, most convincing sound Joshua had ever heard.

Immediately his eyes flew open and he sat straight up in bed. Beside him, Helen stirred and looked at him, eyes blinking. "What was that?"

He stared at the room around him, but it took several beats of his heart before any of it looked familiar. He shot a glance at the alarm clock — it was only 11:30. "I don't know. A dream, I guess . . ."

Helen snuggled up against her pillow. "That's strange —" she yawned — "I thought I heard something."

Joshua's hands felt clammy, and he shifted his attention to his wife. "Like what?"

She was already drifting back to sleep. "I don't know, something loud. Almost like a shout."

His blood couldn't have felt any colder if he'd been standing in a freezer. Slowly, he settled back into bed and lay there, his eyes open, staring at the ceiling. *What's going on, Lord? What are You trying to tell me?*

But all he received in response was an image that seared its way into his consciousness, keeping him focused and denying him any sleep whatsoever.

The image of plywood walls falling to the ground.

Jordan pulled his car up along the side of Jericho Park at 11:31 that evening and stared into the darkness, allowing his eyes time to adjust. He'd stayed with Heidi and her husband until ten minutes ago, and now he needed a quiet place to think. As driven as he'd been that ill-fated winter when his mother lay dying years earlier, Jordan felt compelled to find his way to Jericho Park.

Especially in light of the task that lay ahead.

He fingered the fragile envelope in his hand and reached up to flip on the car's dome light. All that had happened that day was overwhelming, almost more than he could bear. His sister had found him, and in one afternoon they'd recaptured the closeness they'd shared as kids. He'd found Faith, too . . . and despite his determination to see walls around the Jesus statue, she'd been nothing but kind and loyal to the memory of their friendship.

And now this.

A letter from his mother, words straight from her hand intended for his heart alone. Jordan felt himself tense at the thought of opening the letter and he searched himself, trying to understand his reluctance. Was it because of her beliefs? Because he'd turned his back on the One who had mattered so desperately to her? Was that why his hand trembled now?

He gritted his teeth and slid his finger carefully under the flap. The paper inside was pressed thin from years of being unread, and Jordan pulled it out slowly, careful not to rip it. As he opened the folds he thought he caught a faint whiff of his mother's perfume, and his hands fell to his lap. He closed his eyes and allowed himself to go back. Not to the days when his mother lay wasting away in her bedroom, but before that . . .

Back when she would put on a baseball cap, sweatshirt, and jeans and play catch with him in the front yard . . . or sit behind home plate at his games, flashing a thumbs-up whenever he had a good hit. Back when she and Heidi would do hand-claps on the front porch, their sing-song voices ringing out while Jordan and his friends played ball in the street. Happy days, memories that almost seemed to belong to someone else entirely. Times when going to church and loving God Almighty made perfect sense.

The fragrance of her perfume faded. It was getting late, and the temperature in his car was dropping. He tenderly lifted the paper, as though it were his mother's hand in his and not her penned words, and in the brightness of the car light held the letter up and began reading.

Dear Jordan . . .

He could hear her voice, see her face again — and he missed her more than he thought possible. Tears came, and he closed his eyes, not wanting to break down. He could do this — he could read the letter and allow himself to feel her loss as he hadn't done in years. From somewhere deep in his soul he found the strength. Clenching his jaw he drew a steadying breath through his nose and opened his eyes once more.

Dear Jordan,

As I write this I already know what will happen. God, my eternal Father and yours, is calling me home. I've prayed otherwise, asked God to let me stay with you, but He's made it clear to me that — for whatever reason — it's time. I want you to know I'm not afraid to die. I know this will sound strange to you, but I'm actually excited. I've been doing some reading on heaven lately and I understand it as well as I will this side of eternity. Here — this place we call earth — is not our home, Jordan. It's a waiting room, really. The place where we live together until we're called into the grand palace — the place where real life will begin. Our forever home.

And so my fears are not for myself.

Rather they are for you and Heidi. You are young, Jordan, and though you love God now, I fear deeply that you will change your mind. Life as you know it is about to change, and the world will want you to blame our loving God. But Jordan, it's not His fault death and disease reign here in the shadows. He's not the cause of bad things. In reality, He's the only way out . . . the only life rope, the only path from the darkness to eternal light.

The only way home.

Jordan blinked, and what felt like a bucket

of tears fell down his cheeks. When his vision was clear again he continued.

You see, Jordan, I love you and Heidi so much that I've asked God for something very special. If He wants me to be with Him now, fine. I'm comfortable with that. But I feel in my heart He's promised me this: You and Heidi will live a life of faith. You might stray from Him at first, but eventually . . . in His perfect timing . . . you will come back. And one day we will be together again in Paradise.

By the way, I want to say a word about Faith Moses. Her family has been wonderful to us, Jordan. In ways you could not possibly know or understand. If you were older I'd explain in detail how we might not have had food and electricity if it hadn't been for them. As for Faith, I know the two of you care about each other and that you're young. But if . . . just if you should choose to marry her one day, please know this, son: Somewhere up in heaven I'll be giving you the happiest thumbs-up ever.

I'm tired and I need to get some sleep, but I wanted you to know my heart. I may stop breathing, Jordan, but I'll never stop praying for you and Heidi. Begging God that no matter where you journey from here, you'll find your way home again. Because when you do . . . I'll be there, waiting with open arms. I love you more than you know . . . Mom.

The sorrow that welled inside Jordan was so great it was as though someone was standing on his chest. His hands trembled as he read the note again, and finally a third time. His mother had known all along . . .

Forget the fact that Jordan seemed strong and able to handle her loss, that he seemed willing to take on the responsibility of Heidi's well-being. His mother had seen something else, even back then.

She'd seen his heart. And his weakness.

"How could you know me that well?" Jordan's question came in a broken whisper, and he wished with everything inside him he could reach across the seat and hold his mother's hand, hug her like he'd done as a boy. He stared at the letter again, though the tears made it impossible to see. Before he could analyze his thoughts, he began to speak. "Thank You, God . . . for letting me hear her voice again. How can I thank You?"

Return to Me, son. I have always loved you . . . let down the walls . . .

The words that flashed across Jordan's heart were so foreign that he sat up straighter in his seat and glanced around. Switching off the dome light, he inhaled sharply and folded the letter. Then he slipped it back in the envelope and set it

491

squarely on the dashboard, staring out into the evening.

What was he doing? Had that been his voice, praying to God, thanking Him for his mother's words?

Jordan gulped and clenched his hands on the steering wheel. Something felt different, something in the neighborhood of his heart. As though thick, stony walls had surrounded it for years . . . and now . . . now they'd crumbled to the ground, and all in the space of a heartbeat. He sat back in the seat and marveled at the lightness of the feeling. Was it his mother's prayer that had done it? Heidi's prayer? Faith's? Jordan wasn't sure, but he knew one thing. He'd come to Bethany a month earlier longing for three women he'd once loved: Faith, Heidi, and his mother. And now . . . here in the cold darkness of his sports car, alone at Jericho Park, he'd found them all.

His eyes adjusted to the night, and the image of the walled-in Jesus statue came clearly into view. Walled-in just as his heart had been. To people. To God.

Suddenly, more than anything in his life, he wanted to see those plywood walls — walls he'd been instrumental in erecting — come down. He wanted to see the image of Jesus, arms outstretched, beckoning all who had a willing spirit to come to Him . . .

Come, and He would give rest for even the hardest heart, the coldest soul.

Even a sinner like Jordan.

The truth dawned on him then, and his head spun as he struggled to take it in. God wasn't his enemy. No, the only enemy he'd had these past sixteen years was himself. He'd spent all his time, his talents, waging a battle against the Lord as if that could somehow erase the losses in his life. But in the end that battle would have cost him everything.

Jordan blinked . . . it was as if he could feel scales falling from his eyes.

God was real. Of course He was. What other explanation could there be for the way Jordan's mother had found His saving grace before her death? Image after image filled Jordan's mind, and he saw the Lord's hand at work throughout his life — even in the darkest hours. He'd survived the cave incident, hadn't he? And what about the other day in New York City, when the trio of muggers was arrested moments before they would have attacked him? What about Faith's victories? And Heidi's? What about the fact that he'd found his sister after all these years only hours after Faith's prayer?

Even little Rosa had reason to believe:

God had given her one good hand, after all and a devoted friend in Faith.

All of it was proof. Proof he'd avoided with a lifetime of hiding behind walls o anger and bitterness. Walls of fear.

Why hadn't he seen it before, the trustworthiness of God?

His gaze lingered on the plywood walls and he began to shake his head as a heavy mourning swept him. "I'm sorry, Father . . I've gone against You at every turn." He began to cry, deep, guttural sobs tha worked their way up as the sorrow and regret he felt for a lifetime of wrong attitudes and actions threatened to consume him.

"I'm sorry . . . I'm so sorry, God . . ."

The words of the three women he loved most echoed in his heart. He could see Faith, her beautiful eyes filled with sincerity as she whispered, *"You can't stay angry a God forever . . ."* Heidi's image appeared ir his mind and he took in her tearstained face in the hour after they'd found each other heard her earnest words: *"Sometimes ou walk with the Lord gets a little confusing.* The picture faded and his mother's word appeared, words from years ago, words Goc had saved for this time and place . . . a mes sage that Jordan understood now was abso lute truth: *He's the only way out . . . the only life rope, the only path from the darkness here to eternal light.*

The only way home . . . only way home . . . only way home . . .

His mother . . . Heidi . . . Faith . . . their wisdom echoed again and again in the core of his being, and Jordan knew he couldn't last another minute. No matter what he'd said before, no matter how he'd bought into a lifetime of lies since his mother's death, a few truths remained. Deep down inside, Jordan Riley still loved God.

And he could wait no longer.

Compelled by a force greater than anything he could remember, moving with a strength that was not his own, Jordan climbed out of the car and began jogging toward the statue.

The cold air burned his lungs, his loafers slipped with each step, but Jordan moved on, determined, energized with a supernatural desire. He reached the statue, and his eyes darted from one board to the next until he saw several areas where the wood was loose. Working his hand into a crack between two panels, he gripped the plywood and pulled. He cried out from the effort as a section of the wall fell to the ground.

Then he moved to the next piece.

One by one, he gripped the wood, tearing the panels from the place where they stood, barely noticing the splinters that pierced his skin. There wasn't a person in sight, but Jordan wouldn't have minded if there were. They could pack the place with people and air what he was doing live on national television for all he cared.

The walls had to come down. The Jesus statue in Jericho Park deserved to be seen.

Faith wasn't sure what lured her to the park that night, whether it was her desire to soak in all that had happened between Jordan and Heidi, or whether she wanted to pray about Rosa Lee and the upcoming hearing. Whatever it was, she hadn't been able to sleep and at almost midnight, bundled in her thickest winter coat, she stepped out of her car, gazed across the park, and considered whether she wanted to find a bench or get back inside where it was warm.

She'd been standing there only a few seconds when she heard loud cries and frightening noises, as though some terrible fight were taking place. She spun around and stared into the darkness. What she saw made her mouth fall open, her eyes widen with a mixture of emotions. Someone was ripping down the walls around the Jesus statue, tearing at them and pulling them down with a brute force Faith had never seen before. She watched, mesmerized, as the panels of plywood fell in heaps of scrap around the base of the statue. The entire process seemed to take no more than five minutes, and when the man was done, he fell back on his heels and stayed there, unmoving.

Lord, what should I do? A ripple of anxiety coursed through Faith, and she glanced around, making sure no one else had seen what happened. She wanted to hurry over and thank the man for doing what she'd wanted to, but a voice of reason told her what she had just witnessed was wrong. The judge had ordered the walls up, and they should have stayed that way until — by God's design — they were ordered down. She pulled her coat tight around herself and began walking toward the man. Whoever he was, he was on her side and he apparently had a deeply personal interest in the Jesus statue.

The man remained on the ground and finally, when she was ten feet from him, he whipped around to face her.

Faith gasped. "Jordan! What are you doing here?" Her heart pounded and she took slow steps in his direction until the gap between them closed. He stared at her, and there was a light in his eyes that hadn't been there before. "You . . . I didn't see your car."

"I parked on a side street." He was breathing hard, and a layer of sweat glistened on his forehead.

She stared at the statue, at the piles of broken plywood, then her gaze met his again and her voice was barely a whisper. "Why, Jordan?"

He reached out and took her hands in his, searching her eyes as though he was only now seeing her for the first time. "Faith, I'm so sorry . . ."

The ground beneath her seemed to fall away. "I . . . I don't understand."

Jordan motioned to the statue. "The lawsuit, the walls . . . all of it was wrong, Faith. I must have been crazy . . ."

She couldn't decide whether to laugh or cry, and in the end she did both, coming to him as he stood and wrapped her in his arms. It was a miracle beyond anything Faith could have imagined or hoped for. Jordan had torn down the walls around the Jesus statue, but not before God had torn down the walls around his heart. "What happened . . . what changed your mind?"

He drew back several inches and met her gaze. "Heidi gave me a letter . . . from my mom." He shrugged, looking from the statue back to her as though he were still confused himself. "Something happened while I read it, Faith. I don't know how else to explain it." He looked up at the dark, starless sky above them and Faith's heart beat high in her throat from the nearness of him.

God, is it true? Have You really restored his love for You?

Jordan uttered a quiet laugh and shook his head, his eyes still focused on the heavens. "It was all so amazing. I kept hearing you tell me I couldn't be angry at God forever . . . and Heidi saying sometimes our walk with the Lord gets confusing . . . and then my mom's words . . . set aside for me until this exact moment. Right when I needed them most."

He looked at her, and a shiver ran down her spine. "I've been a fool, Faith." He eased his fingers along the sides of her face and drew her gently toward him until their lips met. When they pulled apart, breathless from the cold air and the desire Faith knew they both were feeling, he ran his thumbs gently over her brow, her cheekbones. "Faith, I love you. I always have."

She wanted to shout aloud from the joy that welled up inside her. "I prayed you'd come back, Jordan." She smiled and kissed him tenderly once more. "And now here you are." Her eyes searched his. "Welcome home, friend."

He cupped her face with his hands, framing her with his fingertips as though she were the finest treasure. "I have so much I want to tell you . . ." He grinned, and she saw the depth of love in his eyes. "So much I want to ask you. But there're some things I need to do first. Can you give me a few days?"

Faith didn't stop to consider his words. It didn't matter what he wanted to tell her. Instead, she let her head fall back a bit and laughed softly before meeting his eyes once more. "Are you kidding? I'm so happy for you, Jordan . . . whatever you want to talk about, take as long as you'd like."

Jordan brought his face to hers once more, and kissed it in a way that made Faith's knees go weak. "Come on, little Miss Town Favorite," he whispered near her ear. "You need to get home before you freeze to death."

He put his arm around her shoulders, and they were halfway to her car when he stopped and turned to look back at the Jesus statue. Faith did the same and smiled at the way it glistened under the dim park lights.

Jordan sucked in a breath through clenched teeth and cast her a hesitant look. "You think God'll forgive me for destroying public property?"

Faith hugged him and they started walking again. "To tell you the truth —" she grinned at him — "I think He already has."

Joshua was up earlier than usual the next morning.

He sipped a mug of French vanilla roast as he flipped on the TV and turned it to the local news. He still couldn't shake the strange dream from the night before or the way the shout had seemed so real.

Real enough that Helen had heard it, too.

A commercial break ended and a newscaster appeared on the screen. "In other news, vandals apparently tore down the walls around the controversial Jesus statue in Bethany, Pennsylvania's Jericho Park last night . . ."

Joshua was on his feet, his coffee forgotten. *Dear God, did she say what I think she said?* The picture changed and suddenly Joshua was staring at the statue, standing victorious amid a pile of scrap wood. It was true, the dream he'd had the night before . . the walls really had fallen!

"Helen! Get in here, quick!" Joshua kept

his eyes trained on the screen and in that moment he had the distinct feeling that the walls around the statue weren't the only ones that had fallen the night before.

Father . . . thank You . . . I'm sorry for ever doubting . . .

The battle is Mine, Joshua . . . I will go before you as I always have. Your prayers have crossed My Jordan and now he and the land are both yours.

Joshua drew his eyebrows together as the strange thought drifted across his heart. Jordan and the land were his? It didn't make sense, but then nothing had since he'd first heard about the case. The day he'd seen the golden man in his office. It didn't matter. The Lord would make everything clear in the end.

"Helen!" He shouted again, his voice filled with celebration. The news segment was almost over and he didn't want her to miss it. "Helen, get in here! You won't believe it . . . It's just like my dream . . ."

Twenty-Eight

Twenty-four hours before the hearing and with everything that mattered to him waiting back in Bethany, the last thing Jordan wanted to do was drive east to New York. But he knew with every fiber of his being he couldn't move forward without first tying up the loose ends back home.

He walked into T. J. Morris's office just before noon and shut the door.

His friend was working on a file. He whipped around, his features instantly frozen. "Jordan, what the —"

Jordan held up a hand. "Don't talk. Just listen."

T. J. started to stand, started to open his mouth, but Jordan pointed to his friend's chair. "Sit. You owe me that much."

A look of resignation flashed across T. J.'s face. Slowly, silently he sat back down.

Jordan took the chair opposite him, folded his hands, and rested his chin on the tips of his forefingers. "You look nervous, Teej. Why do I get the feeling everyone in my office is somehow doubting me these days?"

T. J. turned and looked out the window, studying the towering office buildings fighting for position in the city skyline. "This is all because of Faith Evans . . ."

Anger began to boil in Jordan's blood, but he was careful not to let it show. "Her again, huh?"

T. J. sighed and stood up, shuffling toward the window, and then turning to face Jordan again. "I can't believe she's still fighting this thing . . . I mean, Hawkins thought for sure she'd pull out after the network called."

Jordan had the strange sensation he was dreaming. Almost immediately he could see in T. J.'s eyes that he knew he'd made a mistake by mentioning Faith at all. "How'd Hawkins know about the network call?" Jordan leaned back in his chair and stared unblinking at T. J. "And why do *you* know about it?"

T. J.'s expression went flat. He moved to his chair once more, sat down, and slumped back. "Hawkins knows all about Faith." T. J.'s cheeks puffed out as he exhaled through pursed lips. "You can't tell him I told you, but he's . . . he's worked hard to make her change her mind about fighting or the statue."

Jordan clenched his teeth and again forced himself to appear unaffected. "What's he done?"

T. J. crossed his arms and studied his feet. "He got her fired — at least he said he was going to — and he pulled some strings at the network . . . had someone call her and tell her they were interested in her for a national spot if she stayed out of the political limelight." T. J. looked up. "Oh, and that kid she likes, the orphan. Hawkins had her picture yanked from the Web site the day our ad began to run. Just to send Faith a message . . . to warn her there'd be a price if she got too involved in the case."

T. J.'s eyes clouded with shame, and Jordan felt sick to his stomach. He'd always known Hawkins was ruthless, but this . . . He thanked God for opening his eyes to all that had been going on around him.

T. J. leveled his gaze at him, and Jordan had the feeling this was maybe the last conversation he'd have with his old friend. In the past week friendship had taken on a deeper meaning for Jordan, one that left him little in common with someone like T. J. Morris. Jordan watched the man struggle for words to fill the awkward silence between them.

"I should have told you sooner . . . I don't know . . . things have changed around here, Jordan. There's a lot at stake."

Jordan wanted to stick around and find out what T. J. meant, but he knew he needed to get back to Bethany. And he still had one more stop to make. He studied T. J. It made sense, he supposed, that his friend had been quiet about the attack against Faith. HOUR was made up of a determined group of attorneys bent on seeing justice done the only way they understood it. Even if it meant betraying one of their own.

Jordan stood, and T. J. did the same. For a moment neither of them spoke, and finally Jordan reached out and shook his hand. "I've got a case to finish." He held T. J.'s eyes for a moment, praying that one day the man would understand the decision Jordan was about to make. "See ya, Teej." With that, he turned then and walked out into the hallway.

Jordan expected T. J. to protest or stop him, but as he made his way from his friend's office there was nothing but silence behind him. Two minutes later, Jordan stood in front of Hawkins's secretary, an older lady who had been a prison warden in her younger days — and who still carried the same charm and demeanor. She scowled at him as he approached. "I thought you were supposed to be in Bethany."

Jordan wanted to ignore her and head straight into Hawkins's office, but that would ruin his plan. It was important he play his cards perfectly. He smiled at the woman. "The hearing's not until tomorrow. I need a moment with Mr. Hawkins, if you don't mind."

Her frown eased some and she hesitated. Jordan thought she might decline his request, but then she stood and disappeared down a series of hallways. In less time than it took Jordan to rehearse his game plan, Hawkins came into the foyer, a smile pasted on his face. "Jordan . . . come on back."

Jordan followed him into the plush, spacious office, the place where they'd celebrated numerous legal victories in the past. He felt a pang of regret. Those legal victories had put Jordan on the map of human-interest law — and taken him miles from the things that mattered most.

Jordan had sometimes felt intimidated by Hawkins, but this was not one of those times. He understood too clearly the path he needed to follow, the choices he must make in order to finally be true to himself and the God who had never stopped loving him.

Hawkins slammed his forearms onto his desk. The smile was gone. "You're supposed to be in Bethany."

Jordan chose his words carefully. "Sir, I had some things to take care of here."

Hawkins waved his hand toward the door. "Well, take care of them and get back to Bethany. We have a case to win there, Riley. You worry me." He searched Jordan's eyes, as though looking for signs of weakness. "I don't know if you understand how important this case is to HOUR."

"Yes, sir," Jordan smiled. "I think I do know."

Suspicion darkened Hawkins's face. "So what do you want? A vote of confidence? You already have that or you wouldn't be there in the first place." Hawkins's voice was gruff. Clearly the man was unsettled over Jordan's unexpected visit.

"I have a question, sir. I thought you'd be the one to ask."

Hawkins gestured as though a fly were buzzing near his face. "Go ahead."

"About the bonus money . . ." Jordan was guessing, going out on a limb, but it was something he needed to know. "I want to know if the person in public office has promised additional funds for future cases?"

Hawkins eyed him carefully. "Who told

you?"

"Same way you heard, sir." Jordan paused. "Found out the other day."

The scowl on his face deepened. "Look, Riley, what happens behind the scenes at HOUR is none of your business. All you need to do is win the case. The partners will take care of you after that, and one day —" his smile was small, forced — "one day you might have an office on this floor." He chuckled, but the sound made Jordan's skin crawl. "You'll make a fine partner, Riley." The room was silent for a beat. "Now get back down there to Bethany and do the job."

Jordan felt a chill pass over him. So he'd been right. Funds were coming from an elected state official. And if Hawkins had been willing to play Faith like a puppet, what else might he have done? What might he still do? Jordan resisted the urge to end the conversation then and there.

He and Faith were going to pray with Heidi and her husband at Heidi's house that night. Jordan hadn't told them yet what he planned to do, but he had told them about the change that had come over him. They knew, as did he, that whatever happened in court the next day, the former Jordan Riley was gone forever.

He glanced out the window, reminding

himself to be patient. His heart was already halfway down the highway, but he had one thing to tell Hawkins first. After that . . . well, if HOUR chose to sue him for what he was about to do, so be it. "Sir, I want you to know that the Bethany case is very important to me. I . . . well, I have a personal interest in it. And you can be sure tomorrow, when you hear the outcome, it'll be just the way I want it to go." Jordan stood and shook Hawkins's hand. "After tomorrow, I want everyone to know how I feel about that statue."

Hawkins looked like a man warmed by a sudden burst of sunshine. "That's my boy, Riley. You go get 'em."

On Tuesday morning Joshua Nunn arrived at the courthouse an hour before the hearing. A crowd had already gathered on the lawn, and a quick glance showed they were in support of the statue. Joshua nodded at them, waving and pointing a single finger heavenward. "Pray!" he called as he headed into the building. In front of the double doors to the courtroom he found Frank Furlong and several city council members, concern etched on their faces. Frank motioned Joshua aside.

"I got a call this morning from the HOUR

organization." Frank wiped a layer of perspiration off his brow. "It isn't good."

Joshua set his briefcase down and crossed his arms. Since his dream about the walls he wasn't even a bit concerned. Faith had told him there was something different about Jordan now. He'd had an awakening, she'd said. Joshua had no idea what Jordan was going to do that morning, but he believed without a doubt that God was in control.

Joshua smiled at the mayor. "Did the person from HOUR give you his name?"

"Peter Hawkins, one of the partners." The others were far enough away not to hear the conversation. "Joshua, he offered me twenty thousand dollars to make a statement in court . . . to insist that permanent walls go up." Frank raised his eyebrows. "I told him no, but he said he knew for a fact the city was going to lose. He'd seen to it personally."

Joshua took hold of his friend's shoulder. "It's too late to panic. Believe me, the battle of Jericho Park is under control." He patted the mayor on the back and led him toward the others. "In fact, it's already won. No matter what it looks like."

While they were talking a man approached them, someone Joshua had never seen before. In his hand was a stack of papers more than an inch thick. "Sorry to interrupt, Mr. Nunn." He handed the papers to Joshua and smiled. "The townspeople have been working on this for a few weeks. We thought it might help."

In that instant, Joshua knew that everything God had promised from the beginning was about to happen. He would present his case with strength and courage, and no matter what happened, no matter what was said, God Himself would go before him.

Twenty-Nine

Jordan was still reveling from the feeling of praying the night before, but even now, fifteen minutes before the hearing, he wasn't exactly sure what he was going to tell the judge. Charles had shown him the Scripture that said not to worry about words . . . God would provide what to say.

He had two assistants nestled in the row behind him, young attorneys clearly out of the inner loop of happenings back at the office. They were there to make copies or read through case precedents should he need help. Jordan could picture them getting star status as they replayed for Mr. Hawkins the events that were about to play out.

A chorus of whispers and movement filled the courtroom as reporters squeezed into the back and townspeople filled the spectator rows. Jordan made eye contact with Faith, and she nodded to him. He refrained from smiling or winking in response. *She knows my heart, Lord. I can see it in her eyes.*

As he took in the rest of the courtroom, Jordan realized he wasn't nervous. In fact, he felt wrapped in a cocoon of peace that surpassed anything he'd ever known.

Judge Webster appeared at the bench and took his seat. Rapping his gavel twice he shot a frustrated look at several noisy groups. "Order! This court will come to order." Immediately the reporters fell silent.

They don't want to miss the townspeople's tears, Jordan thought. Then he swallowed hard and focused on the judge.

"Very well." Judge Webster looked from Jordan to Joshua and back again. "I have given you thirty days to determine what type of permanent fixture will best keep the people of Bethany, Pennsylvania, from feeling forced to view a statue of Jesus in the middle of —" he checked his notes — "Jericho Park."

A holy presence seemed to settle around Jordan, and he knew instinctively that Faith was praying for him. Faith and Joshua and Heidi and Charles. Most of the people in Bethany for that matter.

The judge cleared his throat. "At our last meeting, counsel for the plaintiff recommended a ten-foot-high, permanent brick wall to resolve the matter." He looked a

Joshua. "But before I can order anything, I promised to give the defense and the —" he arched his eyebrows — "new owner of the statue a chance to speak before this court."

Joshua Nunn, the city's attorney was first. The older man looked ten years younger as he took the floor and moved slowly to a spot in front of the judge. "Your Honor, the people of Bethany believe their voice has not been heard in this matter. It is *their* park and they have enjoyed the statue in question for decades without incident." He pulled out a thick stack of papers and handed it to Judge Webster. "I'd like to introduce these documents as Exhibit A."

The judge wrinkled his nose as though he'd caught whiff of a bad odor. "What is it?"

Joshua smiled. "The signatures of more than five thousand citizens of Bethany and the surrounding towns. People who do not want walls around the Jesus statue." He hesitated.

Across the room Jordan masked the way his heart soared within him.

I'm right there with them, Lord . . . thank You for letting me see . . .

"If I may read the opening paragraph, Your Honor?"

Judge Webster rested his forearms on the

edge of the bench and sighed. "Very well, proceed."

"Thank you." Joshua held the paper out in front of him and studied it. Then he raised his voice so even the reporters in the back row could hear him. "We, the people of Bethany, Pennsylvania, believe it is important for our voices to be heard. The statue of Jesus Christ in Jericho Park neither offends us nor threatens our religious freedom, as some have contested. Rather it is our privilege as Americans not to be subjected to censorship."

Joshua hesitated, and Jordan could sense a chill making its way down the spines of all in attendance. "Placing permanent walls around a statue given as a gift and now belonging to a private citizen — just because it depicts the central figure of the Christian faith — is censorship and it is discriminatory. We are, for that reason, asking that common sense and true freedom prevail in your decision." Joshua looked up at the judge. "The signatures begin at the bottom of the page."

The only sound in the courtroom was that of Judge Webster turning the pages of the petition. Page after page after page . . . apparently until he was convinced the signatures were valid. He cleared his throat and adjusted his glasses, his eyes still on the document. "Obviously I'm unable to count the names, but I'm willing to admit this as Exhibit A and stipulate that it appears to have the signatures of some five thousand people." He looked at Joshua. "However, as I said when hearings first began in this case, I am not obligated to pay heed to this exhibit or the protests or the opinions of newscasters. It is my decision alone." His eyes narrowed. "Anything else, counselor?"

The attorney folded his arms in front of him and cocked his head. "I had an argument prepared, Your Honor." He shook his head once, as though even he couldn't believe the strength in the voice of the people, a voice that Jordan knew would resonate in his heart forever. "But I believe in a government that is of the people . . . by the people . . . for the people. A government our fore-fathers would have recognized as constitutional." He waited a beat and a smile filled his face. "They elected you, if I'm not mistaken."

Jordan glanced at the judge and thought he looked less confident than before.

"As far as I'm concerned, Your Honor, the people have spoken. Anything I might say at this point would hardly be relevant." He looked at Jordan and back at Judge Webster. "The defense rests."

Jordan considered all that hung on the next few minutes. Members of the press held their collective breath, waiting to share the story with the nation. Hawkins no doubt was pacing by the telephone in his plush office, and somewhere a room full of advisors to a shady politician stood by anxiously awaiting the outcome as well.

Despite all of that, Jordan could not remember ever feeling more relaxed.

It was Faith's turn. Judge Webster scanned the spectator section and leaned into his microphone. "The court would like to hear from Ms. Faith Evans."

Faith made her way to the front of the courtroom, and Jordan joined the others watching her as she took the witness stand. She looked professional, like she'd just walked off the studio set at the station, and Jordan wondered if she knew how proud he was of her.

Although Faith made an undeniable presence, Judge Webster did not look affected by it. "Miss Evans, as a landowner and party to this matter, I will allow you to voice your concerns." He sounded unemotional, as though his dialogue were scripted. "You may proceed."

Faith smiled at him. "Thank you, You

Honor." Her eyes shifted to the courtroom and locked onto Jordan's. His pulse quickened. How had he survived sixteen years without her? She looked away, her eyes dancing as she searched the faces of the spectators. "The reason I purchased the property in Jericho Park is because I think the people of Bethany deserve to see the Jesus statue. Every hour, every day of the year. Any time they'd like." Jordan was struck again by both her beauty and eloquence. He stifled a chuckle. Even a crusty old guy like Judge Webster had to dread making a decision against her.

"When the statue belonged to the city, it was a liability the people were unaware of until the judge's earlier ruling." She turned back to Judge Webster. "But now that it belongs to me, I believe I have a right to see it, to access it like any other property owner. By placing a permanent wall around it, that would of course be impossible." She shrugged lightly and looked back at the spectators, this time bypassing Jordan.

"Ultimately I agree with Joshua Nunn and the citizens who signed the petition. Let the people decide. And in this case, my purchase of the property has helped to do just that. The mandatory placement of a permanent wall around my property would be a violation of my right to access it." She leveled her gaze at the judge in a way that was just short of angry. "And that would defeat the whole point, Your Honor. Because you told this court at the first hearing that you were concerned for the *rights* of the people. I'm assuming that means my rights as well." She smiled politely. "That's all, Your Honor."

In the silence that followed Faith's testimony, it hit Jordan that no matter what argument he might present today, God's plans would prevail. Based on the statements by Joshua, the valid points by Faith, the fact that the statue was now clearly private property, and the signatures of five thousand local voters, Jordan was sure he wouldn't have had a chance. He swallowed and looked down at his hands, humbled by the enormity of it all. He would have lost the case — and possibly his job. Maybe even the relationships he'd rekindled with Heidi and Faith.

Most of all he would have missed a chance at new life, the life God planned for him to live all along.

The judge was rambling on about the decision being his no matter what anyone else brought to the table. Jordan's thoughts wandered for a moment and almost immediately his stomach twisted. The loss o this case would cause fallout from the lowest levels of HOUR to the highest levels of state government.

It was entirely possible Jordan might never work as a lawyer again after today. What firm would trust him after what he was about to do? *See me through it, God . . . please. Give me the words to say.*

Faith had returned to her seat, and Judge Webster smiled weakly at Jordan. He knew the judge wanted him to save the day, to give an irrefutable argument strong enough to quell the voice of the people. "The plaintiff will now state his position. Mr. Riley?"

He thought of the hours he'd spent preparing for his career, his fervor at winning battles for the wrong side — and he was assaulted by warring emotions. *These are my last few minutes as an attorney for HOUR . . .*

Jordan took the floor, and his anxiety dissipated, as though he were sailing on a reservoir of peace. He had no idea what he was going to say, but he wasn't worried.

God was in control.

"Thank you, Your Honor." He slipped his hands in his pockets and made his way closer to the judge. "Several years ago when I first became a lawyer, I had one thing in mind." He stopped and locked eyes with

Judge Webster. "Find the wrongs and right them."

Jordan exhaled heavily. "For years I thought those wrongs centered around Christianity, around the people who insisted on being public about their religious beliefs." An image came to mind of Mr. Campbell, the high school teacher Jordan had gotten fired for praying with a student. He cringed inwardly. *Lord, if only there was some way to make it up to him . . .*

And suddenly Jordan knew that there was.

"I thought those things, but that was before I filed suit against the city of Bethany." He turned and faced the curious eyes of the spectators and the concern on the reporters' faces. "I've found out a lot since I started this case." A smile tugged at the corners of his lips. "I found a friend I thought was lost forever . . ." He let his gaze linger on Faith for an instant before looking around once more. "I found a sister who thought I was dead . . . and I found the heart's cry of my mother, who I buried in Bethany when I was just a boy. But most of all I found this."

Jordan faced the judge and took another step closer. *Let him hear me, Lord . . . let all of them hear me . . .* "Most of all I found out that putting walls around myself, or

522

walls around Jesus Christ isn't righting a wrong."

A wave of whispers washed over the courtroom, and from the corner of his eye, Jordan saw several townspeople break into grins and grab hold of the hands of someone next to them. There was no turning back now.

"Order!" Judge Webster was furious. "There will be no talking, no —" he waved his hands in the air — "no outbursts like that, or I'll have everyone thrown out."

Quiet fell over the crowd, and Jordan waited until he had the judge's full attention before resuming. "I could tell you that I concede here this morning. That Mr. Nunn's speech about government of the people, by the people, for the people was right on, or that Faith Evans made a valid legal argument by requesting that her right to access and view her property not be denied." He cocked his head and paced a few steps toward the spectators. "I could tell you the HOUR organization has no right removing a landmark from a city where five thousand people want it to remain." He stopped and gazed past the people to Joshua, sitting serenely at the defense table not ten feet away. "But I don't want to concede."

The courtroom seemed to hold its collec
tive breath, waiting for Jordan's next word
the way a retriever waits for a tennis ball
He smiled at them, praying they could se
the difference in him. "Instead, I want to
add my voice to those who have already
spoken today by saying this —" he spur
slowly around and stared at Judge Webste
— "please, Your Honor, put a *three*-foot
high wrought-iron rail fence around the
base of the Jesus statue, but don't wall it in
I have no right, and neither do you no
anyone else, to censor a park statue becaus
it depicts a religious figure."

Jordan folded his arms and looked down
for a moment, overcome with emotion
When he felt strong again he looked up and
continued. "My days of attacking the ver
beliefs this country was founded on are
over, Your Honor."

Judge Webster's face was chalky white, and
an air of stunned amazement hung in the
courtroom. Nearly a minute passed before
the judge spoke. "Am I to understand tha
you are revoking your earlier request
counselor? That you no longer want this . .
this Jesus statue surrounded by walls?" Hi
voice was quieter than at any time sinc
earlier that fall when the proceedings firs
began.

Jordan felt a twinge of pity for the judge. It wasn't his fault God had opened Jordan's eyes, and now he had little choice but to rule in favor of the people — a ruling he was clearly against. *Help him see the truth, too, God.* "Yes, Your Honor. I'm revoking my earlier request."

For a moment, Judge Webster did nothing but stare at Jordan. Then he rolled his eyes, looking like a man disappointed in a favorite son's bad decision. "Very well. I will take the information shared with the court this day and make my decision. Court is adjourned for fifteen minutes." He rapped his gavel once and then quickly left the room.

Jordan saw the reporters pressing in toward the front of the courtroom, each of them desperate for an interview with him. He looked to the spot where Faith had been sitting, but she was gone. He moved back to the plaintiff's table, sat down, and rested on his forearms. There was a tap on his shoulder and Jordan braced himself. After today, the public sector would never again view him the same way.

He turned around, expecting to find a microphone in his face. Instead he saw Faith, eyes glowing with more feeling than Jordan had ever seen before. Unconcerned about the cameras aimed on him, despite the fact that the entire country would know his feelings by tomorrow, he stood and came to her. A railing separated them, but he drew her close anyway, hugging her, certain that somehow — despite the camera flashes lighting up the room — everything was going to work out.

He pulled back and saw there were tears in her eyes.

"That was perfect."

He lifted his eyebrows. "It wasn't planned." He squeezed her hands, still mindful of the crowd closing in, watching them. "I told God I'd let Him do the talking."

A reporter wedged herself between them and stared at Jordan. "Mr. Riley, did someone pay you to revoke your earlier request?"

"No, of course not, I —"

"Mr. Riley —" Another reporter, this one with a microphone half the size of his face angled in closer and took Jordan by the sleeve. "Now that you've become religious, are you resigning from the HOUR organization?"

"I didn't become religious. I've always known God . . . I just got sidetracked for a few years because of personal —"

"Mr. Riley, what is your relationship with Faith Evans?"

"Did you change your mind about the statue because of your feelings for her?"

"Mr. Riley, tell us why you no longer think human rights are important?"

The questions came at him like bullets from a semiautomatic. Faith cast him a quick look of sympathy and allowed herself to be squeezed back by the media. Her eyes told him they'd talk later. As she moved to the back of the courtroom, a vision filled the screen in Jordan's mind. Faith and him and Rosa Lee in a church full of people. And something else. His mother smiling down at him from heaven, giving him the biggest thumbs-up he'd ever seen.

His heart grew warm with compassion for the throng around him. After all, he'd been just like them a week ago. He turned his attention to the reporters. "Rights are very important to me, but I understand now that I've been *attacking* human rights, not defending them. People have a right to freely express their religious views whether in this court or . . ."

Jordan continued to answer questions, and the fifteen minutes passed quickly. Judge Webster needed only one rap of his gavel to bring the courtroom to order. Reporters hurried back to their spots and a hush gave way to utter silence. The judge looked about, and there was humility in his eyes. "This court is now in session." He glanced at the piece of paper in his hand. "I have reached a decision in the case of the HOUR organization versus the people of Bethany, Pennsylvania."

Jordan clenched his jaw and prayed.

A heavy sigh drifted from the judge's mouth. "Honestly, I had my mind made up about this case long ago. From a personal standpoint, I agreed fully with Mr. Riley's earlier argument." He cast a discouraged glance at Jordan. "But this is not a case I can decide based on my personal viewpoint. Instead I must — according to the law — make my decision based on all possible evidence and points of view." His eyes shifted to the spectators. "As Mr. Nunn reminded us, this is government of the people, by the people, and for the people. And I believe in this case the people have spoken."

He tapped his finger on the paper and looked from Joshua Nunn to Jordan and back again. "For that reason, I hereby rule that a three-foot-high, wrought-iron railing shall be erected around the Jesus statue in Jericho Park, along with a plaque declaring it to be private property."

Jordan wanted to raise his fist in the air.

ump on the table, and shout to all the courtroom about God's faithfulness. Instead, he glanced up toward the window, at the blue sky beyond, more grateful than words could express. How awful it would have been if . . .

Jordan banished the thought. Things had worked out, just as the Lord had promised.

A wave of excited whispers rose through the courtroom, but the judge said nothing. He glanced at Jordan, but refused to make eye contact, allowing his eyes to settle on Joshua instead. "If there are no further questions —" he waited for a moment — "this court is adjourned."

Judge Webster left in less time than it took Jordan to stand and start loading his briefcase. The moment the judge was gone, a cheer rose up across the courtroom, the kind usually reserved for game-winning touchdowns or buzzer-beating three-pointers. The cheers filled Jordan's senses, and he had the distinct impression that the applause of heaven itself was mingled in the sound. He looked behind him and saw that Faith was gone, but that was okay. She and Heidi had agreed to meet right after the hearing since Heidi had stayed home with the baby.

"Jordan . . ."

He turned and saw Joshua Nunn. He reached out his hand, aware that the reporters were closing in again. "Hello, Mr. Nunn. Great job."

Joshua smiled, and Jordan had the strange feeling he'd spoken to the man before. Something about his eyes. Then it hit him. Shining from the older man's eyes was the same peace and warmth and certainty he saw in Faith's, the same he'd seen in his mother's eyes back when he was a boy. Wasn't there something about that in the Bible? The eyes being the window to the soul? Jordan wasn't sure, but he knew one thing. He had a friend in Joshua Nunn.

One that he felt sure had been praying for him.

"Faith tells me you've had an interesting week."

Jordan nodded. "Yes, sir." He dropped his gaze for a moment and then found Joshua's eyes once more. "I'm sorry about all this. I was wrong. There's no other way to say it."

Joshua put his hand on Jordan's shoulder and grinned. "I didn't come over here for an apology, Jordan. I have something to ask you. Now let's get out of here before the press eats you alive . . ."

THIRTY

The warm smell of fresh roasted turkey filled the Benson home, and Joshua Nunn could hardly wait for the meal. In the days since the hearing, he and Jordan had talked at length, and finally Jordan had promised an answer by Thanksgiving Day.

"It's a lot to think about," Jordan had said the night before. "I'll give you my answer tomorrow. Over dinner."

Now, as the others bustled about the kitchen and Joshua and Helen watched the final minutes of a football game, he smiled to himself. The idea that Jordan would tell him over dinner was a good sign. Especially given the group of people gathered there. Heidi and her husband and baby daughter, Jordan and Faith. Even Rosa Lee had been able to come for the day. They were a tight group with everything in common and every reason to celebrate, even if Jordan had been tired the day of the hearing. Jordan hadn't gone into details, but apparently his conversation with the partners at HOUR had not been a pleasant one. He'd planned to quit anyway, and Joshua had a hunch God had better plans for the young attorney than any of them could imagine.

Faith's news had been better. The media groundswell of interest surrounding her had continued to be positive — even after Jordan's statements in court and the photographs of their hug had made the front page of every newspaper for a couple hundred miles. As a result, WKZN made an executive decision to hire her back on a part-time, feature basis. She'd work out of the same Philadelphia studio as before, but her feature pieces would run nationally. It was a dream position that paid twice as much as her previous job and allowed her more time off.

In addition, the previous station manager, Dick Baker, had been relocated to an affiliate in Los Angeles.

Joshua smiled. It was just one miracle after another.

He remembered again the dream he'd had in his office back before Jordan had filed suit, back when he couldn't imagine lasting another day without Bob Moses' help. *You're so faithful, God.* And he realized the

Lord hadn't merely brought down the walls in Jericho Park, He'd torn the walls down from their hearts as well. All of them. His and Faith's, and especially Jordan's. He saw again the portraits he'd seen in his dream. One of himself, and one of a handsome, angry young man. Joshua chuckled softly.

God had done everything he'd promised.

And now that Jordan was smiling more, his picture was going to look absolutely fantastic on the office wall.

Faith set the mashed potatoes on the table and caught Heidi's eye. "I think we're ready."

From across the kitchen, Jordan smiled first at Faith, then at Heidi. He had Rosa Lee by the hand and he bent down and whispered something to the child before the two of them took their places on either side of Faith. Rosa's entire face was lit up, a grin spreading from ear to ear as she took Faith's hand.

Thank You, God. I've never been so happy in all my life. Daddy, if only you could see me now . . .

Over the past two days, she and Jordan had spent hours together, much of it with Rosa. There was no denying the feelings she and Jordan had for each other, and though she wasn't exactly sure of Jordan's intentions, she could see how completely he'd fallen for the little girl as well.

"Okay, everyone, time to eat." Heidi's voice rang across the room, and in the den Joshua turned off the television. The group gathered around the table and held hands. Heidi smiled at her brother. "Jordan, would you say the blessing for us?"

Faith squeezed Jordan's hand as a hundred memories danced across her heart. Memories of Jordan and Heidi and her as kids, believing that somehow they'd be together forever. And now, against all the odds, on a day devoted to giving God thanks, here they were.

Jordan returned the squeeze and bowed his head. "Lord, we come to You this day with full hearts, hearts of gratitude for all You've done." He paused and Faith knew he was struggling to find his voice. "Thank You for the people we love, for bringing us back together. And thank You for this food. Help us to stay close to You now and always, in Jesus' name, amen."

Faith slipped her arm around Jordan's waist and hugged him, letting him know that she understood how deep his feelings were. Laughter and conversation broke out as they sat down and loaded their plates. A full thirty minutes passed before Jordan stood up and grinned, waiting for the others to notice him.

Faith's heart skipped a beat and she put down her fork. He'd hinted that he had something important to announce at dinner, and with all the whispering he'd been doing with Joshua and Rosa, she had no idea what it might be.

When everyone was quiet, Jordan looked across the table at Joshua. "I won't take too long, but I have a question to answer and a question to ask. I wanted all of you to witness both because, well —" his eyes lit up and he smiled at each of them before continuing — "this is one of those moments you remember forever."

People put down their forks, and across the table Faith could see tears in Heidi's eyes. She could hardly believe that a few months ago Heidi had thought Jordan was dead, and now here they were, celebrating Thanksgiving together.

Jordan set his gaze on Joshua again. "Joshua has asked me to team up with him at the Religious Freedom Institute here in Bethany."

Faith's breath caught in her throat. Why hadn't she realized that was what he and Joshua had been talking about? She waited while Jordan continued.

"After praying and thinking through my options, I'm absolutely sure that I want the job."

Joshua stood and reached his hand across the table to Jordan. Their handshake had the definite air of finalizing the deal. "I never had a single doubt." Joshua dropped Jordan's hand, circled the table and gave him a hearty hug. "Welcome aboard!"

Faith clapped her hands, then joined the men, reaching an arm around each of their necks and kissing Jordan on the cheek. "I didn't know you were thinking about working here!"

He squeezed her, his eyes shining with new life, new hope. "Let's just say I've had a lot on my mind and wanted to wait until —"

"Okay," Heidi interrupted. Faith and the others turned to look at her, and Faith lowered her eyebrows curiously. What was that look on Heidi's face? Like she was keeping a secret that was about to burst to the surface. Heidi raised a single eyebrow at Joshua and then leveled her gaze at her brother. "You said you had a question to answer and a question to ask. You've answered the question about the job. So what's the question you want to ask?"

"Give me a minute." Jordan grinned and

motioned for Faith and Joshua to sit down. When they'd slipped back into their seats, he asked Faith and Rosa to turn their chairs out from the table. They did as he asked, and he positioned himself between Faith and Rosa, dropping to one knee.

Tears stung at Faith's eyes and she had to remind herself to breathe. Was this what she thought it was? Was he . . . could he be . . . ? She blinked and two tears slid down her cheeks as she uttered a sound that was part laugh, part sob. "Jordan?"

He took hold of her fingers in response, then reached out for Rosa's hand with the other. "All my life I've searched for a special kind of love . . ." His eyes grew watery and they stayed locked on Faith's, as though they were the only two people in the room. "The kind of love I'd known only once in my life, back when I was thirteen and shared a special friendship with a girl named Faith."

Fresh tears filled her eyes. Was this really happening? Was he going to ask her to . . . ?

Jordan swallowed, struggling to keep his emotions at bay. "And now that I've found you again, I know that I could never share that kind of love with anyone else. Faith, with all my heart I want to love you and cherish you, laugh with you and grow old with you." He looked at Rosa and nodded. She pulled a velvet box from a pocket in her dress and handed it to Jordan.

Faith watched, eyes wide, mouth open. Rosa had been in on the secret the whole time? Her head was spinning, and she felt as though she were dreaming, but she held her questions at bay. Jordan released the hold he had on her fingers and opened the box. From inside he pulled out a diamond solitaire ring. As the others watched — and Heidi cried softly from the other side of the table — Jordan locked eyes with Faith once more. "So my question is this: Faith Evans Moses, will you marry me?"

Across the table, Joshua's wife, Helen, gasped, and her hands flew to her mouth. Her smile lit up that corner of the room, and Faith knew that her parents' friends were as sure about Jordan as she was. She directed her focus on Jordan. Surely there would have been a hole in her chest if she'd looked down, because her heart was gone, given completely to a man she'd wondered about most of her life. Deep in the core of her being Faith knew that this was the holy plan her father had spoken of for so many years. Finally, here in Bethany, when it seemed all hope was lost, God had shown her His most excellent reality for her life.

Jordan held the ring out, and she lifted her hand, allowing him to slide it on her finger. It glistened, casting a spray of light across the dinner table and causing the others to lean closer, looking over the turkey and stuffing and green bean casserole to see how it shone and to wait for her answer.

Faith met Jordan's gaze, praying he could see the way she felt for him, the way she'd always felt for him and always would feel. All the days of her life. "Yes, Jordan Riley, I will marry you and love you, laugh with you and grow old with you."

There was a chorus of cries and applause as Jordan stood and eased Faith into his arms. He moved his mouth near her ear and whispered, "I love you, Faith."

Her words were equally quiet, equally private. "I love you too. Forever, Jordan."

Rosa stood at their side clapping and smiling and tugging on Jordan's sweater. "Is it time, is it?"

He patted her head and helped Faith back to her chair. The others remained standing, wondering what Jordan was going to do next. Faith still felt as though she were floating, but she sat down and took Rosa's hand as Jordan pulled another velvet box from his back pocket. This time he took a small locket from the box and opened it. Inside were two single pictures, one of Jordan and one of Faith.

Faith hadn't thought she could possibly feel happier until now, but as she watched Rosa's face, she knew she was wrong. Jordan was on his knee again. "Rosa, now that Faith has agreed to marry me, we have a question for you." He winked at Faith, and took her fingers in his. "Faith has been praying for a family for you, honey. And now that the two of *us* will be a family . . ." Jordan let go of Faith's hand and leaned forward. He put the locket around Rosa's neck, and when it was clasped, he leaned back on his knee again. "We want to ask you to be our little girl."

Rosa squealed and threw herself into Jordan's arms. Faith couldn't hold her tears back any longer. She wept for God's goodness, for the amazing way that only He could have worked this miracle between the three of them. Faith wished her mother could have been there to share this moment with them, but it would be fun sharing every detail with her by phone that night. With her arms around Jordan and Rosa, the three of them formed a hug. They stayed that way as her father's partner stood and circled the table, putting himself directly behind them.

"I say we all gather around this family-o-be and ask God to bless them."

Heidi was crying, using her Thanksgiving napkin to dab at the mascara beneath her eyes. With Charles by her side, the two of them joined Helen and the others in a circle around Faith, Jordan, and Rosa. Before they could pray, Joshua began to sing. It was Faith's favorite hymn, the one the people had sung on the courthouse lawn back when everything about her life, about all their lives, looked like it was falling apart. She could think of no other song that so aptly fit the moment. She choked back her tears and joined in while Jordan did the same.

"Great is Thy faithfulness, oh God my Father, there is no shadow of turning with Thee . . . Thou changest not, Thy compassions they fail not, as Thou has been Thou forever will be . . ."

Heidi and Charles and Joshua and Helen added their voices as the song grew. "Great is Thy faithfulness, great is Thy faithfulness . . . morning by morning new mercies I see."

Rosa's eyes lit up and she added her voice as well. "All I have needed Thy hand hath provided. Great is Thy faithfulness . . . great is Thy faithfulness . . . great is Thy faithfulness, Lord unto me."

As the song ended, Joshua led them in prayer, and Faith tried to believe it was all true. Jordan had really found her after all these years, he'd really asked her to marry him and asked Rosa to be their daughter.

It was beyond her comprehension. *Lord, Your faithfulness knows no limits. How have You pulled this all together, worked this out?*

My daughter, I have always known the plans I had for you . . . and it is My pleasure to do more than you can ever ask or imagine . . .

God's words echoed in Faith's heart, and she allowed herself to be wrapped in them, covered by them, loved by them. She tuned back in to Joshua's prayer and held tight to the people who would soon be her family, the people she loved more than life itself.

"Finally, Father, we thank You because You work all things to the good for those who love You, for those who are called according to Your purpose. And together, as a family united in Your truth, we look forward to the wonder You have in store for us today . . . and all the days of our lives. In Christ's name we pray . . ."

With the smell of pumpkin pies baking in the oven and refrains of Joshua's favorite hymn ringing in their hearts, they finished the prayer together with a single word:

"Amen!"

THIRTY-ONE

Joe and Jenna Campbell led their three children into Jericho Park and set up their blanket not far from the famous statue, the one that had caused a national commotion almost a year earlier.

"Okay, kids, there it is. The Jesus statue."

Their ten-year-old son cocked his head and stared up at the eyes of the statue, taking in the way Jesus' hands were outstretched, welcoming, beckoning all who were weary to come. "That's exactly how I picture Jesus, Dad."

Joe stared at the statue, liking the way its presence dominated the park. "Yes, son. Me too."

The family moved closer, and Jenna put their picnic basket down as the five of them formed a circle on the ground.

"Why are we here again, Dad?" Their six-year-old daughter smiled through curious eyes. Joe knew she was unaware of all that had gone on since the trial, back when he'd been fired by the New York school district.

"Well, honey, about a year ago Daddy lost his job because he wanted to pray with one of the kids at school." He looked at his wife and saw tears glistening in her eyes. "Mommy and I wanted to come here to celebrate how good God is for taking care of us and getting me a new job."

Their eight-year-old daughter nodded as though she understood the situation completely. "That's why we moved here, right, Daddy?"

Joe grinned and tousled the child's hair. "Right, sweetheart. A few months ago a nice attorney here in Bethany, a Mr. Riley —" he caught Jenna's gaze — "called me and told me about a teaching job at the high school here. He put in a good word for me and I got hired." He looked at the faces of his family and felt his heart swell with gratefulness. "We're here today to celebrate God and all He's done for us, for His provision and love and care."

Jenna took his hand and finished the thought for him. "And for sending Mr. Riley at just the right time."

Joe thought back to that awful day in court, when Jordan Riley had fought so hard against him and he'd lost his job. He could see it as clearly as if it had happened yesterday. There they were, Jenna and him, immediately after the judge's decision, bowing their heads together in prayer, scarcely aware of the chaos that reigned in the courtroom. Joe drew a deep breath and searched the faces of his children, wondering how much they understood. "The day I lost my job, your mom and I prayed very, very hard."

Their oldest daughter angled her head, curiously. "Did you pray for a new job, Daddy?"

"No, we didn't, honey." He smiled at his wife and gently squeezed her fingers. "We weren't worried about that because God always takes care of us." He paused. "We prayed that Mr. Riley might love Jesus one day."

"That was a good thing to pray, right, Daddy?" Their youngest nodded confidently.

"But does he?"

"Yeah, Daddy, does he love Jesus now?" The kids spoke at the same time, and Joe and Jenna laughed.

"Yes." Joe's eyes were suddenly wet. He remembered Jordan's phone call a few months earlier, the tears in the man's voice as he apologized for costing Joe his job . . .

and the joy as Jordan shared the fact that he had joined the ranks of believers. "Yes, kids, he loves Jesus very, very much."

"That's kind of like a miracle, isn't it, Dad?" Their oldest waited for an answer.

"Yes." Joe gathered his family close and gazed up at the Jesus statue. "It's the best miracle of all."

FEDERAL COURT RULES CITY NOT REQUIRED TO HIDE STATUE OF JESUS

(Marshfield, Wisconsin) — An atheist group's request to erect a ten-foot-high wall around a statue of Jesus was denied May 9, 2000, by U.S. District Court Judge John Shabaz. The decision came as a result of a lawsuit filed by the Freedom From Religion Foundation, whose goal was to remove or hide the statue, which has stood in a Marshfield city park since 1959.

The case was dismissed by the U.S. District Court after the city sold the statue to a private landowner in December, 1998. On appeal, the U.S. Court of Appeals for the Seventh Circuit held on February 4, 2000, that the sale of the statue was valid and appropriate, but ordered the city to take steps to differentiate between the property owned by the city and the private property where the statue is located.

Judge Shabaz in his final decision said the Constitution did not require what he called "visual separation" of the statue from the rest of the park. He accepted the proposal from the city requiring the erection of a four-foot-high, wrought-iron fence that will not block the view of the statue. The city will display a sign signifying that the statue and the land it sits on is privately owned.

The city of Marshfield was represented by the American Center for Law and Justice (ACLJ), and by Harold Wolfgram, assistant city attorney for the city of Marshfield. The ACLJ specializes in First Amendment law and focuses on pro-family, pro-life, and pro-liberty cases.

Although *On Every Side* was inspired by this true event, it is not intended to accurately depict any aspect of either the ACLJ, the Freedom From Religion Foundation, or any other person or event involved or associated with the actual incident as it took place.

Dear Family and Friends:

It's good to meet with you again and as always to thank you for traveling with me through the pages of this, my latest book. I must tell you how much I enjoyed writing *On Every Side* — both the heart-stopping research and the way God worked in me, bringing down walls of my own as He brought Faith and Jordan and Joshua to life.

As with all my books, there is a nugget of truth nestled between the lines of this story. The truth is that walls have been around since the beginning of time, whether they belonged to Adam and Eve, who allowed a barrier between themselves and God, or the people of Jericho, who believed they could keep God out by building a wall around their city.

Before I wrote *On Every Side,* I thought walls were more of an Old Testament issue. Walled-in cities; walled-in, stubborn people;

temple wall, that kind of thing. But as the story came to life, God began to make something very clear.

Walls are a part of our lives to this very day.

Oh, we may not think we've put walls between God and us. I certainly didn't think so. But I discovered that without meaning to, I had allowed schedules and responsibilities and the busyness of life to put distance between the Lord and me. In a sense, I allowed walls to form. I'm guessing that this is true for you as well. Though your intentions may have been good, though they may still be good, somewhere along the way you've allowed space to come between you and the Father.

It is my prayer that in reading this book you've had a chance to take stock of your faith life. That where you've recognized walls, you've found time perhaps even now to draw nearer to God, to tear down the walls and enjoy once again that intimate walk with Him.

Of course, for some of you the walls have been in place as far back as you can remember. People might have told you about God, and in the back of your mind you knew you'd have to deal with Him someday. But not yet, not while you were busy with life and planning your agenda without Him. For you, I pray this will be a life-changing moment, here, now. That you will recognize as long as walls exist between you and God your situation is desperate. And that you will beg His forgiveness. Ask Him to knock down the barriers, brick by brick. Believe that He will take you into His loving arms and grant you mercy and grace so long as you take the first step.

If this is you, and if here and now you've made a decision to accept Christ for life and allow the walls to fall, please do this: Get connected with a Bible-believing church and plant yourself in the fertile soil of God's Word. That way you will be sure to grow deep roots, roots that will prevent anything from ever coming between you and the Lord again.

On that note, I'd like to ask for your prayers for our family. We have adopted three precious little six-year-old boys from Haiti. Many of you have journeyed with me through all my books and know a little more about how we came to this decision. For those who don't, let me say it was a two-year process. We began by believing God wanted us to take into our hearts and homes one or two children who were orphans. And so we searched social services' photolisting files online from across the United States.

What we found was sad indeed.

Generally, if a child was up for adoption, and if there weren't already ten or twenty families waiting in line for a child, then our social worker would simply say, "That child can't go to a family with young children in the home." Or, "There are severe anger issues with that child, making him unsafe around other children." Or, "That child has a considerable number of special needs."

In the end, we nearly gave up.

Then God led us to a wonderful Christian orphanage in Haiti called Heart of God Ministries. We found our little boys on a photolisting on their Web site (www.hgm.org) and prayed for God to open the door for us to adopt them if it was His will. Let's just say God has blessed us indeed, opening the door so wide it came off the hinges! Our three birth children are thrilled about the arrival of their new brothers and have talked about them for nine months as though they're already here.

A few days ago, three-year-old Austin said, "Mommy, will you pick up E. J. and Sean and Joshua from their house?"

I said, "No, honey. They don't have a house."

He blinked. "Do they have a castle?"

I smiled at him and smoothed a finger over his cheek. "No, buddy. They don't have anything. Not even a mommy and daddy."

With that, baby tears filled his eyes, and his normally rough-and-tumble child said, "Can we be their mommy and daddy?"

Yes, I believe God has all our hearts ready. We anticipate a God-directed transition, safe travel, and a closer walk with Him because of the privilege of caring for these three in addition to our three birth children. Still, there are bound to be speed bumps along the way (for instance, they speak Creole and we don't). Because of that, please pray for us. I'll give you another update at the end of my next book. Until then, blessings to you and yours, humbly in Christ,

Karen Kingsbury

P.S. As always, I'd love to hear from you. Write me at my e-mail address: rtnbykk@ aol.com

BOOK CLUB OR BIBLE STUDY GUIDE

1. Have you ever prayed for something or someone and felt as though God didn't hear your prayers? How did it make you feel? How do you feel now?
2. Did it surprise you to learn that there really was a Jesus statue case? Why or why not? Where do you think our country stands today in terms of religious freedom issues?
3. How are you or your family and friends affected by restrictions on religious freedom in the United States?
4. To which character in the book can you most relate? Why?
5. Consider the main characters. How did they change over the course of the story? In what way is God trying to change or grow you at this stage in your life?
6. Read Joshua 5:13–6:20. What are the parallels between that story and the story in this book?

7. Jordan lost much as a young teen. What losses have you dealt with and how have you responded to them?

8. Have you ever been angry at God because of those losses? Have you ever walked away from God? If so, how are things now between you and God? Why are they that way?

9. Read Romans 8:28. God always has our situation under control. His control, not ours. Has there been a time in your life when all seemed lost, but God — in His timing — worked things out for your good? What was that like? How did you feel about God during that time?

10. Why did the letter from Jordan's mother change his life? Has anyone ever written you a letter that changed your life? Describe that situation.

ABOUT THE AUTHOR

Karen Kingsbury is the bestselling author of seventeen books with a total of more than a million and a half copies in print. Her titles include *A Moment of Weakness, Waiting for Morning, Where Yesterday Lives,* and *When Joy Came to Stay.* She is also a recognized author with the Women of Faith Fiction Club. One of her books was made into a 1997 CBS TV-Movie-of-the-Week. She lives in Washington state with her husband and six children.